A Handful of Coppers

A Handful of Coppers

Collected Early Stories, Vol. 1: Heroic Fantasy

Charles de Lint

SUBTERRANEAN PRESS · 2003

FIRST EDITION

ISBN
1-931081-73-5

Subterranean Press
P.O. Box 190106
Burton, MI 48519

email:
subpress@earthlink.net

website:
www.subterraneanpress.com

Contents

Grateful acknowledgments are made to:

Happy Rhodes for the use of the lines from "Words Weren't Made for Cowards" from her album *Warpaint*. Copyright (c) 1991 by Happy Rhodes; lyrics reprinted by permission. For more information about Happy's music, contact Auntie Social, P.O. Box 162, Rifton, NY 12471, or go to: www.auntiesocialmusic.com

Robin Williamson for use of the lines from "The Iron Stone" which originally appeared on the Incredible String Band album *The Big Huge*. Copyright (c) 1968 by Robin Williamson. And for the use of a line from "Five Denials on Merlin's Grave" from the book of the same title published by Pig's Whisker Music Press. Copyright (c) 1979 by Robin Williamson. "Five Denials on Merlin's Grave" can also be heard on Robin's album *A Glint at the Kindling*. For more information about Robin's music, poetry, and stories, contact Pig's Whisker Music, P.O. 114, Chesterfield, Derbyshire S40 3YU, England, or email them at info@pigswhisker.com.

this one's for my pal
Charles R. Saunders

I won't say I wouldn't have
become a writer without knowing him
but he sure made it
a lot easier for me

and for Gorden Linzner & the late Gene Day
who gave so many of us a chance
when no one else would

Once There Was A Man with No Name

If you were one of the people who helped make *Triskell Tales* sell out so quickly, and especially if you're one of the readers who wrote to me or the book's publisher, Subterranean Press, asking to get more of my early fiction back into print, then you're to blame for this book you hold in your hand.

Indeed, it seems that some of you are gluttons for punishment, so once again I come before you with old stories in hand — some dating right back to the beginning of my career. I find it difficult to make a fair value judgment on these stories. Some I still like, others are quite painful for me to reread now. But each was the best I could do at the time. Each was about something that interested me, or that I cared about, and there's not much else a writer can promise his or her readers than to deliver the best, heartfelt stories that they can.

If these same stories happen to fall flat on their faces, for any of the number of reasons that stories can, they don't do so out of authorial neglect or disinterest. They do so because talent and craftsmanship had yet to catch up to vision. Because the real difference between this book and *Triskell Tales* is that you won't find a progression here from the work of novice writer to one more assured with his craft. These are *all* early stories — awkward and earnest, and desperately in need of a good editor.

I've taken out a few of the many adverbs and exclamation marks, dropped some of the clumsy dialogue attributions, played a bit with the paragraphing, but otherwise, what you find here is pretty much the way these stories were presented in their initial publication. In many cases I desperately would have liked to work on the plots and characterization, but soon realized that to do so, I'd basically have to throw' the whole story out and begin again from scratch. I have new stories I want to write, rather than retelling these.

Besides, half the time I don't even *know* the person who wrote these stories. He was (to quote Steve Earle in reference to people in their twenties) "not done yet." He had no great wealth of experience or insight to help him, though what he lacked in either, he more than made up for in enthusiasm.

I'm not sure I'm "done yet" even now, but hopefully I get the words down on paper so that they read better. I do know that it takes me *far* longer to write than it did that kid.

∞

You'll notice, if you're the sort that reads the copyright page, that many of these stories initially appeared in small press magazines ('zines) — some of them with *very* small print runs. Back in the seventies when I first began to market my fiction, the small press 'zines were the proving ground for new writers — probably the way that the Internet is today, although back then, someone actually had to pay to get the issues printed, maybe pay the contributors (as a little as ¼¢ a word, or sometimes only a copy of the 'zine), and readers had to buy the finished product.

∞

If you're wondering what the title of this introduction means (although I suppose it could refer to me before I started getting published and finally began to acquire a readership in my chosen field), it comes from my realization that heroic fantasy stories really weren't all that different from spaghetti westerns, the most famous (when I was writing these) being the films featuring Clint Eastwood as the mysterious bounty hunter/adventurer, "the man with no name."

The difference was, heroic fantasy had magic.

I kept that in mind as I was writing these stories, so much so that I'm surprised I didn't give Aynber a cheroot to chew on, along with the serapé she wore in some of the stories.

What strikes me the most as I reread the material here to prepare it for publication is how brutal all of this is, especially the Aynber and Damon stories. In them, if you gave someone a wrong look, you could expect to have the point of a sword stuck in your face. Or worse.

C33ED

For my part, the real pleasure in the existence of this book is the lovely cover that MaryAnn has done for it, and how it's provided an opportunity for me to rejoin forces with my old friend John Charette, whose art originally appeared with many of these stories. John and I used to sit around in the old house on Lewis Street where MaryAnn and I lived, working on these stories and pictures on my day off from the record store. Although the John of today has issues with some of these old illustrations, I still enjoy looking at them, as much for the memories they call up as for anything else.

I also got a kick out of revisiting the two Liavek stories, one of which was a collaboration with my friend Lee Barwood. I think it's here that one first gets an inkling of the camaraderie enjoyed by the repertory company of characters you can meet in my Newford books.

I hope you enjoy the art. I hope you enjoy the stories. If this is (God forbid) your first visit to my fiction, I think I'm telling better stories these days.

C33ED

One last thing: perhaps one of you can help me. There was an unpublished novelette I wanted to include in this collection, but unfortunately, I've long since lost touch with my collaborator on it. His name is Jim Coplin and back in the seventies, he was writing as "J.E. Coplin." If any of you know how I can get in touch with Jim, please let either me or the publisher of this book know. Hopefully we'll then be able to include that story in a future volume.

C33ED

If any of you are on the Internet, come visit my home page at www.charlesdelint.com.

Charles de Lint
Ottawa, late Autumn 2002

Aynber

The Fair, the Foul & the Foolish

...the birds came in a crowd,
wing upon widening wing, until the air
wrinkled with sound...

—Roy McFadden

The Huntress awoke suddenly to an unfamiliar sound. Her wide eyes opened to peer about the darkened chamber, searching, until they rested at last upon the slim young man who lay sleeping by her side. As she teased a curl from his smooth brow, the sound came again. Clearer now, she heard it as a rattle upon the shutter. She rose without a sound from the bed. Wrapping a blanket about herself, she crossed the room, stopping only to unsheathe her dagger from where it lay in its sheath on the floor. She stepped over the profusion of clothes that lay where they'd fallen—a pleasant reminder of the earlier part of the evening—until she stood at the window.

There came a scratching on the shutter as she put her hand on the bar to open it. A low voice muttered:

"Hist! Hist! Aynber!"

It was Thorn, she realized, recognizing his voice. She gave the shutter a rough push, almost tumbling him from the sill as it swung open.

"It's long past midnight," she said in a low voice. "What do *you* want?"

"I've found him, I've found him," he answered in a breathless whisper. "In The Mug & Tankard. And he's alone, too."

"Who is?"

"Who is?" Thorn repeated. "Why, Halin is, that's who is. Come on. Get yourself dressed and we'll go. If we hurry, we've a good chance of taking him without too much of a struggle."

Aynber thought of the young man asleep in her bed and of the almost full purse of gold that lay on the table beside. The bounty on the highwayman Guil and his men had served her well this past month, and there was enough left for at least another week or two.

"Na, na," she said, shaking her head. "Another time perhaps."

She began to close the shutter.

"Aynber!" Thorn cried in a hoarse whisper. He put his hand out to stop the shutter from closing on him and almost lost his balance in the process. "That's two hundred gold pieces you're saying 'na, na' to."

Aynber looked at Thorn clinging precariously to the sill. He cut a ridiculous figure and a smile slipped across her lips.

"Well...why not?" she said at last. "I'll meet you below."

She closed the shutter and turned back into the room. Fumbling in the dimness, she coaxed life into a coal from the dying fire with which to light a candle. Slowly, the shadows spilled away from its light, bathing her features. She had an oval face, with full lips, a small nose, and dark sea-green eyes. A thin scar marred her left cheek, while long tresses of honey-gold hair swept down her back in an uncombed tangle.

Dropping the blanket, she began to dress: shirt and knee-length trousers of thick cotton, leather boots and jerkin. Then she gathered her weapons. On her belt, she hung her dagger, sheathed once more, and a leather pouch filled with death-stars — small five-pointed discs of star-silver that the Aelves called *lessen-yaln*. She paused as she reached for a sword.

She had a choice of two: her old familiar short sword, and a long slender length of steel that Thorn had convinced her to buy before they set out to hunt Guil, almost two months ago. She reached for the long blade. Of late, too many of her opponents were tall men and she needed its extra reach. She never believed in giving another the advantage, not when lives were at stake. Especially not when one of those lives was her own.

18

Moments later, she blew a kiss to her still-sleeping companion, slipped through the door, and padded downstairs to where Thorn was waiting on the street. The sky was filled with twinkling stars and a moon that was three days from being full. Thorn stood under a dimly lit sign that read the Inn of the Worn Scabbard, melding into the shadows as though he were a part of them. He stepped from that dark and scowled at her, his mustache quivering, his narrow bright eyes gleaming as the moon caught them in its light.

"You took your own sweet time," he complained, lifting his peaked cap to scratch at his scalp. "I feel like I've been waiting for hours. And that climb to your window…"

"Well, la-di-da," she said. "You might've come by the stairs— but, na, that's not dramatic enough, is it?"

"I…"

"And if you're tired of waiting, why didn't you go on your own? Surely, there's some great spell you've not tried yet, or if all else fails, your might at arms would see you through. Parry…thrust…" She mimed the actions as she spoke.

"I should have," he mumbled. "I should have, and showed you what I can do on my…no wait, Aynber!"

She turned from the door of the inn that she'd been about to re-enter.

"Aye?" The questioning raise of her eyebrows was lost in the dark.

"Let's go, shall we?" he said.

"Lead on, O Wizard," she replied with a low flourishing bow.

CRSO

Calthoren's streets were dark at night. Lit only by the feeble light of Woldenar's stars and the light thrown from open windows, when there was no fog, and the pale glow of the moon, when it was full enough to cast any light. Shadows abounded, and through them, the Huntress followed Thorn. He led her through twisting alleyways, along the night-shrouded streets, until they finally arrived at the Mug & Tankard.

The inn was situated in the Thieves' Quarter, along the sea wall. Aynber began to wonder at the wisdom of their coming here, just the two of them, and not so well-armed at that, should they meet with more resistance than just a few thieves. Thorn appeared nervous as well, though there was nothing unusual in that. But all along their way, he'd cast fearful glances about them as though he expected them to be attacked at a moment's notice and it was beginning to get on her nerves.

"What is it?" she asked him once, trying to keep the exasperation from her voice.

"Nothing," he replied quickly. Perhaps a little too quickly. "I thought I heard something...but it must've been just a rat's scurrying. Nothing to fear."

Now they'd arrived. The end of this night's rainbow lay just beyond the door, awaiting their arrival.

Aynber loosened her blade in its scabbard and took a death-star from her pouch. Stepping past Thorn, she entered. Behind her, Thorn drew a long length of steel, almost ludicrous for his fairly short stature. Throwing back his cloak, he drew a breath and followed her in.

There were four men inside.

Behind the bar was the inn's keeper, stout and half-bald, a man who obviously wanted no trouble, though what he would do should trouble arise was open to question. By the door sat a brawny barbarian, probably from the foothills of the Peredur Mountains, at least so Aynber surmised from the looks of his tattoos and the long curved blade that rested by his knee. Across the room was a thin man in a large cloak who looked up nervously when they entered, frowned and then returned to a brooding surveillance of his near-empty wine mug.

And by the kitchen door was Halin, tall and ragged in his shabby clothes, a dirty mantle lying on the table by his sword. He looked up as well when they entered, his eyes going wide as he recognized Aynber.

"Bounty hunter!" he cried, rising from his seat.

"No need for dying," Aynber said.

Seeing the panic in his eyes give way to desperation, she spoke quietly, hoping to avoid bloodshed.

Halin's only response was a curse. Grabbing his still-sheathed sword, he bolted for the kitchen.

Aynber flung a *lessen-yaln* at his legs. She was a split-second too late. The death-star ripped into the door frame at calf-height just as Halin dove out of sight.

"Buggering luck," Aynber said.

She raced across the room, weaving nimbly to avoid the profusion of tables and chairs in her way. When she reached the threshold of the kitchen door, she peered inside, throwing herself back as a throwing knife arrowed for her chest. She twisted aside, the dagger's hilt brushing the fabric of her shirt, and tripped over Thorn who was directly behind her.

They fell to the floor with a clatter and crash.

Aynber looked up. The thin man in the cloak was gone and the landlord hid behind his bar, but the barbarian by the door was coming for them, the long curved length of his blade glinting in the taper light of the inn. He staggered as he walked, and when he spoke, his words were slurred.

Dead drunk, thought Aynber as she scrambled to her feet.

"Sho you'd deal in mensh livesh?" the barbarian said, waving his sword in her face.

Drunk or not, he could do damage.

Aynber stepped in closely to him. The barbarian backed up slightly, trying to bring his sword into play, but with a quick movement, Aynber caught him in the groin with her knee. As he doubled over, the hilt of her blade met the nape of his neck and he collapsed onto the floor with a dull thud. Ignoring his gurglings of pain, Aynber turned, hauled Thorn up by the scruff of the cloak and propelled him through the kitchen door.

Tonight was not going well, she decided. She should have stayed in bed, but it was a little late for that now.

The back door of the kitchen swung ajar. She stepped through it to stand with Thorn. He pointed to the right from where Halin's footsteps could still be heard echoing. Aynber nodded and they sped after him.

The inn was soon lost far behind as Halin led them a merry chase through the dark cloaked streets of Calthoren. Once when he took to the rooftops they lost him until he, thinking he was clear, dropped down almost in front of them and the hunt was on again. Up Helder's Alley he ran, down through the Merchant's Quarters, to the wharves. Aynber breathed heavily, almost spent from the chase, and Thorn's face seemed drawn and pallid in the moonlight. But Halin would be faring no better.

Around another corner they raced, running full tilt into a silent figure, hooded and cloaked all in white. The three fell a sprawl in the roadway. Without pausing, Aynber was upon her feet and on. Thorn stayed long enough to pry loose a heavy pouch that clinked hopefully from the fingers of the cloaked figure, before he followed suit.

"Vermin!" cried a voice from inside the cowl. "Return it, or pay for the cost of its taking with your life."

But Thorn was already too far away to hear.

And not so long thereafter, he realized that he'd lost both Aynber and Halin. He was in the midst of the wharf area. Tall ships loomed just off shore and the wharves themselves were a clutter of bales, caskets and chests. He made a stealthy route among them, coming at last to where a bridge spanned Kessind, the first of the five great canals that ran through Calthoren.

Ah…and there was a furtive sound from below in the shadows.

For one moment Thorn's breath caught in his throat. His pulse raced as he peered into the dark. Steeling himself, he stepped into the inky blackness, stolen pouch safely hid in his belt. His sword was bared in his hand.

It must be Halin, he thought, half smiling to himself, and half fearful. His confidence won out over his fear.

He'd show her. He'd bring Halin in alone and collect the whole reward for his trouble. Then they would see who mocked who. Ha! With steel alone he'd take Halin…no spells, no tricks.

Thorn's smile grew into a grin. Already he could see himself as the hero of the day. She called herself the Huntress, did she? Well, he could see it now: Thorn the Hunter.

He paced forward, cautious, moving like silence itself. Holding his sword in front of him, he lunged forward when he heard a slight sound before him. A jolt in his arm told him that his blade was engaged. He imagined his opponent's steel speeding for his throat. Just in time did he brought his own blade back into play to deflect it. Immediately, the other's sword could be heard cutting the air in front of his stomach. Thorn sucked his belly in and struck out, his blade ringing on another.

A weird battle this, fought in the utter dark with an almost silent foe. The man was good, damn him, and Thorn cursed himself for a fool to have engaged an unknown opponent in the dark like this.

Slowly, he was being forced back. Nearer and nearer he could feel the whistling breath of his opponent's blade almost upon his cheek.

He stumbled over a loose cobblestone and was nearly impaled by the invisible sword before he recovered himself. And he continued to be forced back.

Again he threw himself into the assault, weaving a deadly net of steel, but his foe kept edging forward and he, in turn, had to step back. In one such retreat, the moonlight caught his features for he'd stepped from underneath the bridge. His opponent gasped, dropping his guard for a second.

With a triumphant cry, Thorn lunged forward. As his foe twisted out of the path of his thrust, Thorn lost his balance and his body followed his sword. Stumbling, he felt a cuff on the back of the head and was knocked headfirst into the canal. He rose spluttering only to hear an all too familiar voice saying:

"Damn you for a sow's dried teat, Thorn Hawkwood. You could have killed me."

With a sinking feeling, he realized that it had been Aynber he'd fought in the dark. She reached down, helping him out of the water. He grinned ruefully at her from where he lay wet and bedraggled on the cobblestones.

"We've lost him for sure," she added. Then a thought glimmered in her eyes. "Unless...he might be making for the city gates. West I'd say. Come on. We've still a chance, I'll wager."

"Gods, Aynber...I'm half-dead," Thorn complained. "Can't we put it off for tonight?"

He was about to tell her of the pouch that he'd pilfered earlier from the cloaked figure.

"Na, na," she said, without giving him a chance to speak. "You've got me out of a warm bed tonight to fetch Halin, and bedamned to how you feel, it's bring him in we will. Are you coming?"

Up Caples Street they raced, down through Minon Alley, past two closed market places and another market of an entirely different sort where a woman in a thin shift beckoned Thorn within. He was about to go, savoring her smile and knowing that the pouch bouncing at his knee would pay for a fine evening indeed, until he was brought up short by a sharp call from Aynber. Shrugging as he ran, he marked the place down for future reference and sped after her.

Dawn was just breaking when they saw a figure fleeing before them.

"I was right," Aynber said, pointing him out to Thorn. "See? There he goes!"

She drew a pair of death-stars from their small pouch at her belt and put on an extra burst of speed. Ahead, Halin attempted the same:

There was a crossroads, in front of the house of Linn the head of the Sea-masters' Guild, where two roads crossed, mingled for a moment and then slipped off on their separate ways. Halin was just about past Linn's house when one of Aynber's *lessen-yaln* caught him in the leg, sending shafts of sudden agony rippling through his body. His leg collapsed under him and he skidded across the rough cobblestones. Before he could get his bearings, or bring his blade into play, the pair were upon him. Aynber was businesslike, kicking Halin's sword from his fist, while Thorn danced about waving his blade.

"Put it away before you skewer him," Aynber said. "I'd rather bring him in alive than…"

She stopped in mid-sentence, turning about as some sixth sense warned her of another's presence.

Behind them, a tall figure stood, wrapped in a cloak and hood all of white, a grim threat glinting in his eyes. He threw back his hood and pointed a long withered finger at them.

"I'll have what you stole from me," he said in dry raspy tones, "and I'll have your lives as well."

Aynber stared at the figure in bewilderment, recognizing him for the man they'd knocked down earlier but unable to guess what he was talking about. She glanced at Thorn, catching his guilty downward glance. At his belt hung a pouch that'd not been there before.

"Thorn…" she began.

She stopped as three other men approached them with bared steel from another side-street, death in their eyes as well. They were town merchants from the look of their clothing and the aprons tucked into their belts.

"Who..?" Aynber asked

"I owe them some coins," Thorn admitted. "Not much, really. It's just that a couple of small spells that I'd promised them never quite worked out and there was a little trouble over them. It seems

that the love potion was actually a potion to help a beard grow quicker and the maid to whom they gave it..."

Now Aynber realized why he'd been so nervous earlier on in the evening. The three merchants were probably also the reason why he'd climbed to her window rather than come up the stairs, and why he'd been hiding in the shadows outside the inn. She stepped over to him, ripped the pouch from his belt and threw it toward the man in the white cloak. It landed with a muffled clink and split open. Gold coins rolled out onto the cobblestone, as well as a number of small vials filled with a dark liquid, one of which broke into shards. Tendrils of smoke rose from it as the liquid met the air.

The man in the white cloak snarled, deep anger awakening in his eyes. His hand snaked out of the folds of his cloak to pluck at the air. Deliberately, he closed his fist as though grasping something that he alone could see.

Aynber felt a tightening about her heart and a low gasp of pained surprise escaped her lips. The more he contracted his fist, the greater was the pain. She cried out as her legs gave way beneath her and dropped the death-star still in her hand to tear at her jerkin in convulsive motions. A great darkness welled up within her.

"So it's spells, is it?" Thorn cried, reaching under his sodden cloak to where his own pouch of vials and powders hung.

Aynber's tormenter glanced disdainfully at him, striking at the air with his free hand. Thorn felt a blow out of nowhere and went tumbling to the ground. The momentary lapse of attention had Aynber hopeful. The pain slipped away and she half-rose, but before the motion was even really begun, the wizard's attention was upon her again, the force of his power driving her back to her knees.

All this while, the three merchants and Halin stared open-mouthed at what was taking place. They saw Thorn desperately scrabbling about in his cloak, Aynber writhing in an invisible death-grip, and the tall cloaked figure casually slaying the Huntress. But his offhand attitude was belied by the beads of sweat that dropped from his brow and the intense concentration that was written plainly in his face.

Now whether, as Thorn forever after swore to, it was a spell of his; or whether, as everyone else who heard the story agreed, it was just chance, at that moment a great flock of pigeons rose up from their roost in the eaves of the house of Linn of the Sea-masters' Guild, sweeping over the crossroads. The rising sun awoke a thousand colors in their grey and white feathers. The sudden sound of their wings was like thunder in the still dawn air, broken only by small cries of pain from Aynber and mutterings from Thorn.

The pigeons swept into the air, circled once, and swung off across the city. Behind, they left a downpour of bird droppings that splattered down among the players of this one-act scenario, one landing—wetly and with great force—upon the uplifted face of the strange wizard.

Blinded, he cried out and wiped the excrement from his eyes. His concentration broken, Aynber felt a loosening of the death-grip upon her. Her fingers searched the cobblestones for the *lessen-yaln* she'd dropped earlier.

One moment it lay glinting among the grey stones, the next it was imbedded in the wizard's throat. He fell with a choking sputter to those same cobblestones, his blood smoking as it met the air, much as the strange liquid in his broken vial had.

The scene held for yet another moment before the three merchants who had been chasing Thorn leapt forward, gathered the dead wizard's gold, and sped away. Thorn—surely without thinking on his part—was immediately in hot pursuit of them, never reflecting on what he would do with them, when and if he ever caught up to them.

As for Aynber, she stared at the wizard. She found her breath again and the pain in her chest receded. Slowly she rose and turned to see that Halin had fled as well, leaving a trail of blood from the wound in his leg. She'd have been surprised to still find him there. It didn't seem worthwhile to continue hunting him.

The night was a total loss, she realized until she thought of the young man she'd left in her bed chamber above the Inn of the Worn Scabbard. Perhaps he was still there, sleeping.

"I wonder," she said aloud, tracing the scar on her cheek thoughtfully.

With the possibilities of a pleasant morning to make up for the indignities the night had laid upon her, she started back to the inn with almost a spring to her step.

Wizard's Bounty

I

She came in out of the cold rain, her dark cloak steaming in the sudden warmth of the inn. It was called the Rose Door — run by one Hanar, late of Caeldon — and straddled the crossroads north of Calthoren. She drew back her hood with one slender hand, to reveal long tresses of golden hair held back with a thin strip of leather, and made for a table by the fire which crackled merrily on the far side of the room.

As she wended through the tables, the wayfarers and locals that filled the hostelry took in her obvious charms with open admiration. She favored them with a general withering glance. Throwing her cloak to the bench beside her, she sat down with a sigh.

"Curse this weather!" she complained to no one in particular.

She was no sooner seated than Hanar the landlord was at her table with a goblet of mulled wine.

"Can I help you, mistress?" he asked.

"I'm looking for a man —" she began, but stopped at his grin.

"Well, we've plenty for you to choose from here, eh lads?" he said with a chuckle.

The men who were near enough to hear him laughed with him until her short sword whispered from its sheath in a swift sure movement. Its point hovered an inch from the paling landlord's throat.

"His name is Nemenor," she said. "And when I find him, I don't plan to embrace him. Do you know him?"

"I...I..."

Hanar had no answer, but he didn't want to seem uncoopera-tive—not with that point of sharp steel at his throat.

"No, that would be too easy," the woman said.

Her blade disappeared as suddenly as it had appeared and she reached for the wine. Hanar beat a hasty retreat and a lanky man in a dusty brown robe approached her table to take the spot where the innkeeper had been standing.

"I know the man you seek," he said.

She turned to look at the newcomer, marked the fierce eyes that burned in a lean wrinkled face.

"There's gold in it for you," she said, "if you can tell me where he's to be found."

The man sat at her table and placed his goblet upon it.

"Oh, I can tell you where he's to be found," he said. The slit that served him for a mouth twisted into a wicked smile. "But who is it that seeks Nemenor the mage?"

"It's more like Nemenor the sorcerer with five hundred pieces of gold on his head—or so 'tis offered by a merchant in Calthoren." She fingered a thin scar on her left cheek and added: "I am Aynber— some call me the Huntress. And you?"

"Boadar."

She took a sip of her wine, dark grey eyes measuring him over the rim of her goblet.

"Well, Boadar," she said. "Where's he to be found?"

"He has a tower to the north of here, hidden in the Weneren Hills. I can take you there if you like."

There was a glint in his eyes as he spoke that bothered her.

"Na, na," she said, "there's no need for that. Just tell me how to find it and you've earned your gold."

He smiled again and held out his hands, palms up.

"It's a long road," he said. "One that two can fare with greater safety than one."

Aynber shrugged her slim shoulders. "You seem ill-equipped for a sell-sword."

The man was weaponless. He looked down at his worn robe, then over to her. He had watched her with the others when she came in and it was time well-spent. Her golden hair framed an oval sun-browned face with wide-set eyes and full lips. She was tall and wore a doe-skin shirt with a mail vest overtop that did little to hide the swell of her breasts. Beneath her shirt, short trousers of the same material met knee-high leather boots, while around her slender waist was a wide belt from which hung her short blade, a dagger and a small pouch.

"I have no need for mail or weapons," he said.

She gazed at him thoughtfully, one finger absently tracing the scar on her cheek. She never considered it a blemish for it had been won in a hard-pressed struggle from which she had emerged with but that one cut — and her life.

"Why so eager to guide me?" she asked.

"For a share of the gold. I'll guide you — and that's the only way you'll find his tower — and I'll take but a half of the reward for my trouble."

"A third."

"Let us meet part way between the two — give me three-sixths."

"That's still half. A third, or I find my own way."

"Fair enough," he said. "Will you have me for your guide?"

Aynber laughed. "Aye, why not? But mind you: I have no reason to trust you. And I have ways of dealing with treachery, so take care."

She tapped the hilt of her sword to emphasize her meaning, but Boadar only smiled. She shrugged, adding, "So be it. We'll leave at dawn then, if you're able."

Finishing her wine in one long swallow, she gathered up her cloak and left the table.

"Ho! Landlord!" she called out as she crossed the room. "A bed — for one — and quickly!"

Hanar scurried over and led her to the bed-chambers above.

Behind at the table, Boadar grinned into his wine cup. "Oh, aye, Huntress," he said, his voice soft. "I'll be able."

II

It was still raining the next morning when the mismatched pair left the inn. Boadar was in a foul mood and rode an ill-kept nag that looked near death compared to his companion's prancing mare.

"By the Goddess," she said as they rode northward. "It hasn't let up for a week."

In no time at all, they were wet to the skin and splattered with the mud that splashed up from their mounts' hooves. Still, the rain was more of a discomfort than a hindrance and they made good time.

"How far is this tower?" Aynber asked, breaking their long silence later in the day.

"Two days' journey, perhaps three," her companion replied with a thin smile.

She didn't like that smile of his but there wasn't much she could do about it. He alone knew the way and until they arrived he was needed. Yet, if he tried anything along the way...well, there'd be one less Boadar in the world, of that she was sure.

CRŁO

"We'll go no farther today," Aynber said later in the day.

Drawing back on her mare's reins, she sat easy in her saddle and surveyed the stretch of wood that they had come to. It was a dismal scene even though the rain had let up around mid-afternoon — petering off into a thin drizzle. But there was shelter beneath those dripping boughs. She felt wet and miserable and longed for a fire and a stomach full of warm food.

She turned to her companion. Boadar was slumped over his mount's neck, a sullen smile still playing about his mouth. The dusk was coming upon them now — a grey clouded sky growing darker — and then he sat up straighter.

"I'll start a fire if you'll fetch us some wood," he said.

Aynber shrugged dismounted.

"If you can start a fire in this wet, you're well-worth that third of the reward," she said and went off to gather the wood. When she returned, he had a small spark hissing in damp kindling.

"How did you — " she began.

Boadar looked up at her from where he crouched by the growing flames.

"Na, na, never mind...I don't think I want to know."

She dropped her armload of wood and knelt beside him. That small fire seemed unnatural and smelt of sorcery, but why bother questioning how he could make wet fuel burn? It was enough, for now, that she had its warmth. Cupping her hands, she held them out to the flames. Boadar chose that moment to speak.

"We've been followed," he said.

"Who?"

He nodded to the road behind her. She turned and looked past their tethered steeds to see three mounted men approaching. Brigands. They leered and rattled their swords in their scabbards. One made a lewd motion with his hand and the three laughed uproariously. And came closer...

"And will you give me a hand with them?" Aynber asked her companion.

Boadar grinned. "For a half of the reward?"

She cursed and, with feline grace, rose to meet the oncoming riders. From the pouch at her belt she drew three five-pointed stars wrought of silver.

Behind her Boadar's eyes widened in surprise. Death-stars, he thought. But they were an aelfin weapon, only found in their haunts far to the north. How had she become versed in their use?

But now wasn't the time for questions.

The brigands thundered toward her where she stood balancing on the balls of her feet, her legs slightly apart. The death-stars flew from her hand. The first ripped into the foremost rider's throat and nearly cut his head from his shoulders. Blood spurted from the ghastly wound, blinding the second man with a thick spray so that he never saw his own doom. A death-star pierced his left eye and took off the side of his face. And then Aynber slipped in the mud.

The last rider was upon her too quickly to take a cut with his long sword, but his steed's shoulder caught her as she slid and flung her aside. Boadar scrambled from the horse's path and was showered with sparks as the beast's hooves scattered their fire. The brigand wheeled his mount about and charged Aynber where she lay with her breath knocked from her.

She had clutched the third death-star in her hand when she fell. Head spinning, she staggered to her feet. Her sword slipped from its sheath and her own blood oozed from between her fingers for the death-star had cut deep into her palm. She gripped the slick hilt of her blade — wincing at the sudden pain — and met her remaining assailant's attack.

Blue sparks cut the night air as their swords rang together and then he was past and Aynber reeled backward again. For the first time the man saw the fate of his companions. Howling with rage, he threw caution to the winds and leapt from his saddle. He mouthed obscenities as he charged her—all reason fled now.

Aynber's right arm was numb from his last blow. She transferred her blade to her left and met him with a flurry of steel. Boadar stood to the side and watched the two trading blows. He had been in the midst of a small spell to aid her, but now he checked himself to watch the outcome. He marveled at her skill and even her foe seemed daunted for she was as capable with her left hand as most men were with their right.

Both the brigand and Aynber were breathing heavily now—skidding in the uncertain footing, yet matching each other blow for blow. Then the man left himself open for the briefest of seconds. Aynber's sword seemed to sing as it slipped through his defense and plunged into his side. He cried out as he felt his life spin from him and then he fell forward in a pool of his own blood. Boadar hurried to the girl's side, his face carefully masked with the appropriate expression of concern.

"Let me help you," he said, taking her arm.

She shook off his supporting hand. "Na, na...you'd give me no aid earlier—I'll have none from you now."

Then she fell forward across the body of her last foe. With surprising strength for his frail frame, Boadar carried her limp form to where their fire had been. There he laid her down and added more fuel to the few embers that yet remained. Gently he bound her wounded hand and covered her with her cloak.

As he crouched over her, a hungry gleam came into his eyes and he reached out with a claw-like hand to pull aside her cloak. In the dim glow of the fire her body seemed to welcome him and he cupped one half-revealed breast—his breath heavy with desire. But then she stirred and, replacing her cloak, he drew back hastily. The remainder of the night he spent in alternatively staring at her sleeping form and then gazing into the dying fire, humming tunelessly to himself.

III

The next day dawned grey and cheerless. Aynber awoke to the throbbing pain in her right hand where the death-star had left its mark. She sat up, shaking the sleep from her head, and glanced across the fire to where Boadar squatted. He seemed more surly than ever this morning and no wonder — what with this weather. She inspected her hand and, seeing the bandage on it, she realized that he must have seen to it after she had fallen across her foe last night.

Considering how little help he'd given her in the fight she was damned if he'd get any thanks from her.

Boadar looked up as she stirred and nodded to the small pot of stew that bubbled on the fire. It was then she recalled that she had never eaten last night. She reached for a bowl of the steaming stew.

"Who is it that offers so much gold for an insignificant wizard like Nemenor?" Boadar asked.

She shrugged and swallowed a mouthful.

"He's hardly insignificant," she said as she spooned another mouthful.

"Oh? And how's that? What's he done?"

"Well, I can't say what he's done to whoever's offering the gold for I don't know the man. I've been dealing with a merchant who handles another's affairs. But I do know that Nemenor is responsible for at least a dozen slayings in Calthoren — and those are just the known ones. I've seen his handiwork myself...if you could have seen what I've seen...a whole family it was in the quarter of the Weaver's Guild, butchered in some foul rite."

She shuddered as she remembered that grisly sight. There came a silence then and she put down her spoon — her appetite gone.

"And how do you mean to defeat this sorcerer, Huntress?" Boadar asked.

Her hand came down from her cheek where she had been fingering her scar and she patted the pouch at her belt.

"I have an amulet that can strip him of his powers," she said.

"Have you tried it yet?"

That mocking smile was back as he spoke. Aynber shook her head.

"Na, na, no more questions. Come. It's time we were riding."

They broke camp and mounted their horses as a fine drizzle began to fall once more. ·

CRSO

By nightfall they were high in the Weneren Hills making another wet camp. The evening passed without incident and the next morning found them traveling — still northward — under an overcast sky. The hills through which they wended were thick with coarse brush. They kept to the upper ridges where they could, for thickets of gnarled ash, birch and cedar choked the small valleys and in places the twisted boughs grew so closely together that the way was scarcely passable.

The pair straggled out of one overgrown valley and topped another rise. At its crest they paused for a moment. Aynber craned her neck, trying to make out the distant speck of a bird of prey that hovered high in the gloomy sky. Then Boadar nudged her and pointed down the slope before them.

"There it is," he said.

In the midst of another heavily wooded valley, a tall tower of grey stone rose above the trees — lofty and narrow like a claw tearing at the sky. Aynber fingered her scarred cheek with a stiff hand and peered down.

"Well, no use biding here," she said after a moment.

She shook her reins and steered her mare down the incline. Boadar followed close behind her, his ever-present smile playing about his lips.

When they came to the base of the tower, Aynber dismounted and cautiously approached it. There was no sign of life, in fact it looked as though it had been uninhabited for years.

"You sure this is the place?" she asked Boadar.

He nodded, so she turned to examine the tower again. She ran her hand along its weathered stone and then followed the wall with her eyes as it rose before her. Knotty vines crept up the tower's side and ended just before the first set of windows, which were placed about midway up its length. There was no door.

"Now here's a puzzle," she murmured. "How does he get in and out of this tower?" She glanced at Boadar, eyebrows raised quizzically.

He grinned. "Why don't you ask him?"

He was staring over her shoulder. She turned and followed his gaze to face the woods behind her. A tall man came walking from between the trees, eyes on the ground, white hair and beard fluttering in the wind. Aynber reached into her pouch and drew forth a curious stone with heavy runes scratched onto its face. She held it before her and began to mutter in a low voice. Boadar strained to make out the strange words, but she spoke too softly for him to make them out. Still, the approaching man heard them well enough.

His body jerked spasmodically as if he was being struck repeatedly by invisible blows. Piercing blue eyes sought out Aynber and glared at her with shock and consternation. Tiny beads of sweat broke out on her brow and then the full brunt of his defense hit her. She staggered back and murmured the words once again—more forcefully now—and he dropped to his knees. Involuntary twitches ran their course up and down his body. Those fierce eyes of his beseeched her now.

"Why?" The word issued gratingly from his throat as though he were unused to speech.

Aynber stepped closer to him—her amulet still before her.

"Why?" she repeated. "For the gold, Nemenor. I'm being paid well to bring you back to Calthoren where you'll be made to pay for your sins."

He was a handsome man and seemed younger than she had supposed he would be. Only the stark whiteness of his beard and hair showed as signs of age. That and his eyes—and they seemed older than time itself.

He was growing weaker now—supporting himself on his hands and knees. He wasn't as evil-looking as she had thought he would be, either. He looked up at her again, a strange look in his eyes. Words spilled haltingly from his throat:

"Fool you are...I, Old Winter...not Nemenor..."

She leaned forward to hear what he said. His voice was no more than a rasp when it reached her.

"He...is...with you..."

Then something hard struck her from behind. A darkness welled up in her mind and the last thing she remembered was falling beside the white-haired wizard with the echo of a too-familiar laugh ringing in her ears.

IV

When she finally regained her senses, she found herself leaning against a stone wall — her arms and legs bound in heavy chains. There was a dull throbbing in the back of her head and she could just imagine the size of the lump that was there. Across from her, she could make out the shape of the man she had come hunting. His head rested on his breast — for he was still unconscious — and he was chained in the same manner as she was.

Looking up, she saw that what little light there was in this room came from a small window set high in the wall.

They must be in the tower, she thought. But how?

She remembered how she had been struck just as she had defeated the wizard who now lay helpless across from her.

It had been Boadar. But why?

She tried to remember what the wizard had said just before she was struck, but then she saw that he was stirring.

One moment he had been unconscious and in the next, two blue eyes were appraising her with intelligence and a hint of amusement. She strained at the links that bound her — realizing her helplessness should he care to take his revenge for what she had done to him. There was no give in the chains; they were just too strong. Boadar had taken her weapons as well — not that they would have been of much use at the moment. At last she looked up and returned the wizard's gaze.

"How do you feel?" she asked. "Are you all right?"

"Not...unwell. I have...not...spoken...for...many years. It is...unfamiliar to me...this method...of communicating..."

"How do you talk, then?" Aynber was curious about this man whom she had stalked for the last two weeks.

Through the mind, came his reply.

"Oh — " she began and stopped short.

His lips hadn't moved and his words echoed in her mind. How could that be? But, of course...he was a wizard. Nemenor of — she stopped short again as she remembered what he had said during their struggle. She stared at him through the half-light. From the window above her, she could hear the soft patter of rain on its sill.

"Who are you?" she asked.

38

My true name is not for this world and, once heard, is best forgotten. Yet I will tell you. I am Tamar Greyskin, although the folk near here call me Old Winter.

And then she knew: Boadar had been Nemenor all along! The realization struck her like it blow.

"You don't seem that old," she remarked at last.

The years fade in my memory but I have seen the passage of three centuries since first I came to the hills of this world. Long and long ago that was, indeed, in the count of mortal years.

Aynber drew in a sharp breath. Her mind filled with dread superstitions which she forced from her.

How is it, he continued, *that you search for Nemenor and yet travel in his company?*

There was laughter in his eyes.

"I was blind, that's all," she answered irritably.

A faint flush spread over her face as she thought upon her foolishness. At least the dim light within the chamber hid her embarrassment.

"My name's Aynber," she said to change the subject.

Amber?

"No, with an 'n.' It's pronounced Ann-burr." Her thoughts drifted for awhile and then she said: "I wonder why we're still alive."

Nemenor seeks my knowledge, came Old Winter's reply. *As for you—* he ran his eyes along her full figure—*I'm sure he'll find a use for you, though I'm afraid, it's one that won't be much to your liking!*

Aynber wrinkled her nose in disgust as she thought of her former companion.

"Still," she said, "knowing what he wants us for won't help us now. It's a way to escape that I'm looking for, but these chains are too strong and I, for one, don't have a key to the locks…"

A thought came to her as she was speaking and she fell to peering through the dim light that illuminated the floor, searching…

What do you seek?

"Well, since that amulet stripped you of your powers and we don't have a key…I'm looking for something long and thin with which to pick the locks. In my trade, I've had a lot of practice at lock-picking. Now, if I can only find something like—ah!"

She moved away from the wall and inched her body along the floor. The heavy chains impeded her progress, but at last she was

40

able to reach her goal. With her teeth, she picked up the sliver of wood that she had seen and laboriously made her way to where Old Winter leaned against the opposite wall. Then she went to work on the lock that held the chains which bound his hands...

The sliver kept slipping from between her teeth until, at last, she fitted it into the lock. She twisted it within, straining to hear the welcome click of its release, when the sliver broke. As did the next two. The fourth cut her gums as she forced it within the lock, but there was a faint snap and she was rewarded for her efforts. With his hands free, Old Winter followed her directions and soon they both stood — albeit wobbly — and faced the door to their prison. The lock for it was on the other side.

There is another way, came the wizard's words, and he turned toward one of the walls.

As he felt along its rough surface searching for a hidden catch, Aynber stood rubbing her wrists and planning her vengeance upon Nemenor, whom she had known as Boadar. There was still an aching in the back of her head from where he had struck her and her thoughts were none too pleasant.

Then she heard Old Winter's delighted cry within her mind: *Ah! Here it is!*

He pressed a stone that seemed no different from any of the others and a section of the wall slid to one side, revealing a dark passageway. Motioning Aynber to accompany him, he strode forward and was swallowed by the shadows. Aynber took a deep breath and coughed, for she had breathed the stale air that issued forth from the opening. With a resigned sigh, she followed him. Behind her, the opening in the wall closed again with a dull rumble.

V

As the darkness swept in around her, Aynber stepped forward and walked into an old spider web. The gossamer strands clung to her face and, as she jumped back, she could feel goose-bumps all up and down her arms and shoulders.

"Ugh!" she muttered, brushing them from her. "Don't you ever clean in here? And how about some light so that we can see where we're going?"

Normally, came her companion's voice, resonating in her head, *I have little need to walk through these passageways, so why clean them? And I could form a light for us; however, since you were kind enough to take my powers away earlier...*

"Never mind," she broke in. "Let's be on our way."

She took hold of the edge of his robe and trailed along behind him as he set off. As they made their way, she thought of sunlight and meadows to take her mind from this dank corridor, only to remember that it was still raining outside. With that she felt even more depressed and walked straight into Old Winter's back when he came to a sudden stop.

There are stairs here...watch your step.

The stairs were circular and wound upward for many turns. At last they came to the top one and the pair were in another corridor. There was a faint glow at the end and the sound of chanting echoed up the gloomy passageway.

Silence now, came the wizard's voice. *We approach my private chambers.*

The chanting rose and fell; at one moment, high and clear as a young boy's voice and in the next, guttural and scarcely human in timbre.

That is Nemenor, continued the wizard. *He wastes no time in making use of my sacred circle.*

Soundlessly, they crept along the corridor until they came to the source of the glimmer of light. It was a peephole set in the stone wall. Aynber dusted the cobwebs from it and peered through. Sure enough, there was Nemenor.

He crouched in a circle of arcane symbols and ideographs that were sketched on the floor. The symbols and runes were innocuous on their own, but he had added to them so that they stood out stark and obscene in the dim candlelight that lit the room. There were eldritch objects set at certain positions within the circle. Aynber recognized some of them and knew their magical worth, but again, Nemenor had corrupted them to his own use. Some were inverted, while others had been reshaped or otherwise profaned. Quelling an instinctive shudder, Aynber turned to Old Winter.

"Is there a door in this wall as well?" she asked, her voice a whisper.

Aye, but hold your wrath for a few moments longer. Soon he will be at the height of his invocation and sufficiently distracted so that we might at least have a small chance to get within the chamber ere he discovers us.

She could wait, she decided, and returned her attention to the scene within the chamber.

From Nemenor's crouched form, her gaze searched the room. Ah! There were her weapons and...the amulet as well. It would be of no use against Nemenor now, but perhaps if she could destroy it, Old Winter's power might be returned to him. It was worth a try at least, for after all, what else could she do?

Along the edge of the circle, the symbols and runes began to glow and a thin line of green light traced its way. There were five candles that stood in certain positions just beyond the perimeter of the circle. They flared up without warning and then died just as suddenly without a splutter. The room plunged into an eerie darkness and an oppressive gloom settled over the green-lit circle, where Nemenor stooped, shrouded and still chanting.

Old Winter touched Aynber's shoulder and in her mind she heard his voice: *Now is the time.*

He moved past her and pressed a stone in the wall, just above her head. Slowly a section of the wall slid to one side. As soon as there was enough space, Aynber leapt into the darkened chamber and made for where she had seen her weapons and the amulet. Old Winter was close behind her.

No sooner had they stepped within the room, than the candles flared brightly again and Nemenor was facing them. Behind him a shadow detached itself from the wall and approached them, menacingly.

"You!" Nemenor cried as he saw who it was.

Aynber ignored him and raced for her weapons. The shadow took on shape and shuffled across the chamber so that a powerless Old Winter faced the thing. Out of the corner of her eye, Aynber saw a glow form about Nemenor's hands. Swift as thought, a bolt of greenish light sped from his fingers to explode where she had just been.

Aynber had thrown herself to the floor and rolled to her feet, all in one sure quick motion. Another bolt shot over her head, singeing her hair, but then she'd reached her weapons. She grasped neither her sword nor her death-stars. In her hand, she held aloft the amulet and, as a third bolt of hell-fire splintered the wall behind her, she dashed it to the floor where it shattered in a flare of brilliant golden light.

"Damn you!" Nemenor cried, all control fled as his rage consumed him.

In the midst of his cursing, Old Winter cried out in triumph, for his own power had returned. Now the shadow-thing fell back from him as blinding golden lights spilled from the white-maned wizard's fingertips, piercing the formless murk of the creature until it was no more.

"Na, na," Aynber said, "it's not me that's to be damned."

There was a ruddy glow in her cheeks from the heat of her battle-fury and a deadly gleam in her dark eyes. In her bandaged hand she held a death-star and she flipped it with deceptive ease at the man she had known as Boadar. Nemenor tried to ward it off with a gnarled claw, but it was to no avail.

"No—" he began, then the word was lost in a gurgle as the death-star tore into his throat.

Brackish blood spewed from his mouth and smoked as it came into contact with the air. Tendrils of that smoke wreathed his anguished face and then his flesh crumbled and peeled, to fall from him. In a moment there was just a small mound of dust where he had stood.

CR&O

It's a long strife, we've had, Old Winter was explaining the next morning as they sat outside his tower under a clear sky with just a hint of cloud. *I was always stronger than Nemenor. In you he saw a way to better me at last, so it's fitting that you should have been his downfall as well. Still, I should have been more on guard. But I hadn't seen him for at least a score of years and my studies have been taking up more and more of my time of late. Ah! well…his threat's ended at last, anyway.*

"Mmm," agreed Aynber, listening politely—one finger tracing the scar on her cheek.

She was more eager to return to Calthoren, rather than sitting here and listening to him, even if his company was pleasant enough. Above them more clouds began to gather. It would be good to sit in a tavern, drinking mulled wine with her feet up on a bench before a roaring fire. Aye, that reward money would last her for at least a month, if not a bit more, she mused. The reward money!

"Damn," she said and rose to her feet.

What's wrong? inquired the wizard.

"The reward! I've no proof that I killed Nemenor and so I can't collect it!"

As she spoke, it began to rain once more. She looked up at the sky and shook her fist at the clouds.

"Damn," she muttered again.

Stormraven

"A tower," Aynber said, "and a maze within. Guardians you can put no name to — nor give a reckoning as to their numbers. Put that together with the fact that you're not even sure that whatever you seek is there..."

Frowning, she leaned forward, resting her chin in the hollow of her cupped hands. Her corn-gold hair spilled about her face, hiding the small scar that ran down her left cheek. Her clear grey-green eyes stared into her half-empty ale mug.

She wore trousers and a tunic of heavy cotton this evening, with calf-high boots of Tanic leather. A slightly curved sword with a guardless hilt lay across her knees. In a pouch thonged to her belt were a handful of throwing stars.

"Na, na," she finished. "It scarce seems worth the risk."

Harper Rhynn sighed. "Must I remind you of an unpaid debt then? Five years ago..."

Aynber nodded. She looked Rhynn over as she remembered.

His garments were threadbare, his face lined and weary. His instrument's case was weathered and battered. He'd not seemed near so down-at-the-heels that night he'd helped her escape from Haj'n's Keep. But that was five years ago indeed. A lot could happen in five years. A lot *had* happened. Still. She could do worse than try this adventure with him to repay the old debt. He was fair enough to look upon at least, not like the hang-abouts that tended to drift through Calthoren these days. Mind you, you had to look past the

47

road dust that grimed him now. Cut away some of those matted tangles and give the beard a trim...

She shook her head.

"But why me?" she asked. "If there's sure loot in the offing, I can find you a dozen or more blades who'd jump at the chance. With a strong company..."

"I must have a guide within the tower."

"Me?"

The harper nodded.

"But, Rhynn. *I've* never been there before. Anann knows I've never even heard of the place before today!"

"You have untapped depths, Huntress. Any with an inkling of deepsight can see that. The moon shines through your eyes, blessing you."

Aynber laughed. "Blessing me? Hardly! More 'n' likely it's an ale-glow you see in my eyes."

Rhynn sighed. "And yet the moon is there. For that reason, and the debt, I ask your aid. I have sought entrance to this tower for many years. Three months past I dreamed a harpdream. Woven amidst the strands of its music was an augury. It showed me that only with one of the moon-blessed as a guide can I breach the tower's riddle. I cast about for one such and then remembered you. Would you deny me?"

"I..."

Aynber took a sip of her ale. She looked about the inn, mentally cataloging the new faces. Her thoughts turned back and she recalled how Rhynn had tricked Haj'n into giving her her freedom. Strange harping and a cunning riddle—had Haj'n ever guessed it? But now there were new riddles and she was the one left guessing. What did she stand to lose?

"You can tell me no more?" she asked.

Rhynn shrugged. "I know little enough myself. I can scarce promise that we'll come to no harm. But I must enter that tower. If not..."

"If not?"

"If not I must walk the roads of Woldenar until I die."

"But...ah, never mind." She raised her gaze in mock despair. "Why is it that all mages and harpers can only speak in riddles?"

"I'm not sure what you mean..." Rhynn began.

Aynber waved him into silence.

"No more riddles," she said. "I didn't expect an answer, though Anann knows there must be one." She smiled suddenly. "But I do owe you one, Rhynn. And if the truth were told, I've been bored stiff these past weeks. When Thorn and I bought this inn—well, it seemed like a good idea at the time. Only Wedley and Kendra run the Darkwood well enough on their own and I'm only so much excess baggage. With Thorn attempting an honest trading venture and gone for at least another month, and Calthoren so dead you'd think it was a monk's tomb…"

"Then you'll come?"

"Did I mention I'm bored half to death? Indeed I will."

"I'm glad," Rhynn said, his voice soft.

Aynber lifted her ale mug. "To the moon then!" Her eyes held a gentle mockery.

Rhynn clanked his mug against hers.

"To the moon!" he agreed, though there was no mockery about him. "For it is said that only the moon may breach the walls of Stormraven with impunity."

Aynber gave him a questioning look, then shrugged and tossed back her ale.

ଔଞ

Deep into the northlands they fared. Rhynn took them by hidden ways—"Easy enough to find, if you know enough to look."— until, near the end of a day in the middle of their third week of journeying, they reached the tower.

They sat their mounts on the brow of a low hill and regarded it. Twilight hung like a mantle upon the structure. It straddled its own hill, rising tall and dark into the shadowed sky—a grey finger of rock silhouetted against a crimson sunset. High on the side facing them, the bas-relief of a raven's profile watched them with its one eye.

"It doesn't seem evil," Aynber said. She leaned across her pommel to stroke her mare's neck. "Old, aye, and a little otherworldly— but that's no more than the mood the dusk throws over it. It's more…hallowed…"

"I did not say it was evil."

50

Aynber shot Rhynn a dirty look. Her temper — never the most even — was fraying at the edges of late. It had been like this the whole of their journey north. Rhynn was as friendly as ever — oh, aye — and as full of tales and songs as might be expected by his trade, but whenever she'd questioned them more about their destination — or even discussed it — he would reply with infuriatingly cryptic evasions.

"No," she replied. "You never did say it was evil — bless my soul! But tell me. Why have you dragged me all this way? To protect you from the wind in the trees? The sunset? And as for guiding — you've been the guide these past weeks, not I. I feel about as useful as a teatless sow trying to feed her litter."

Rhynn eyed her steadily. "Your time for guidance will come and there may yet be danger. In what form, I cannot tell, but there will be a struggle, though the way through may not necessarily be won by a skill with weapons." He shrugged. "Aye, there will be a struggle. How else to win freedom?"

Aynber gave a snort of disgust. She shook out her reins and cantered down the slope.

"Shall we see, then?" she called back over her shoulder.

Rhynn sighed and followed at a more sedate pace. When he joined her she was standing before the tower's portal fingering the brass bindings of its huge oaken door. Her mare was ground-hitched by the simple measure of tossing her reins so that they trailed on the ground. The well-trained mare grazed peacefully unconcerned. Rhynn swung from the back of his own mount.

Aynber turned as he approached.

"Have you the key?" she asked sarcastically.

Rhynn shook his head.

Aynber stared at the broad door. It dwarfed them, standing at least twenty feet from base to top-most edge. She could see neither latch nor keyhole. How thick was it? A half foot?

"Then how...?"

"Let us set up camp and eat," Rhynn said. "Later will be soon enough."

Aynber shrugged. "It's your tower."

They saw to their mounts first — rubbing them down with sweet grasses then letting them graze. Their own meal passed in silence.

Throughout it Rhynn gazed at the tower, his face strangely alien in the light of their small fire.

Aynber watched him, feeling mixed emotions. Throughout their journey she'd been torn between frustration and wanting to leave, and a need to see this thing through. Now that they were come to the tower, she could understand some of Rhynn's feelings. There was a sense of wonder about the structure. Now having seen it — felt its presence — she was drawn to it in a way she couldn't quite define.

Rhynn rose suddenly and fetched his harp. As he drew it forth from its case, Aynber was again amazed at its beauty. Perfectly crafted, it shone and gleamed in the firelight. There were a number of jewels set into its supports — "If we find nothing else, you can have these," Rhynn had remarked one night, leaving Aynber calculating their probable worth for about an hour. But his harping always dispelled her more mercantile instincts leaving her dreamy and restless, with a bittersweet longing she couldn't place. Strange feelings would tug within her. She would find a silence within the music that was warm and pulsed with the deep air of the woods about them.

Tonight was no exception.

The music swelled, filling with mystery. It told the riddle of the tower that loomed over their campsite. Aynber was sure that amidst the harping — if she could only understand — she would *know* the answers to all her questions. She never quite did. But whereas Rhynn's cryptic replies never ceased to irritate her, the harping soothed while it wove its riddles.

Rhynn watched her as he played. When the moon rose — when he could see its horned crescent reflected in her eyes — he let his fingers fall from the strings. Silently he replaced the harp in its case, stood and shouldered it.

"It is time," he said.

Still caught in the music's dying echoes, Aynber stared at him uncomprehendingly. Then she scrambled to her feet. She buckled her sword to its shoulder harness, adjusting the hilt so that it was positioned just behind her right shoulder. Opening her pouch, she took out three throwing stars and clipped them to her belt. Satisfied that she was as ready as she could be, she joined Rhynn by the door.

"Well?" she asked.

"Remember in Calthoren," he replied, his voice intense, but low, "when I spoke of the moon? That only it could breach the tower?'

Aynber nodded.

"Feel it within you, Huntress. Let it grow. The bright wise moon. Can you feel it?"

Aynber shook her head. But she turned and looked skyward to where the silvery crescent rode the night skies. It seemed to tremble as she watched it. She felt a tingle run through her.

"Touch the door," Rhynn said.

Obediently, Aynber lifted a hand, then paused. She took a step back to regard Rhynn with suspicion. She opened her mouth, but the questioning protest died on her lips. Rhynn's gaze met hers, frank and open. She found that, try though she might, she could not distrust him.

Breaking eye contact, she stepped forward and touched the door with a hesitant hand. It swung open silently to reveal a large anteroom. The room was immense. Misty globes hung from a high ceiling, throwing a dim pale light that spilled out the door.

"They are dalin," Rhynn said. "Dwarf-wrought and so neverfailing."

He stepped inside. Frankly curious—with her suspicions lulled if not vanished—Aynber followed him inside. The door closed behind them. Aynber whirled, right hand streaking for her blade's hilt, left to her throwing stars. She saw only the door—firmly shut. She turned to Rhynn.

"What is this place?" Her voice rang hollowly in the large room.

"Many things," Rhynn replied. "Different things, perhaps, to every being that enters." He met her gaze openly. "I have an inner sight, Huntress, a deepsight that can see through the glamors of this world. But in here I am blind. There is too much mystery—Middle mystery. I know the ways of the Light, understand the Dark. But the Grey Middle Kingdom—it is the moon's realm. I am lost here. But still, I need to find that…that which I seek. You have a different sight. There is a fey wisdom in you and the moon knows your spirit. Here you are the guide. I hope to find my freedom here."

Aynber shook her head. "Why can't you just tell me what we're—you're—looking for? Anann, I've come this far on speculation. Do you think I'd back out now?"

"If I told you," Rhynn said, "you would not believe. And that disbelief would affect your ability to guide us. Huntress, you have trusted me so far. Trust me a little longer."

"You leave me little choice. Having come this far —"

Rhynn cut her off. "Do not say that! You *do* have choice! You are the guide."

Aynber looked away from him. Across from the entrance were three doors. Save for them, the room was unadorned. She pursed her lips, looking from the doors to Rhynn.

"The left one then."

At the door, she paused, lifting an eyebrow. Rhynn motioned her forward. Shrugging, she put her palm against the dark-grained wood, scarcely surprised when it swung silently open at her touch.

They entered a long hallway, lit from above by a row of dalin set at intervals of twenty feet. The walls were bare stone, save under each dalin. There were bas-reliefs of intricately-carved ravens in various positions of flight. The floor and walls were dry; the air slightly musty, though not uncomfortably so.

"These carvings," Aynber said, stopping to examine one more closely. "Are they dwarf-wrought too, do you think? Ravens have the name of evil in the old lore, and yet...these seem beyond that."

"There *are* dark dwarves," Rhynn replied, "though I doubt this is their work. They would scarce take the time. And I would not call ravens evil, either. Proud, aye, but untouched by our moralities. They belong to the twilight realms — the Middle Kingdom. There are many such misunderstood beings, Huntress — longwolves and moonhares, the grey bears of the highlands, aye, and others more magical still: the spirits of moor and hill, the tree-dwellers, stonesmiths, windriders..."

Aynber regarded him thoughtfully. This was the closest she'd come to a direct answer from him since they'd left Calthoren. She wondered if she should push her luck. But something else was nagging at the back of her mind now. The hallway they fared down seemed to run on forever. It curved slightly to the left so that their entranceway was lost to sight.

"There's something not quite right here," she said. "This hallway. It can't possibly be this long. You saw the size of the tower from the outside..."

Her voice trailed off. She shivered suddenly. Rhynn caught her mood, but was quicker to shake it from him.

"It is part of the mystery of this place, I suppose," he said a little uncertainly. "Yet there is a feeling of 'rightness' about it. As though it were indeed a crossroads…"

"Of what?" Aynber asked when he didn't finish. "A crossroads of what?"

"Of worlds," Rhynn replied and he would say no more.

Aynber sighed. Well, she'd learned more in the past few minutes it seemed than in the whole of their ride north. The trouble was she understood her new knowledge no better than if Rhynn had never spoken. How could anyone be so damned secretive and still expect to be helped?

She sighed again and took the lead. The hallway branched a short while later. Aynber peered down the new corridor's length.

"What now?" she asked more to herself.

"You must choose."

She shot him a sour look.

"We're liable to get completely lost and end up wandering through here for the rest of our lives if you're so keen on following my guidance. Anann, I haven't a clue which way to go."

"Let yourself go quiet," Rhynn said. "Inside. Fill yourself with silence and let the moon speak to you."

"The moon! The moon! You can take your moon and shove—" She broke off, shaking her head. "Ah, what's the use. I suppose it can't hurt to try."

She closed her eyes and tried to still the inner conversation that rambled through her mind. It seemed to be an easy enough thing to accomplish, but the more she tried, the more totally irrelevant thoughts clambered to the surface of her mind, disturbing her concentration. She frowned and took a few deep breaths, letting the clamor run its course.

She stood enrapt for long moments and finally there came a time when her mind held stillness more deep than any ocean depths. A golden radiance seemed to fill her, squeezing into her every pore. She basked in its quiet wonder. When the questions arose once more, she knew an answer to at least one. Whether it came from within herself — an insight — or it was moon-born…

"We go on," she said.

They passed three more branching hallways, then a crossing. At the next turnoff, Aynber stopped.

"This way," she murmured with growing confidence. She felt now as though she had a built-in compass inside her, pointing the way.

The new hallway ended after three turnings. Before them was a large wooden door with iron hinges, though no latch. Aynber smiled. She stepped up to it, palm face-out. As the door swung open she stepped through, then stopped dead in her tracks. In the sparsely furnished room stood a tall shaggy creature.

Its body hair was long and matted in grizzled tangles. About its loins was tied a strip of leather. Yellowed fangs protruded from the corners of its mouth, pulling the lips in a hideous grin. Aynber met the creature's unblinking gaze. Though it put her in mind of the great apes of Kasque, there was a burning intelligence in these eyes that never an ape had.

She drew her blade suddenly and side-stepped, but made no other threatening gesture. The creature had reach on her, but with her blade — a sharp feint left, twist, in on the right…

She paused, uncertain. The same sense that had guided her through the hallways was trilling a low warning. She remembered something that Rhynn had said. It would not necessarily be a struggle of weapon's skill. But what then?

Lightning swift, her thoughts ran through her. The tableau held. The beast continued to watch her, shifting position slightly. Aynber struggled with her uncertainty. She felt she was being tested. But the confidence that had filled her in the halls had deserted her…deserted her or demanded something other than her natural reaction to such a confrontation. She could hear Rhynn breathing behind her. Her own breath sounded a little quick. She sighed. Still uncertain, she lowered her blade.

"Lord," she said quietly. "We ask entrance."

For all her outward composure, her heart was pounding.

Here dies a fool, she thought.

One did not face shaggy brutes and bespeak them politely and with her blade lowered, she was now at a disadvantage. She couldn't bring the same strength to play in an upswing.

The creature smiled, baring the full length of its fangs.

"Lady," it said, inclining its head slightly, "I bid you welcome."

Aynber stared in shock, unable to believe her ears. Rhynn smiled and let loose a long sigh.

"We seek…ah…"

She looked to Rhynn for aid.

The beast motioned to the doorway behind it. "Through there."

"Ah…thank you."

Still shaken, she edged around the creature, making for the door. It opened under her touch and she and Rhynn filed through. As soon as the door whispered shut behind them, she whirled on Rhynn.

"What *was* that thing?"

"A guardian, I should think," the harper replied.

"Some guardian," Aynber said. "It let us through without batting an eye. If that's the best this place can throw against us…"

Rhynn touched her arm. "I do not think the guardians are necessarily against us. But again, there is some test involved. How you approach the problem depends upon…"

"I know, I know. How well I listen to the moon. But what do you think? Is that the trick? A non-combatant's stance…?"

Rhynn shrugged.

"I do not know," he replied honestly.

"Na, na. Of course you wouldn't."

Her sarcasm was lost on the harper.

They went on. The corridor turned, ending at the bottom of a flight of stairs. At the top was another door. More cautiously, Aynber opened it, standing well back until the whole of the room could be viewed.

This chamber was empty of life, though well furnished. Heavy tapestries hung from the walls. There was a hearth in one corner and a half-dozen chairs scattered throughout. A long table ran the length of the wall to their right. There were a number of flasks and goblets upon it, gleaming eerily in the dalin light. Across from them was another door.

They passed through more chambers, each untenanted, each richer furnished than the last. The corridors between them had wooden floors and their boots rang softly upon them. The walls were adorned with more and more bas-reliefs. The ravens were still present in them, but now a whole plethora of mythical creatures shared the stone.

Time dragged. They found room after room. Always Rhynn shook his head, indicating they must go on. Aynber would shrug, marking the riches, but not wanting to burden herself down at the moment. On the way back, she decided.

After awhile the chambers began to take on a more Spartan look once more. Four flights of stairs and more rooms than she cared to remember later, Aynber wondered if they would ever find an end to the place. A barrow stillness hung over the rooms and corridors. They sensed no other living presence. At the next door, Rhynn stopped Aynber's hand before she could touch the smooth wood.

"I sense life within," he said.

Aynber nodded. She sensed it too. Touching the door, she stepped back as it swung silently open. The revealed chamber was of bare stone: ceiling, walls, floor. In the very center stood a handsome man in a monk's habit. Blade still sheathed, Aynber moved slowly into the room, eyes on the monk.

"Greetings," she said. "We seek entrance."

The monk bowed. As he moved, his habit shimmered and fell from him. He was clad now in white leather and in his fist was a sword identical to Aynber's. He smiled strangely.

"Then find death!"

He attacked with such suddenness that Aynber barely had time to throw herself aside, catching the blow on her swiftly drawn blade. Her attacker drove in relentlessly and she was fighting for her life. She had no time for her own attack. It was all she could do to defend herself from the warrior's lightning blows.

"Rhynn!" she cried out once during a rapid flurry of feints and dancing thrusts. "Rhynn!"

She caught a glimpse of the harper out of the corner of her eye before her assailant demanded the full of her attention once more. Rhynn stood ashen-faced in the doorway. He was struggling to come to her aid, but an invisible force held him helpless. So be it, then. She could count on no aid.

Her inability to lay a blow on the warrior baffled her. Her every thrust was parried with a skill that made her feel like a rank amateur. The warrior taunted her with an arrogant smile. Aynber smiled back, her eyes cold and hard. Swiveling she engaged his blade, gripping her hilt with one hand. Her free hand unclipped a throwing star from her belt.

Up and around went her blade. The warrior stepped in to follow the movement, but she was already leaping to one side. She flung herself across the room, rolling to her feet and turning. The throwing star left her hand—cutting a bright arc across the room. It caught him square in the chest. His face blanked in surprise. His blade-arm sagged, blade-tip touching the stone floor.

"Scarcely sporting," he murmured and fell forward, his sword clanging against the floor.

Aynber straightened slowly, drawing in large gulps of air. With her blade in her hand, she faced Rhynn. The harper's face was still pale.

"I could not move," he said. He drew his own blade.

Aynber nodded. She worked a kink out of her neck with her free hand, then motioned to the new door. They faced it together with drawn steel.

"Why did this one attack and the other not?" mused Aynber.

Rhynn shrugged. "Perhaps to show that things are not always what they seem."

He looked back. Aynber followed his gaze and drew in a sharp breath. The warrior was gone. On the floor lay her throwing star…and the warrior's sword. She passed the back of her hand over her brow.

"Let's get this over with," she said softly. "This'll be the last door." Her intuition was speaking within her.

She touched the wood panel and the door swung open to show another empty room—empty except for a small dais in its centre. On the dais stood a plain wooden harp with bronze strings. She caught the look on Rhynn's face.

"For this?" she asked.

Rhynn nodded, his eyes shining.

"But your own harp…it's so much finer."

Rhynn touched his harpcase. "This is not my harp. Just as Woldenar—this world—is not my world. That is my harp. For thirty years I have been trapped in these violent lands, seeking my way homeward. But I am a Harper…to spell my passage I must have my own harp."

"But how did it get here? How did *you* get here?"

"I was cast here in the backwash of a great spelling on my own world. It…" He shrugged. "The reasons for that spelling would mean nothing to you and would take a lifetime to tell—for it was a thing of many lifetimes that the spelling sprung from. Suffice that I was trapped here and must needs adjust myself to this world until the chance to return home might come my way."

"And the harp?"

"I could only hope," replied Rhynn. "This tower stands on many worlds, Huntress. It is a crossroads...a gateway. With my desire strong enough, the harp could be here. But only one such as you could gain me access to the tower itself. It is a testing ground, you see. It belongs to the Middle Kingdom. My way is the way of the Tuathan, the Fair Gods. They have no strength in this place—I have no right to be here unless accompanied by one of the Middle Kingdom's moon-blessed."

Aynber shook her head. "You're still not making any sense. I tell you, I'm not blessed—by the moon or otherwise."

"Then what guided you through the maze? What stayed your hand with the one guardian, yet let you prevail against the other?"

"Myself," replied Aynber firmly.

"To those of the twilight it is often one and the same." Rhynn smiled. "I must take my leave, Huntress."

He sheathed his blade, then unstrapped it from his belt and laid it aside. "I will have no need for such a weapon in my own land," he explained." He unshouldered his harpcase, drawing out the beautiful instrument within.

Aynber frowned as she compared the two. It seemed a poor choice to make, the worn weathered harp for this bejeweled one. She regarded Rhynn and her frown grew deeper. This talk of worlds and gateways....The riddle was growing deeper and still there was no answer in sight.

Rhynn reshouldered the empty case. He took up the old harp from the dais and, sitting on the edge, began to play. With the first chords, an amber light came creeping about him, pale and gossamer. Aynber stepped back, unsure of herself.

"You survived the testing," said Rhynn across the sound of his harping. "You have the right to claim your freedom."

Freedom? Freedom from what? She *was* free. Only...

Her eyes misted as the harping grew deeper. It pulled and tugged within her, then left her in a pool of silence. Within, she was wrapped in a quiet so still it left her breathless. She blinked and the room shimmered about her. When the shimmer was gone, she was in a strange place of silence and grey-amber mists. Before her...She shook her head.

A huge raven, its feathers streaked with grey, the tips golden, was before her. In its eyes an amber storm raged. Its beak seemed to curve into a smile.

"You..." she began.

The word fell like a pebble into the silence, tiny ripples of sound widening around it. The raven's smile grew broader.

"I?" it asked with humor.

Aynber rubbed her eyes. "Are you real? *Can* you be real?"

"I am named Rootwing," the raven said, "and I am as real as you."

Aynber digested that. The bird had put a strange emphasis on its words so that she was unsure of what it meant.

"It was not a grand testing," continued the raven, "I'll admit to that. And yet...if you saw the dangers and bypassed them, I can scarcely complain that your testing was too easy. Now what would you have? Your freedom? Or do you seek passage?"

"Freedom from what?"

The feathered shoulders moved in a shrug. "Reality. Illusion. Who can say?"

"And the passage?"

The raven's smile grew mocking. "Why to the other worlds. Where else?"

"I..." Aynber paused.

Her mind was broiling with questions, but her insight told her that this moment—however strange and unreal it might seem—would still not last long. She must make a decision and make it soon. But what? She scarcely understood what was going on. All the riddling seemed to lead to this moment and here was she not knowing which way to turn. This was something that Rhynn was better equipped to—

The answer came rushing into her mind.

"Passage," she said firmly. "For the harper."

"So be it," said the raven. Its voice held a tone of slight disappointment. "That was fairly spoken, I suppose. For had you not offered your companion the passage, he would have drifted all his years through the grey spaces between the worlds. With your generosity you have saved him, but lost your own chance. Where now *your* freedom?"

As the raven spoke, her eyes misted once more. For a moment her vision cleared. She saw the harp chamber once more. Rhynn was gone, though his jeweled harp and sword remained. Then the room faded and she felt herself falling.

The sensation lasted for brief seconds that appeared to drag into hours. Her head spun and her eyes closed. When she felt something solid form underfoot, her legs buckled under her and she stumbled to lie in...grass?

She opened her eyes to find herself outside the tower. It was midday and the sun was high and bright overhead. On the grass beside her were Rhynn's harp and sword. And Rhynn? He was bound homeward now, she supposed.

She thought she heard a sound then—an echo within her mind like the ringing of a distant harp. She smiled as she recognized the tune for one that Rhynn had composed on their first night out of Calthoren. He had called it: "The Harper Thanks the Lady."

"You're welcome, Rhynn," she said softly.

The tune played on for a few more bars, then faded and disappeared.

Aynber sighed. She felt a shiver of loss run through her, but...

The grass under her felt good. There were shoots of clover and thyme growing underfoot as well and their scent filled the air with a sweet, heady fragrance. The sky was a brilliant blue that could only make her smile.

CR80

Aynber twisted in the saddle, her mare restless under her. She steadied it with the firm pressure of her knees. Rhynn's mount tugged lightly at the reins wrapped about her pommel and nickered.

Behind stood the Tower of Stormraven, grey and slender in the afternoon light. Aynber regarded the raven's profile and smiled a little. Dealing with faery was always chancy, for those denizens of the Middle Kingdom were capricious and willful—proud and given to strange quirks. And this raven...

"You're wrong, stonebird," she said, her voice ringing in the still air. "I never lost my freedom. It's just that I've finally understood the riddle and so discovered it. Illusion...reality...the truth lies inside me. In the silences — *and* the confusions. Rhynn's harping tried to tell me, aye, and the moon as well, I suppose. So I've no need for your 'freedom' when my own's been inside me all along."

Her smile broadened. She patted the pouch that hung at her belt — stuffed full of the gems she'd pried from Rhynn's harp.

"Aye!" she added. "And I've these as well!"

Laughing, she shook out her reins and rode southward.

The Valley of the Troll

And Old Troll picked o'er spoils long pawed
and worried travellers' bones long gnawed
and listened ever o'er the roar
for horses hooves as they'd come before...

—J.E. Coplin

They've a two hour lead on us, Thorn, perhaps three," Aynber said.

She lifted her eyes from the trail, pushed her hat back, and mopped her brow.

"I tell you," he replied over the dull clopping of their horses' hooves, "that it's treasure we should be seeking, not some piddling bounties."

"No more talk of treasure." She shook her head resolutely. "There's a surety of a thousand gold pieces on Guil's head, with another hundred for each of his men. The last treasure hunt you led us on near' cost me my life..."

"But just think of the treasure," he continued glibly. "Mounds of it, Huntress. More than we could spend in a score of lives."

Aynber sighed. His spiel had become all too familiar over the last two weeks of hard riding through this misbegotten wilderness, following the trail of the highwayman Guil and his band. She sat loosely in the saddle, fingering a thin scar on her cheek. Surely the gods would have mercy on her and he'd come down with laryngitis, or perhaps his tongue would fall out? She shot a hopeful glance in his direction.

Under the brim of her hat her hair was the colour of sun-ripe corn, framing an oval face with full lips and wide-set eyes, before it fell down her back in long unbound tresses. She wore a doeskin shirt, with knee-length trousers to match. Overtop was a woolen tabard, while at her belt hung a dagger, a long thin sword, and a leather pouch holding a half-score *lessen-yaln* — Aelfin death-stars, small five-pointed discs wrought of star-silver.

"Jewels with which we could ransom a kingdom," Thorn was still saying. "Aye, and gold and silver beyond counting..."

"Na, na," she said a touch irritably, scowling at him.

His clothing was somber, all greys and blacks. He was dark-haired, with a thin nose, high cheek bones, and a wisp of a mous-tache that quivered cat-like when he spoke. A dusky cloak hid the rapier that was sheathed at his side. From under a small peaked cap his eyes, narrow and a piercing blue, glittered with an unmistakable passion for the aforementioned wealth.

"It's just this endless bedamned road," she added, "through lands so uncivilized that I haven't seen a tavern, aye, or had a drink, since we left Calthoren. And as to your treasure, doesn't it seem just a *little* bit odd to you, that all we've got to do is ride in and collect it?"

"Well, so said old Grimble," Thorn replied, "and in all the years I've known him he's never steered me wrong."

"Aye, so you say. Still, if it's such a simple matter, why hasn't he shook his fat arse and come traipsing out here himself? Eh?"

"Aynber, Aynber...he's an old man, and unlike us, he's not fit to rough the wilds. Besides, in return for his map, I promised him a third share..."

"You what?"

There was a definite rising anger in her voice. Knowing her tem-per all too well, Thorn ignored her and took to whistling tunelessly through his teeth.

"Thorn..." she began threateningly.

"A lovely countryside really, don't you think?" he replied with a grin. "'Minds me of my homeland, it does, though it's a touch more wild and not nearly as cheery. Hist, what's that?"

He pointed to the shadows at the base of an old ash tree leaning precariously over the roadway. Aynber followed his finger with her

eyes, one hand streaking for the hilt of her sword, when a large jack rabbit sauntered out from the shade. It took one look at the pair, ears twitching, before it bounded away. Thorn laughed.

"A third's not too much, really," he said.

Aynber loosened her grip on her sword's hilt and glowered at him.

"Just saying that we're searching for the treasure—which we're not—and just saying we found it—which we won't—do you think for a moment that I'd share it with that fat sniggering toad? Na, na, there'll be no fool's quest for me. Guil's bounty will be quite enough, thank you very much."

Thorn made no reply.

❧

The next morning found them resting their horses, still on the trail of the highwaymen. Aynber leaned forward, resting her palms on the pommel of her saddle.

"They've split up," she said. "See, Guil and the one with the poorly shod mare follow the roadway, while another's cut across the field there." She pointed out the tracks as she spoke, her eyes raking the roadside. "Ah! And the other two have headed south. Well, it's Guil I want."

She shook out her reins and her mount stepped briskly forward, along the roadway. Muttering, Thorn followed.

Their way led through copses of pale grey beech, bordered by thick-bushed hawthorns and briars, until they topped a hillock. There the road led into a small vale. At its bottom was a river that cut like a slash through the length of the valley; deep, though not wide. Crossing the water was a wooden bridge held together with thick ropes, and by it, a rude cot of turf and stone.

"This is it!" Thorn cried.

Aynber turned in the saddle to see him scrabbling about in his pouch. Soon, he was busily perusing a map written on a scroll of animal hide, the corners of which kept turning up on him. He mumbled eagerly to himself as he struggled with it. Looking up at last, he said:

"It matches the map, see? Well, save for the bridge. It must be newly built, or at least since the map was made."

Aynber sidled her mount up to his to look at the map herself.

"So it is," she mused. "I wonder who lives there?"

Thorn shaded his eyes to peer closer.

"There's such a rubble about it that I'll wager no one's been there for at least five years...except for...no!" He turned to Aynber, anguish written plainly on his face. "Do you think Guil's been there and snatched the treasure before us?"

"Well, his trail leads that way, and if he's not got it, I'm sure anybody who's come by here before us has had a crack at it."

"Without the map?" Thorn asked disdainfully, recovering his composure. "Come. Let's go."

He put heels to his horse and trotted ahead. Aynber shook her head, following at a slower pace. The cot might well be a sanctuary for pursued outlaws. Aye, and the brush along the roadside grew high and thick enough to hide an ambush.

"Seems a bit precarious," Thorn said as she joined him by the bridge. Two thick strands of heavy rope, tied about a pair of stumps, were all that anchored the poorly made structure. "Still, I'm sure it'll take our weight. See there?" He pointed to the opposite bank where the mouth of a small opening stood out darkly against the grey granite of the cliff, just above the waterline. "That'll be the cave that's on the map."

As he started across, Aynber held back, looking about the deserted cot and its surroundings once more. There was an odd taint in the air that didn't sit right with her. An intangible essence that she couldn't quite put her finger on. Giving up, she sighed, started to follow Thorn, and saw it: a long craggy arm snaking from underneath the bridge, reaching for the leg of Thorn's horse.

"Thorn!" she cried. "Look out!"

He turned with a smile to see her gesturing at the side of the bridge.

"Oh, no," he called back gaily. "You'll not trick me so easily."

Remembering the scare he'd thrown into her the day before with the jack rabbit, he shook his head at such an obvious attempt to get back at him. His horse squealed, cutting into his reveries. Gasping with shock, he felt it being pulled from beneath him.

"What...?" he began.

Falling from the back of his mount, he saw a huge grinning face leering at him; in one hand was his horse, whinnying its terror, while the other was reaching for him.

"An ogre!" he cried.

Scrambling back, he almost fell off the opposite side of the bridge. In a flurry of panic-swift movement, he raced back to where Aynber waited. Once there, he looked back and saw his horse being pulled from the bridge, its legs pumping madly as it strove to escape its captor.

"No, I think it's a troll," Aynber said, regarding the panting form beside her from the back of her mount.

"But my horse…"

"Gone now, I should think, O great Thorn Hawkwood, mightiest of wizards, fiercest of warriors," replied Aynber with a mocking laugh. "What now? Have you a spell to lay low this monster? Or will you fare forth and slay it with one blow of your matchless sword-arm?"

"Bedamned to the troll. What of my horse?"

"Ah, but with the troll's treasure you'll be able to buy a stable of noble steeds. All you need do is waltz in and collect it."

Thorn was silent for a moment.

"I think we should forget about the treasure," he muttered at last. "I've heard tales about troll's gold. It's cursed, 'tis said. Gives you warts, turns into mud and…"

"Na, na," broke in his companion. "It appears that there is a treasure after all, and I for one, think it's time we studied on a plan to get it."

CR£O

Later, they rested amongst a stand of birch and maple by the crest of the hill where first they entered the troll's valley. Thorn's enthusiasm returned, as well as his modesty. That Aynber was actually interested in the treasure now was just another feather in his cap.

"So," he was saying, "as soon as my spell takes effect—a most difficult spell, I might add, one that only the hardiest of adepts would ever attempt—you will creep down to the troll's cave, step lightly over his sleeping body, and bear away armloads of gems and gold!"

"There's a little weakness in your plan," Aynber said, absently tracing the scar on her cheek as she spoke. "Mainly, that your spells have a tendency to either not work at all, or backfire to ill effect. Usually on me, if I'm not mistaken, like that time in the Dead Marshes near Franwath, when you were going to turn a giant lizard into a hummingbird and instead all my hair went—"

"This is different," he broke in. "It's only the simplest of spells, one that even an apprentice's apprentice might try without too much difficulty."

"Ah," Aynber said with a smile. "If that's the case..."

Thorn scowled and muttered something inaudible into his mustache.

CRSO

Aynber stood on the cliff's edge, glancing from the way below to where Thorn sat pulling vials and small bags of strange powders from his journeysack, setting them out in a neat order before a low fire. She took a deep breath and doffed her tabard and boots. Laying her sword and hat on top of them, she tied a sack to her belt—in which to store the hypothetical treasure should she find it. With a last look at Thorn, she slipped over the rim of the cleft. Gingerly, she made her way down to the river. At its edge, she patted her pouch of *lessen-yaln* reassuringly, checked the thong that looped her dagger in place, and dove in.

She gasped at the icy chill as her body met the cold water. The shock took her breath away, though she soon warmed with the effort of her swimming. Before the mouth of the cave, she clambered onto the rocks, her underclothes dripping. She wrung the water from her hair, looking again to where Thorn sat brewing his spell over the fire as she did. When he waved confidently to her, she faced the entrance once more, and stooping, entered. No sooner was she out of sight, than a great cloud of green-tinged smoke erupted from Thorn's fire. As it billowed about him, he slumped forward, narrowly missing the fire, to lie fast asleep on the grass.

Inside it was dark; damp and dark with a fetid troll-reek in the air that made her gag. She longed for a light, cursing herself for not having thought of it sooner. Undoing the loop about her dagger, she took a death-star from her pouch and moved on, her fingertips tracing the wet slimy surface of the tunnel. Slowly, she made her way.

The damn place made her skin crawl.

Memories crowded her mind, jostling the senses she needed to warn her of the troll's presence. Yarg hunts in the dark woods above the moors of Boscawen vied with reminders of a dozen other skirmishes and battles. Aye, and that time the marsh-dwellers rose up against her foster-clan and young Kalin was slain.

Oh, Kalin...

Suddenly she stumbled over something that lay across her path. She leapt back, dagger and *lessen-yaln* ready. She stood unmoving, stilling the surge of adrenaline that shook her. Only the sound of her own raspy breathing filled her ears. Cautiously, she crept forward once more, tracing the object before her with trembling hands. It was the troll and — thank the Gods for miracles — it was asleep. For once one of Thorn's spells had worked.

She was still nervous as she stepped over the sleeping form, only to plant her foot into what must be the remains of Thorn's horse. A nauseous feeling rose from the pit of her stomach and she was sick. Shuddering, she moved forward, the foul taste of bile still in her throat, and tripped over a jumble of bones. The clatter of the bones seemed to raise a terrible din in the narrow confines of the tunnel. Aynber poised motionless until she was certain that the troll had not awakened. When no sound came from where it lay, she let her breath out and hurried on.

As her receding back disappeared around a corner, a glittering eye opened in the still face of the troll. Grinning hugely, he stood in a silent whisper to follow her.

Aynber's way sloped downward now. The footing of the tunnel became progressively muddier and so soft that her bare feet sank into it. Low plopping sounds echoed dully about her when she lifted them. She shivered as she imagined what sorts of pale leeches, or other slimy creatures, might be hiding in the mud and...was that the sound of someone treading through the muck behind her? She stopped to listen. Shrugging, she put it down to an echo of her own footsteps and went on.

Ahead, a dim yellow glow showed against the heretofore utter darkness of the tunnel. Aynber smiled to herself as the way grew brighter. Before her she could make out glitters and sparklings in the pallid light that could only be the treasure. Now here was something indeed. Not only had its spell worked to good effect, but Thorn's information was correct for a change as well.

Her smile grew broader when she stepped within the chamber. Walled, floored and ceiled with mud it might be; still it was filled with such wealth that she gasped for sheer pleasure. She walked about, lovingly lifting here a gold necklace hung with sapphires and jade, a tiara set with an enormous diamond, there an ornate goblet of some unfamiliar glinting metal, imbedded with precious jewels that bespoke of a king's ransom. Everywhere, coins of silver, copper, gold, glinted and shone, some with markings that placed their age at least a century in the past. Here was one, even, with the visage of Lord Tanlan upon it, the founder of Calthoren in the dawn days of the Eastern Kingdoms. Aynber filled the sack at her belt as swiftly as she might. Knowing full well that it would take at least a lifetime to gather up the whole treasure, she chose only the best.

So caught up was she, that she almost missed the unobtrusive sucking sound, like a heavy foot being lifted from deep mud. When it did register, a chill ran down her spine. Slowly she turned to see the troll in the threshold of the chamber, the phosphorescent light of the treasure room outlining it against the deeper dark of the tunnel.

"Garna's got ye, pretty gold-hair," it said with a hideous chuckle, its voice low and cracked with little use.

Aynber backed away from the monstrous form that was advancing upon her. Feral red eyes glared unblinkingly, huge in its misshapen face, and yellow teeth showed through the tangle of its filthy beard.

"Garna want ye," it chuckled again.

The troll stepped forward, matched by a similar step backward by Aynber, only now her back was against the dank slimed walls of the chamber. There was no further she could go. *Lessen-yaln* and dagger leapt into her hands from where she had lain them while she gathered the treasure. The sack was full and heavy, fastened to her belt.

Damn that Thorn Hawkwood, she thought. She was going to kill him if she ever got out of here.

"Pretty gold-hair," the troll said. "Garna wants to play wi' ye."

It advanced again.

"Aye," Aynber said through clenched teeth, "you misshapen coupling of a pig's arse and a wart! But first you'll have to catch me."

As she spoke, she loosed the death-star in her hand. Straight and true it flew to embed with a sickening thud in the troll's broad forehead. The troll shook its head bemusedly, as though only a gnat had landed on its brow, and reached for her. Gold goblets and crowns broke under its tread as it shambled toward her. Aynber stared in horror as the creature bore down on her, the *lessen-yaln* stuck in its skull to no avail.

She slipped under its grasp at the last moment. Bolting for the door, a long arm caught at her shirt and pulled her back. Desperately, she hacked at the front of her doeskin with her knife. The troll fell back, clutching her shirt. Bare-breasted, she flew up the tunnel, knife in one hand, the other steadying the treasure sack that bounced at her thigh.

"Come back, gold-hair!" the troll bellowed from behind her.

It threw a jewel the size of a man's fist after her. The gem struck her in the arm, numbing it so that she dropped her dagger. She gave no heed to the loss, though, and sped on.

Behind her the troll raged and shrieked, tearing at the rough walls of the room, until it lumbered after her. At first she made good headway, having both a head start and the swifter limbs, but the mud bogged her down, and once moving, the troll's speed increased until it fairly shot down the tunnel after her.

Finally the ground became more solid under her feet so that she made better time. But the troll did as well. She cast a useless glance over her shoulder, for it was too dark to see her pursuer. Still, she could hear its raspy breath and pounding feet not two dozen yards behind her.

She fell a-sprawl over the remains of Thorn's horse once more. Floundering in the gory remnants, her one thought was that safety was now near. In a moment, she was up, the treasure sack yet secure. Though bile rose in her throat, she was too much in fear of her life to pause and relieve the sickness that hovered in her stomach. With lungs gasping, sharp pains lancing her sides, she managed a last burst of speed and tumbled out of the cave's mouth, almost falling into the river. The instant before she dove in, she realized two things: one, that the treasure sack would slow her down, and two, the troll could probably swim faster than she anyway. In the time it took for the thoughts to flash through her mind, she spun about, scrambled for handholds on the cliff side, and clambered up.

The troll was at the cave's opening before she'd gone half the distance. Looking back, Aynber saw it shrink back from the water. The troll caught her eye, grinned horribly, and followed her up the cliff-face. As she reached the top, she threw down a heap of rock, striking the troll so that it fell heavily down to the water's edge. A sudden idea was burning in her thoughts.

It feared the water, did it?

She raced for the bridge, as the troll scaled the rocks once more, reaching the overpass just as its head topped the rim.

Across the bridge she pounded. Reaching her pile of clothes, she tore her sword from its scabbard and returned to the swaying causeway. With heart pounding wildly and lungs desperate for air, she cut away at the supporting ropes, while the troll loped across it toward her. She could almost feel the troll-breath upon her, when she sawed through the last strand. The whole structure fell away from where she stood. With a thunderous crash, bridge and troll thudded into the opposite cliff. The troll scrambled to its feet, shaking with fury and choking on the dust. It hesitated at the water's edge — Aynber knew it longed to plunge in just to get at her — before it raced up the rocks to roar its fury at her. She paid it no mind.

After she called her horse, she lashed the treasure sack to its saddle and slipped into her boots and tabard. She picked up her hat, glancing at Thorn's sleeping body as she did.

"Wizard! Bah! I should leave you here for all the help you've been."

With a sigh, she wearily lifted his still-sleeping form, laying it across the neck of her horse. One last glance she threw to where the troll stood. Laughing, she blew it a kiss, shook out her reins, and set her steed at a gallop along the homeward trail.

Behind, the troll bellowed still. When she was out of sight, it squatted on its haunches, tearing at the ground. Shards of rock and clumps of dirt sprayed about its figure, until a thought slowly entered its dim mind. Thick fingers rose the rubble to cut the air in crude cabalistic figures, and all the while it muttered to itself:

"Garna no get gold-hair, gold-hair no get gold...Garna no get..."

CRSO

Aynber drove her over-burdened mount as fast as she dared. Only when she felt confident that they'd put enough distance between the troll and themselves did she ease it to a slow walk. Cursing the still-sleeping Thorn Hawkwood, she mused on the whereabouts of Guil and his men. More than likely they'd rendezvoused somewhere beyond the troll's valley, and by now, were far away.

How many miles had they ridden since Garna's valley was left behind? She puzzled over that as well, giving up when her weariness became so much that it was all she could do just to stay in the saddle. She ached all over, was still damp, and the rough wool of her tabard chafed her skin. Ah, still the treasure was worth a few small discomforts. Coming to a halt in a small track just off the wood road, she dropped Thorn to the ground, almost falling from the saddle herself.

How long is this bedamned sleeping spell supposed to last, anyway? she asked herself.

She dismounted, rubbed down her horse and staked it out. The twilight was edging the sky with night, when she thankfully collapsed onto her blankets, not even bothering to have a look at the treasure. As her weariness washed over her, her last thought was that she was only courting danger sleeping in the open like this. Half-determined to rise and find a safer spot, she fell into a deep sleep.

CRSO

"On your feet, doxy!"

The harsh voice disturbed a pleasant dream of a youth with curly hair and strong lean limbs.

Aynber struggled to waken.

"What...?" she began.

A chorus of rough laughter and a booted foot against her side was the only answer she got. Someone grasped the folds of her tabard and lifted her to her feet. Her eyes flickered open and she strove to bring awareness into her sleep-fogged brain. It was night. A pale moon hovered above the trees, seeming to mock her helplessness.

"So this is the great Huntress, is it?"

She focused on the speaker, recognizing him with a shock. It was Guil! Aye, Guil, and with him, four of his men. They swaggered before her in the dim light, gaudily clad in stolen finery — a sharp contrast against the dirt of their skin and the filth matted in their beards and hair. She twisted in the arm-breaking grip of the one that held her. Another stepped up and cuffed her savagely across the face. Sniggering, he tore the tabard from her shoulders. Her breasts heaved in the moonlight as she struggled powerlessly. He smiled with appreciation and bent down to loosen the ties of her trousers.

"She's a woman, right enough, for all her man-like ways," he muttered.

Aynber lunged at him, dragging the man that held her forward. Her knee rose up to catch the man bending before her on the chin. He fall back, his eyes glazed. Shaking his head, he rose and struck her in the face with the full of his fist.

"Leave her be, Draln!" Guil cried. "Damn, are you all fools? Ten thousand in gold Kesser's offered for her in one piece, unhurt. He wants to wring every last ounce of pain from her for what she did to the thieves' guild in Nalbur."

Aynber stared at the bearded highwayman in shock.

"Aye," he said laughing. "Does it surprise you? A bounty offered for a bounty hunter? You'll see soon enough. 'Twas a pretty racket you broke up then, and Kesser's not forgotten. Thieves are thicker than water, my brave Huntress, and gold is gold. Ha! And so easy in the taking."

Aynber strained in her captor's grip, to no avail.

"Tie her up. Like the other one," said Guil with a disdainful wave of his hand. "And just remember: they're both worth money. Two thousand for her, with an extra fifty for any in her company."

She fought like a tigress, but for all her efforts, they soon had her trussed. She gnashed her teeth in helpless fury. Once bound, they let her fall, so that she lay on her stomach, her arms tied behind her. With a sudden surge of hope, she felt the pouch with her death-stars beneath her.

"What's this, then?" cried Draln, ripping the treasure sack from her saddle. Guil approached him as he tore it open.

"Damn," muttered their leader. "The bitch had a treasure on her." He rubbed his hands with glee. "What a night this is, oh, what a night!"

They retreated to where they'd readied a fire; flint and steel soon had the tinder blazing. By the light of that fire, the highwaymen pored over the troll's treasure. Wineskins were taken from saddles, exclamations filled the air, and through it all, Aynber attempted to get at the knife-sharp discs in her pouch. She cast an eye to where Thorn lay bound, just on the edge of the firelight.

He looked up as he felt her attention upon him and smiled. Shadows that might have been bruises splotched his face. He rolled about so that she could see the ropes that bound him and her eyes went wide with wonder. Thin tendrils of smoke rose from the cords. After a moment, he pulled his hands apart. He was free. She shook her head in disbelief as he cautiously loosened the ropes about his feet and crept across the grass to her.

"How did you do that?" she asked in a whisper, when he was near.

"A simple spell," he said with a shrug. There *were* bruises on his face.

"You'll have to show me sometime," she said.

"It takes years of self-discipline," he explained and proceeded to launch into a long discourse until Aynber's sharp whisper brought him back to their surroundings.

"Enough, damn it. Will you just set me free?"

He crouched behind her and began to work at her bonds.

"Leave me a little skin, would you?" she said.

She glanced nervously to where their captors lounged by the fire, their voices getting progressively louder and more slurred as the wine seeped into their blood. Bounty or no bounty, she was sure that once the alcohol took much more effect, they'd be upon her.

"That's the last," Thorn said.

Aynber flexed her arms with a grimace. Her head still rang from the blows she'd received.

"How are we going to take them?" Thorn asked.

Aynber stared at him, unable to believe his words.

"Are you mad? I've but two death-stars left, and without other weapons, how long do you think we can hold them off? Na, na, their time will come soon enough. For now…we flee."

Silently, they crept from the boundary of the campfire's glow until the darkness of the surrounding woods swallowed them.

CRSO

Draln shook the empty wineskin and threw it away with a curse. He scratched at the stubble on his cheek and rose to relieve his bladder. Pulling at the thongs that held up his trousers, he glanced over to where Aynber should have lain.

"She's gone!" he cried.

Guil stumbled to his feet.

"Bedamned to the lot of you!" he bellowed. "Who was on guard?"

"Ha!" Draln said, inspired by the vast quantities of wine he'd consumed. "You were, Guil."

"Aye," added the others, quick to take his lead, "it was you."

Guil glared at them, fury roaring in his eyes, until he broke into a wild laugh.

"Mount up," he said at last, still gasping for breath. "Gods! I'd never have thought you'd have had the wits to think of that. Come, now, if we hurry we can still catch them…" He caught himself, glanced at the treasure sack, and laughed again. "Ah, to hell with her. We've all the gold we'll ever need right here."

CRSO

A week later, outside of The Serpent's Tongue in the small coastal town of Thistral, there were six weary steeds tied to the hitching rail. Inside there was an argument.

"You can take your dung and mud, me buckos, and pawn it off elsewhere," the proprietor of the inn cried.

Behind him stood a half-score of the local men, tall brawny lads — able, willing, and more than ready for a tangle.

Guil and his men stared aghast at the treasure sack. How had it changed to this, from the gold and jewels they remembered? There was no time to look for an answer to that riddle just now, though, for the men behind the inn keeper were advancing upon them. The highwaymen beat a hasty retreat through the door, making for their horses.

Suddenly, Draln clutched at his throat. A fountain of blood poured from between his fingers, and gurgling, he fell to the ground. As his hand dropped from his throat, Guil and his remaining men saw the *lessen-yaln* imbedded there.

"I can take you dead or alive," came a familiar voice, resounding over the street.

They looked up to see the Huntress facing them, her tabard caked in mud. In her left hand was another death-star, in her right, a long thin blade. Leaning casually against a building behind her was Thorn Hawkwood, a grim smile playing on his lips, a blade in his hand. He stepped forward to stand beside her.

Four swords whipped out of their sheaths. In that time, another *lessen-yaln* sped from Aynber's hand, ripping into Guil's chest. As he fell forward, a cry dying on his lips, the others moved forward, thought better of it, and dropped their weapons. A few years in the gaol in Calthoren was better than sure death.

Aynber laughed as she crossed the street.

CR80

Later, in the inn, she handed her sword to a youth.

"My thanks for the loan," she said.

With an elbow propped on the table, Aynber threw back a mug of ale, wiped her mouth appreciably, and smiled to hear the tale of how Guil and his men had tried to buy drink and food with a sackful of dung. Yet when she thought of the treasure sack that she'd filled with her own hands, a frown furrowed her brow.

"How...?"

"The curse!" Thorn said, snapping his fingers. "Remember I spoke of a curse? The troll put a curse on the gold!"

Aynber raised a refilled mug to her lips. Fingering the scar on her cheek, she glanced through the inn's door to where the highwaymen were tied to their mounts.

"Well, there'll be no curse on that gold," she said nodding to them. "At least that's certain."

The Road to Jarawen

By noon the markets of Calthoren are packed with jostling bodies. The strident cries of the vendors lift over the hub-bub of voices: cajoling, arguing, bargaining. A thousand scents and colors assault the senses amidst that clamor. There are the peddlers and hawkers, the ragmen and merchants, husbandmen and their wives in dull cloths, noblewomen in blinding apparel, laden with jewels, and handmaidens in shifts of dappled chintz. The odor of meatcakes and pastry, of berrykelms and sweetloots, wafts across the squares.

Where the Crafter's Quarter leads into Yalmin Square, a tall, cloaked figure worked his way through the crowds. As he moved, the folds of his cloak fell back from time to time showing the richness of his raiment. Handsome leather boots scuffed the worn cobblestones; dark eyes raked the crush of folk. The man had wealth: that was certain. The beggars and merchants saw this clearly enough and he was hard put to force his way through them. Curses spilled from his lips as he pushed one particularly obstinate fellow in rags and tatters from him. Looking over the man's head, he saw what he had come for.

By a weapons stand was the one he wanted. She was tall and golden-haired wearing a plain thick cotton shirt, knee-length trousers and a leather jerkin. As he stepped closer, she tossed her head back, laughing at the vendor. The press of bodies was less about the stand, for men stood about hefting blades in their hands, swinging them experimentally.

"It's well-balanced," she said as he approached, commenting on the long sword in her hand. "But, Koln, the edge is badly honed. See here, and here? A poor job."

The merchant Koln protested.

"Na, na," she continued, "don't try and tell me that this is the Palinick blade you promised me."

"And what would you know about a blade, wench?" asked a burly man who stood beside her.

He'd been looking at a set of daggers and was laughing in his beard.

She turned her face to him. Grey-green eyes appraised him disdainfully. Pursing her lips, she smiled. She stepped back with a sudden movement and flicked the blade at his face. He jerked back with a curse as a tuft of his beard fell to the cobblestones. His hand darted for the blade at his belt, yet she was swifter. The point of the long sword rested against his chest, directly over his heart. She put a little pressure on it.

"Try it," she said softly.

He stood as though he was carved from stone, while about them, there fell a hush.

"I meant nothing," he said at last.

His eyes belied the statement and she laughed.

"Let's keep it so, then, shall we?"

Tossing the blade to the vendor, she turned to go.

Behind her the man went for his sword. She whipped about, her boot lashing into his groin. Eyes rolling, he doubled over, gasping from the sudden pain. As he bent, the edge of her hand smashed into the nape of his neck. He fell like an ox. When he tried to rise, she kicked him again. This time the boot caught him dead in the face and blood spurted from his crushed nose. A blade appeared in her hand. The onlookers gasped. So swift had she drawn it, that none had seen the movement. The man began to rise once more, only to fall forward, unconscious. The woman sheathed her blade and turned from him.

"Damn fool," she said to herself as she stepped away.

"You are the Huntress?" asked a voice at her shoulder. "Aynber the Huntress?"

She looked at the tall, cloaked man who had spoken to her. His cowl was thrown back and she took in his finely chiseled features.

She dropped her hand from her sword hilt as she judged him, knowing that he was not there to continue the skirmish as she'd half expected. A noble, she thought, or a merchant from the Isles of Nalin. His red curls fell about his high brow and his eyes were so dark they were almost black.

"And if I am?"

"Then I have a proposition for you. The service of your sword," he swiftly added, seeing the quick anger in her eyes.

She was beautiful, he decided, no doubt of it. Long golden hair swept unbound to her waist. Her oval face, with its full lips and wide-set eyes, was marred only by the thin scar on her left cheek. Still, her slim figure accentuated legs that were more muscled than those of the court ladies that he was familiar with. Her wrists were thicker, too. Glancing at the long sword that rested against her thigh, he realized that it was bladework that had made them so.

"Well," she said, "when you're done gawking, perhaps you can tell me about it."

"My pardon," he said flushing. "I could not help…"

"Aye," she said with a wry smile. "That's what they all say."

"I have a caravan going north to Jarawen," he said, suddenly businesslike. "I need a swordswoman to guard it."

"I chase bounties myself. I know a few lugs out of work, though…"

"No. I have men a-plenty. It's my daughter. I would like her to have a companion as well as some extra protection on the journey."

Aynber considered it.

"Let's talk about it over an ale, shall we? I know a good inn that's not far…"

CRSO

His name was Nyrin, Aynber learned as they waited for their ale. The light in the Worn Scabbard Inn was poor, though bright enough to set the broaches and tassels of Nyrin's garments a-sparkling when he doffed his cloak. At least he looked rich enough to pay her way.

"I'll not be your daughter's — what was her name again?"

"Valera."

"Aye…Valera. I'll not be her maidservant."

"There'll be no need. She has one. Rhea's dull, though, and not fit company for Valera. No, I'm looking for a companion — one who can wield a sword if need be. She's heard of your exploits and when we came to Calthoren, she sent me searching for you. No other would do."

Aynber regarded him. Thoughtfully, she traced the scar on her cheek. The pay was good and her own purse was light. There'd been a noticeable lack of bounties offered of late and, though she wasn't a sellsword, there was no reason why she shouldn't become one. It wasn't like she was being asked to assassinate someone. Aye, and Calthoren had become so dull of late that her swordmate Thorn had left for the eastern lands in search of employment. She was to meet with him in Kopple, in three months time. Till then, though...

"Fair enough," she said. "I'll ride with your escort."

Nyrin smiled and tossed a small pouch to her. It landed on the table with a satisfying clunk. Undoing the fastenings, Aynber appraised its contents. The dull yellow of gold glinted in her eyes.

"For now," said Nyrin. "The balance when you reach Jarawen. We'll be leaving by the north gate at noon tomorrow — or rather the caravan will. I'll be staying on here to complete some business."

CRŁO

Aynber rode through the north gate of Calthoren an hour before the nooning. Over her cotton shirt and trousers she wore a vest of mail; overtop of that, a plain brown tabard, simply embroidered with threads of dull green and rust. A wide-brimmed hat held back her hair and shaded her eyes from the sun.

Along the outer wall she spied her party and shook her head mournfully. There was a large wagon, so brightly painted that it hurt her eyes to look at it. Golden tassels hung from its corners, bright silver fleshed along its edges. They might as well have painted a large sign on its side, reading: "Please rob me. I am rich with gold, silver and jewels, with the possibility of a large ransom for my occupant."

About the wagon milled a good score of men, perhaps a few more. They were plainly dressed in light mail and leathers, with swords strapped to their backs or hanging from wide belts. Here and there she saw a longbow. A tall man stood amidst them, bellowing orders. His ragged red hair was bright in the sun as he twisted about to see that his orders were being obeyed. The men sprang into action at the sound of his voice. A huge grin spread over Aynber's face as he turned in her direction.

"Conn, you old dog!" she cried, stepping her mare forward.

He looked up at her call, grinning as well when he recognized her.

"Annie!" He strode up to her. "Damn, but you're looking well. When Nyrin told me you'd be riding with us I couldn't believe my ears. How many years since those days with Talon, eh?"

Aynber dismounted and stepped up to him, throwing her arms around him, and was enveloped in a great bear hug.

"Too long, Conn," she said. "And where'd you get this?"

She flipped his large mustache with a finger.

"Shhh!" he said in an exaggerated whisper. "I'm in disguise." His eyes went wide and he rolled them about fearfully. "The priests of the dread hedgehog cult seek me for blasphemies too sordid to mention. Woe would befall should they ever..."

"Away with you!" said Aynber, laughing delightedly. She tapped him lightly on the chin. "You've not changed a bit. Remember..."

"So this is the Huntress," said a low voice from behind them, breaking into their reminiscing.

Aynber turned. Facing her was a woman almost as tall as she was. Her skin was pale—closer scrutiny showed the use of certain powders—and contrasted sharply with the long dark hair that fell past her shoulders. She wore a white robe with a scarlet cloak over-top. A large brooch fastened the cloak at her throat: a sapphire set into a gold fitting. The fitting alone was worth Aynber's wages thrice over.

This must be Valera, thought Aynber.

The woman's eyes were large and as dark as her father's with purple shading heavy on their lids. Her complexion was smooth, her lips full and a deep red. Behind her stood a maid in a simple shift. Her hair was a plain brown, her features plainer still. There was a glimmer in her eyes, though, that told Aynber this maid was not as dull as Nyrin thought her to be.

"You're all I thought you'd be...and more," Valera continued.

85

Aynber started as a strange look passed over Valera's eyes. She had seen men stare at her all too often, desire plain in their eyes. To see a woman look at her so...

"We must be leaving," Valera said, her voice breathy. "Perhaps you will join me this eve when we are camped for the night?"

When Aynber nodded, Valera swept away to her wagon, Rhea in tow. Two men helped her up the stairs. Aynber turned to Conn who shrugged at the question in her eyes.

"She's a strange woman," he said. "Minds me of a whore with her painted eyes and lips. She's got a tongue, though. I don't envy her husband-to-be."

"Husband-to-be?"

"Aye, didn't you know? She's to be wed in Jarawen—and not too willingly on her part, I've heard. All this,"—he nodded to the gaudy wagon—"is to be her dowry. Polawer—another merchant— is the lucky man. Her father wants to win him over because of trade matters. Seems that Polawer has much influence in Jarawen and if Nyrin can get some special dispensations through this wedding, he can treble his wealth, if not more."

He needed to say no more. It was an all too familiar story among those of the merchant class. Aynber frowned. She had no special regard for Valera, true enough, but this wedding smacked more of slavery than anything else. A wedding should be more than just a way to seal a business deal.

"I don't like it," she said.

"Aye, but what's to do, Annie? Can you stop it?"

"Na. na. It just makes me ill. She doesn't seem that upset over it, though."

"She'll fill your ears with it tonight, mark my words. Probably, she'll try and convince you to help her escape along the way."

"Aye," Aynber said. "And if she wasn't such an obvious bitch, maybe I would."

"Eh?"

"It's in her eyes, Conn. She'd stop at nothing to have her own way."

CR80

86

Two days along the trail northward found Aynber in a foul mood. The idea that she was a party to a forced marriage was working on her sense of injustice. Valera hadn't asked for her help, she'd demanded it. Save for that, Aynber might have helped her. Now she was torn between her dislike of Valera and her sense of fair-play. Without her, Valera wouldn't get far in these wild lands. There was no doubt that she would try, though. And where would she go? Or more to the point, if Aynber aided her, where could she take her?

Then there was Golan, one of the guards. The man was a thug, nothing more. He'd been troubling her ever since the first day; his advances were crude and offensive, his speech vulgar, and his attempts at courtship had all the finesse of a rutting bull. She'd thought, more than once, of letting his gut taste the kiss of her blade. There was no point in killing him, though. There were men like him everywhere and you couldn't kill them all. But she was tired of that sort of advance. Not to mention Valera...

"Why so glum, Annie?" Conn asked. He'd spurred his mount forward so that he rode at her side.

Aynber looked at him unhappily.

"You've not said a word since yester'eve," he added. "What happened when you met with Valera?"

"Well, you were right," Aynber said, "she asked me to help her escape. Then she tried to seduce me."

Conn's eyebrows rose quizzically.

"Aye," she continued, "as if that fool Golan were not enough. She'd heard tales of me here and there and decided I was to be her lover. Can you imagine that?"

She remembered going to Valera's wagon. Rhea served them wine and withdrew behind a curtain. Valera leaned forward, speaking softly in her husky voice. Aynber had not quite connected that she was being seduced until Valera began to stroke her thigh with a long slim hand, its jeweled ring sparkling in the taper light. Aynber had jumped to her feet, spilling her wine and sending Valera sprawling in the process. Storming out, she ran into Golan who started up with his usual uncouth advances. He still had a black eye from where she'd struck him ere she stamped off, fuming.

"I think I'll return to Calthoren tomorrow," she said, shaking the memories from her. "This whole expedition has left me with a sour taste in my mouth. Why can't they just leave me alone?"

"You're an attractive woman," Conn said.

"Aye," she replied ruefully, "and a curse upon that fact."

"You're not really going to leave?" he asked after a few moments of silence.

Aynber looked at him, disappointed that even he, her friend of old, couldn't understand. Without answering, she put her heels to her mare so that she rode well ahead of him—well ahead of them all: the wagon, Valera, Golan, the whole lot.

C33SO

If Aynber was even a little undecided about her decision to leave, what befell that night made up her mind for her quick enough.

Conn called a halt well before dusk and the men broke camp at his direction. Not wishing any company, Aynber rode on ahead for awhile, gathering her thoughts. When she returned to the camp at last, it was dark. She took the saddle from her mare and, while she was rubbing her down, she heard the scream—a man's scream. Deep and throaty, it was filled with unbridled terror.

Aynber dropped what she was doing and ran towards the sound. By the time she reached the spot, a crowd had gathered. It was near Valera's wagon, beneath a stand of trembling aspen. She pushed her way through the men to where Conn stood, a torch raised high in one hand.

The torch flickered as a light wind caught its flame. It lit the scene amply for all that. Aynber gasped as she saw what lay there. Once it might have been a man. Now it was naught but the husk of a man. Skin hung loosely on its bones, eyes that were popped huge and fearstruck bulged in its skull. The corpse's hands were deep in the earth, as though it had clawed spasmodically in its death throes.

"Who...?"

As she asked the question, Aynber felt a chill crawl up her spine. The night seemed overhung with a growing dread, as though a huge fist was slowly closing about them.

"Markm," Conn said softly. "By the clothes, I'd say 'twas Markm. But what could have done this?"

Aynber had no answer to that. She looked around, her eyes raking the shadows. Her gaze passed over the crowd, resting on Valera where she stood in the threshold of her wagon's door. Valera's eyes seemed to glow in the torchlight with something unreadable in their depths. She smiled warmly at Aynber, beckoning to her. Shuddering, Aynber made her way through the crowd. She stopped when Golan loomed up before her, blocking her way.

"Would you want the comfort of my strong arms?"

He laughed stupidly, as though he'd said something very witty. Aynber snarled at him, her frustration and rage boiling over.

"Anann damn you!" she cried and drew her steel.

Golan was as quick with his own. Their blades rang loudly in the night air. Aynber stepped back to give herself some room. Poised on the tips of her toes, she was about to thrust forward when a roar erupted. It was Conn.

"What're you doing?" he bellowed. "Have you taken leave of your senses? Here's a good man slain and you two'd fight and cut our defenses even more?"

Aynber lowered her blade. Golan followed suit.

"Someday," Golan said, "you won't have Conn about to mollycoddle you — and then we'll see. Aye, then we'll — "

Aynber's blade flashed for his face and only Golan's quick reflexes saved him. His blade came up, caught hers to flick it aside, and darted forward in its own attack. Conn was suddenly between them, slapping the blades apart, nearly getting skewered in the process.

"Stop!" he roared. He looked from Aynber to Golan. "If it's a duel you want, we'll do it properly, in a paced out circle and with judges."

Aynber shrugged her shoulders in exasperation. Anann take them all, she thought. A duel! By all that's holy, they'd been watching too many plays. Duels were all the rage among those of the Actor's Guild these days.

Golan laughed, eager to begin.

"Fair enough," Aynber said, "only no judges. The one that can walk away will be the victor."

The men that made up the wagon's guard shouted their approval. Conn frowned at the turn of events, plainly unhappy. As for Aynber, she looked to the shell of what had once been a man, then to Valera where she still stood by the door of her wagon. Valera's lips were slightly parted and Aynber could read eager anticipation of the coming duel in the woman's dark eyes. Something was stalking them,

Aynber thought. Looking at Valera, she was uncertain as to whether it came from without or within their own party.

CR80

Aynber and Golan faced each other across a roughly marked dueling yard. Golan stood with a grin fixed on his face. For all that he knew of her battle skill, he still found it vastly amusing that they would be dueling. Aynber took in his muscular frame. Watching his quick sure movements as he flexed the stiffness from his limbs, she cursed herself for getting into this in the first place. This was what came of hiring herself as a sellsword, rather then wending her own trails, with no company save for Thorn Hawkwood's.

She took her hat off, laying it on her tabard by her feet. Scabbard followed as she drew her sword. The bared blade glinted in the light thrown from the five large fires set out to mark the borders of the dueling yard. The men of the party stood along the sidelines placing bets with each other, eager looks on their faces. To their right was Valera and her handmaiden. Aynber frowned when she saw them. Their faces sported the same blood-lust as the men's.

As an afterthought, Aynber stuck the point of her sword into the dirt to draw two *lessen-yaln* from the small pouch that hung at her belt. These were aelfin death-stars — small discs wrought of star-silver, perfectly balanced for throwing. She slipped them into her belt where they could be reached easily, took up her sword and stepped forward.

From behind she heard Conn whisper: "Good luck." She was watching Golan as he moved from his side of this makeshift arena and was too bemused to reply. She hadn't missed the whip coiled about Golan's waist, nor the small dagger he wore at his wrist. For this reason — although they were to fight with swords only — she had her death-stars ready.

They circled warily as they approached each other, watching for an opening. Beneath her feet Aynber felt the rough dirt. The uncertain footing and poor light were little help. She watched Golan's eyes, waiting for that infinitesimal betrayal that would spell an attack. It came so suddenly that she was almost caught off-guard. Blades whirred, clashed with a jar so that sparks flew, and disengaged. They broke apart, each more wary now.

Damn but he was good. He had the reach on her as well. Normally her own swiftness made up for another's strength and reach, but Golan matched her for speed and he was obviously the stronger.

Again their blades met. For a moment, Aynber was hard-pressed, beating back Golan's blows with all at her command. She danced back to break away. Feeling a small nick in her shoulder, she knew he'd drawn blood. Events seemed to slow down for that instant. She was aware of Valera's dark eyes drinking in the sight, of the smile that blossomed at the sight of Aynber's blood.

Aynber lunged suddenly. She caught Golan's blade with the edge of her own and twisted it aside. In a blurring motion, her sword leapt from her right hand to her left, striking out before Golan could parry it. A thin line of red opened up on his forearm. He grimaced, more from anger than pain, and thrust forward. A flurry of blows and they broke apart again. He was disconcerted with her left-hand attack. Still, he'd caught her thigh with the very tip of his blade in the completion of his last blow. Though it wasn't serious, Aynber knew that it would slow her down in a prolonged fight.

They were both breathing heavily now, backing away. Aynber mopped beads of sweat from her brow. Stepping forward again, she saw Golan unwinding the whip from his waist. A cry of protest went up from the onlookers. Cursing at that long length of leather, Aynber charged him. His blade caught hers, twisted and spun it from her hands. She threw herself sideways in a desperate attempt to retrieve it, when the whip cracked in the air over her head.

The sound ripped into her mind, awaking memories best forgotten. The scar on her cheek seemed to burn. Once again, in her mind's eye, she saw the slaver who had given her that scar, saw the long whip in his hand and the flames of her foster-kin's holding roaring behind him.

"Hold!" Conn's voice rang over the shouting of the men.

For a moment, he'd been too enrapt in the duel to react. Now he was moving forward in an attempt to stop Golan. He wasn't fast enough.

The whip snapped at Aynber and she rolled across the dirt to dodge it. Her hand streaked for the *lessen-yaln* in her belt. The whip cracked again. She came up from her roll with a death-star in each hard. The first disc spun flickeringly across the distance that separated Golan from her to embed with a sickening chunk into his belly. Eyes wide with shocked surprise, he dropped the whip—the hand that had held it striving uselessly to stem the flow of blood that poured from his gut. The second disc caught him in the throat and he pitched forward, limbs thrashing.

Slowly Aynber crossed over to him, a far away look in her eyes. She retrieved her sword and stood over him. No need for the sword; Golan was dead. A soft touch at her arm made her start. She turned to see Valera there, her hand stained red from where she'd touched the wound on Aynber's shoulder. Repelled by the action and disgusted with herself for having slain Golan—pig though he'd been—Aynber's fist launched out and struck her. Valera fell back, stumbling; her mouth twisted in rage.

"Slut!" she cried. Raising her voice so that the men could hear her, she added: "Kill her! I want her dead!"

Not a man moved, save Conn who came to Aynber's side.

Aynber laughed. "You'll have to do better than that," she told the woman.

Stepping to Golan's corpse, she retrieved her death-stars, leaving Valera fuming behind her.

"You'll pay for this affront," said Valera, trembling with fury that her orders were not being obeyed.

Aynber paid her no mind.

ᘓᘔᘓ

The next morn another man was found slain, his body only a husk as Markm's had been the night before. He'd died silently, though no less permanently. Aynber was saddling her mare when she heard the news. Conn approached her as she stepped into the saddle. About the campsite, she could hear the men muttering fearfully. Against a mortal foe, their ability was unquestioned. Most of them were mountain-bred, though, and superstitious to excess. Facing these strange deaths, they were like children: uncertain, frightened and looking for guidance.

"Annie," Conn said. "You'll not leave now?"

"Why not?"

"I need your help. With you leaving, the men are ready to flee as well."

"So? Perhaps it's better this way. Why don't you saddle up and join me?"

"I can't," Conn said. "I've a responsibility to fulfill. How could I leave Nyrin's daughter here alone?"

Aynber thought of Valera, of the husks of what were once living men. Valera would survive easily enough, she felt, but Conn...Whether it was for old time's sake — for Talon and the oath that had bound their band together against all ills — or whether it was pity, Aynber could not help herself.

"I'll stay then," she said. "But only for you, Conn. Keep Valera from me, that's all."

"That I can do," said Conn.

I hope, he added to himself.

CR☙

An hour later they set out. Aynber sat astride her mount and silently watched the party pull out. Conn and four men took the lead, followed by that damned gaudy wagon, with the rest of the men taking up the rear. Sighing, she put her heels to her mare till she rode at Conn's side.

They rode in silence, each wrapped in their own thoughts. The trail wound its way through the rough terrain of the foothills of the Peredur Mountains. Tall crags of granite loomed over them and the remnants of old shale slides bordered the trail itself. The vegetation was sparse. Only the hardiest of rowans and briars were growing. Brown grass, dull grey weeds and clumps of sparse gorse dotted the slopes.

Aynber was striving to come to a decision. Much as she disliked Valera for the spoiled child she was, she yet felt pity for her, being led northward to a husband only to further her father's aims as she was. Yet there was more now. What was Valera? Aynber couldn't shake the memories of the slaughtered men from her mind. Could this frail city-bred maid have done this? The sexual advances Valera had made to her did not cloud Aynber's thinking. Once the strangeness of being desired by a woman had worn off, she had put Valera along with all the leering men and dismissed that aspect from her mind.

93

The senseless deaths of the two men troubled her. It was not that they were kith or kin. Still, they were men and deserved a cleaner death. She was almost positive that Valera was responsible, only how? The word vampyre slipped into her mind. She dismissed it immediately. They were night creatures, unable to face the light of day. There were other beings that were close to vampyres in many ways, could she but recall them.

The word came into her mind like a flash flood. Succubus. The blood began to pulse in her temples. For one moment the thought made her dizzy. She glanced back to the gaudy wagon and shook her head thoughtfully. It was possible.

"Conn?" she said aloud.

"Mmm?" Conn was watching the guard who rode point, his eyes fixed on the little puffs of dust that rose from the hooves of the man's mount.

"Have you known Valera long?"

"No, not long." He regarded her curiously. "I was employed by her father just for this trip. Why?"

"Have you noticed anything strange about her — besides her wanting to lay with me that is."

When he shook his head, she added: "Well, do you think she could have slain those two men last night?"

"No," he replied after thinking the question over. "She's spoiled, right enough, and cares not a whit for this marriage her father's arranged, but I can't see her having killed them. What makes you think so?"

Aynber remembered the look in Valera's eyes when they were fixed on Markm's corpse; aye, the lust that awoke in them when Golan drew her blood during their duel. She remembered Valera's hand on her shoulder, the blood on her fingers as they came away from the wound.

"Nothing really," she said.

Conn looked askance to her. She said no more and they rode on in silence.

CR80

That night another man died. Young Halj stepped from the company of Oolie, his fellow guard, to relieve himself. When he took more than a couple of minutes, Oolie called out to him. A sudden thrashing in the brush was the only reply. Crying an alarm, Oolie plunged forward in time to see Halj's body tumble to the ground while a shadowy figure slipped from sight. Oolie reached Halj's body and went no further. Standing over his dead comrade he called out to the men who were already approaching, brought by the sound of his first cry.

Conn and Aynber were among the first to reach the scene. Aynber took one look at what remained of the youth and sped back to the camp, making for Valera's wagon. The darkness seemed to close in on her as she ran, thick shadow tendrils arising before her path—reaching out—only to dissipate as she was upon them. The presence of something wholly evil was in the air. The night fairly pulsed with it.

Reaching the wagon, Aynber tore up the steps and kicked the door open. Valera looked up, startled at her sudden entrance. Rhea came out from behind a curtain and her eyes went wide at the sight of Aynber's sword. The blade gleamed in the taper light and Aynber held it as though she expected to use it.

"Shut up!" Aynber said as Valera opened her mouth to protest.

Aynber stared at them with furious eyes. They were both composed. Rhea a little frightened, perhaps, and Valera glaring. Aynber didn't know what she'd expected. Valera to be gone, or breathing heavily from the race to beat her back to the wagon—perhaps some blood on her robe. There was nothing. The blade drooped in Aynber's hand. Wordlessly, she turned on her heel. Conn was outside.

"Nothing," Aynber said in reply to his unspoken question. She sheathed her sword and pounded fist against palm. "Damn, I can't understand this. I was sure it was her; that I could catch her redhanded."

"But Annie," Conn said. "Surely if it was Valera, these killings would have begun earlier?"

"Na, na," said Aynber. "She could have been biding her time. Aye, and what do you know of her before you joined this party, eh? Perhaps her father's getting rid of a threat as well as furthering his own aims. Aye, perhaps she is his means of slaying this Polawer in Jarawen, so that he can take over Polawer's holdings. How could we know?"

A movement on the threshold of the wagon caught their attention. Turning, they saw Valera there, her face twisted with rage.

She'd be on to them now, thought Aynber, and they'd be next.

"You think that *I* am responsible?" she asked, incredulous.

"No, mistress," said Conn.

Aynber snorted, holding her own comments in check. It was unnecessary though. Valera knew they suspected her. Worse, her eyes lifted to look behind Conn and Aynber to see the men gathering. They were in an ugly mood. Looking at her, framed against the lit doorway, she was the embodiment of all the evil witches in all the tales that they'd grown up with: the black hair, waist-length and unbound, framing the thin features of her face; the long white shift, the alabaster skin, the dark burning eyes. Here was the original temptress come to life. In their fear, the men wanted her dead.

"Who else could it be?" asked a voice.

Aynber recognized it as Oolie's.

"Burn her!" shouted another.

They moved forward. Rhea appeared at Valera's elbow and clung to her mistress's arm, shaking with fear. Cursing, Aynber leapt onto the stair to turn and face the crowd. Her sword appeared in her right hand and was transferred to her left, while the right gathered three *lessen-yaln* from the pouch at her belt.

"Back off, dogs!" she cried. "Where's your proof that it was her?"

Inwardly she swore, disgusted that she was protecting the very one she thought was responsible. In the back of her mind there was a tiny nagging doubt. Until that was resolved, she would not let Valera be butchered.

One of the men dragged forth Halj's remains.

"Here's all the proof we need," Oolie said.

He drew his sword.

Conn moved to stand before Aynber. Every hand held a blade now. In another moment, Aynber knew, the scene would turn into a bloodbath and there was nothing either she or Conn could do to prevent it.

"You are dismissed!" came Valera's voice over the crowd's shouting and catcalls. "I will find my own way. All of you: you are dismissed!"

Aynber couldn't believe her ears. Was Valera mad? As if a simple dismissal would stop them. The dawn was almost upon them.

What a way to die, Aynber thought as the men edged closer.

Behind Aynber, Valera realized the foolishness of her order and backed into her wagon, pushing Rhea ahead of her. The bedamned wagon. It seemed to encompass all the uselessness of this entire affair and, such a bright beacon it was, she was surprised that they hadn't already been attacked by brigands, lured by its promise of wealth and riches there for the taking.

As though in answer to her musing, the dawning was broken with battle cries and the sound of many horses riding down upon them.

This finished it, she realized. The mob might not get them, but the highwaymen would.

The men began to scatter.

"Get the women ready," Aynber said to Conn. "I'll saddle some horses."

"But the wagon," he protested, "the gold..."

"To hell with the damned gold! Maybe it'll keep them long enough so that we can get a good head start. Now, will you move?"

Without waiting for his answer, she ran for the picket lines. Already she could hear the sound of battle rising up from about her. A mounted man reared up out of the morning shadows. She cut him down with a deathstar, hastily flung, yet true. It tore into his face. Clutching upward with his hands, he toppled from the saddle.

Aynber ran for the horses. She saddled her own mare, had Conn's saddle on and was buckling it, when two more riders appeared. In the growing light, Aynber recognized them. They were barbarians, mountain men from the Peredur Mountains. Their blue tattoos seemed to glow in the half-light, rendering their faces and bared chests ghostlike and weird. Another death-star took the first man. The second was too close. He rode down on her and she dodged at the last possible moment. Her sword swept out as he passed only to strike uselessly on the heavy leather of his stirrup.

He came about. Suddenly Oolie was there before him. Not to protect her, Aynber was sure, yet he would serve as a diversion. Like the rest of the men, he was trying to escape. They were hopelessly outnumbered. That had been obvious from the first moment. Now he faced the oncoming rider with an upraised sword. The rider twisted aside from Oolie's blow, cutting down with his own blade. It half-sheared through Oolie's neck, pulling free with a shower of blood and a wrench that should have dislocated the rider's shoulder.

He lifted his sword skyward, roared out a battle-cry and turned to charge Aynber — totally oblivious to the pain in his shoulder. A *lessen-yaln* met him as he was half-turned, biting into his neck. Knowing he wouldn't trouble her anymore, Aynber raced for Valera's wagon. There were too many attackers. She'd have to get Conn and the women out of the wagon. At the picket lines they could either catch a couple of the attacker's mounts or ride double on the pair she'd already saddled. Whatever. They had to get out of here.

She reached the steps of the wagon. Taking them three at a time, she burst in, only to reel back in shock.

Conn!

He had been served as Halj and the others had: all that remained was a husk, loose flesh over the bones. Tears blinded her. They'd been separated by years, aye, still Conn was dear to her. Those days of riding with Talon were long past, but Conn had been like a father to her then.

"Damn you, you soul-sucking whore!" she cried.

She tore a taper from the wall and turned to face Valera, her rage washing over her like a bursting dam. But Valera…she cowered back against the further wall, her eyes terror filled. She was staring behind Aynber. The truth burnt in Aynber's mind: it had been Rhea. All along, it had been Rhea. She whipped about in time to catch the handmaiden along the side of her head with the fist that held the taper.

Rhea was transformed. Veins stood out on her face and neck, blue against the flush of her features. Her teeth were bared, showing small pointed tips, and her tongue…it was like a snake, long and sinuous, with a small hole at its end from which she fed.

Shuddering, Aynber lashed out with the taper again. Rhea dodged it, a huge grin spreading over her face. Her fingers had become long claws. She leapt for Aynber, seeking to lock her in a death's embrace. Aynber slipped under the grasping arms, swung out a fist and sent Rhea crashing to the floor. Outside the wagon, she could hear the battle still raging. She had no way of knowing in whose favor it went. She could guess, though. Rhea was upon her again, and conjecture gave way as Aynber fought for her life.

The clawed hands latched onto Aynber's arms, making her drop the taper. The tongue snaked towards her face as she twisted uselessly in the creature's grip. Slowly she was drawn closer. The more she struggled, the deeper the claws dug into her arms. The carpet of the wagon was aflame now. In horror, Aynber watched the tongue weaving before her face, the lips of its small hole pulsating in anticipation of the feast to come.

A flaming brand appeared between the tongue and Aynber's face. Valera bore it and drove the taper into the creature's gullet. The claws released their grip on Aynber. She fell to the floor and watched Valera do battle with it. The claws tore at the taper, at Valera. Long welts opened along Valera's wrists and forearms, yet she kept a firm hold. The flames caught in Rhea's hair and the creature fell back. Valera let her fall, dropping to her own knees to nurse the long rips in her arms.

Rhea twisted and writhed on the carpet; the flames that fed on her hair and shift mingled with the burning carpet's. Aynber staggered to her feet and dragged Valera backwards, beating the little sparks that had caught fire to her robe. Turning to Rhea, Aynber saw the flames consume her.

The head of a barbarian appeared in the doorway. With fast-ebbing strength, Aynber dove for her sword, rising in time to block his first swing. Their blades clashed together. The flames crawled across the carpet towards them. Desperately, Aynber hacked at the barbarian with a flurry of blows.

"Get to the horses!" she called to Valera.

Valera only moaned.

The attacker swung a huge blow that Aynber caught on her blade. She buckled under the impact, yet slipped her blade along the edge of his steel as her knees gave away. A quick twist and she cut into his wrist so that the great sword fell from his hand. Smoke was filling the wagon and the heat grew unbearable. Aynber rolled to her feet and cut the attacker down before he could retrieve his blade. With sword in one hand, she hauled Valera to her feet with the other and made for the doorway. Choking from the smoke, they made it down the stairs.

The camp was in chaos. Some few guards were still alive and fighting. Dragging Valera, Aynber sped for the horses. A man swung in front of them and Aynber dropped Valera to meet his attack. His horse swerved from her at the last moment and her blade cut only air. Turning sharply, he swept back towards them. Out of the corner of her eye, Aynber could see others taking note of them. This would have to be quick or they'd have no chance to get away.

"The horses," she said to Valera who was a little more aware.

The rider was upon them. Aynber dodged his blow and realized with a sudden bitterness that he was only playing with her. She could not afford the loss of time. Still, this made it easier. If he was only toying with her.

She laughed as he passed her again. Catching hold of his arm, she anchored herself against the weight and pulled him down. Before he could gain his feet, she'd skewered him.

Valera had reached the picket lines. Aynber raced to join her. She helped Valera mount and had to almost drag herself onto her own. At least the horses were fresh, no matter how weary they themselves were. Other attackers were charging them.

"Ride!" Aynber cried, slapping Valera's mount. "Ride like you've never ridden before."

They had a chance with the small lead. It was a slight one, though. Leaving the trail, they pounded away, riding westward and away from the foothills. In a moment, they were swallowed by a gully and out of sight. Still, their pursuer's hoof-beats were loud in Aynber's ears and the dawning was almost full, lighting the gully.

The way before them split. Without considering—there was no time—Aynber chose the right branch, praying that it wouldn't be a dead end. The sound of pursuit was growing less, though not safely so. Aynber drove the horses mercilessly. They were lathered with sweat and frothing at their bits. One misstep on this rough ground would be certain disaster. But so would capture by their pursuers.

At last, twenty minutes later, Aynber drew up. Between her legs, her mare's sides heaved for breath. Aynber dropped from the saddle and put her ear to the ground, listening for the telltale sound of pursuit. They'd made so many turns and twists that she had no way of knowing where exactly they were, so maybe they had...

"We've lost them," she said, looking up to Valera's bedraggled figure.

Valera had never looked less composed. Her robes were stained with blood and smoke. Sweat soaked her head and had made her hair all stringy.

CHARETTE 7

"I don't know how we managed it," Aynber repeated, "but we lost them."

CRSO

They walked their mounts slowly until they came to a seep of water where the gullies gave way to a heath dotted with small clumps of blackthorn. In the far distance Aynber saw the haze of a forest's borders. With that water, they cleaned each other up as best they could, bandaging their ugly wounds. The horror of the succubus that they'd faced together had erased the tension between them. Valera's anger was gone, though not her desire.

Her hands were gentle as they tended Aynber's wounds and the Huntress sighed. When the hands strayed from the wounds, Aynber gently pushed them from her.

"Valera," she said, suddenly breaking the silence, "how could you not have known about Rhea's...affliction?"

"How could I? Father hired her just before he sent me north."

"She would have been pleased," Aynber said. "You were her ticket to an easy life. I don't think she would ever have harmed you." Looking quizzically at her, she continued: "I owe you a debt and I'd like to repay you for saving me from her."

Valera smiled at Aynber's words, desire soft in her eyes.

"Na, na, not that. It's just that I know of a holding that lies far enough off the beaten track where your father would never find you. You'd not have to go to Polawer's bed, either. They'll take you in there, though you'll have to do your share of work—they don't care much for haughty airs or lay-abouts. They're kind folk and would treat you well. Can I take you there?"

"How...how far is it?" Valera asked, her voice uncertain.

"Far enough. At least a month, riding easy. We'd have to with these wounds."

Valera thought about a month in Aynber's company and smiled. Surely she would break down in that time.

"I'd like that," she said aloud.

Aynber smiled as well, though inwardly she sighed. She knew Valera's thoughts well enough. Somehow she'd have to divert her attention. Maybe she'd take up swordplay? A month would be long enough to teach her the rudiments and keep her too busy to think of other activities. As she thought of that, she realized it wasn't very likely. How did she ever get into things like this in the first place?

A Handful of Coppers

The Darkwood Inn was quiet that night. Its dozen or so customers filled the high-ceilinged room with the murmur of conversation and the odd clink of mug against wooden tabletop. When the dock workers got paid at the end of the week it would be a different matter. Then the room would resound to coarse songs and peals of laughter. There would be shouting and fights and roars of approval if the entertainment proved even middling fair. But tonight it was quiet.

In a candlelit alcove by the hearth, one of The Darkwood's proprietors was sitting, her feet up on a stool, long corn-gold hair falling down the back of her chair. Aynber studied her ale mug's damp rings on the tabletop and wondered where Thorn had got himself lost this time. He was at least an hour late, if not more. Not that it surprised her. The only thing that did surprise her was that she kept expecting him to show up on time.

She had half-decided to go up to her room and make an early night of it for a change—Glacker and his damn challenges could wait—when she spied Thorn framed in the entrance of the common room. He caught her gaze and grinned broadly as he made his way through the clutter of tables to where she was sitting.

Sitting down, he produced a small object from the folds of his cloak and set it down on the table with a flourish, then studied her for a reaction. Aynber fingered the scar on her cheek and looked at it in boredom. The object was eight-sided and appeared to be made of some sort of bone that gleamed oddly in the candlelight.

"What do you make of that?" Thorn asked finally.

"A gaming die," she said, "except it has—"

"Eight sides instead of six!" Thorn finished triumphantly.

Aynber lifted her gaze to regard him. His whole face was beaming. His thin mustache quivered with barely suppressed excitement. She reached for her mug.

"So?"

Thorn's face fell. "So?" he spluttered. "So? I'll tell you what's so!" He looked carefully around for spying ears then leaned close. "Tonight—along the Walkways—I was following a cowled figure—while I was on my way here, I might add—when this object fell from the folds of his mantle. He never noticed so I picked it up—and no, he didn't see me and he won't come looking. I took care of that, I can tell you, and found a safer route to get here—which is why I was late, you see? Anyway—"

"Thorn Hawkwood," Aynber said in a tired voice. "What are you babbling about?"

A barmaid appeared with more ale for Aynber and a mug for Thorn. The small man fumed inwardly until she was gone.

"Wizardry!" he said in an unconscious stage whisper. "That's what I'm talking about. This, O mighty Huntress, is a wizard's bauble!"

Aynber sighed. "So wizards game with two more sides to their dice than we do. So what?"

Thorn's face contorted as though he would explode. Aynber grinned until he held up his hand with authority.

"Touch it," he said softly. "Before you laugh at me, just touch it."

Aynber shrugged and put out her hand. When the tip of her finger touched the polished bone, a tingle of suppressed power sparked up her arm—not painful, just startling. She drew back her hand and studied Thorn.

"So what do you plan to do with it?"

"Ransom it—if I can find out who it belonged to. That, or sell it do the highest bidder."

Aynber shook her head. "Sell it? Na, na. You don't even know what it does. It could turn wine into sow's milk for all you know. Let's talk instead about Glacker and his loud-mouthed claims. If we're to have any peace with the Thieves' Quarter, we *have* to do something about him."

"Later," Thorn said, not really listening. "I'm going to test this tonight. If it's any good at all, we can just get sacks of gold for it — you just wait and see."

"More like a handful of coppers," Aynber muttered under he breath. "If that."

Ignoring her, Thorn picked up the die and rolled it thoughtfully in his hand. He liked the tingles it set off on his palm as he rolled it back and forth. The curious runes cut into each side danced hypnotically in the candlelight. Without thinking about what he was doing, he let the die roll from his hand.

He froze as it hit the table with a dull clunk. A wizard's die. What would it do? *What* had he done? A queasy feeling rolled about in the pit of his stomach. His gaze locked onto the die's movement. He could sense Aynber's sudden attention. The crackle of some intangible tension closed in about them as he reached across the table to take her hand.

The die finally balanced on one corner, quivered, then rolled over. When it stopped, one strange rune stood out, black against the pale bone. Thorn met Aynber's gaze across the table. They both exhaled thankfully, relieved that nothing had happened. Then, just as their tension was draining away, The Darkwood Inn faded about them and they were spinning in a grey void.

"Thorn Hawkwood!" he heard Aynber roar. "I'll roast you on a spit for this...."

Her last word dragged out to echo on and on. A sense of vertigo finally spun the sound of her voice out of his mind. Raw fear rasped against his thoughts, making it impossible to think. He held tightly to Aynber's hand. When he felt her other arm brush against him, he caught hold of it too, clinging to her like a leech.

He wished he could learn to leave well enough alone. He wished he was anywhere but here — wherever here was. He wished he was back in bed, safe in the confines of his room....

The greyness disappeared with a rush that took away his breath.

CRSO

They landed in a pile on Thorn's bed. Thorn lay on top of Aynber, still clinging to her. She pushed him off and looked around, eyes wide with disbelief.

"Anann!" she murmured. "What happened?"

Thorn sat up. "I...I just wished to be back in bed again," he said. He gave her a look. "Now that we're here...."

Aynber slapped his hand away. "Na, na. None of that. Where's the die?"

It lay between them on the bedclothes. Gingerly, Thorn picked it up.

"There must be some sort of teleportation spell laid on it," he said. He peered at it, holding it up to his eye. "Why...why with this...with this...." His voice grew shrill with mounting excitement. "We could do anything, Aynber. *Anything*!"

He climbed off the bed. Grinning from ear to ear, he began to dance around the room.

"Who's going to call me a third-rate wizard now, eh?" he asked.

"Thorn."

He ignored her. "And Glacker," he chortled. "Says we can't find a way into his place, does he?"

"Thorn!"

He broke off to look at her. "What?"

"Will you sit down and think for a moment? If that thing can do what it's just done to us, then there's got to be more to it than what we know so far. We can't take chances with something like that." She thought for a moment. "You had to picture where you wanted to be, didn't you?"

Thorn nodded.

"So that must be part of it. I'll lay odds that if you've never been somewhere, then you can't go there with this. Have you ever been inside Glacker's place?"

"No."

"Neither have I—so that puts it out of the question. Now will you put that thing away and let us get back to business?"

"But, Aynber...." A sudden smile creased Thorn's face. "I've got it!" he shouted and began to roll the die in his hand.

"Thorn!"

"You don't understand," he said. "Hillie's been there. In Glacker's."

Aynber rose from the bed. Thorn stepped back and let the die fall, ducking Aynber's fist. She sidestepped and moved in with a rush to grapple with him. They fell to the floor with Thorn pinned under her, unable to move. But then the die stopped moving and the greyness swelled around them once more.

CRSO

Horge Jolfull stared with dumbfounded amazement at the two figures that appeared on the head of the bed in front of him. His straining face clouded with superstitious awe and he scrambled out of the way as the two tumbled towards him. They landed on the bed in a heap, the bed's protesting rattle drowning Hillie's surprised cry.

Being a merchant, Horge had the sort of mind that could take an instant stock of the profit or loss in a given situation. Being low on valor—and considering where he was—he beat a hasty retreat out the door, tugging on his trousers as he went. He stumbled across the floor, fought the door's latch for a long three seconds, and was thundering down the hallway with all the speed his overweight form could manage.

Thorn found himself lying in between two women. Aynber glared at him on his right. She snatched the die up before he could and cuffed him. On his left, Hillie gathered up a fold of the bedclothes and held them up to her neck. The shock in her eyes was rapidly fading to be replaced with a furious look that matched anything Aynber could muster. Caught between the two, Thorn could only shrug and bring to play his most winning smile. It went over like honeyed vinegar.

"Thorn Hawkwood!" Aynber and Hillie shouted simultaneously, then paused to look at each other.

Thorn took that opportune moment to squeeze out from between them and lunge for the relative safety beyond their immediate reach.

"I can explain," he began weakly, backing away from them. "Look beyond the moment—that's all I ask. Think of riches beyond count. Think of fame and fortune."

Think of anything but me, he added to himself.

Aynber took in Thorn's quaking figure and her anger drained away. She began to laugh and rolled back on the bed.

"What is going on?" Hillie asked, her own anger unappeased. The bedclothes fell from her as she started to get up, hands clenched into tight fists.

Aynber reached over and caught the courtesan's arm. "Let me explain," she managed to gasp. "If you listen to him, we'll be here all night."

Hillie glared at Thorn, then settled back on the bed, modestly pulling the bedclothes back up to her chin. As Aynber explained, Thorn gingerly eased his way to a seat at the end of the bed, prepared to bolt at a moment's notice. Hillie didn't look quite so angry by the time Aynber was done, but she did turn to Thorn, one hand stretched out to him.

"Five silvers, witling. That's what you cost me so far this evening."

Thorn frowned and dug into his pouch, coming up with twelve coppers. He looked beseechingly at Aynber who was trying to keep a straight face. A smile leaked through for all her effort.

"Oh, why not," she said at last and counted out the silver from her own pouch. "But it'll come out of your share, my fine wizarded friend — plus interest."

Hillie nodded and rose from the bed, forsaking her false modesty. "Let me get something on," she said as she dug through a tangle of clothes in a corner of the room. Thorn stared at her with all the open-mouthed awe of a country bumpkin until he remembered who he was with. Reddening, he looked away and began to whistle tunelessly through his teeth.

Hillie shrugged a long shirt over her head and shoulders and snatched up a pair of tight-fitting trousers. When she was dressed, she sat beside Aynber and looked at the small die.

"So all I have to do is roll this and think of a room in Glackers? I thought magic was *much* more complex than that, taking years of long hard study." She shot Thorn a withering look.

"So I've been told as well," Aynber said, her eyes twinkling with humor.

Thorn squirmed restlessly, painfully aware that he was reaping too many just rewards this evening.

Hillie shrugged. "Well, let's give it a try then, shall we?"

She caught up a dagger and belted the sheath at her waist. Then with her right hand in Aynber's, she rolled the die. Thorn scrambled to take his place beside Aynber as the greyness rose about them again.

CR℘

They felt stone underfoot. Their nostrils filled with the sharp sting of incense. When the sensation of vertigo passed, they found themselves in a large chamber. Hundreds of candles lit the room. Carpets from Jallawm hung from the walls, their traditionally brilliant color patterns dazzling in the bright light. There were no furnishings except for a low bench directly across from them. Its legs ended in carved lion's paws. There were three doors, one for each of the other walls.

"This is…?" Aynber asked, lifting an eyebrow to Hillie.

"An antechamber to Glacker's inner rooms," she replied. "That door'll take you through to them. The others lead down to guardrooms, but I'm not sure of the way. We're usually blindfolded when we're brought here."

"We?" Thorn asked.

"The others on the Street," Hillie said shortly, as though lecturing a fool. By "Street," she meant Courtesans' Avenue that led from the docks into the Merchant's Quarter. She stooped and pocketed the die before anyone else could reach it.

Thorn shrugged. "Well, we can find our own way from here," he said to her. "Give me the die and we'll be about out business. If you hear a knock on your door around dawn, it'll be us, fresh from a successful venture."

"And how am I supposed to get back?" Hillie asked.

"Ah…." Thorn turned to Aynber for help.

She grinned at his continuing discomfort. "Not really your night, is it, Thorn?" She loosened her sword in its scabbard, adjusting the hilt of the blade so that it was within easy reach, topping her right shoulder. There were three throwing stars clipped to her belt, with another half-dozen or so in the pouch that hung from it. "I suppose it's the three of us," she added, turning towards the door that led to Glacker's private rooms.

"Four," a voice said from behind them.

Aynber turned, hand flashing for her sword hilt. Standing by one of the doorways leading to the guardrooms was a tall, darkly-clothed figure. When she saw his thumbs hooked in his belt, she relaxed a bit, then frowned as she recognized him.

"Stark. What are *you* doing here?"

Silas Stark smiled mockingly. He moved from his position by the door with a pantherish grace. "After the prize, same as you. Did you think Glacker's boasts had only reached your ears? Every rogue on the streets is after that prize."

Aynber eyed him carefully, watching his hands. She'd seen Stark in action before and knew just how fast he could draw and throw the pair of knives that were sheathed in shoulder harnesses under each arm.

"How'd you get in?" she asked.

A small brass key appeared like magic in Stark's palm. "I saw Glacker's hallsmith drop this in the market today. Turns out it opens the small postern gate on Haggles Street."

"It wasn't guarded?"

"It isn't anymore."

Aynber nodded. "Well, now that you're here —"

"Aynber!" Thorn broke in. "This close, you're planning to give away another share of the prize? Let this lout find his own treasure."

Stark's eyes narrowed, But Aynber spoke soothingly.

"A four-way split's fine by us," she said, overriding Thorn's protests. "Besides, we don't even know what the prize is."

Stark nodded. "Considering it's Glacker offering it, it could be anything."

"It's the principle of the thing that's got me here," Aynber said. "I'd like to see Glacker call me a gutless wonder when I'm standing over his bed with four feet of steel caressing his neck."

"He's earned that," Stark agreed. He paused for a moment, considering his next words, then added, "The Mole's trying this place tonight as well. Overheard him in The Wizard's Prentice not four hours ago. Knowing him, he'll find a way in."

"Has found'd be a more realistic way of putting it, Stark."

Aynber wasn't even surprised at the new voice. She turned to see the Mole standing in another doorway, blinking furiously at the bright lights. His grey shirt and trousers were wet and streaked with filth. In his hand was a small oiled blade that was known as a sticker in the Thieves' Quarter.

"And how'd you get in?" Aynber asked wearily.

The Mole smiled. "Up the drains — what did you think? Had to kill a few of Glacker's pets, though. Never did like snakes anyway."

Aynber sighed. "Well, there's five of us now. Shall we try for the inner rooms while there's still space for us to move?"

Muttering to himself, Thorn led the way. If he just knew *one* good all-purpose blasting spell, he thought, loosening his sword in its sheath, then he'd show them all. But a five-way split.... Why not just go home and save the bother?

The others followed him through the doorway into a short hallway. When the last of them crossed over the threshold, a loud clatter roared in the hall's narrow confines. Behind them, an iron grating thundered into place, effectively blocking their retreat. Aynber looked back, lifting her hand to the hilt of her sword.

"Looks like we were expected," she said drily and let her hand fall free again.

The voice that replied was husky as the scales of snakes on stone and seemed to come from the air around them.

"Expected, dear Huntress? Why, of course. Though I hardly expected to catch such a fine collection of fools the first night out."

"Fools?" Thorn spluttered.

"Ah," the voice replied. "Thorn Hawkwood — the less than usless wizard of our little group. What would you call yourselves, if not fools? A word whispered here, another there, a challenge thrown, and I knew your sort would be falling over yourselves to get in here after the prize. It's a pity that you'll never learn from this lesson."

"Now see here," Thorn began, feeling a little foolish replying to a disembodied voice. But to be called a less than useless wizard — never mind if it was true — was the final straw to this night's disaster. "Why don't you show yourself?" He fumbled with his sword. In such narrow quarters, with Aynber and Hillie so close to him, he had trouble drawing it. "I'll show you who's useless."

"Shut up, Thorn," Aynber said.

"Yes, please do," the voice agreed. "And put away that ridiculous length of steel. If you wish to meet me, you've only to continue down the hallway."

Exchanging glances, the company moved down the hall towards the door at its far end. As Thorn opened it, he was pushed aside. Aynber broke to the left, bared steel in one hand, a throwing star in the other. Stark flanked her movement, the Mole on his heels. Glacker waited for them, a broad smile on his jovial face. A knife left Stark's hand at the same instant that Aynber threw one of her stars. Both weapons hit something a yard or so in front of Glacker and ricocheted off to fall with a clatter on the floor.

"Well done," Glacker murmured, clapping his hands. "Oh, well done. But I'm afraid I'm far too well protected for you to do me any harm. And please don't use your swords — you'll only blunt them. That would be a pity as I'm sure I can get a fair price for them in the market tomorrow. Imagine the looks on the punters' faces. The Huntress' own sword. A matched pair of Silas Stark's throwing knives. The Mole's sticker."

Thorn stood glowering by the door. Then he noticed the cloak that lay across the chair behind Glacker and he nudged Aynber.

"See that cloak," he whispered. "He's the same man I saw on the Walkways. The charm was his." He turned slightly so that his soft words could reach Hillie. "Use that charm to get us out of here."

Hillie nodded and reached into her pocket. "It's gone," she said with a frown, pulling out an empty hand.

"What's the game?" Stark demanded of their captor.

Glacker shrugged. "I want the Thieves' Quarter and I won't share it. Mind, I'm not talking about petty filchers and pickpockets and the like. Organized, I could do wonders with them. No, it's folk like you that I need to be rid of. I mean to rule the city, with the Thieves' Quarter as my headquarters. What I don't need is to have the 'heroes' of the Quarter banding together to drive me out."

"We're not heroes," Aynber said.

"Granted," Glacker replied. "I use the term lightly. But you're not the sort to bend your will to another's either, now are you? Would you give me a cut of every bounty that you took in?"

"Well, no. But that's not the same — "

"It's all the same," Glacker said firmly. "Any wealth coming into the Quarter must first come to me, although those who work for me would get their cut, of course. But your sort would never agree to that, and even if you did, I wouldn't trust you. And therefore, I felt forced to eliminate you, deciding that it was better that I met you on my own ground, at my own time, rather than wait for however long it would take for you to finally all agree to wage a concerted attack against me.

"This challenge business was rather a bit of a brainstorm, I thought. Playing on your pride, as it were. I offered a non-existant prize, insult your skills, and sure enough, you come running like bees after honey. And what makes this plan of mine so deliciously perfect, is that it feeds on itself. Once I've finished with you lot and prove your deaths to the rest of the Quarter, I'll have every rogue in Calthoren running in to try to succeed where others have failed."

He smiled. "Until, of course, there are no more heroes left. Only those who belong to me."

They listened to Glacker rant on with various emotions. Plans rose in their minds, only to be discarded. There simply wasn't enough information available to make a worthy plan.

Thorn was particularly angry. What rankled the most was that he'd known Glacker for years — not personally, but to see him about the city. Where had this fat fool acquired such wonderous powers? And then he realized — Glacker never had. But with his already considerable wealth, it would be no hard task for him to hire a wizard.

He eyed Glacker carefully, then scrutinized the room. To work his spells, the wizard had to be near by, and since the room's furnishing, while ornate, could not possibly hide a rat, little say a wizard.... His gaze centered on a doorway behind their captor that probably led to Glacker's bedchamber. The wizard had to be there. Gathering his courage, Thorn leaned close to Aynber.

"Don't ask questions," he whispered. "For once, just trust me. I need a diversion. Count to twenty and then do it. Will you?"

Aynber gave him a quick questioning look from the corner of her eye, then nodded imperceptively. What did they have to lose? She'd meant to try something anyway. If she had to go down, she meant to go down fighting. The whole situation held a farcical element that disturbed her, but she couldn't deny the very real danger. Perhaps whatever harebrained scheme Thorn had cooked up would be just what they needed to counter Glacker's megalomania. She counted under her breath, pretending to listen to Glacker ramble on while trying to catch Stark's eye.

When she reached twenty, she let out one of the fiendish warwhoops of the Peredur Mountain barbarians and charged. Stark, the Mole and Hillie lagged only a breath behind her.

When Aynber shouted, Thorn dashed for the other doorway. He dug into his pouch and came up with his twelve coppers. Not enough for Hillie's favors, perhaps, but they'd do. He hit the door with his shoulder and burst into the bedroom. Across the room, a small wizened man looked up at Thorn's entrance. He lifted his hands in an arcane motion and Thorn flung his coppers. They scattered as they left his hand and the wizard instinctively moved to brush them away.

That moment was all Thorn needed.

He crossed the room in three bounds and stuck his sword straight into the wizard's chest. Smoke issued from the wound. The wizard's mouth cracked open with pain. He began to mouth a curse, but Thorn thrust his fist into the opened mouth. The wizard bit down on Thorn's hand, but couldn't mouth his spell. He writhed as Thorn thrust the sword in deeper and tried again to bite through Thorn's hand. Thorn held on, resolutely ignoring the pain.

Not until he was sure that the wizard was dead did Thorn let go of his sword to pry his other hand from the wizard's jaws. He remembered hearing a scream in the other room. He heard a step in the doorway.

"Thorn?"

He turned to face Aynber. The look of worry in her eyes deepened when she saw his hand. She crossed the room quickly.

"Sit!" she commanded, steering him towards Glacker's bed. Tearing strips of linen from the sheets, she bound Thorn's wound. The raw flesh had an ugly look to it. "We'll have to get this properly looked at when we get home," she said.

"Did...did you get him?" Thorn asked.

"The Mole did." Aynber finished binding the wound. Putting an arm around his shoulders, she helped him to his feet.

"I'll be fine," he said. "It was just a scratch. My sword?"

"I'll get it." When she'd fetched his blade, she returned to his side. "How did you know?" she asked, putting an arm around his shoulder again.

Thorn gave her a weak smile. This was his moment. "I suppose it takes a wizard to know this kind of thing," he said.

Aynber smiled back. "I suppose it does," she said. She gave his shoulders an affectionate squeeze. "Shall we tell the others it was a spell?"

"Only partly," Thorn replied. "I could use a little respect for my swordsmanship as well...."

Colum mac Donal

CHARETTE 78

Night of the Valkings

Ah, my heart is weary, all alone
and it sends a lonely cry
to the land that sings beyond my dreams
and the lonely Sundays pass me by...

—from "Ard Ti Cuain"

I

It came with the dawn, and from the wood, that sound of one running toward him. One, and more than one, by the noise of them. The youth in the glen roused himself from a light sleep and put one hand to the long sword that lay sheathed beside him. Swiftly he rose and strapped its scabbard to his wide belt. With a small round buckler on his left arm and spear in hand, he faced the wood and waited what might betide.

He was seventeen this summer yet, for all his few years, he was a man full-grown. He stood tall and wide-shouldered, clothed in leather leggings and woolen shirt with a tunic of mail overtop that hung to just below his knees. A bronze helm covered his rust hair. He had a square handsome face with broad brows and quiet eyes — green-grey they were and full of confidence — and the few days growth of his beard did little to hide the fresh scar that started to the left of his chin and ran down onto his neck.

119

The spear in his hand was of oak with an iron tip and drawn back it was, ready for casting, when a figure broke into the clearing wherein he waited. It was a young girl, auburn-haired and as fair as one of the sidhe. He had scarce the time to hold back his cast before he realized that she posed no threat to him. She collapsed onto the sward in a tangle of limbs, her shift ragged and torn and doing little to hide her well-filled form from his gaze. Amber eyes sought his own.

"Aid me," she said in a husky voice and her breath came in short gasps.

There was no time for a reply.

Almost on her heels, three weapon-men broke from between the trees. One bore a long-handled axe, the others swords, and all three had shields of polished wood and were clad in mail. He took in their yellow hair and horned helms and knew them for what they were: raiders from Norseland. Valkings. With a snarl they launched their attack on him.

Straight and true he cast his spear and caught the foremost man in the chest with it, then he drew his blade. The Valking staggered in a shower of his own blood, tripping one of his companions, but the other was upon the youth. He struck the lad with so mighty a blow that his wooden buckler was split in two with a great rending crash and he fell back. Now the other Valking was upon his feet, he that bore the axe, and the two closed in on him. Faced with these odds, only the youth's own strength and speed could save him. He could feel the battle-rage growing within him and the red mist fell across his sight.

He tossed the remains of his buckler at one and feinted toward the axe man. The Valking's shield swung up to meet a blow that never came for already the youth's blade was speeding toward his companion and a boot lashed out and caught him in the groin. Dropping his axe, he doubled over with pain while sword rang against sword. Then the axe man fell groaning to the ground, even as his mate backed away from this sudden onslaught. The odds were evened now.

A flurry of strokes, an unguarded moment, and the youth's blade sunk into his opponent's neck. He gave the sword a quick twist and pulled the bloody blade free to meet the axe man who was strug-

gling to his feet. The axe was half-raised when the youth's sword thrust through mail and leather to pierce the man's heart.

The red mist of battle was yet before his eyes when he heard a low exclamation from behind him.

"Och!"

He wiped his blade clean on the raider's leggings and sheathed it before he turned to meet the owner of that voice. The maid he had rescued was sitting up and breathing more evenly now. Forgotten were the remains of her shift that she had held to her breast throughout the battle. Her arms hung loosely at her side as she stared at the youth.

"It's a swift and sure blade you wield," she said with admiration.

The youth nodded brusquely in reply to her compliment and felt a flush redden his cheek.

"Is there a tongue in your mouth then?" she added with a smile. "I'd know your name, you who have saved my life."

There was silence for a moment, forged with a wary look in the youth's eyes. Then he said:

"Do you ken the folk of Down and their lord, Donal mac Conn, and how he led his people against Fergus High King but five days past?"

"Aye," she said. "The whole countryside talks of naught else. It was all his men save one of his sons and a score of his carles that died in that battle. Fergus himself dealt Donal's son a wound that should have slain him, but still he escaped."

"Then know you that I am Colum mac Donal and the King's own bounty is on my head."

"He is but a youth..." she began. Then she took in the figure that stood before her. Her eyes were wide now and there was a fear in them that she could not hide. Without thought, she gathered the folds of her torn shift to her breast. That scar...

"What will you do with me?" she asked at last.

"Ah, lass, you be too fearful," Colum said with a laugh. "I mean you no harm."

He glanced meaningfully at the three corpses that littered the glen. Already the flies were settling on them. She followed his gaze and sighed.

Aye, no harm so far, she thought. But if he knew who she was.

"What do they call you?" Colum asked.

"I am named...Meave," she answered with only the slightest hesitation. "I was faring homeward from Conogh with my father's men and it's by the sea road we were going and we but five, myself and four others. We came upon a camp of Valkings. Unexpected was that meeting for how were we to know that they raided so early in the year? Och! But there were four long-ships pulled up on the beach and its my companions they slew and myself to be their captive, did I not flee far and fast from them." A thought struck her then. "Anann! There'll be more of them upon us and that too soon. We must flee!"

"And where do we flee?" Donal's son asked. "Where is your home and father, Meave?"

"In Emain Macha, the High King's holding."

"The High King's holding..." Colum repeated.

His mind filled with thoughts of the vengeance he craved of Fergus. Donal fallen, aye, and Comyn and Cailean and Hakon the Gath — all dead. It was luck alone that had placed his sister Aine in Briunal's keep in South Muman. She would be safe there. Safe and alone, stripped of all her kin. A reckoning he desired, a blood-letting to ease the passage of all those who fell 'neath the blades of Fergus' men and now must cross the great river of death. And...

Too soon, too soon, cried the voice of reason within his breast and he cursed it even as he heeded its rede.

"It is far, the road that leads to Emain Macha," Colum said.

Meave nodded her head in agreement. "Aye. Do you but bring me to a steading where I may find men to lead me home and its my gratitude you've earned."

As she spoke, Colum regarded her steadily and a longing arose in his heart.

Ah, and she was fair, he thought, as fair as any maid in Aerin or elsewhere. And was this then his destiny? To leave land and maids such as these forever when he crossed the seas? Ochone! And how could he do otherwise? How to return? Ochone, ochone!

Then his ears caught the sound of heavy footsteps and swords rattling against shields. Swiftly he caught up one of the slain men's shields.

"We'll talk more of that again, Meave," he said, "for Tyrr damn them, the raiders are anigh. Come, we must flee indeed."

His cloak he wrapped about her shoulders and, after retrieving his spear, he steered her out of the glen. And then they ran.

II

"How did the others die, Colum?" Meave asked.

They lay on the brow of a wooded hill. Below them was a large clearing surrounding a hillock in its middle. Upon the raised ground was a small rath with a high earthen wall about it, but from their vantage point they could see all that went on within.

It was a peaceful scene. There were cattle grazing to the north, and the fields in the clearing were filled with folk tending their crops. Barley and other grain, scarce a foot high, reached for the sun, clad in bright green, while smiling women and children went up and down the rows, rakes and hoes flashing as they went cheerfully about their work. The men were armed, though not heavily, and were just finishing their day's labor on a new section of the wall.

Colum turned to look at his companion. By early afternoon they had lost the raiders—clumsy and inept at woodcraft as the great sea-rovers were—and now, just before dusk, they had come upon this holding.

"Others?" he asked.

"The men who escaped from the battle with you."

"It was strange and terrible, the way of their dying," he said and there was a bitter edge to his voice as he spoke. "It came in this way. Not far from where Lagan touches Uloth's borders, we were, and faring steadily southward all the while, when we came upon a mismatched band of Valkings and the High King's men."

Meave was about to protest, but Colum raised his hand that she be silent and went on. "Nay, tell me not that such a thing cannot be, for it's with these eyes I, myself, saw this. They were not many, a score of the raiders and perhaps eight of Fergus' men, and with them was a druid of the Valkings' faith. We readied our weapons, for we saw no way we could escape save through battle, when the druid raised his arms and spoke in a strange tongue. Ochone! It was a fear that came upon us that would have shamed a child.

"Our manhood became like water then and our limbs were all frozen and not ours to command so that we might not attack, or even defend. Then were the axe men and sword-wielders upon us and we dying and there was nothing we could do. My heart wept within my breast and how this came, I ken not, but the anger grew in me and the red mist fell upon my eyes so that my mind was blinded to the druid's spell.

"My limbs became my own and I took one of my good Down-made spears and slew the druid with one cast. Ochone! It was too late. My comrades were slain or dying and eight and twenty men faced me so that I ran to save my life, though not my honor. So here am I, the survivor of two battles and victor of none! Ochone!"

A mask seemed to settle upon the face of Donal's son, for as he spoke he was reliving those battles.

"Damn them!" he cried. "It's vengeance should be mine. Fergus, Coemgen's son, it's my wrath will slay you. Och, and that the High King should be such a man and when the throne is rightfully Coinneach mac Conan's. It is in Temuir that the High Seat of Aerin is, not Emain Macha, and not some bitch's cur to sit in it."

His wrath flowed over until, red-faced and quivering, he lapsed into silence, dark eyes flashing. Meave sat quietly beside him.

"Colum?" she asked when he was calmer.

"Aye?"

"Will you not come below with me? I fear for you and with the woods full of foes. Aye, and what if they treat me ill there below?"

Colum shook his head thoughtfully.

"Nay, lass, I think not. Sure it is that those below will be my foes as well and I'll not be reddening my blade with the blood of men Aerin-born, save for those that wear the Livery of the High King."

"But, Colum..."

He turned to look at her.

"Do you truly fear for me, Meave?" he asked.

She nodded and returned his gaze, large amber eyes brimming with tears.

"How can this be?" Donal's son said. "So soon you care for me and we strangers, aye, and have I not a bounty on my head, being outlawed and all?"

"Oh, Colum," she said and then he drew her into his arms. The cloak fell from her and there, as the dusk fell upon the woods and the lights were flickering in the rath below, they knew each other as only a man and a woman may.

CREO

When the morning came, bright and dew-laden, they descended from their hiding place and made boldly for the rath. Perhaps he was a fool for going down with Meave, but being this far south of Down, Colum felt reasonably secure that none here would know him. And if they did? Colum sighed. Ah well, he would face that time when and if it came.

Folk came forth to greet them and all seemed well but, as they neared the rath, the smiles on the welcomers fell from them and in a moment Colum and Meave were surrounded with menacing spears and hastily drawn swords. Colum's heart sank and he cursed himself. And how could they not have known him? The whole countryside would know the tale of his part in the rebellion, aye, and his description as well. But now it was too late.

"It is he!" cried one. "It is Colum mac Donal!"

"See the scar!" cried another.

"Slay him swiftly, ere he draws his blade!"

Meave drew closer to Colum and he threw a protective arm about her slim shoulders. A man with an unmistakable air of authority approached them. He ran a hand through his thick shock of black hair as he looked them over.

"Lay down your arms, Donal's son," he said. "You are outnumbered."

"Fear not," Colum told him. "There is none here that I wish harm upon."

He tossed down his spear and was gingerly drawing his blade when another man came running up and he was shouting:

"Triona! Och, Princess! Anann be praised! You are safe."

He was calling to Meave. Colum gripped the hilt of his blade so tightly that the blood fled his hand.

"This is true?" he asked Meave.

"Aye," she began, "but, Colum..."

He turned his back upon her and through the wondering murmurs of the rath-folk, he addressed the dark-haired man who had first spoken to him.

"Your name?"

"Kevin mac Seamus, of Clandalk," was the reply.

"Then, Kevin," Donal's son said, drawing his blade and impaling it point first in the ground, "do you lead me to your gaol."

So as his blade stood quivering, sheathed in Aerin's rich soil, Colum mac Donal was bound and led into Clandalk, and a prisoner was he.

"Colum!" cried the one he had known as Meave, but he answered her not save for a look so cold that it chilled the blood that ran through her veins.

Fergus' daughter, thought Colum bitterly as they led him away. Cursed be the day that he'd lain with the daughter of his father's slayer. Ochone!

III

Three came to visit him that day as he lay in the dark gaol of Clandalk. Triona was first and to her he would not speak.

Och, Meave, he thought and his temples pulsed with his grief and anger.

When she had gone, Kevin came.

"I have sent word to Emain Macha," he said. "The man who recognized the Princess was Lughaidh, a councilor of the High King's, and it is he who has gone to take the word to the north. They will send a troop, says he, to bring you there for your judgment and to collect the High King's errant daughter."

"What do you mean by *errant?*" Colum asked.

"Och, and did you not know? This is the third time she has run from her father's hall and she will do the same again, she swears."

Hope rose in Colum's breast and then dashed itself to the stone floor of his gaol. And she the High King's daughter and now his blood enemy, as must be all of his kin.

When Kevin was gone, one came with food and drink — neither of which Colum accepted — and then he was left alone. The afternoon slipped by and wore heavily on the youth. Confused he was and longing for his father's council. Och, what to do? Southward he should have sped, as swiftly as his feet might carry him. There in Briunal's keep he would have met with his sister Aine and they could have fled from the isle of their birth to safety.

Aye, from South Muman over the sea named Nial's Arm to Endland and from there they might have taken a ship to Aerin Nua. Far to the westward lay that great land, over the watery wastes of the Ocean of Atlanta, and there they might have made a name for themselves and lived in comfort. Aye, and one day to return and to take back what was rightfully theirs, and in the taking, they would have overthrown Fergus and set Coinneach upon the High Seat.

Colum shook his head wearily.

It could never have been. How could he have taken Aine upon the life of a wanderer? Homeless and landless, that was not for her. He shook his head again. No need to worry about that now. His future was planned and plotted for him and its ending was all too sure and near.

With a sigh, he laid his head down upon the straw mattress of his cell. Stretching his weary frame, he slept then.

CR&D

Some sixth sense roused Colum a few hours before midnight. The short hairs at the base of his neck stood up and there was a tingling in his nerves that spelt danger and seemed familiar at the same time. And then he heard it.

From outside the earthen wall that surrounded the rath of Clandalk, there rose a roar of battle cries and weapons clashing on shields and then Colum knew that the Valkings were come. He rose to his feet and made for the small window of his cell. As he peered without, his nerves prickled again and his limbs felt cold. Suddenly, he knew. This was how he had felt when the druid had bespelled him and his men in that small glen where all save he was slain. Och, and the men of Clandalk would be unprepared for it. For against such magic, what defense was there?

Savagely he grasped the iron bars of his cell window and put all of his strength into tearing them free. The muscles of his neck and shoulders bulged and rippled and he grunted with the strain, but the bars were solid and would not move. Again and again he strove to no avail. From the wall, he could hear the raiders clambering over the earthworks and there was no sound of combat. The men of Clandalk were as frozen with that sorcerous fear as his men had been. The red mist tore across his eyes and he strained all the harder at the unyielding bars of his gaol window.

"Colum."

A familiar voice broke into his concentration and he whirled about. There stood Triona, the High King's daughter, shivering and quaking with her fear, but that she had the use of her limbs showed her inner strength. She held something glittering in her hand and beckoned to him.

"Oh, Colum, take these. They are the keys to your cell. Take them swiftly for Clandalk is falling and the fear of your death is in my soul!"

He crossed his cell in three swift strides and ripped the keys from her hand. One moment of fumbling and then the door swung open and he was free. With a snarl of rage he lunged from his cell and stood outside like a beast at bay. Triona shrank against the wall of the gaol and another fear than that brought by the Valkings swept over her, for the berserker rage was upon Colum.

Still growling from low in his chest, Colum padded toward the earthen wall. Already some of the raiders were within. Great horned helms flickered in the dim light as the bear-like weapon-men ran rampant through the rath, striking down men and women who stood frozen and could not defend themselves. And the first that came upon Donal's son, found himself facing a maddened beast.

With a cry that stuck in his throat, Colum leapt upon the raider and tore the man's axe from his grasp. The Valking rose only to feel his own axe cut through helm and skull-bone and sink into his brain. Colum stood over the body of his slain foe, the great Valking axe held in both hands, and howled a victory cry.

With dripping axe, he made for the earthworks and there was none that could stop him and few that tried. In the dark half-light, he was like some avenging ghost, here one moment and there the next. Soon he was over that wall of earth and stone and among the raiders and men of the High King that were not yet in the rath. Surrounded as he was by some two-score foes and more—and they mostly in the livery of Fergus High King—he had but seconds to do what must be done.

Within the red mist that shrouded his mind, there was yet one clear thought. Frantically he peered through the gloom, even as he fought the men that swarmed to take him. The disadvantage was theirs for, in their eagerness to slay him, they hindered each other and it was not just one man that was slain by a comrade's blade in that wild melee. There was a fear in them too, for they knew only too well what the berserker rage might do to a man, how far it could drive him.

Colum had no qualms and struck out blindly, all about him, the Valking axe reaping a grim harvest of his foes. Then he saw that for which he searched: the druid of the Valkings, arms upraised and chanting in that unholy tongue that was neither of Aerin nor the frozen Norselands.

Screaming curses, Colum made for him.

In moments the axe was torn from his grasp, imbedded deeply in a foeman's chest, and he had been dealt enough blows to slay a normal man. His head rang as blow after blow rained on his helm and sword points thrust against the strong mail that protected chest and back. But the red mist was in his eyes and the rage drove his body beyond pain and him forward.

Another Valking was before him and Colum's fist struck the man in the throat, even as he caught up the man's axe. Two men in the colors of the High King, fell before a great sweep of that axe and then the druid became aware of Donal's son. For a moment his concentration broke and then he focused his will upon the youth and this was his undoing. Colum was berserk and beyond control, but in the rath of Clandalk, the men were freed for a moment and great was their rage when they saw what had befallen their comrades and, aye, their women and children as well.

That wrath drove them against their attackers and a great cry went up from within the earthen walls. The Valkings outside halted for a moment as they heard their fellows being slain within. It was then that Donal's son tore free of his attackers. Up went a bloody arm, axe in hand. Sure and true it sped through the air and buried itself in the druid's breast.

And then Colum mac Donal fell forward on the battlefield and lay as one dead, while about him a howl of dismay rose from the Valkings and High King's men as the folk of Clandalk sallied forth from their rath and there was murder in their hearts for those who had attacked them so cowardly and ruthlessly slain their kith and kin.

IV

A week and a day it was that Colum, Donal's son, lay in the grasp of death's sleep. Clandalk's druid, and he was of Aerin's faith, saw to his wounds and shook his head over the youth's body. He had not long for this world and would soon be crossing the great river where his spirit must bide till he be reborn again. And then who would know the savior of Clandalk when he was returned as a new-born babe and he himself recalling naught of this life?

A week and a day it was, and the High King's daughter sat by his bed where he lay in Kevin mac Seamus' hall. And then did Donal's son awaken from his death sleep and gaze into Triona's face. Long auburn hair framed her features and they were set in sorrow's lines. But when he stirred, the full lips smiled widely, the tear-stained eyes sparkled with joy and all the wrinkles of concern fled her smooth white brow.

"Oh, Colum," said she and buried her arm in the crook between his head and chest. One hand of his rose feebly and patted her arm.

"It's living I am, lass," said he and then he fell back into slumber.

CRSO

Each day Triona, and she still named Meave by Colum, sat by his bed and it's long they talked and told each other their dreams and tales and fancies. And though she was the daughter of his enemy, it was love that blossomed in young Colum's heart. Sometimes the talk drifted to Fergus, Triona's father, and then they would wonder what was keeping his troop and when they would be taken away.

Then there came a day, and Triona was spooning a beef broth for him, when they heard the thunder of hooves in the yard outside and they both knew that the day they had dreaded was come. Colum reached for his sword, but so weak was he that he could not even grasp its hilt, little say wield it. Triona drew his arm back and said:

"Stay your hand, love."

They heard the jingle of men dismounting outside the door of the hall and the impatient stamping of the horses' hooves on the hard packed soil of the courtyard.

"Kevin mac Seamus," a voice called out. "And are you here?"

"Aye," they heard Kevin say, "and it's ill tidings I have for you."

"What mean you?"

"The Valkings struck here but two weeks past and it's Colum mac Donal was slain in that battle."

"Then where's the body? Fergus will pleased enough with just his head."

Was there the hint of suspicion in the man's voice?

"And it's his head you're after, is it?" said Kevin. "Then go you and take a look without the rath. You'll find it buried neath the mound there, along with his body and all of those who fell in battle with the raiders."

"And did the Princess die as well?"

And now there was no mistaking the disbelief in the man's voice.

Triona bent down and kissed Colum on the lips and it was a long and desperate parting kiss she gave to him. She pressed a small gold ring into his hand, taken from her own trembling finger, and rose from his side.

"Should they leave with me," she said, "they'll not think long on you. I go with them, love, and if we meet not again on fair Aerin's shores, then look you for me in Endland or Alban, for sure you can be that I'll come searching you. Aye, and even in Aerin Nua, if that's where you'll be."

"No, Meave, no," Colum cried and his voice still weak and not carrying far.

She looked at him and there were tears in those large amber eyes as she slowly shook her head.

"Triona!" he said then, but she turned from him and stepped out into the courtyard, and if it was hard for Colum lying abed and help-less, it was three times as hard for her and she so filled with love for her Down youth, Donal's son.

Colum heard naught of their leaving, his heart so filled with grief that naught might shake him from his sorrow. And as he lay there, clutching the ring that she had given him, Kevin entered his own hall and walked to where Colum lay. Long it was that he stood there until at last Colum looked up.

"It's a brave lass you have, Donal's son," he said then.

"Why, mac Seamus, why?" Colum asked and his voice was bitter. "Why let her go? It's myself they should have taken. It's myself that should have gone with her."

"Aye," Kevin said, "and it's yourself they would have slain. What of her going? Think you that Fergus will put to death his own blood? No, she'll be safer there than faring o'er the sea with you, lad. And fear you not. If your hearts are true, it's reunited you will be, though it be some few years till that day."

Colum stared at Kevin and slowly nodded his head in agreement. Then a look came into his eye.

"And yourself, mac Seamus. Why do you harbor an outlaw and not so long past you were willing, aye, and more than willing to send me to Emain Macha and to my death?"

"Och, lad," Kevin replied, "and do you think me so hard and cruel a man? It's yourself saved my people from the axes of the Valkings and for that alone I'd not give you up though Fergus and all his men come to take you. And you such a man in battle, och, all Aerin would mourn the passing of such a brave man.

"And heed this as well, Colum mac Donal; it's long I've talked with Triona, and she the High King's own daughter, and it's she has told me how Fergus himself is in league with those raiders from Norseland. Now, I've never held much love for Coemgen's son and how he took the throne, but when all's done, what can I do? He is the High King now—never mind that some folk feel that it is Coinneach mac Conan's throne by right—and it's Fergus I must obey, for his is the rule and his is the strength in these days.

"Yet you can be sure, that the tale of his unholy alliance with our blood foes will be told across the length and breadth of all Aerin, and it's myself will start the telling of it. Tyrr's blood, that such a thing could be, lad, for mark this: when we were burning the slain Valkings, there were Aerin-born among their ranks and they wore the livery of Fergus mac Coemgen himself."

Colum nodded. Even through the haze of his memory, that he could yet recall. Not even the red mist could hide it from him.

"But why?" Colum asked. "Why would he do it?"

"I've thought upon that myself and it's a simple enough reason I've found. There are more than your father was that are discontent with his rule and it's my thought that he seeks outside strength so that others that may rise up against him may be put down the easier. Ochone, these are hard times that are come upon us, Colum."

Donal's son gazed steadily at Kevin, but his thoughts were far away. Father and brothers slain, aye, and many another good man of Down. And love, new-found, swift-lost, and all that remained for him was exile for years beyond counting. He fingered Triona's ring.

"Aye, Kevin," he murmured at last. "Hard times have come indeed."

⊂℞℠⊃

Five months did Colum spend in Clandalk and then there came a day when he was finally strong enough to leave. Three times during those months, the men of the High King had come unexpectedly in search of him, but it was not a trace of him they found. The folk there kept his secret well.

On the day of his leaving, he had stood outside Kevin's hall absently stroking his long moustache, rust as the hair on his head, grown to add years to his looks, aye, and to disguise him as well. The folk met with him there to bid him farewell and it was with the blessing of all those brave folk of Clandalk that he parted from their rath and fared eastward for the sea. No longer could he bide in Aerin, this he knew now.

He had sent a message to Aine and word returned from the south saying that all was well with her and he had Briunal's own oath that he would see to the caring of her and her safety. They were to be wed in the spring, bedamned to any who might say them nay, save for him. Would he agree?

He sent his goodwill to them gladly.

So he came to Benen, on the east coast where Aerin's soil touches the waters of Nial's Arm, just north of Conogh. There was a fisherman on the shore hauling his small coracle from the sea, his day's catch on the sand by him. He looked up as Colum approached and his eyes narrowed thoughtfully.

"It's a passage I'm seeking," Colum said. "Across to Endland and I've gold to pay my way. Will you take me, man?"

The fisherman stood up from his labour and there was a short spear in his hand.

He grinned. "It's gold you have, is it? Well, I'm thinking...the gold you have, would it be a match for the price on your head, Colum mac Donal?"

As he spoke, he leapt at Colum and his spear darted for the Down youth's breast.

There was a weakness in Colum's limbs, a weakness born of wounds not fully mended, and it served him ill. He slipped to the right, knocking the spear aside with one hand as he fumbled for the hilt of his sword with the other. The movement proved too much for him and he went stumbling to the sand, blade half-drawn.

"Behl-Stoirm take you," he cried as he struggled to rise.

Then the fisherman launched his spear. Colum twisted in the sand and the spear bit his cloak. He came to his feet with a sudden rush and a rending of cloth and his blade was in his hand. But the fisherman was upon him.

Colum felt the weight of the man's huge hand smash into his temple and the beach began to swim before his sight, and his sword dropped from his hand. Again he was struck and he fell back to the sand, but now the red mist was in his eyes and the pain of old wounds and the fisherman's blows fled his body.

Ochone, he thought even as the battle fury welled up in him. Did every man in Aerin know Donal's son? Was every man of his own homeland risen against him?

The fisherman's coarse features blurred in his sight and the head of High King Fergus topped the man's burly form. A bestial growl rose from Colum's throat and then he was upon the man. They rolled in the sand, plummeting blows upon one another. Then the Down youth's strong fingers found the fisherman's throat and squeezed.

As suddenly as the red mist had fallen upon Donal's son, so did it slip away. He loosed his grip on the fisherman's throat and rose to his feet, staggering and shaking his head savagely.

He would not knowingly take the life of a man Aerin-born, no matter his greed, no matter his treachery, he thought as he looked down upon his fallen foe.

The man's chest rose and fell as he gasped for air.

Colum turned from him and fetched his sword. With the long blade in its sheath he returned to stand over the man. Reaching into his belt, he withdrew two gold coins and tossed them onto the fisherman's chest.

J.CHARETTE 78

He was no thief, no matter that there be a price on his head, was his thought as he turned and walked to where the fisherman's coracle lay by the water's edge. Pleased was he that, unlike most small craft he had seen, it sported a small sail, though it be no bigger than a large cloak.

So it was that the twilight was shrouding the coast when, with a heavy heart, he paddled it out from the shore, cursing as he fought with the sail. It was little experience he had with the ways of the sea.

Praying that he would not run into some hidden shoal, he gazed back at the land he was leaving and his heart was breaking at the sight. A breeze caught his feeble sail and, as he steered eastward to what he hoped was Endland, he fingered a small pouch that hung about his neck. There was a gold ring within it, too tiny for his large fingers, and as he felt it, he cried out:

"Ochone, farewell, Meave, slan leat. Farewell, Aerin, homeland, oh blessed isle. Slan leat, ochone…ochone."

The Ring of Brodgar

Cold is the night on the Great Moor, the rain pours
down, no trifle; a roar in which the clean wind rejoice
howls over the sheltering wood.

—from the Irish, 8th-9th century

I

He came from the west in a small boat to meet the first storm of
the autumn where Nial's Arm lashes Cymrn on the east coast of the
Grim Isles. Colum mac Donal was his name, late of Aerin, fleeing
his homeland with the wild weather on his heels. It's no sailor was
he. As the waves shook his craft, and the wind tore at his tiny sail, a
dismay was born in his dark eyes. Tufts of rust hair crept from underneath his helm, the wind whipping them against his cheek as he
strove to make out the approaching shoreline.

Scowling, he set his broad shoulders against the brunt of the
storm's force, held the tiller to his will with an iron grip, and steered
to where the sudden white of a sand beach stood out starkly amidst
the darker rocks and craggy shoals. The sea was like a living thing.
It struck his craft again and again with its fury. He had strength,
true, though what use without knowledge of ship or sea? The storm
was proving too much for him. Colum cursed under his breath as
the boat slipped from his control.

A wave lifted the craft, dashing it against a jutting outcrop. Above the din of storm and sea, the sound of wood rent asunder tore at his ears. Willy-nilly, Donal's son was flung into the waiting water. He wore heavy mail — suitable enough for battle with a more tangible foe — yet the weight of it, added to that of the long sword scabbarded at his belt, dragged him downward now. Strong arms flailed against the current to no avail. Relentlessly, the sea pulled him to its bottom in a tumble of helpless limbs.

Darkness grew in his mind as a sudden gasp for air drew in a lungful of salt water. He felt his spirit becoming one with the storm and the sea, aye, fleeing his body it was....

Time held no meaning in that darkness. His next remembrance was of lying on the thin strand of white sand that he had steered for earlier, ere tiller was torn from his grasp, ere the sea pulled him to its bosom. There was little strength in his sodden and weary body, yet his alert ears caught the warning scuffle of horses' hooves on the soft sand long before the riders came into view. He knew none in this land. Were it his homeland he knew that a stranger — more so one fresh from the sea — would be welcomed with suspicion, if at all. Sea-broken and helpless, they might well slay him out of hand. He cursed himself that he was not afoot with sword in hand to meet whoever it might be that neared him.

Two riders came within the limits of his vision, mounted on proud steeds. Such horses...one as dark as a shadow's heart, the other the golden hue of sun upon sheaves of ripe corn. Their manes fluttered in the wind. Colum marveled at the power that lay unconcealed in their mighty frames.

The riders were fair men in silver mail; two bright lords of some golden realm. Their cheekbones were high and delicately formed, beardless their noble faces. Their many-colored eyes shone and held some long forgotten mystery clasped deep within, a mystery shrouded with the telling of countless ages. The one most nigh doffed his plumed helm, running a slim hand through his curly hair. As he did so, Colum gasped, for the man's ears tapered into fine points.

Of the sidhe, they are, he thought. Ochone! Now is my life's end upon me.

"Greetings, brave sailor," said the man with the helm yet in his hand. There was an underlying mockery in his voice. Before it could settle fully into Colum's dazed consciousness, the man smiled, add-

ing: "I am the Aelord Albion, my companion is Gerran na Fertha. Would ye have our aid?"

"What...are...you...?" The words stuck in Colum's throat, coming out in a broken rasp.

"We? We are of the Aelden," was the reply.

There was a weakness upon Donal's son, born from his ordeal with the sea and old wounds not fully healed. Truth to tell, he knew not whether he lived or died. Yet, at those words his heart sank. Many and fearful were the tales of his homeland concerning the sidhe, the aelfin folk...and the Aelden...the Aelden were the eldest, to be feared the most. They gave aid, aye, if it suited their fancy. The price, though, the price was oft too high for a mortal to pay.

"What...would you...of me...?"

The Aelord regarded Colum seriously, measuring his youthful strength. He locked his gaze to the lad's dark eyes.

"There is a mark upon ye," he said at last, "a mark of the bright gods of the Green Isle. I see a time when we of the Aelden will have need of a champion favored by the gods. How do ye name the First Born of the Old Ones?"

"Tyrr...Behl-Stoirm..."

"Well spoken. I see the old blood runs true in you. Tyrr was the first born, before the Norsemen's Wodan, before the Dead God that has risen in the east."

Albion turned to speak to his companion in a tongue that was foreign to Colum's ears. When Gerran nodded agreement to what was said, the Aelord returned his gaze to the lad sprawled helplessly on the sand before him.

"Heed my words," he said. "Heed them well, Colum son of Donal mac Conn." — How knew he my name? Colum thought — "Ye lie at this moment in the grip of Nial's Arm, deep beneath sea and waves. There will come a day when we will ask ye for the strength of thy arms. Agree now that ye will come when we call and we will bring ye to a safe haven, freeing ye from death's eager grasp. We will not ask ye to forsake honor. It will be a deed of valor. But when we summon ye, ye *must* heed our calling. What is thy answer?"

...deep beneath sea and waves...

The words echoed in Colum's head. How could this be? Disbelief ran though his mind, angry as a river swollen with spring flood. And yet...there were tales....

His body held no strength; he could not move.

Tyrr aid me, he thought, for death's madness is upon me.

An unreasonable fear of the unknown rose up in his heart. Reason and madness, indeed, seemed to war within him. There was no ending it save by....

"It's a bargain...you have...man of the Aelden..."

The effort to speak those few words left him even weaker than before.

Albion smiled, lightly dismounting.

"When we summon ye, then, be ready," he said.

The Aelord lifted Colum as though Donal's son were a babe, laying him across the neck of his steed. He mounted behind, spoke a strange word into the ear of the horse, and suddenly they were in motion. Darkness swept over Colum once more, dark dreams quickening in his soul.

CR&O

The shadows shifted before his eyes. Beneath him he could feel straw and dirt. Opening his eyes, he saw he lay in a large courtyard, high stone battlements encircling it. Looking down at him was a huge man, his hair black and shaggy, tinged with grey, his beard falling halfway down his barrel chest. Over his shoulders was a great cloak of bearskin, in his eyes: a weighing, a reckoning, then a judgment.

"Take him from this holding, Aelden." Though Colum could not understand the words, the contempt in the man's voice was plain enough. "Take him before I have him slain. Erse!" He spat on the ground. "They're no better than the cursed Norsemen!"

Erse and the spitting Colum could understand. Redness rimmed his sight as anger grew within him. Had he only the strength to stand....

From behind this man, a slender figure stepped. He was dark-haired as well, yet his locks were straight and thin, tied back with a strip of leather; his face clean-shaven. Dressed in hunting leathers, he bore no weapons and appeared to be more a man of learning than a warrior. He reminded Colum of the Druids of his own Isle.

143

"Why so hasty, Bear?" said the newcomer. "The youth looks strong, and we have a need for men." He smiled at Colum. "What is your name?"

Feebly, Colum shook his head to indicate that he could not understand. When the question was repeated in his own tongue, Colum managed to answer.

"Col...Colum mac...Donal...."

"My name is Myrddin," the other replied kindly, still speaking Erse. He turned back to the man in the bearskin cloak. "I say take him in. In my bones I feel an omen. You will not regret it."

"Myrddin, Myrddin," he grumbled. He stared at Colum once more, sighed and added: "Do you give me a choice? I thought not. So be it then...but you, Myrddin, you I hold responsible for him."

He was obviously a man accustomed to having his own will. Plainly unhappy, he strode off. Myrddin smiled at Colum again. Donal's son knew then that he'd been accepted, albeit begrudgingly. Behind, he heard the sound of horses shifting feet.

"Remember," came the Aelord Albion's voice, "when we summon ye, be ready."

As Myrddin bent down beside him, he heard them depart.

CℛℰᏅ

And that is how Colum mac Donal came to the holding of Artor Foes-slayer, whom men name the Bear; that holding which sat like a crouching lion upon the heights of Caeme Tor in the land of Cymrn. Slowly, Colum learned the tongue of this new land, tutored by both Myrddin and a fellow countryman, Tadhg mac Art, from Colerawe in north Uloth.

"It's not much love the Bear has for we of Aerin," said Tadhg once. "He had a comrade slain by Erse raiders five years past."

"And you?" asked Colum.

"It's fresh from Aerin I was, striding through deep woods a-nigh here when I heard a crashing and din through the trees before me. I met Artor there at the mercy of an enraged boar. Spear broken, axe out of reach...'twas not much he could do." Tadhg shrugged. "So I slew the boar and he took me in."

In time, Colum came to admire Artor, and what he sought to do. Artor had a dream of uniting all of the Grim Isles under his banner.

Cymrn was his, with many of the folk of adjoining Kernow and Thumbria flocking to him. He knew the others would come, the folk of Midstland, Alban to the north, Endland, even the dour Fenfolk, could he but deliver his promise of a lasting peace. He had a cavalry of nine hundred; archers and footmen numbering two thousand.

Whenever the longships appeared along the coasts, he sent his armies at them. Valkings, Gaths, Jutes and Fynns fell 'neath his men's blades and shafts. North in Alban, he harried the Picta tribes; the length and breadth of the Grim Isles he put to the sword the plundering bands of brigands and strong-thieves. From the south a new threat reared: ships upon ships of well-ordered soldiers, originating in a land of sun on the shore of an inland sea. These too, he repelled, and ever his army was growing. Slowly, he was welding the Grim Isles into one land, under the banner of the Bear.

He had three chief commanders in those days: Gawen, Barlin's son, from the Midstlands; bold Ancelin of far Ys; and Drustans of sunken Lyonesse, lately come from King Marke's court in Kernow, fleeing an indiscreet affair with the Queen.

Artor drove Colum to his limit, willing him to fail. When the Bear was not personally on the training field, he had whichever of his commanders who was there, work him hard. Yet the training, the endless skirmishes and warring, turned a brawny lad of seventeen summers into a seasoned warrior who feared no man, answering to but one, and that Artor. He gave his loyalties to the Bear.

In training, he excelled; in battle, he was a terror to the foes. All this Artor noticed and remembered. He learned to ride and fight from horseback. Not sturdy ponies, Aerin-born; these horses were great rangy steeds, while from their saddles they had a foothold called a stirrup, making it possible to retain all control and balance, even in the midst of a pitched battle. Rather than swinging his long sword, he learned to use its point; as well, he worked with smaller, more subtle, blades, where skill was called for, not just brute strength.

At last, Artor had to concede that Myrddin had been right once more. The youth Colum was a youth no more; rather he was proving to be better than his instructors. Try as he might, Artor could no longer dislike him. Talking with him, Artor soon found that he had a keen mind that could readily grasp stratagems, offering intelligent suggestions where he disagreed. After three years, Colum arose up from the ranks to become one of the commanders of Artor's ever-growing forces.

Tadhg mac Art died in a skirmish with a band of Gaths just outside of Tintegal, a year and a half after Colum's coming to Caeme Tor. Yet he had other comrades now. Once the initial distrust wore off, he became a favorite about the holding, save for those times when thoughts of his homeland and the sweet maid he'd left behind reared up in his mind, leaving him morose and brooding for hours. Gentle Meave, his slim lass with her auburn hair and flashing amber eyes; oft was she on his mind. Yet not for him now, was she. They were sundered by distance, and more than distance, for she was the daughter of his most deadly foe: cursed Fergus, the High King of Aerin.

In that same battle that took Tadhg's life, his own was saved by the quick blade of Tarn O'Linn from Alban. Long and lean he was, his light brown hair ever windswept, his eyes bright with the promise of adventure. He saluted Colum with his bloody blade, wheeled about, and plunged into the fray once more, a gay smile on his lips. They became fast comrades, bold and rowdy. There was Garn of the Fens as well, broad-shouldered, massively built unlike most of the Fenland folk. They met through a disagreement in the barracks, fighting it out hand to fist. Through perseverance alone, Colum came out the victor. Garn, who had never been beaten before, grinned through his tangled dark beard, pledging friendship to Colum from that day forth. Long after the reasons for the quarrel were forgotten did that pledge hold true.

Three years were passed since first he came to Artor's holding. Yet, though his life was full, it always lacked. Colum could not forget his homeland and the debt that must be settled there.

Och, Meave, he thought time and again, swiftly stilling the upsurge of emotion that arose with her name.

The day of his return would come, though it seem so far away. Still, someday...first to Aerin and Meave he would fare, doing what must be done; then, across the wide swelling seas to Aerin Nua, where already the Erse had settled colonies. A wide free land 'twas said to be, and it drew Colum, as a flower draws a bee. Aye, one day.... He would decide to return, prepare to tell Artor that he must away, until the promise that the Aelden held over him would echo softly in his mind.

When we summon ye, be ready.

Cursing, he would put his plans aside.

There came a day, though, when the three years were past and done, when the spring was alive in the air, that the Aelord Albion rode in through the gates of Caeme Tor.

II

Colum saw Myrddin approaching from the corner of his eye, parried a thrust that Tarn aimed at his belly, and stepped back, motioning for a rest.

"The Druid's here," Colum said lightly, mopping the sweat from his brow. "Besides which, it's too good you are with these flimsy blades." He tossed the light sword he held to Tarn, who caught it deftly.

"Aye, the Druid's here," Myrddin repeated, "and one other as well, Colum The Aelord Albion awaits you in the courtyard."

The humor drained from Colum's face to be replaced with a scowl. So the moment had come.

"Keep the men working, Tarn," he said.

He turned from the practice yard, falling in step with Myrddin. They crossed the straw-strewn courtyard, alive with the bustle of Artor's retainers, to where the Aelord awaited them by his mount. Colum pulled at his mustache, as rust as the wild shock of hair on his head, remembering again that day when the man of the Aelden and his companion had pulled him from the sea. Abruptly, he shook his head to clear the memories from it.

"So you have come." he said, "and it was not a dream."

He studied the man before him with brooding, half-attentive eyes.

"Ye thought it a dream?" asked Albion with a grim smile. There was a haunted look about him. He drew a breath before he continued. "Would that this were but a dream as well. Years past we made a bargain, ye and I, and now the time has come that I must summon ye to do battle for me. Would ye know where thy geas will lead ye?"

Colum nodded brusquely. It was strange to hear the tongue of his homeland from the lips of this man, this Aelden. Hearing it again brought a longing in him, a longing for home and —

Again he shook his head, striving now to hear what the Aelord was saying.

"These are the Days of the Wolf, my friend. When the Mead Moon is full, it will be ten months since our Lady Brenwen was stolen from the Golden Hall in Yalnya, where we of the Aelden gather for our Great Meets. Stolen, I said? Nay, she was torn from us in a ruin of blood and death! Our heroes were slain, the Golden Hall was burnt in a storm of flame, and she — the light of our lives — was taken from us, never to be seen since.

"From the north came the horror that wrought this upon us — Graldag is its name, a monster in humanlike form that was created by the Picta Druids. From stone and sea, they shaped it. Ten months she is gone. Ten months have we sought her. But our young blades return not, our magics are of no avail. And now…from the Druids of the Picta the challenge has come. On the largest of the Ork-nair Isles there is a circle-henge named the Ring of Brodgar. There will our champion meet theirs to do battle till either one or the other is slain.

"When the Mead Moon is full and Anann rides the stars sky-clad, the Picta will come forth from their hidden holdings to meet with us in that circle of longstones. There will the fate of Brenwen be decided. They have yet to name their champion, still we can put a name to him…Graldag."

Colum's brow was wrinkled, his dark eyes boring into those of the Aelord.

"And it's myself you'd have do battle for you?" he asked. "Myself to be your champion and find the victory that all of your kin, spell-laden magic wielders that they are, have tried, aye, and failed in the trying?"

"Aye," Albion said. "But see, Donal's son. These are the Days of the Wolf. It is not thy death we seek. Ye are a wolf of the Green Isle — thy gods will see ye through."

"My gods are mostly noted for their absence in my affairs," Colum remarked.

"The geas…" Albion began.

"Och! Speak no more of it. My word was given. But it seems that the Aelden are not all they are made out to be." He laughed bitterly, adding: "And to think I feared the mere mention of your name when I was a child!"

The Aelord made no reply.

CREO

"What?" bellowed Artor Foes-slayer, and he named the Bear.

He sat on a great chair of carved oak inlaid with brass ornamentation, a full hand taller than Colum when standing, and Donal's son was not a short man.

"Colum, Colum," he said. "How can you do this? The raiding season is upon us, and you'd take yourself on a fool's errand to the north? Who'll lead your command? Let the Aelden fight their own battles. When have they aided us?"

Colum stood before the dais in Artor's hall. Garn and Tarn stood by him, the Aelord behind, while Myrddin sat at Artor's side. Save for them, the hall was empty.

"It's little aid they've given you, Bear," Colum said. "But it's myself they drew from a watery grave and left me here, now three years past."

Artor nodded agreement. "Aye, they did that, right enough."

He cast a cold glance to where the Aelord Albion stood. There was scorn in the Bear's steel-blue eyes, scorn that a man should call on another to fight his own battle.

"You'd take them?" he asked nodding to Garn and Tarn. "Aye, I thought you would. Well, then...."

"I will ride north as well," broke in Myrddin.

Artor turned, amazed at this, though not half so much as Colum. True, the Druid had spoken up for him when first he came to Caeme Tor. Since then, though, he'd had little to do with him, save aiding him with the language. Artor shook his head, protesting.

"You'd leave as well, Myrddin?"

"The land is restless," he replied in a quiet voice, "and strange tidings ride the winds. This is not a small matter, I think. There is a great dooming in the air, and it speaks in my bones. I must go."

"Then I will send a great force," Artor said. "Five hundred horse, at least. Aye, and perhaps I'll ride at its head myself. It's long since I've ridden the great moors of Alban."

"Send such a force, and the Picta will slay Brenwen!" the Aelord cried, breaking his long silence.

Artor looked up angrily.

"He speaks the truth," Myrddin said before the Bear could speak. "Fear not, we will be enough."

"So be it, then," Artor said, heaving a sigh. "But see you, Colum, and you too, Myrddin. When you're done with the Aelord's beastie, I charge you to return here with haste. There's work to be done and time enough for slacking when the winter's upon us. Ullr, take me! I must be a fool to let you go."

He rose from his chair and stepped down from the dais, clapping a huge hand across Colum's shoulders so that the Erse staggered 'neath the impact.

"See that you return speedily, Colum," was all he said. "Speedily and safe."

III

The next morn, as the rising sun washed over the stone works of Caeme Tor, a small company set out from its west gate, riding northward. Albion led the way, closely followed by Colum mounted on a tall chestnut mare. Riding easily behind him were Tam—already seeing his beloved land of Alban in his mind's eye—and Garn. The Fenman had a longbow slung over one shoulder, a quiver filled with arrows hanging from his saddle. Myrddin brought up the rear, a silence wrapped about him as though the wind that ruffled his hair was speaking with him.

Their way led through the Great Wood, a track of forest that spanned this largest of the Grim Isles from its southernmost tip in Endland through to the highlands and rolling moors of Alban. Gnarled wych elms, yews, towering oaks and ash trees, stands of slender birch and rowan filled that wild forest, their boughs freshladen with springtime finery in all its many dappled shades of green. Blossoms sprung up to be trampled into the long meadow grasses 'neath the hooves of their mounts. There were the yellow blooms of the primroses, the long-stemmed bluebells and sudden patches of bright wood sorrels; a myriad flowers in this wild garden—a feast for eyes that had spent long winter months ploughing through the harsh wind and snow upon endless patrols, or drilling on the frozen courtyard of Caeme Tor.

For two days they made their way steadily northward, faring at an easy pace. Night brought rough camps. With the horses rubbed down and hobbled, a simple meal filling hungry bellies, they rolled themselves up in their cloaks, leaving always one of their company on watch. The wild lands through which they fared were the havens for more than one band of outlawed men. To cross it with safety, caution was needed.

On the third day they rode out from the eaves of the Great Wood and entered a wide meadow. At its far end the wood began once more; in its center stood a circle-henge of longstones, tall granite monoliths that rose skyward, ancient and proud. Colum stared at them through hooded eyes, thinking of the coming combat, of what would befall should he fail. He owed a debt to this man of the Aelden, true, yet what if its fulfilling took his life? What of Meave who awaited him in his homeland, what of his duties to the Bear? It was not death he feared — that he'd faced a score of times — only the deeds undone that he must leave behind. If the Aelden, the ever triumphant race of childhood tales, could not prevail, what hope was there for him?

That evening, as the sun sank like a dying ember and the twilight slipped across the land, they rode into an ambush. Feathered shafts leapt out from between the trees, cutting the air about them, whistling by their faces as the sharp twangs of their assailants' bowstrings echoed in the growing dusk. Tarn took an arrow high in the leg, and it was only Colum's mail that saved him from the three shafts that struck his chest, tumbling him from the back of his horse.

As he fell, he turned in the air to land on his feet, charging the wood with a terrible growl growing in his throat. Here was a way to lose the doubts that plagued him. The red mist of battle fell across his eyes. In the dark, his foes were shadow shapes, yet his long sword bit flesh and he felt the spray of their life's blood warm upon his cheek.

Some second sight warned him of a danger from above. His buckler rose up almost of its own accord to catch the assailant that leapt on him from an overhanging bough. The force of the impact drove Colum to his knees, spinning his sword from his fist. Savagely, he twisted from beneath the greased body of his foe. Half rising, he drove his buckler two-handedly into its throat. The attacker died with a rattling cough. Still growling, Donal's son rose to his feet, dragging his dagger from his belt as he searched for his sword.

He glanced about himself to see that the swift battle was done. There was a faint shimmer about the hands of the Druid Myrddin and a manlike shape lay before him, smoldering in the half-dark. Tarn knelt, clutching his thigh and a bloodied sword. Garn stood over him, breathing heavily, peering into the shadowed wood; there were no more foes for the arrow he had notched and ready in his longbow. And Albion...the Aelord sat astride his mount, his brow wrinkled with concentration. Colum realized that he had not aided them at all.

He sheathed his dagger as he caught sight of his sword. He retrieved it and made for where the Aelord sat on his mount. Albion's eyes blinked once as Donal's son approached. He shook his head as though to clear it.

"Do not loose thy anger upon me," he said in a low voice. "I have no weapons and could not have aided ye."

The red mist drifted from Colum's eyes as he saw—with a shock—that the Aelord spoke the truth.

"Well, what of your magics?" he asked.

"I have been busy," Albion replied.

Colum turned away, muttering to himself. He cleaned and sheathed his blade, saw that Myrddin was tending Tarn's wound, so he went with Garn to have a look at their foes. He turned one over with the toe of his boot, his eyes going wide. The twilight was almost faded from the sky, yet enough light remained for him to see them.

They were small beings, manlike in shape with a pale white pallor to their spindly forms, though their strength far belied their size. Enormous eyes—even in death—seemed to glare with a ferocious hatred. Their only clothing was a strip of dirty leather wrapped about their loins; their weapons were mostly rudely-fashioned short bows and wooden cudgels. Here and there, though, there was one armed with a flint knife or a roughly-cast sword.

"They're not men!" Colum said. "Tyrr damn them! What manner of being are they?"

Myrddin joined Donal's son and looked down at the still corpse.

"'Tis a wicht," he said, "an unseelie wicht. They dwell in the highlands of Alban, hidden in the wastes of the dark moors. Never have I seen one this far south."

Colum tore his gaze from the creature.

"And yourself?" he asked Albion. "What do you make of this thing?"

"It seems that the Picta strive to win this combat by forfeit," was the Aelord's reply.

'Neath the bush of his thick moustache, Colum's lips twisted into a grin.

"So it's fear for me they feel, is it?"

Albion merely looked northward, shrugging his shoulders.

⊂⊰⊱⊃

Twice in the next few days they were set upon by small bands of the creatures. Except for Tarn receiving a second wound — this time in the shoulder — they came through both attacks unscathed. The ambushes suddenly ceased after the third one. Colum put it down to the Aelord's magics, for Albion had grown steadily more withdrawn, as though he were calling upon his inner strengths to keep the wichts at bay. Either that, or they were getting sick of dying 'neath his blade, thought Colum.

IV

On the first night of the new moon, they passed over the borders of Thumbria into the lowlands of Alban. Midst low hills and rambling woods, on the very edge of the Great Moor, they made a camp and bided there for three days, garnering strengths and giving Tarn a little of the rest that his wounds needed.

Donal's son stalked the campsite restlessly, muttering to himself, mulling over thoughts of this coming contest, aye, and of his homeland as well. Here he fought battles for others, whilst in Aerin, his own troubles went unavenged. There was a growing maturity in him, though. He knew it would take more than a strong arm to topple his hated foe from the throne that was rightfully another's, rightfully Coinneach mac Conan's. Could he convince the Bear to aid him.... Ah, when the strife was done, to walk again the quiet hills of Down, take sweet Meave into his arms, then away to Aerin Nua. He sighed as he paced through the campsite, these possibilities for the future alive in his mind.

On the third night of their camping, a great storm broke over the moors. The wind howled like a thousand daemons, tore at the thicket that sheltered them. Rain pounded the hills, broke through the leafy overhang above them, soaked them to the skin. Huddling in his cloak, Colum heard the Druid Myrddin muttering to himself.

"Aie! The storm breaks, and what will become of us?"

Hearing those words, a cold chill clasped the heart of Donal's son.

The Druid spoke not of the weather, that he knew. As they fared through Thumbria, he had felt the presence of a waxing disquiet; now, the Druid's words rang too true. Something stalked the land with them, something that frightened even the wichts from attacking them. No longer could he pretend that it was the Aelord's protection. Albion was proving about as useful as a sow with a litter of piglets and no teats.

Lightning broke in the sky, thunder roaring out directly overhead. Colum remembered looking upon their back trail once, seeing there the misty outlines of a great host of riders silhouetted against the sky. He'd rubbed his eyes, looked again, and they were gone as though they'd never been. Who or what they were, he had no way of knowing. Something traveled with them, fed upon the storm, and he feared it boded ill for them.

But useless though the Aelord was to them, his silence was so intense that Colum knew he planned something. Perhaps to betray them to the Picta? He shook his head, looking at the Aelord through the rain. What cared the Picta for this small company? If not that, though, what then?

The downpour lessened for a moment. In the sudden lull, Colum heard a stealthy footfall behind him. His sword was bared in his fist as he spun to meet the approaching foe. Picta! His eyes narrowed. A sharp cry halted his attack in mid-step.

"Hold, Colum!" It was Myrddin. "They have come to guide us."

He lowered his sword. Perhaps the Druid spoke the truth, for although the Picta numbered a half score, their weapons — long crude knives — remained in their belts. Their hair was black and stringy, held back with strands of braided grass; their dark skin was painted in their tribal markings, beads of moisture glistening on its greasy surface. The loin-wrappings shaped from animal hides were sodden as well. How far could they be trusted, was Colum's thought.

"To guide us?" he said, reconsidering. "We know the way well enough...."

"Hist," Myrddin said, stepping swiftly to his side, his voice low. "You see but ten. How many more are hiding further out?"

Colum understood the Druid's stratagem readily enough. Now was a time for waiting; later could the bloodletting begin. He sheathed his sword and hunched against the bole of a tree once more. The Picta settled into their camp, toothy grins spreading over their faces, small feral eyes gleaming.

"Guide ye, aye," one of them said. "That be a trueness. We be here to guide ye."

The storm grew in force again, rendering further conversation impossible. About them, Colum could feel the fates ringing them in; Picta in their company, the trial awaiting with Graldag, aye, and something else...something that stalked them just beyond sight....

CRSO

On the day that would lead into the night of the full Mead Moon, they came at last to Groat's Head, the northernmost point of Alban. A thin drizzle had accompanied their trek across the highlands, the worse for the Picta that loped beside their horses. Nerves were worn, a dooming seemed to rest upon their shoulders.

They crossed Pentwan Firth in a low barge, reaching the Isle that held the Ring of Brodgar, just as the dusk was approaching. Behind, a dark mist followed, slipping over the waters as it had through the hills. Leaving the barge on the shore, they remounted and rode till they came to the Ring.

The growing twilight cast an even more evil aspect to that already cruel scene. There were three who awaited them within the circle of longstones. Bound to the king-stone was a woman, golden-haired and fair to look upon, though her limbs bore the weight of months of deprivation so that they were thin and weakened. Still, her beauty shone through the welts that crisscrossed her once unmarred skin, and it was an unbroken spirit that gazed through her eyes when she looked up at their approach, trying to smile.

"Brenwen!" the Aelord cried, his anguish plainly written on his ashen face for all to see.

In that moment, Colum forgave Albion for all as he thought of how he would feel had it been fair Meave bound there. A wolfish growl rumbled in his throat. His resolve was strengthened tenfold that he would overcome the Picta champion.

By the king-stone stood two others: one a chief of the Picta, and the other — Colum stared at the manlike creature in disbelief — the other could only be Graldag. It stood as tall as Colum was mounted, its arms as thick as the span of both the Erse's legs. There was no expression in its face, save for two yellow eyes that burnt with an unthinking lust for death; its skin a sickly grey hue, like pale granite and ocean froth mingled. The power apparent in its limbs shook Colum's confidence.

"Stone and sea," Myrddin murmured, "born of stone and sea...."

The Picta chief leered at them.

"Ye are last," he cried gleefully, pointing at the Aelord. "Last Aelden chief, last that die. We slay," — he pounded his chest — "end rule. Ye dead, we take all land for Picta. Picta rule. No more gold-men keep us on Isles."

Suddenly, Colum understood, understood why Artor had needed such a small force to patrol the northlands, to hold the Picta at bay. The Aelden had forced them onto the Ork-nair Isles and kept them there. Once their rule was broken, the Picta would sweep down across the Grim Isles, slaying and destroying anything in their path. Yet why had they not sent Graldag after the Aelord? The Picta chief answered his unspoken question.

"Ye hide, hide. How slay ye? She brings ye, say Druids. Ha! Look!" He swept his arm back and up. At that signal, hundreds of Picta warriors and wichts swarmed from the long grass of that flat land that made up most of the Isle, knives and spears clashing above their heads. "Picta gather, watch ye die, gold-man." Hundreds of throats chorused their approval.

"Betrayed!" roared Colum. "Tyrr damn them, there was to be no contest. We're betrayed!"

He spurred his mount forward, leaping from its back to meet Graldag with a jarring crash. The creature threw its mighty arms around Donal's son, bringing to play all their power as it squeezed. A sharp cry issued from Colum's throat as he felt his ribs groan 'neath the pressure, the harsh metal of his mail rubbing his skin raw as he struggled uselessly in the monster's grip.

Once Daithi, the Druid of his father's rath, had told him that the berserker rage was a gift of the gods. The red mist of that rage blinded him now, ripping into his spirit so that his pain fell from him and he lived only to slay his foe. He exulted in that sense of power. Like some maddened beast, growling from low down in his chest, he strained in Graldag's grip, digging his fingers into the creatures throat.

As Colum fought with the Picta champion, the Aelord Albion looked down at the Picta chief from the tall back of his mount, smiling grimly. Beside him Myrddin lifted his arms, pointing his hands palms out at the dark man. As he did so, the chief's eyes went wide with fear. From behind them, he could see a host forming in the darkening twilight. Mists swirled and roiled, becoming Aelden knights. It was a host of the dead, a host of all those Aelden slain by Graldag, by the Picta, by the wichts. A host come to take a final vengeance upon their slayers.

The terrible cost of holding these shades was telling upon Albion. Across the long journey northward he had gathered them, bidding them to follow, holding them in check until this moment. A shaft of golden light lashed from Myrddin's palms, burning the Picta chief in an arcane blast until he was a charred corpse lying in the shadow of the longstones.

A howl of despair arose from the Picta and they charged. At that moment, Albion loosed the Aelden dead to sweep down upon the Picta and wichts. One glance he gave the meeting of the two armies. Laughing terribly, he spurred his mount to where Brenwen hung from the king-stone. Tenderly, he cut her down.

The Picta fought with all their unbridled fury. Yet their blades passed harmlessly through shadow forms, while shadow blades cut deep into their flesh. The battlefield was soon a welter of moaning and screaming. The battle swept into the circle-henge. Teeth gritted with pain as his wounds opened once more, Tarn's blade was busy. Myrddin fell 'neath the first onslaught. Wielding his longbow as though it were a stave, Garn cleared the Picta from about the stricken Druid.

No matter their blood-rage, though, the Picta kept well away from where the struggling forms of Colum and Graldag swayed. Slowly, Colum's back was being bent to where it would snap. The strain showed in the line's of his sweat-stained face that was twisted into a berserker's death-mask.

Suddenly, Colum loosened his grip on Graldag's throat, smashing both hands with a ringing force against the creature's ears. It bellowed, tightening its grip. Again and again, Colum battered it's ears until Graldag screamed, dropped him to the ground, and fell back to clasp its head. Colum charged it. As he did, Garn loosed a shaft in the midst of a short lull in his defense of the Druid. An arrow sprouted from Graldag's eye. The creature stumbled to the ground. Colum leapt into the air to land with crushing force on its chest. Bones splintered 'neath his boots. The thing bellowed its pain.

Garn loosed three more shafts in quick succession and to no avail, ere he needed to sweep his bow about him to clear another wave of Picta. The monster rose once more. Colum lashed out with a foot as the thing towered over him once more. The kick numbed Colum's foot yet it sent Graldag sprawling, one huge hand sweeping out for balance. It struck a standing stone, shattered it, and the creature fell into the midst of the rubble. Colum grasped its still struggling form by its groin and neck. Grunting with the exertion, he lifted it above his head. For a moment they poised so, ere Colum dashed the monster across the shards of the broken longstone to break its back.

Graldag lay across what remained of the longstone...and lived still, its limbs twitching as it strove to rise and strike Colum. Donal's son drew his long sword for the first time during the struggle. Roaring in his berserker fury, he hacked at the creature until there was nothing left of it but a bloody tangle of grey flesh.

"Look!" Albion cried in a terrible voice.

The word slashed through the red mist and battle lust that blinded Colum. Staggering, he stepped back from Graldag's remains. One eye still gazed with life upon Donal's son, one eye blazed with hatred. It appeared undying. Slowly, the life slipped from it, though. Colum tore his gaze from the mangled body — the bile rising in his throat — and obeyed the Aelord's word. He looked. He looked past where Myrddin stood shakily amidst a knee-high pile of Picta corpses, past Garn aiding Tarn to his feet, past Albion himself, covered in Picta blood, to the flat plains beyond the Ring of Brodgar.

The Picta were broken. Wide-eyed he recognized the warriors that rode through the fleeing ranks, slaughtering the survivors. They were the dead of the Aelden.

"How...?" Colum began. "Och! How can it be, that the dead ride?"

He knew though. It had been the Aelord that had summoned them. This was the reason for his intense concentration along their journey north. He felt weak as the berserker rage left him. His limbs ached and every rib seemed broken.

Garn looked at Colum.

"You might as well ask how it is that you still live after battling that creature," he said.

Colum shook his head slowly. He glanced at Albion, catching his eye. The Aelord smiled at the approval in Colum's eyes. He tossed a Picta sword from his hand and drew Brenwen to her feet, knowing that Donal's son was remembering his words, spoken now three years past.

There is a mark upon ye, a mark of the bright gods of the Green Isle....

"Who can tell, Garn, who can tell?" was all Colum said at last. As he spoke, he felt a warmth flow over him, the warmth of his homeland, Aerin, the blessed Green Isle. Aye, perhaps those gods had been with him.

The Iron Stone

I

I want him dead!" bellowed Artor Foes-slayer whom men name the Bear.

The words spat from a mouth hidden in a grizzled beard that hung halfway down his enormous chest. He rose from his throne of carved wood inlaid with brass workings and pounded the butt of an oaken staff against the rush-strewn surface of the dais.

"Dead! You understand?"

Colum mac Donal, late of Aerin and now one of the Bear's chief commanders, pulled at his rust bush of a mustache and frowned. He stood tall and red-haired, the links of his mail hauberk glinting in the torchlight. He was in his twenty-first year, this Erse wolf, broad-browed, wide of chest, and with eyes as dark as the grey longstones that dotted the Grim Isles, from their southernmost tips, as high north as the Shetland Isles.

161

"Aye," he said with a sigh. "It's clear enough your meaning is."

CR80

It was Ancelin of Ys they sought, when Donal's son and a small band of companions rode out from the keep of Caeme Tor the next morn. The Lordling of Ys had stolen Artor's queen, the fair Lady Gwenore, who was the daughter of Lodigrean of Camelyard. Stolen her from 'neath Artor's very nose and fled to the Fenlands where he had both kin and was well-loved. Somewhere in those marshes he was hidden now. Rumor held that he was holed up in the fabled Castle of Lomar, so to there was Colum bound. He had no choice. He was charged with the rebel's death and the return of the Bear's wife.

Yet it was a bitter task, this one set before him. Ancelin was a true friend of his; a firm comrade. He it had been who had seen to his training in the ways of organized war and leadership when first the Erse youth had come to Caeme Tor. Unlike Artor's other commanders — the dour Drustans, or the overly noble Gawen — Ancelin was ever of good cheer and loved by all...and too well by the Lady Gwenore. Ah, many's the night of carousing and wildness, of long campaigns and quiet talks they'd shared. Colum was loath to turn against his friend, no matter that the Bear was his Lord.

Straight through the long tracts of the Great Wood was the quickest road, so Colum turned his men to the coast, meaning to ride the longer way whilst he pondered a way out of this coming strife. Somehow there must be a way that the two could be reconciled. Och, but when it came to a woman, men's wits grew addled and reasoning was ever thrown to the four winds. Colum shook his head mournfully. If only the Druid Myrddin were here to give counsel. But he was not. It was Colum himself would have to talk with Ancelin, ere he worked out a fitting and final solution to this riddle.

He chose the men who rode with him carefully. Tam O'Linn, the laughing Alban-born warrior, was left behind to lead Colum's company that remained in Caeme Tor. With him were Garn of the Fens and a half-score hand-picked men — all of whom were loyal to him and well-disposed to the one they sought. It would not do to have an over-zealous sword-thrust or arrow-shot spoil his chance to speak peacefully with Ancelin first.

Garn looked askance to Colum when they turned from the road that led through the Great Wood and headed south, toward the coasts of Kernow. He ran a hand through his dark hair, thought for a moment, then laughed in his beard. He knew his commander's mind full-well. They were to delay themselves, were they? He settled his massive build more comfortably in his saddle, took a loose hold of the reins, and prepared himself for the long ride before them.

ᏮᏏᎥᏭ

A handful of days later, they were beyond the wild mountains of Cymrn and riding through the rolling hills and moors of Kernow. And then the sea was before them: the Ocean of Atlanta. Wild and turbulent it spread out before them, losing itself in the horizon. As they fared along the cliffs that overhung the tumbling waters, Colum's mind filled with thoughts of his homeland, of the wild shores of Aerin, of the troubles that had driven him to flee the Green Isle, aye, and more often, of the sweet maid he'd left behind there. In Aerin Meave awaited him, amber-eyed and auburn-haired. She was the daughter of his hated enemy Fergus, the High King — and wrongfully so — of all Aerin, yet still she was very dear to him. Did Ancelin feel for Gwenore but one tenth of the love he felt for Meave, Colum could forgive him all.

The sight of the great sea wastes pounded through his veins, reminding him of his desire to take ship with Meave and sail across those waters; westward, and further west again, to where Aerin Nua lay. Wide open lands were there, long settled by both Norsemen and Erse. Lands where the High King's weighty hand was but a fading memory and men lived their own lives, to their own loss and gain. Savages dwelt there it was said, aye, and peoples older than any in the Grim Isles as well. Still, a better place it seemed to him than all that the Grim Isles or his own homeland might have to offer.

Along the coast they rode, the men silent as their leader lost himself in his brooding. Reveries and planning swam through his thoughts; bittersweet memories that he could never loose from himself. Nor had he the wish to.

On the third day after their first sighting of the sea, they crossed the borders of Kernow and rode into Endland. Woods grew now from the once-moored hills, heavy thickets of briars and thorn-trees reared up along their way. That night they ate well on a doe brought down by Garn's longbow. The next day they fared eastward again, ever along the coast. By midafternoon they were hot and sweaty, for the woods seemed to hold the summer's heat, save in the deepest shades, where coolness hung like a blessing in the air.

The sky grew overcast. When the rain came, it seemed to burst from the sky directly above them, drenching them in seconds. The trees did little to protect them from the onslaught. They broke through a thick stand of beech and young birch to where a long stretch of sand bordered the stormy waters of a small bay. Through the rain they saw a sight that turned their blood cold. In the midst of the strand were two cross beams thrust into the ground, and a man was nailed to them.

They put heels to their mounts and thundered across the beach, the wet sand flying from their horses' hooves. Colum and Garn rode straight for the man whilst the others broke into two parties and fanned out across the strand. As he rode forward, Colum made out rills in the sand nigh the water's edge. Dimly through the downpour he saw them, yet Colum knew that sign well enough. Longboats had been drawn up on this beach. There were Norsemen abroad.

He was at the man's side now. Swiftly he dismounted and rushed forward to give what aid he might. The man was of Endland, and so, one of their own.

"T-too...late..." came his voice as Colum reached for the spikes that impaled him.

His body was wracked and torn, a hundred wounds open and bleeding in the rain. About his feet was a pool of blood that not even the heavy downpour could wash away.

"Gaths...half...score ships...c-caught me..."

His head fell forward to his breast, his breathing labored. Colum reached for a spike and gently began to work one loose. The man gave a cry at his touch and lost consciousness, making Colum's job easier. At least he wouldn't feel the pain. Garn supported the limp body as, one by one, Colum tore the spikes from the protesting wood.

"Cloth!" he cried as the last spike came loose.

As Garn lowered the man to the ground, Colum took a proffered shirt and tore it into strips to bind the man's terrible wounds. Above, offering what little protection from the rain as they could, some of his men held a blanket by its four corners. Under Colum's hands, the wounded man began to stir. His eyelids fluttered and a moan escaped his throat.

"Your name, man," Colum asked. "And is it true? The Gaths have served you so?"

He nodded feebly.

"H-Halwedd...my name...Gaths...must warn...village..."

He gasped suddenly. Foam bubbled up from between his clenched lips. A convulsion shook him and he grasped hold of Colum's arm. With his fingers digging into the Erse's flesh, he gasped once more before he died. Colum pried the dead fingers from his arm and rose with a curse. He stared seaward through the rain and shook his head.

"Garn?" he said at last, "do you know of this village?"

"Aye," the Fenman replied with a brusque nod. "At least there's one a mile or two up the beach that might be it."

"Take some men with you — three — and ride for it. Warn the folk there, if they yet live." Colum paused and looked about himself. "Aye, and then ride for Ancelin and tell him what betides. He knows you well enough. We need help here, and have no time for quarrels as to who is who's wife." The full impact struck him as he spoke. "Tyrr damn them! A half-score longships, with eighty men at least to a boat. It's an army of eight hundred that's floating somewhere off the coast." He turned to his men. "Withed, take the rest of the men to Caeme Tor. Tell the Bear of what befalls and make no delay or half the land will fall to the Gaths ere we can lift a hand to stop them. I'll await you both here. By the time you've returned I'll have scouted enough so that we can lay some plans. Now go, man, and ride swift!"

There was no lagging at Colum's commands. Garn began to protest, thought better of it and mounted, leading three men eastward. Withed took the others and returned the way they'd come. Colum watched them until they were out of sight, before he returned to the corpse. He knelt by it, meaning to lift the sodden blanket, when he felt a sharp pain in his knee. There was a stone hidden in the sand.

Wordlessly, he dug it out. He was about to throw it from him when he held it up to take a better look. The rain soon washed the dirt from it, setting flecks of metal glistening in its seeming granite surface. Norse runes were cut into one side. Holding it thoughtfully in his palm, Colum looked again to the crossbeams whereon they'd found the dying man. The stone stunk of ritual. Why he couldn't say.

Had this been a sacrifice then? he wondered.

Motion from behind him broke his reverie.

He whirled, drawing his longsword as he did, to see a tall man walking toward him from out of the woods. Gaunt and hollow-eyed he was, with a haunted look about him. His hair was plastered to the sides of his face, and the rain had soaked his cloak so completely that it hung in heavy sodden folds about his body. There seemed to be no danger from him, for he was unarmed, so Colum sheathed his blade. At first he'd taken the stranger for a Druid, yet now he saw clearly enough from the harp slung over his shoulder, that he was a Bard.

"Who is it that you are, man?" asked Colum as he drew nigh.

The stranger spoke not. Slowly, he looked about the strand, taking in the corpse, the empty beach. His gaze rested at last upon the stone in Colum's hand.

"Who am I?" he repeated in a low voice. He smiled grimly. "Homeless I am, aye, and unknown to most. Llew is the name I bore once. And you, warrior? Who are you to stand here on the shores of Endland, an Erse by your features, with the death-stone of Wodan in your hand?"

Colum started. His fingers clenched instinctively over the stone to hide it from the stranger's sight. The stone became cold to his touch, the tighter he gripped it. He relaxed his grip with an effort.

"It's Colum mac Donal I am, Bard," he said. "One of the Bear's men." At the blank look, he added, "Artor Foes-slayer; the Bear."

"Artor the Bear," said Llew musingly. He locked his gaze on Colum's. "Do you know one named Drustans, then?"

"Aye, what of him?"

"He is an unfriend to me and my people that once were..." He raised his hand in protest as Colum reached for his sword. "Nay, draw not your steel on me...my quarrel is with him, not with you or any other of Artor's men." He changed the subject abruptly. "Let me see this stone."

"What do you know of it?" asked Colum.

Llew remained silent until Colum handed it over, suspicion yet flaring in his eyes. Gingerly, Llew took it.

166

"You found this you say? Here on the beach?"

Colum nodded. Llew looked from the stone to the corpse that lay at their feet.

"Poor soul," he said at last. His eyes met Colum's. "This is the *tod-stein* of Wodan's—he is the Norsemen's god. Knew you that? Aye, well as I was saying, this is Wodan's death-stone, an artifact of great power in the hands of the Norse Druids. When the proper words are spoken, and blood has been spilt, it weaves a bane of storm and sea over their enemies..."

As the Bard spoke, Donal's son felt a chill rise up from the shoreline, as though brought on by the man's words. The rain, which had been petering off, renewed its onslaught. Strange images clouded Colum's mind. First there was greyness, the sound of rising winds, and the beating of wings. Through the growing shadow, he made out ravens—were there hundreds or but two? The visage of an old man appeared. One eye glittered and seemed to bore into Colum's soul; the other was an empty socket. Behind the image of the man, winged steeds bore armored women who held corpses to their breasts. Colum knew them now. He'd heard tales of the Norsemen's god and his reapers of the dead. Savagely he shook the images from his head.

"...cast it from you," the Bard finished, "for the Norsemen will return for it, aye, or their god will. 'Twas part of the ritual, I think, that it be left here. Cast it from you."

Colum muttered a curse in his own tongue and thrust the stone into his belt.

"I feel that I'll find a use for it," he said.

Llew gazed on him sorrowfully.

"It will bring you naught but madness and death," he said. "I know, for I bear a curse of the gods on my own head. Aye, and they are older than the upstarts of the Norse. The Daketh, the Dark Elder Gods..."

Colum was no longer listening. He cared nothing for talk of gods and doings beyond mortal realms. Little enough he knew of them, but that little was enough to set him seeking other paths when the ways of the Old Ones seemed to open up before him. He bent down, lifted the corpse, and strode for the wood, calling over his shoulder:

"Will you aid me lay this man to rest?"

With a nod, Llew followed him. Later, when the body was buried and a small cairn raised above it, Colum turned to his companion.

"Saw you these raiders that were on the shore?" he asked.

"Raiders? Nay, I'm but newly come here, seeking forgetfulness and rest, though my seeking is ever in vain. I sensed something here, miles back, some terrible power, and my curiosity brought me. At first I thought it was you — until I saw the stone, that is."

"Had you no fear?" Colum asked. "If this power is so dire, why dared you to come? The Gaths would spare you no more than they'd spare a seasoned warrior."

"I told you once, Erse, I am cursed. They could not have harmed me. I cannot know death, aye, or rest, or hearth or home."

"You tell a stranger tale than ever this stone could," Colum said, patting his belt. "Well, it's scouting I must go so that when the Bear arrives we'll be able to strike back at the damned Norsemen. What of you, Bard? There's a Druid in Artor's court might aid you, if it's help you seek. Myrddin's his name."

"Do you but 'mind me to Drustans," Llew replied. "Tell him his Bard of old sends greetings, aye, and a curse as well. And you, man of Aerin, cast away that stone ere its doom falls upon you. To be cursed by the gods is not something that may be lightly borne. I should know, for..."

"Farewell, Llew," Colum said, cutting into the Bard's speech:

He slipped into the wood with only the slightest whisper and was gone from the graveside. Llew watched him go with a sad shake of his head. Turning, he strode away as well.

II

For two days Colum stalked the coast nigh where they'd found the first traces of the Norsemen. Sometimes on foot, other times mounted, he moved like a ghost. Yet it was always in vain. There was no trace of them. At times he cursed the length of time it would take Artor and Ancelin to arrive — when he wasn't wondering about the wisdom of bringing them together. Other times he brooded over the strange dreams that had been haunting his few hours of sleep.

Whether they were brought on by the stone, or the words of the strange Bard, he knew not; yet they were always of the one-eyed man and his riders. Through his dreams they seemed to stalk him, searching for...the stone? For him? Always, Colum awoke just before the shades of his dreams caught up to him. He would sit awake then, staring into the dark woods or the benighted sky and ponder. He would think of throwing the stone from him, only at the last minute he would refrain and slip it back into his belt.

On the morn of the third day he came upon his first signs of the Norsemen. A village lay before him, gutted and ruined. The charred remains of the cots and huts still smoldered sullenly in their ashes. Bodies lay strewn about — men, women and children — and the sight of their mutilations wrought a deep anger in the heart of Donal's son. Warily, he rode through the remains, his horse nickering with fear as the sharp rank stench of burnt flesh, of blood and fire, met its nostrils. Upon the northern edge of the village, he found tracks of the Norsemen. They were faring northward, deeper into Endland. Again Colum cursed that he had not an army with which to pursue them.

CR80

Ancelin arrived on the seventh day of Colum's lonely vigil with three hundred mounted Fenmen. They were weary from their long trek, yet they were still eager to meet with the raiders. Garn and Ancelin dismounted and walked to where Colum awaited them. Behind him the crossbeams were still implanted in the sand, their red stains bright in this day's sunlight.

"Well met, Wolf," Ancelin said with a trace of wariness in his voice.

"Aye, well met," Colum replied, his own voice grim. Then he laughed suddenly. "Och, Ancelin, and will you be saving the distance in your voice for the Bear and not let it fall upon those who would yet name you friend? It's no concern to me that the pair of you bicker over his wife — though Artor might have aught to add on that score seeing how it's myself was sent to bring him your head. Na, we've more pressing matters before us with these raiders. Besides, the both of us know that there's been trouble between Gwenore and he since before I even arrived on these shores. It's only the Bear's pride that sets his heart a-yearning for your death."

"I'll not give her up," Ancelin said. "Aye, and neither would she leave me."

"And is it myself that is asking you to, man? Behl-Stoirm's blood! We have a war on our hands and you'd bicker over a wench?"

"Gwen is no wench..." Ancelin began with rising anger.

"Aye, aye, I know that well enough. Would you just be putting her from your mind and settling your thoughts on what's to be done with these Norsemen?" At Ancelin's brusque nod, Colum continued: "There's almost a week ere the Bear's forces can be with us, yet I'd like to strike a blow or two against our foes ere he comes, rather than skulking in these bedamned woods for any longer. There's a village nigh that was leveled by them. There were no more than three or four hundred in that party, and though that leaves a half of them to be accounted for, I believe we have enough to take them. At the very least we can harry them until the Bear arrives."

"They marched north you say?" asked Ancelin. "And their ships? The longships?"

"I found traces of a landing nigh the village," replied Colum, "but the ships are gone. There was plain sign that they marched north."

"Then mount, Wolf, and we'll ride north and find them."

CRESO

For the next four days they rode northward through Endland. Though there were signs a-plenty of the Gaths, they had yet to meet with them in battle, or even catch a sight of them. The trail led them in a wide sweep so that, on the fifth day, they were faring southward again, along a swath of burnt villages and slain country-folk. The wrath grew in their hearts with each mile they fared.

"The folk here are helpless," Colum said to Garn as they rode through another small steading. "With no Lord to aid them or gather them together they fall like chaff before these damned raiders." He shook his head thoughtfully. "And for what gain? It's nothing but senseless pillaging they're doing. Where's the wealth, the booty?"

"I've heard," Garn replied, "that they mean to settle this land for their own. They'll want those settlements to be safe and what better way is there than to slay all who might oppose them?"

Colum made no answer. The truth in Garn's words was plain enough, little though it pleased him. There was another matter that troubled him as well. The matter of the iron stone—as he called it. The *tod-stein* that was tucked in his belt. It tormented him in his dreams; wrought a gaunt and hollow look to his eyes. Though Ancelin and Garn questioned him, he was loath to speak of the matter to them. Yet he found no relief. The one-eyed man came ever nearer to him, stalking across the wind-swept land of his dreams with a raven perched on either shoulder. He spoke now as well. The tongue he used was foreign to Colum's ears, though it bore a resemblance to the language of the Norsemen.

CR80

On the day they looked to meet with Artor's forces, they were again within sight of the sea. The scouts returned with two reports. The Norsemen were gathered on the beach as though awaiting their ships, and the Bear—with but two hundred men—was camped to the west abiding their coming. Aye, and the Bear was dead drunk as well, they warned.

"Two hundred men?" Colum roared. "Tell me you counted wrong, man. Tell me the Bear's not gone mad to bring so few, aye, and to be lost in the cup as well."

The scouts backed away from the glowering figure before them.

"We speak only the truth, Wolf. As Ullr is our witness."

They hurried away as Ancelin dismissed them with a thoughtful wave.

"What do you think, Colum?" he asked.

"I know not what to think," Donal's son said, his brow furrowed with anger, "but I know well how to find out. It's ahead to Artor's camp I'll be riding and you to follow slower. Aye, and mayhap, before you're come, I'll know what betides."

As soon as he spoke, he put foot into stirrup and was off with a thunder of hoof beats. Once he rode his initial anger from him, he slowed down to a pace-eating trot, worrying at the riddle of Artor's strange behavior. It was well-known that Artor loved his ale...yet

171

he scarce drank during a campaign. Had the loss of Gwenore troubled him more than Colum had thought?

He was still without an answer by the time he rode into Artor's camp. Straight through the encampment he rode, not even nodding to the men that greeted him; straight through to Artor's tent. The Bear was seated before it with a tankard of ale in his hand, his beard wet with froth.

"Ho! Colum!" he cried. "What news of Ancelin?"

Colum dismounted and strode forward.

"Were you not told?" he asked with anger in his voice. "Were you not told of the Gaths — eight hundred strong — who seek to ravage all the coast, aye, and are succeeding as well? Where's the men you should have brought?"

Artor lurched to his feet, quaffed the remaining ale in the tankard with one gulp, and threw the empty cup from him. He wiped his hand across his mouth.

"Who commands here?" he asked.

"Why...it's you are our leader," Colum replied, puzzled.

"Aye!" Artor bellowed, pounding his chest. "I'm the leader indeed. I give the commands. Now where is Ancelin?"

"He follows with three hundred of his own horsemen to give us aid against the Norse."

"Three hundred men? I want him dead. I don't want his aid against a handful of raiders. I'll have his heart for this, aye, and yours as well!"

"You're drunk," Colum said quietly, stifling his anger. "I'll speak with you again when there's sense in your words."

"Drunk? Drunk? Who's drunk? I gave you an order, Colum mac Donal, and I expect it to be carried out!"

Colum nodded.

"Aye, so you did."

He drew back his fist and smashed Artor square in the face. The great man reeled backward falling to the ground, and glared stupidly at Colum. As he tried to rise, Colum stepped forward and hit him again. The Bear lay still. The two blows and the vast quantity of ale he'd drunk laid him low where two dozen foes would have been hard-pressed to do the same.

Men approached Colum with their weapons drawn. He drew away from them, not wishing to pull steel on those he'd name friend.

"Hold!" he cried, lifting his empty hands as he spoke. "Hear me out. It's not the Bear's overthrow I'm seeking, but the man's dead drunk. There are four hundred Gaths on the beach, with another like amount on their way. With Ancelin's aid—no matter that the Bear's wife has sundered them—with his aid we can take the ones on the beach." He looked over the heads of the men who threatened him as he spoke to see the first lines of Ancelin's men riding into the encampment with Ancelin himself at their head. "Is it war with your own you'd be wanting, or death to the Norse?"

The Bear's men muttered to themselves. They glanced from Artor's still form, to Colum, and back to the approaching horsemen who outnumbered them. Aye, and Tam O'Linn was there as well. With a score of Colum's own company he pushed through the throng to stand by Donal's son.

Degar of Thumbria stepped forward.

"You speak the truth, Wolf," he said. "Artor's drunk, indeed, and the matter of Gwenore should be settled 'tween he and Ancelin. We have our own foes to fight. Lead us, and we'll meet the Gaths with you."

"Na," Colum said, shaking his head. "I'll not be leading you. That is for the Bear to do. Do you but give me your aid in convincing him of the right of this matter."

Degar smiled.

"Well spoken," he said as Ancelin rode up. "Let's sober him up then and ride upon the Gaths."

CRWSO

"Aye," Artor said later that night, "I'll agree. What choice have I with not a loyal man here to side with me?" He held a hand up to his aching head and frowned as he rubbed it. Pointing to Ancelin he added: "But I'll have your head when all this is done. Mark my words. And you, too, Colum. Do not think that I'll forget...bah! My head's pounding too much to talk. Leave me...all of you. Ready yourselves for battle in the morning."

The commanders filed out of the tent. Colum paused as Artor called him back. He faced the Bear, his brow furrowed.

Och! And what now? he thought.

Artor looked up at him and tried to smile through the drink-brought pain. He succeeded only in grimacing.

"You've a heavy hand, Colum, and one that I take no pleasure in feeling upon my own chin. This matter of Gwen...it is between Ancelin and myself. I thank you for reminding me. How can a man — be he plowman or Lord — seek to order the heart of a woman? 'Tis this that has troubled me, aye, like a festering sore that grew into madness." He shook his head sorrowfully. "For all the trouble between us, I love her still, and it breaks my heart — aye, and wounds my pride — that she should go to another. I know not what to do, for this is a matter in which I cannot play the king." His eyes locked on Colum's. "Aye, all I've succeeded in doing is to play the fool, though I'll never admit that to the men."

The look in Artor's eyes was fond as he spoke. He looked of Colum as the son he never had, and so could speak to him of the things that troubled his heart without the fear of losing face. For Colum's part, he felt a rush of pride for the bear-like man that sat before him. He understood Artor's mind far better than the Bear imagined. Though Artor could never replace the father who had died at his side in Aerin, he was yet the one man Colum respected above all others.

"My thanks," Artor said at last, breaking the silence. His eyes twinkled and Colum knew that the Bear of old was with them again. "Now go...ere I remember too well how you struck me down and — Ullr damn you! — with but two blows!"

Colum chuckled as he left the tent.

He walked about the camp, checking the guards, ere he took to his own blankets. As sleep swept over him, the dream returned again, heralded by rain-heavy winds that tore through his soul and left him gasping. He strove uselessly to wake himself. The dream seemed to tighten about his mind the more he struggled. The one-eyed man was there, one raven on his shoulder, the other circling about his head. Behind, in the storm-wracked sky, the riders on their winged steeds were silhouetted against the lightning that ripped across the dark clouds.

The man stepped closer and closer, his movements like the turns of some dark tune, deliberate and ponderous, yet snake-swift at the same time. He came within a hand's-breadth of Colum.

"*Het tod-stein...*" he said in a chill voice. The thunder rumbled a harmony to his voice as he spoke.

A chill entered Colum's soul, like a wedge of ice being driven into his heart. The words were Norse, yet not Norse. Regardless of their origin, Colum knew their meaning. The man's hand reached out to Donal's son.

If a man died in a dream, thought Colum, his mind suddenly clear as time seemed to slow down to a crawl, did he live yet in waking life?

He never learned the answer. With a surge of inner strength he ripped himself from sleep, from the dream and the clutches of the one-eyed man.

Awake now, he lay panting on his blanket. The sky was clear and star-laden above him. He felt in his belt. The stone lay there still, strangely cold to his touch.

III

The next morn, Artor led his men onto the beach. The Islanders were five hundred strong, well-armed and mounted. Before them were the Gaths, chanting and clashing their swords and axes against their oval shields.

"Wodan! Wodan! Wodan!"

The sound swept over the strand to the ears of the waiting Islanders. The banner of the Bear fluttered over their heads. They were proud, these men who rode and fought neath Artor's banner. Yet there was a dismay a-borning in their hearts now. It was not born from the bellowing Norsemen before them, though. Behind the Gaths, a half score longships were coasting in from the open sea. The Islanders were soon to be outnumbered.

Colum glanced to where the Bear sat astride his great war-horse, his arms resting on the carved wooden pommel before him.

"It bodes ill," he said.

Artor turned to him.

"Aye," he replied, "but if we move swiftly, we might yet have a chance."

He sat up straighter, drawing a huge war-club from its thong on his saddle. Of oak it was, iron-spiked and bound with great rings of iron. He held it above his head and pointed to the beach.

"Charge!" he cried

A mighty roar arose from the throats of the men who rode neath the Bear's banner, drowning out the Gaths' cries to their god. For one moment the Islanders poised, mounts straining at their bits, ere they charged forward sweeping down upon their foes. The two forces met with a shock that shook the very foundations of the strand.

The Gaths fell back against the initial onslaught, regrouping quickly. When the first impetus of that charge was spent, they swept about the Bear's men. They faced the horsemen afoot, or pulled them from their steeds to grapple with them in the sand. In the midst of the swirling battle, Artor's huge form could be seen. His arm swept his war-club about him in wide mighty strokes. None could stand before him. By him rode the men of his personal bodyguard, and among them was Colum mac Donal. His face twisted into a deadly mask of death as the berserker rage fell over him, the red mist blinding his eyes.

The Islanders were being torn from the backs of their mounts. A third of them were afoot now, fighting in the uneven footing of the sand, slipping in the blood, stumbling over the dead that were soon piled about them. The battle broke up into countless individual combats, save where three or four Gaths at a time would charge the Bear. They were loath to face him alone, for he wrought a deadly havoc with his club. And the Erse that fought at his side was no laggard either, caught up in the berserker rage as he was. They knew that battle-madness all too well.

Still, the Gaths were many and the longships were pulled up on the shore now. Ancelin led a charge against the men who were leaping from the decks. He had to draw back, though, for they outnumbered him greatly. Desperately, he urged his men to block the newcomers from joining the main battle.

At Artor's side, Colum lost his sword in the breast of a foe, the man falling forward too heavily for the Erse to pull it free. He laid about himself with his buckler, drawing his knife as he did. The madness was full upon him now. The point of his dagger broke against the mail of a Gath. He booted the Norseman in the groin, flung the useless hilt at another and raised his buckler to block an-

other blow. Instinctively, his hand leapt to his belt, seeking a weapon. When it came away it bore—rather than steel—the iron stone that haunted his dreams.

The man directly facing him, faltered in his attack and drew back when he saw the stone in Colum's hand. Donal's son paid him no mind. He leapt upon him, striking the Gath with it. Red was the blood that glistened suddenly on the stone's iron-flecked surface. Another Norseman caught sight of what Colum bore. Slowly the Gaths backed away from Colum. He stood panting, battle-blind, and roared curses in the tongue of the Green Isle.

A murmur appeared to run through the lines of the raiders. In moments, a lull descended upon the battlefield as the Gaths retreated, staring at the stone in Colum's hand. Through his battle-madness, Colum sensed something of what was befalling. An icy stabbing in his hand brought him back, clearing the red mist from his eyes. By him stood the Bear and...another? With his free hand, Colum rubbed at his eyes. No, only the Bear stood there. Approaching them from the lines of the Gaths was a tall, bearded man, a bared sword in his hand. He held it by the blade, high over his head—the sign of parley.

"Redhair!" the Gath cried to Colum. His voice was roughly-accented, yet he spoke in the tongue of the Grim Isles.

"Aye?" Colum replied, the blooded stone still in his hand.

"You have profaned the god-stone of Wodan with Norse blood. Aye, and more, you have disturbed the Ritual. You must return it. No more blood must be spilt on it."

"So it's the stone you'd be wanting, sea-cur?" Colum said.

He shook his head unbelieving. He was to give them back their amulet and for what? So that they could slay them and continue their pillaging? He spat on the stone.

"This is what I think of your holy stone!" he cried.

A cry rose up from the ranks of the Norsemen. At first, Colum took it as a reaction to his blasphemy. His grey eyes raked their lines to see that they were gazing upward. From behind—from the men of the Bear—another cry went up. The sky was greying. There were no clouds scudding in from the sea, enwrapping the sky. The blue merely turned steel-blue, then grey in the passing of a moment. A cold keening wind sprang up from the sea to sweep over the strand.

178

Colum felt light-headed and swayed on his feet. Riding that wind, to the cacophonic shrieking of a thousand ravens and wailing winds, were maidens on winged horses. They brought with them a greater darkness, these handmaidens of Wodan, his reapers of the dead. A foreboding stole into Colum's heart as he recognized the figures from his dream. A great cry and clashing of weapons arose from the Gaths.

"Wodan! Wodan! Wodan!"

In the midst of the greyness the visage of a one-eyed man appeared, with ravens hovering about it. Colum cursed. The stone in his hand was like ice; his hand was numb with cold. Frost covered his hand. Desperately, he loosened his fingers from their grip and threw the stone so that it landed on the sand between the Gaths and himself. The icy prickling did not abate. Colum knew then that the Bard Llew had spoken true. He should have cast it from himself earlier. The face of Wodan grew clearer, though mist and greyness swirled about it. The god's voice ripped into the air.

"THE CURSE OF THE FROZEN WASTES IS UPON THEE, ERSE."

The hand that had held the *tod-stein* grew so cold that there was no feeling at all in it. The freezing continued to spread up his arm.

"DEATH BE THINE, DEFILER OF THE SACRED. WHERE NOW THY BOLDNESS?"

The breath in his lungs seemed to freeze as Colum felt the ice enter his chest. His teeth rattled and a greyness was growing in his mind. Without needing to look, he sensed that the Bear and his men were frozen as well, as though time had stood still. The Gaths were yet roaring their war-cry.

"Wodan! Wodan! Wodan!"

The cold spread over his other limbs. Still Wodan's voice shook the skies with its utterings.

"BLOOD CALLS ME, FOOL. THE STONE IS THE FOCUS OF MY POWER. I SAW THY TAKING OF IT FROM NEATH THE FEET OF THE HANGED MAN, THE SACRED HANGED MAN. I SOUGHT TO HUNT THEE, WHEN LOOK HERE...YE HAVE DRAWN ME TO THIS BATTLEFIELD. IT IS BY THY ACT THAT THY COMRADES WILL DIE. BUT THOU FIRST, O BRAVE MAN, THOU FIRST..."

Aye, thought Colum, his body was freezing and a blackness was welling up in his mind. He pitched forward. His body hit the packed sand with a shock, yet he felt it not at all. His time was come. His last thoughts were a curse upon this god of the Norse and the sorrow that he might never see his sweet Meave again.

The blackness wove itself tighter and tighter about him. As each fold encompassed his spirit, he began to hear a music. It was distant, as though it fared over hills and from far away ere it met his ears. Its tonality awoke a strange feeling in Colum. The sharp notes stung his ears. Frozen though his body was, blinded by an unnatural dark, he sensed still that there was a struggle unfolding. It was not his doing though, for he was as helpless as a newborn babe. Then who?

The darkness shifted to grey. Through the dimness he saw the Norse god facing a bent figure which seemed to hover in the mists. His back was turned to Colum, yet he recognized the man. It was Llew. Where had he come from? Colum remembered the fleeting impression he'd had of a man standing by Artor. Wodan's voice broke into his thoughts.

"YE CANNOT HARM ME WITH THY HARPING, BARD."

"Oh, aye," came Llew's voice, "I know that well enough." His music continued to play as he spoke. Colum could almost see the notes now, flickering in the grey air. "And yet," continued Llew, "you cannot harm me either. I bear one god's curse already. What care I for another?"

Colum could sense the Norse god's disconcertment. The harp music swelled suddenly. As if in slow motion, the *tod-stein* floated up between Bard and god. Wodan's eyes went wide.

"NO!" he cried, his voice rumbling like thunder.

He was too late.

Golden harp notes wrapped themselves about the *tod-stein*. The music swelled once more. There came an explosive sound as though a mountain was falling in on itself and the *tod-stein* flew apart into a thousand shards. In that same moment, a stillness fell upon Colum's ears. He'd closed his eyes as the *tod-stein* burst asunder. In the ensuing quiet, he opened them to find himself alone, save for the Bard. Llew approached him, his harp slung over his shoulder once more.

Why? asked Colum, shaping the word in his mind. The paralyzing ice still held his body in thrall. *Why did you aid me?*

"I took pity on you, Colum mac Donal," replied the Bard with a shrug. "I know all too well the burden of a god's curse. Had you died 'neath his power, there'd have been no rebirth for you...only death eternal. There was no risk for me, aye, and I would not see another burdened so. Perhaps, though, had you been Drustans..."

He left the sentence unfinished.

I will help you break your own curse.

"No need," replied Llew with a bitter laugh. "See you to your own folk. They have need enough for you."

He looked down on Donal's son. Lifting a hand in farewell, he strode away. Colum strove to make his body his own, to rise and follow Llew. Only darkness answered his mind's call.

He fought that dark for what seemed like ages. As it fell from him at last, he became aware of his limbs once more. He drew a deep breath and almost choked on the sand he took in with it. He looked about, still coughing. There stood Artor Foes-slayer, whom men name the Bear. His great war-club was in his hands and he looked with satisfaction at the smashed remains of the *tod-stein* before him. Colum stared in bewilderment. It was obvious that Artor had destroyed the stone. But what of Llew?

Artor lifted his eyes to the long lines of the Gaths before him. The Norsemen were staring skyward, unable to comprehend why their god had forsaken them. A ripple of anger passed through them as they focused on the Islanders and the broken *tod-stein* at Artor's feet. Without a war-cry, they charged.

"Lock shields!" Artor cried.

He lifted Colum to his feet, dragging him backward. The Islanders were soon in position, shields locked. Those who were still mounted drew aside, away from the main onslaught. The Gaths met the wedge of Islanders and broke against it. Under Ancelin's command, the mounted men swept in upon them. The wedge held for just a few moments longer. At the Bear's signal, it broke and the Islanders fell upon their foes.

CR&O

That battle raged into the setting of the sun. Bodies littered the beach and the Norse fought to the last man. Their hope and drive was gone from them; they were men forsaken by their god. Wherever Artor or Colum were, they fell back in consternation at the two who had driven Wodan from their side. As the twilight washed over the strand, the beach was still lit from the burning longships and men were scouring the woods for the small bands of Norsemen who had given up the battle and fled.

Artor and Colum stood in the glare of the burning longships and gazed at the ruin of the Gaths' army. Yet Colum's mind was filled with thoughts other than the carnage before him. Thoughtfully he worried at the riddle of Llew and the *tod-stein*. He thought he understood. Where Llew had faced Wodan—that had been the same land as the one of his dreams. Deeds which befell there were reflected in this world. So when Llew's harp notes destroyed the stone, in this world those same notes had caused Artor's body to lift from the frozen embrace and crush the stone with his war-club.

Colum rubbed at his head. It was confusing, no doubt of it.

"Any reports?" the Bear asked, breaking into his thoughts.

"Aye," Colum replied, gathering his wits. "They're broken and we've won indeed…but the cost has been heavy. We've lost a half of our men, and of the others, there's hardly the one that doesn't bear a wound of some kind."

Artor looked at Colum in the flickering light. The Erse nursed an arm that was broken and stood favoring one leg. His mail was rent in so many places that it was a wonder that he yet lived. Aye, and the Bear himself was sore hurt from a shoulder cut. His bronze breast-plate and armor had been served no better than Colum's mail.

"Ancelin?" Artor asked. There was a flicker of emotion in his eye as he spoke.

"He fares back to the fens," Colum replied. "You'll wait to settle with him?"

"Aye, I'll wait…but not long. No armies though. Just the two of us this time."

Colum grinned.

They stood in silence for a long time thereafter as their men bustled about them. The wounded were tended to. The slain were gathered in a great pile so that they might be burnt, their ashes offered to Ullr and the winds of the Grim Isles. Colum thought back on the past few years as he watched the men cover the pyre with brush. He shook his head wearily. There was more to life than endless slaying, especially when a man had a maid awaiting for him. This land was not even his own, though their foes were one.

"Bear?" he said at last. "Will there ere be an ending of this?"

Artor turned to look at Colum.

"Aye," he said, "but not till we've cleansed these Isles from shore to shore, aye, and seen to it that they remain safe and in the hands of our own people. But that day is a long way from us still, Wolf. A long, long way."

The Fair in Emain Macha

This is the noble truth of the arising of sorrow. It arises
from craving, which leads to rebirth....

—from "The Pali Canon,"
sacred scriptures of the Theravada
Buddhists (c. 500 - c. 250 B.C.)

Above and below all weir the Green Man makes his play...

—Robin Williamson,
from "Five Denials on Merlin's Grave"

I

Twilight fingered the sky with grey threads of cloud as the horseman stepped his mount from the wood. He skirted a jumble of rock, avoiding the trail that led down into the marshes, and made his way to the chalk cliff that lay ahead. From that vantage point he could look out over the Erse Sea, that body of water separating Aerin from the main body of the Grey Isles. His own kin called it Nial's Arm.

A frown twitched on his brow.

Kin. Best not to remember; impossible to forget.

He had no kin now.

Seven years ago, his father had led him into a Kingbreaking—a justified rebellion that ended in failure, death its only reward. The horseman had been the sole survivor of that final battle. He was the last of his clan; an outlawed wolf of Aerin, alone on a foreign shore. And soon to be outlawed here as well.

The horseman sighed. He dismounted wearily, swinging his right leg across his mount's forequarters and dropping lightly to the ground. The grass, blades bowed low by the sea winds, was springy underfoot. He stood in the quiet for a moment, listening, grey eyes watching his back trail with a wary gaze until he was satisfied that he hadn't been followed. Only then did he drop the reins and continue on foot to the lip of the cliff. Left to its own devices, his mount nibbled contentedly at the salted grass.

Aerin, the man thought, looking westward. Do you remember me still?

Seven years was a long time.

He stood tall and straight-backed, one hand plucking at his mustache, the other loosely resting on his sword hilt. The links of his mail tunic caught the last rays of the sunset and made a glitter of its captured light; his hair was as red as the sun itself as it now sunk seaward. His gaze fixed on the misted distance, hoarding thoughts behind his eyes.

He yearned for justice as a blind man yearns for sight. Yearned for justice, and for a welcoming smile from his own Meave whom he had been forced to leave behind.

His frown deepened at the thought of her, for he could not think of Meave without recalling her sire as well: Fergus mac Coemgen, Ard-righ of Aerin; the unbroken King who'd had the horseman's father slain and set his King's Curse on the horseman himself. In the years since his exile, word had come from the Green Isle: How his father's rath was less than a memory, how the clan's fields were salted and barren now, how their cattle fattened the Ard-righ's herds, their great black bull—his father's pride—servicing the Ard-righ's weaker stock.

Men, women and children had all been slain. In the duns of his people, in the raths of the Kings, not even the harpers kept alive the memory of his clan. His sister Aine lived, but was wed into Briunal's clan, no longer a Fiolan. Of the Fiolan clan, only he remained, Colum mac Donal, truly his father's son, for the father's hatred for the unbroken King still lay unchecked and simmering in the son's heart. But retribution remained beyond his grasp. He was an exile, a chieftain of Artor Foes-slayer, with three companies of horse under his banner, his own keep, more land and gold at hand than his own father had ever known, but he was no closer to vengeance now than when he'd first left Aerin, a lad of seventeen summers and green as the woods in spring.

Staring westward, watching the sun set behind the green isle that had once been his home, he knew he had to dare Artor's anger and return. He had no choice. For all the honor he had earned under Artor's Bear banner, he was still an outlaw, still wore a King's Curse in the land his heart named home.

Who was the Bear to forbid his going?

During his seven years of exile he had faithfully served the Bear as Artor's banner was carried across the Grey Isles. Cymrn lay under its protection now, and Midstland. Kernow, Endland and Thumbria to the very borders of Alban. They named Artor the Pendragon in the duns and raths of his liegemen. Chief of chiefs, King of Kings. What Norseman did not fear the sound of his horse companies come a-riding? What brigand stole through the Great Wood and did not keep a wary watch for the Pendragon's men? The chiefs of every tribe except those in the Highlands bowed their knee to him.

They had won peace, Artor and his horse companies. What need was there for an Aerin wolf when the battles were all done? To which did he owe his fealty now — liege or homeland?

Colum knew which call was stronger.

CRSO

He remembered an evening two nights past when he and Artor had been out to take the night air, standing together on the high battlements of Caeme Tor. The conversation had turned to Aerin and Colum had spoken of returning, but the Bear shook his head in response.

"No," he said.

His voice was quiet, but it crackled with an edge that would brook no argument. The Bear was used to commanding, and expected his commands to be obeyed. It could be no other way. But that night Aerin stirred strongly in Donal's son and a queer streak of feyness made him argue.

"The Norse have stopped their vikings for a full season," he said. "The tribes are quiet—even the Picta. The whole summer long I've been at nothing but drilling and training recruits."

Artor nodded in agreement, but said nothing. He looked away, across the green slopes below Caeme Tor that lay cloaked in darkness.

"Why do you deny me?" Colum asked. "I ask for leave—a season at the most. Not to be forsworn."

Artor turned to him again.

"We're not all fools here, Colum," he said finally. "Use the good common sense that Ullr gave you and think of what you are saying. You'd go to an isle where every man's hand is against you...to accomplish what? Revenge? All you'll gain in Aerin is your death."

"But—"

"Give me one more year to see that the peace we worked so hard to win here holds and then I'll sail with you myself."

Colum shook his head. The darkness hid the bitterness in his eyes, if not that in his voice.

"You said that last year, *and* the year before, and still we train troops in Caeme Tor and I'm no closer to home than I ever was. If you'd go, go now. Let me scout ahead of you. There are still those loyal to Coinneach mat Conan. Think of it, man. You'd be a liberator."

"And I say it's still too soon," Artor replied. "If I left now the tribes would be yammering at each others' throats within a fortnight. We'd return liberators of Aerin with the task to begin all over again at home."

"But—"

"Ullr take you! Are you deaf? I've said no."

They faced each other, veins throbbing in their temples, fists clenched at their sides, each willing the other to back down. Colum found himself considering the sword sheathed at his belt and was half minded to draw it and damn the consequences, when he realized what it was that he was contemplating. He dropped his gaze from the Bear's, reason prevailing, the anger untempered.

"Follow your own head," Artor said softly, "and you'll be out-lawed here as well as in your homeland, mac Donal. I'll hound you from shore to shore and never give you a moment's pause."

Colum looked up as the Bear stalked away from him. He bit back further argument. Under his anger, sorrow ran like a wide river, for he knew what he must do; knew as well that neither Artor, nor the threat of a second King's Curse would stop him now.

He had to forget that they had been friends, the Pendragon and he.

After this day, they could only be enemies.

CR℘

On that western cliff top, Colum shook his head, remembering. Caeme Tor was behind him now and the King's curse was on his head — or would be, as soon as he set foot to ship's deck. Before the word went out, he must be gone from these shores. He would miss the Bear and his other comrades, but they would have to make do with each other for their company from now on. Tam O'Linn and Garn of the Fens. Ancelin with whom Artor had at last settled the difference as to whose wife Gwenore was to be. The druid Myrddin.

He would miss them, but Aerin's call had the stronger pull now. It was as though his homeland had lain a geas upon him, a geas to return that he could no longer set aside.

He returned to his horse, mounted and rode down the narrow twisting trail that led, on one side, into the fens, on the other, to Clynnog-fawr sprawled along the coast below. There would be trad-ers docked there, a passage across Nial's Arm that he could buy. He unrolled his cloak from behind his saddle as the night's chill deep-ened. It was a plain cloak, woven from wools dyed a muted green and blue. His scarlet cloak — that which marked him as one of the Pendragon's captains — lay rolled around his commander's torc in his keep near Caeme Tor.

He no longer had a need for either.

II

He sailed on the morning tide, the gulls haggling like fishwives overhead, the salt spray in his hair. Cymrn fell away behind him, but he looked only westward, waiting for his first glimpse of Aerin and her green shores.

He wondered vaguely at what course the Bear's anger would take. Would he sail to Aerin to reclaim his errant captain? The notion pulled a grim smile from Colum's lips. What dark humor that would be, if his desertion was what it took to influence Artor to cross Nial's Arm.

But mostly he let the past seven years slip away, just as the shores of the Grey Isles slipped away behind the wake of the ship, and turned his mind to what lay ahead.

Was vengeance so important?

He remembered his father's face, features twisted in a death mask as he lay on the battlefield, and knew that, if nothing else, retribution was necessary for his father's sacrifice not to have been in vain. The harpers should be singing the great deeds of the Fiolan clan. When their songs told that Donal's son had set Coinneach mac Conan on his rightful throne, that a Fiolan had returned the High King's Seat to Temuir where it belonged, then the bitter taste of his clan's defeat would finally be washed away. They would be remembered with honor once more and their ghosts would finally know peace.

But what of Meave? Would she still be waiting?

Colum shook his head. There it was not such an easy thing to guess how it might end. He had sent no word—how could he? But seven years was a long time for silence. That he had taken no other woman to his bed during that time...how was she to know? But if she would still have him...there were the far western lands, across Atlanta, where Bruinal had taken his sister Aine; to them, to Aerin Nua, he'd take Meave if she was willing. But first....

He sighed.

First there was the small matter of who should sit in the High King's throne.

"Your thoughts seem heavy, for one who's returning home."

Colum turned at the voice. There was a man at the rail beside him, his features hidden in the hood of his brown cloak. Colum wondered at the man's silent approach, then gave a mental shrug.

He'd been so lost in thought that a longship of Valkings could have come alongside the ship and he wouldn't have noticed them.

"Home," he said softly, looking west again.

He must have the look about him of a man returning. The way his gaze strained ahead into the distance. The sense of anticipation that hung over him like a bright cloak that could not possibly be missed.

"It's a long time since I've seen Aerin's shores," he added.

The man at his side murmured sympathetically. They stood at the rail silently for awhile, gaining their sea-legs. The sun was warm on their faces, the salt spray cast up from the bow, invigorating. The rigging creaked as the sailors raised the ship's sails. The gulls continued to follow in its frothy wake, filling the air with their raucous cries.

"And what will you do when you arrive home—Colum mac Donal?" the stranger asked suddenly.

Colum stepped back from the rail, hand falling to the hilt of his sword.

"Who—?"

The stranger lifted back his hood and let it fall to his shoulders, revealing features browned by sun and rough weather. The man's long dark hair was tied back with a leather thong; his eyes were a startling pale blue when measured against his complexion and flickered with secret knowledge.

Colum knew those eyes, knew that face.

"Myrddin," he breathed.

His fingers tightened on his sword hilt and he took another step back.

"Has the Bear sent you to bring me back?"

The druid shook his head. A half-smile touched his lips, then he looked away across the waters again as though nothing had interrupted their conversation.

"Who is Artor to command me?" he asked.

"Then why are you here, man?"

Myrddin was quiet for a long while. Finally he shrugged. When he spoke, his voice had a wistful note in it.

"Perhaps," he said, "to bid farewell to a friend too much in a hurry to come to me himself."

"Ah...."

Colum's voice trailed off and his wariness fell from him. He took his place beside the druid once more.

"And how could I, Myrddin?" he said. "How could I know that you wouldn't tell the Bear? He would have stopped me before ever I stepped through the gatehouse of Caeme Tor. I wouldn't willingly raise my sword against him, but...."

"And I?" Myrddin asked. "Could you raise it against me?"

Colum shook his head. "Of all men....I've heard the story often enough of how you argued with Artor to take me in when this same sea washed me ashore by your camp. It was an omen, you said then."

"It *was* an omen," the druid said. "And wasn't it fulfilled? The Isles are peaceful now and will you tell me that your hand was not in the making of that peace? But our work is done. The Bear can hold his land without our help now. It's time we went on to fulfill the destinies of our own lives."

Colum nodded thoughtfully. "And the Bear? You spoke to him of this?"

"I did."

"And he said?"

"You've his King's Curse upon you, Colum. He said he'd warned you it would come to this."

Colum made no reply, only stared at the waves.

"Surely you know it would be so?" Myrddin said. "How could you expect the Bear to take back his word?"

"I knew," Colum replied softly. "It wasn't a...thing I desired. But I expected it. He warned me plainly enough."

"What will you do now?"

Colum sighed. "I'm bound for the rath of Coinneach mac Conan. And you?"

"I'd go with you — if you'll have my company."

Myrddin smiled at Colum's surprise.

"And why not?" the druid added. "Does the wolf disdain to travel with the fox?"

Colum grinned and shook his head. "Not this wolf. But why? Another omen?"

"Not as such. It's been years since I've walked the low green hills of Aerin. I've found myself wanting to hear her harpers and the sweet music of the Erse tongue once more. I grow tired of Cymrn, tired of Artor's brooding since he sent Gwenore off with Ancelin.

"Tired of war and the endless talk of war...."

"Then you travel to the wrong isle," Colum said, his grin vanishing. "I mean to start a Kingbreaking in Aerin and I won't rest until I'm dead or the deed's done. You travel into war, Myrddin, not from it."

"War?" the druid repeated. "Perhaps. But is it war when only two men fight?"

"What do you mean?"

Myrddin shrugged. "Sometimes the words simply come—and not at my bidding. But look, Colum. Isn't that the coast of Lagan that I see?"

Colum looked to the west. Rising from a bank of low hung mist was a long streak of grey and green. Land. His homeland. As he looked upon it, all questions were forgotten.

"It is," he murmured.

A great joy settled in his heart. Trials lay ahead. Death crouched at his elbow, awaiting the harvest that was surely to come. But in this moment, Colum knew only that a part of him that had been lost had now been found once more.

"It is," he repeated. "It's Aerin we see...."

III

They made landfall at Howth on the coast of Lagan, the easternmost of the five kingdoms of Aerin. From there they rode north to Temuir, Coinneach's rath. Once it had been the High King's Seat, the rath of the Ard-righ over all Aerin, but when Fergus took the throne, he moved the King's Seat to Emain Macha in Uloth, leaving Temuir deserted except for those of Coinneach's clan.

The man at the rath's gates stared with wide eyes at the pair when Colum named himself and his companion. He made the Sign of Horns, in case it was a shade of the dead that had come calling on his lord, but let them in, sending word into the rath of who it was that had arrived. Only moments after the gates opened, Coinneach himself was there to greet them. Wordlessly, Lagan's King stepped forward and clasped Colum to his breast.

"It's been too long, Donal's son," Coinneach murmured. "Far too long since these eyes looked upon one of the Faolta. Though the dun of the Wolf lies open to the sky and its winds, though the King's Curse lies upon you and your clan, still you are welcome."

As they broke their embrace, Colum stared at this man—his father's friend and the rightful Ard-righ of Aerin. The years had not bowed Coinneach. Though now in his late fifties, he stood tall and straight as a young sapling, but with an old oak's strength in his limbs. His hair was black, his brow wide, and the gaze that met Colum's was as piercing a grey as Colum's own. Though Coinneach was recognized as a King—of Lagan still, if not all Aerin—he was simply clothed in leather leggings and a wool tunic, but his manner was generous, as befit an Erse King.

"Lord," Colum said respectfully and inclined his head.

He could say no more.

After Coinneach had been introduced to Myrddin, he called for retainers to stable their mounts. Then he took Colum's arm and led the two across the dirt courtyard and into the Mi-Cuarta, the great banqueting hall of Temuir which was Coinneach's own dun.

Inside, there was room for two hundred men, though now it housed barely three score. It had a high roof with broad beams supporting its heavy timbers. The walls were wood as well, except for the stone foundation which was to a height of three feet. Long tables stretched the length of the hall, with sleeping cubicles along either wall. At the far end, on a low dais slightly above the rush-strewn floor, was Coinneach's own cubicle near the central hearth.

Lagan's King gave the two travelers the guest cup himself, then smiled as they sat to eat. A harper played, sitting on a stretched piece of speckled doe-skin near Coinneach's cubicle, and Colum listened to the man sing as he ate. The Erse lilt in the harper's voice and the strong mead—drawn from a vat near the door—brought home the fact that he had returned, truly returned, with far greater impact than setting foot at Howth had ever done. Even the venison had a subtle difference of flavor that set it apart from the meat of Cymrn and the rest of the Grey Isles.

When he could finally eat no more, he pushed his platter aside, cleaning his greasy fingers on his leggings.

"What news is there?" he asked, after waiting for the harper to complete the song he was half-singing, half-chanting. "I've been away seven years with nothing but rumors and memories to feed my hunger."

Coinneach regarded him, a troubled look in his eyes.

"There's little new," he said. "Fergus still holds the throne and the land withers under his rule, but his position is strong and the druids can do nothing to remove him." He paused, then added, "Did you know your sister escaped to Aerin Nua?"

Colum nodded. "Has there been word from her?"

"None that we have heard."

"And what of Meave?" Colum asked.

"Who?"

At Coinneach's confusion, Colum realized the mistake he'd made. Meave was the name he would always know her by, but her father had named her otherwise.

"Triona," he said. "Fergus' daughter."

Coinneach gave him a shrewd look. "So it *was* you."

"What do you mean?"

"The harpers' songs tell how she went into the wilds with an outlaw, though there's not one man knows who he might be for she won't name him." Coinneach smiled. "You've a son, Colum. Did you know that?"

"A...son?"

Coinneach laughed. "Yes, a son. And now I understand the riddle of his name. She called him Connal—named him for both you and your father."

"Connal...."

Colum stared into unseen distances, a foolish grin spilling over his features. He turned to Myrddin.

"Did you hear?" he asked. "A son!"

The druid smiled. "I heard, Wolf."

"Where is he?" Colum asked. "And his mother. Meav—Triona. Where are they?"

A shadow crossed Coinneach's face.

"I don't know where your son is," he said softly. "It enraged Fergus—not knowing who the father was. He would have killed the babe out of hand except that the druids forbade it. They laid a geas on him that was so strong not even Fergus could dare break it."

"And?" Colum prompted. "Tell me, man. What happened to him?"

"Beineon took the child to keep him safe from Fergus. The tale is that he fostered the boy with the sidhe. And Colum...as for Triona.

Fergus chains her to the wall of his Mi-Cuarta each night until she will name the boy's father. He means to marry her off to one of his Valking allies—a man named Guttorm."

Colum's features tightened with anger.

He had a son, fostered by the sidhe? The boy would be no more than six—if he still lived.

And Meave. Chained in her father's hall. Married to a Norse....

"No!" he cried. He pounded the table with his fist sending mead-mugs scattering to the floor. "How could no one stop it? Are the Erse all cowards?"

Coinneach's face darkened with his own anger.

"Talk as you will, Donal's son," he said. "But tell me this: Where were you these past seven years?"

"I? I'm but one man alone."

"And so is each one of us," Coinneach said. "And when have the clans gathered to a common cause except at the peace-swearing of the Fairs? When Muman's Fachtna is feuding with Oran over a cattle-raid three years passed and gone, and Seanan—the wealthiest man in Connacht now—will not speak with his own King....Do I need to go on?

"And even could the clans unite, the High King's Gailana are everywhere with Fergus's Valking allies at their side. The druids are silent and there's not a man in Aerin who will step forward now—not since the Faolta clan were defeated; their dun no more than a memory and their last son with the King's Curse on his head."

"But—"

Coinneach cut him off. "We work towards a King-breaking, but it's slow work. It takes time. I have men training, the smiths are readying my war chariots, but I can't raise an army overnight—not even over seven years of nights. Not when I have my own borders to protect as well.

"The day will come when we will march on Uloth and take Fergus's throne, but it's not come yet."

Coinneach looked away, his sense of frustration bringing a dark bitterness to his eyes. In the silence that followed Coinneach's argument, the immediacy of Colum's anger ran from him. In its place burned a slow smoldering fire that he knew wouldn't die until he had Fergus's head hanging from his belt.

"How can I help?" he asked finally.

"The Fair," Coinneach replied. "The Great Fair in Emain Macha. I meet then with Muman's King. If I can win him to my banner, the others will follow his lead."

"And I? What is it you'd have me do?"

"Best his champion. Fachtna won't listen to me otherwise."

Colum nodded, understanding. He remembered his father speaking of Muman's King. Best him fairly and he would follow you ungrudgingly.

"And who is his champion?" Colum asked.

"Donnan mac Ailin," Coinneach replied.

"I don't know the man."

"He hasn't been beaten once," Coinneach said. "Not in the four years since he became Muman's champion."

CR80

Colum slept little that night. He lay restlessly on the furs in his cubicle for long hours, thinking of a young woman with chestnut hair. A young woman as fair, in the eye of his memory, as any queen of the sidhe.

Meave.

Their time together had been short—a few weeks stolen in the aftermath of a Valking raid and the pair of them little more than children. She'd be a woman now, as he was a man. What did she think of Donal's son and the seven year long silence that lay between them?

Colum sat up. Taking his sword in hand, he laid its sheathed length across his knees.

Whatever she thought of him, he would win her her freedom. No Erse maid deserved to be wed to Valking. He would see her free and then let her make her own choice. If gentle Angus Og thought to look kindly on them, perhaps, just perhaps, she would go away with him. Away from these isles. Away from wars and the bitterness of old griefs that haunted them.

They could sail to Aerin Nua. It wasn't Tir na nOg, to be sure, but a blest land still, if half the tales he'd heard of it were true. It was a place without Kings. A land of wide open plains and tall forested mountains. A land of promise and hope. Together they could go, and with then, their young son....

Connal.

A deep warmth stirred in Colum. He set aside his sword and stretched out on the furs once more.

Connal mac Colum.

He knew that it was more imperative than ever that he reclaim the honor that had once belonged to his clan's name. For how else could his son wear it with pride?

IV

Colum and Myrddin were with Coinneach mac Conan's party as it rode north to the Great Fair in Emain Macha on the following day. Colum wore the leaf-green livery of Lagan's King. Myrddin had dyed the Wolf's flame-bright red hair, moustache and eyebrows a stark black. The simple change was so remarkable that his own horse company in Caeme Tor might well have had trouble recognizing him. His name was Seadna mac Fionntan now. Seadna, Fionntan's son, in the employ of Coinneach mac Conan, King of Lagan.

Myrddin wore the robes of an Erse druid—drab and brown, though decorated with a subtle embroidery of red, gold and green thread. He carried a holly staff.

The company rode at an easy pace, across flat pastures, skirting the bogs and dark woods. On the morning of their third day, they came at last to the gentle hill lands of the north and finally, nestled in among them, Emain Macha. Colum scratched at his scalp—the dye was making his skin itch—and stared at the structures that dotted the hills before them.

He regarded the buildings and tents with mixed emotions.

Meave was there, but so was Fergus.

Patience, he told himself. But he had never been a patient man.

Fergus had patterned Emain Macha after the rath of Temuir. He had made use of the original twin stone towers that had stood there long before he was born and built around them. His Mi-Cuarta was all of wood and commanded the space between the towers. Outward from it spread the secondary halls: the houses for the lesser Kings; the Grianan, or sun-house, for their Queens; the Stronghold of the Hostages where Meave would be kept when she wasn't on display in the Mi-Cuarta; and the Star of the Bards. Further outwards still, spreading down the hill, were the halls of Fergus' retainers and the people of Emain Macha, while beyond them were a host of newer structures.

As they approached, Colum cursed when he realized that these latter buildings housed Fergus' Valking allies.

People from all across Aerin were camped around the hill, their tents and encampments extending to the slopes of its neighbors. Wherever Colum looked, he could see preparations being made for the Fair. There were cattle grazing between the tents, watched over by small bands of boys with staves in hand. Gaudy tents displayed crafts and wares. There were areas marked out for tests of strength and other contests. Everywhere was a bustle and flurry of people hurrying to make ready. But for all the holiday trappings of their clothes and gear, there seemed to be little happiness in the air — nothing like the Great Fairs that Colum remembered from when he was a boy.

Coinneach's company made their way through the crowds, aiming for the hall that had been set aside for Lagan's King and his people close by the Mi-Cuarta. Colum fretted in his saddle, straining hopefully for a glimpse of Meave, but fearing what he would do when he did see her. Could he hold in his rage? When he thought of her shame, chained in her father's hall, offered up to one of her father's Valking allies....

Guards in the deep yellow livery of Fergus' Gailana took their horses when they reached the Mi-Cuarta and escorted them toward the hall. As they drew near its threshold, there was a sudden movement from inside and then Fergus was there.

He was dressed in a rich robe interlaced with gold wire and jeweled studs. There was a torc of gold about his neck and a girdle inlaid with precious stones at his waist. Armbands and rings glinted in the sunlight. But for all his finery, his coarse features belied his claims to the throne of the Ard-righ. His cheeks were heavy-jowled, his eyes small and gleaming, his hair thin and a plain brown. His figure was stocky — more a merchant's body than that of warrior, or a High King of a race of warriors.

"Greeting, Coinneach," he said, stepping from the doorway. His voice had an oily, perfumed quality to it. "You are the last to arrive."

In his guise as an Erse druid, Myrddin regarded the Ard-righ dispassionately. How had such a man taken the throne? he asked himself. Taken it, and held it.

He glanced at Colum and saw the rage that was building up in his companion's face.

Not now, Myrddin thought.

The druid could understand Colum's wrath, but to allow it free rein at this time would only abort their plans and undoubtedly be the death of them all. There were too many Gailana about — armed and waiting on their King's slightest order.

With his hand at his side, hidden from the gaze of the Ard-righ, Myrddin made a small motion with his fingers. It went unnoticed by the Gailana and either of the Kings, but Colum felt the power of it work on him. His limbs froze and his face composed itself. The hand that had been inching towards his sword's hilt fell limply to his side.

"You will be at the banquet this evening?" Fergus was saying.

Coinneach nodded in reply.

"Good. Perhaps afterwards we can take a walk together. I have much to speak of with you."

He turned aside, indicating that he was done speaking. Coinneach made a brusque bow, then led the way into his own hall. With Myrddin still controlling him, Colum felt his body fall into step with the others and enter it with then.

V

Colum could easily have done without the banquet in Fergus' hall that night. Surrounded by what he could only consider his foes, he felt naked without the mail he usually wore. Coinneach hadn't allowed it because it would give him away as an outlander when he was supposed to be Seadna mac Fionntan, a Lagan man. Few Erse wore mail, or any armor, considering it unmanly to fight in it. Colum's father hadn't scorned this when he went up against Fergus and Colum agreed with his father's thinking. Why give the foe an advantage?

But neither mail nor armor had helped the Faolta that day.

No, they had died to the man, except for him, and sitting here, like a corpulent spider at the center of its web, was the man responsible. All Colum asked for was a few moment's alone with the man. Then he'd—

Colum caught Myrddin watching him. With an effort, he put the thought away and concentrated on the hall and the people in it.

The men and women serving them wore plain brown tunics. They were unsmiling—but cowed, rather than unfriendly. There was no order to the seating this night, so harpers sat with shanachies, the files recited their poetry from where they sat with the warriors and the scholarly ollams. Only at the far end of the hall were men seated according to rank. There the Kings ate and drank with their Ard-righ, their captains and retinue near.

Colum had his anger better in check now, though it still threatened to break free at any moment. Again and again his gaze raked the hall, looking for Fergus' daughter who should have been chained to the great oaken central support by now. But tonight the oak post reached high to the rath's roof, unattended.

Where was she? Colum asked himself. Still in the Stronghold of the Hostages? Was Fergus being cautious in how he shamed her—here before the gathered Kings of Aerin? Or was it that she was betrothed now and he mustn't lessen the worth of the gift she would make to his allies?

He lifted a hand to pull at his mustache, dropping it when he remembered the dye. He tapped his fingers on his thighs, tension building in his shoulder muscles. He could feel Myrddin's gaze on him, wary, watching.

Then finally the meal was done and Fergus took Coinneach aside. They left the hall to walk in the courtyard that encircled the Mi-Cuarta, Fergus attended by two of his Gailana, Coinneach bringing Colum. Three yews grew in the shadow of one of the towers. Fergus paused when he reached them and sat on the stones under the boughs, motioning Coinneach to sit with him. Colum and the Gailana took up positions nearby.

"I know what your feelings are towards me," Fergus told Coinneach. "And yet I can forgive their treason, if you will stand with me tomorrow."

"I...."

"Guttorm comes then," Fergus went on before Coinneach could speak. "He arrives with three longships of warriors from the Norselands. When this Feis comes to its end, I mean to give him my daughter in marriage — to bind our friendship for all time."

"It's no secret what you mean to do," Coinneach replied, his anger only barely contained.

A few paces away, Colum's fingers clenched into fists.

No, he told himself. Listen. Wait. But ochone, it was hard.

"But do you know why?" Fergus was saying. "The Norse have always been our foes — is there a man in Aerin that ever questions this? We are two warrior peoples, forever at odds. Only think a minute. With them as our allies — Erse and Valking united — what could stand before us?

"We could take the Grey Isles, then move from them across to the mainland itself. Even Aerin Nua could be ours. It lies across Atlanta and calls itself free, but an iron hand could bring it as quickly to heel as we will soon bring Artor's people."

"What...has this to do with me?" Coinneach asked after a long moment of silence.

"I offer you this," Fergus replied. "Aid Guttorm and I in our endeavors and as soon as the Grey Isles have fallen and we begin our assault on the mainland, I will give you the High King's Seat to do with as you wish. You will be the Ard-righ — you must only swear on your word never to strike against us."

"My word."

Fergus nodded. "Your word is legendary, Coinneach. It will be enough."

"If you know that," Coinneach said, "then you know as well that I've sworn to overthrow you, once and for all."

"Yes," Fergus said. "Let us speak plainly. Do you think me blind, deaf and dumb? I've been aware of your plots and your plannings, but why would you set your countrymen at each other's throats when I offer you a way in which you may have this throne you covet so much, and be rid of me as well, *without* bloodshed?

"I have men loyal to me and, with my Norse allies, enough strength to hold this island under my rule for as long as I wish. But my ambitions are greater. To fulfill them I need your support. The other Kings will listen to you, Coinneach. They will never support your Kingbreaking for no matter how much they hate me, their loyalty to the High King's Seat is stronger, even with myself on that throne. But if you swear peace, they will keep it with you."

"You can't send a front to attack the Grey Isles while dealing with a rebellion at home, can you?" Coinneach said thoughtfully.

"Exactly. So give me your answer, Coinneach mac Conan. Can you be patient a year or two longer, or must we have war here on your beloved green isle? Can you not swallow your pride for such a short time?"

Coinneach would not look at him. He lowered his gaze to his feet. Colum stepped closer so that he could hear Coinneach's reply. Fergus's plans were the grandiose raving of a madman and yet…and yet he could succeed. Not even the Bear with his horse companies could hope to prevail against massive invasions on either coast.

"Your word is all I require," Fergus repeated.

Coinneach lifted his head.

"My word?" he said. His voice was hard and sharp as a blade's cutting edge. "My word's been given once. What honor would it retain if I were to take it back and then give it out again? Lugh show us some light!"

"Peace, Coinneach," Fergus murmured.

"How can there be peace? Speak plainly, you said, so I ask you this: How can you speak of sworn oaths, you who have never kept the one? Shall I sell my people as though I were a merchant? Ask them for peace yourself, High King. Speak before the people and let them give you their answer."

Tension thickened in the night air. Fergus' guards clapped hands to their sword hilts and Colum watched than carefully with a narrowed gaze.

Had Fergus grown so mad that he would allow his men to break Fair-truce? he wondered.

But when Fergus spoke, his voice was soft—like a peddler's.

"Think upon it, Conan's son."

"I have thought upon it—for as many years as my hands have fingers." Coinneach's voice softened now, too. "Think, Fergus. Think of what you mean to do. Not even the druids will allow it. Remember your daughter's child. This time the druids will set such a geas upon you that—"

"The druids are mine to control!" Fergus cried. "I do not ask—I command. Did you think I cared for that child of my daughter's?

The grub could choke on its own spittle for all I cared. I obeyed the druids then because it was *my* will to do. To show the people that I still upheld the old ways. But those ways are changing. The druids will obey me in this — as will the people.

"I give you a chance, Coinneach. Do not throw it away. How many of the Kings do you think will come to your aid if my Norse were to storm Temuir this winter?"

"Don't threaten my people," Coinneach began, but Fergus overrode him.

"Concerned with their own lands, their cattle and the hunting and the cleaning of weapons....Do you think the other Kings will come to your aid when the winter's deep and the roads are bound with mud? I don't think so, Coinneach. Your dun will be torn down around your ears and you in it before they ever arrived — *if* they could even agree to come in the first place."

"If it's war you want!" Coinneach cried, leaping to his feet.

"It's war — but not with you."

They stood face to face, Coinneach towering over the Ard-righ, his face flushed with anger; Fergus's jowls quivering, his small eyes ferret-bright. Colum and the Gailana stood uncertainly to one side, hands on their weapons, fearing a Truce-breaking or worse, but not one of them willing to make the first move until they knew that their respective King was truly in danger.

"No more," Fergus said. "Think on this, Coinneach, and give me your answer on the last day of the Feis."

"You have my answer now."

"And I will have it again then."

Coinneach glowered at him.

Fergus shook his head. "You should have a wife to temper your angers, Coinneach," he added. "A babe to bounce on your knee."

"I—"

Fergus lifted one hand imperiously. "Go drown your anger in ale," he said. "I won't hear another word of this until the Feis ends. Go."

Coinneach's shoulders shook with anger, his hands opening and closing at his sides. For a moment Colum thought he was going to strike the Ard-righ, but then he turned abruptly and strode away. Colum hurried after him, his head spinning with all he'd heard.

Coinneach was the one to caution patience, he thought with black humor. Just listen to him tonight.

But Colum knew as well as Lagan's King that time was running out for them. What else could Coinneach do but speak plainly?

They returned to the hall set aside for them without speaking to each other. Silence hung the length of the building, long and brooding as Coinneach paced back and forth. When he finally paused and spoke to Colum, his voice was calm again, but edged with iron.

"The lesser contests are tomorrow," he said. "Watch them. Fill your head with them. But guard your strength for on the day after, you meet Fachtna's champion and him you must beat. With Muman's King beside us, the others will listen to me."

"You'll go to war?" Colum asked.

"No."

Coinneach stared into the fire, his face an expressionless mask.

"Not war," he said. "It will be a King-breaking. But I don't doubt that the Morrigan's ravens will still feed their fill on the flesh of too many of Aerin's sons."

VI

Colum and Myrddin wandered the Fairgrounds the next day, pausing to watch the various chariot races, spear-throwing, sword play, foot races and wrestling acrobatics; noting the wealth that changed hands as the chiefs and their warriors wagered on the various outcomes. The bustle and confusion of the Feis surrounded them, no matter which way they turned. There were voices raised high in laughter. Fiddling, piping and harping. Songs sung, poems told, genealogies recited. In the stone circle on the hilltop above the rath where at Beltaine the summer fires burned high, a day-long moot was in its sixth hour. Below, in the farmer's mart, men hired out and cattle were traded or sold. Hawkers cried their wares, selling ale and mead and whiskey, venison and boar's meat, cakes and breads.

Though they kept to themselves, they were still greeted by many, for at Fair-time, there were no strangers. Near the foot races, Colum met the King of Muman's champion. Donnan mac Ailin was a tall, wide-shouldered man with a wild thatch of red hair and a grin as broad as his face. He measured Colum with a keen gaze, for he knew that they would be rivals tomorrow; then he laughed. Thrusting a large tankard of ale into Colum's hand, he clapped the Wolf on his shoulder.

"Drink up, Seadna," he said, "for tomorrow's not today."

Colum smiled as he took the ale. Here was a man. Big as life, like the heroes of old, with a generous heart and a laugh like spring waters tumbling from the wintered hills. Tomorrow they would compete, but today they could be friends.

This, embodied in the one man, was the Aerin that Colum remembered.

They spied Fergus twice in the crowd.

The first time was when Colum was disengaging himself from a young Connacht woman with ale-merry eyes. The Ard-righ smiled at him as the woman ruffled Colum's hair for proving to be such a poor sport. Colum nodded to the High King, then turned to watch a new foot race begin as the woman sauntered away, so he never saw her look at her hands and the black marks on them. She lifted a finger to her lips and tasted the dye, then laughed and wandered off.

But Fergus was watching her and he recognized the dye as well without needing a taste. Thoughtfully, he studied Colum for a time before moving on through the crowd.

The second time Colum noticed the High King was near a harping contest. Colum lifted his gaze from the red and silver strings of one harper's instrument to find Fergus watching him from the back of the crowd. When the Ard-righ saw that he was marked, he smiled and lifted a hand in greeting before walking off.

"He troubles me, that man," Myrddin said in a low voice.

"Small wonder," Colum said. "He's little loved and he knows it. He troubles everyone."

Myrddin frowned. "It goes deeper than that."

His gaze took on a far-off look, as though he saw into distances that lay far beyond the Fair at hand.

Colum touched his arm.

"Somhairle," he said, calling the druid by the Erse name he'd taken in Temuir.

Myrddin blinked. His gaze settled on Colum.

"Who is Beineon?" he asked. "Is he here?"

Beineon, Colum thought. Who'd fostered his son to the sidhe.

"He was my father's harper. Coinneach told us of him — remember?" Colum took the druid's arm, fingers tightening. "What did you see?" he asked. "Connal. My son. Is he...?"

"Fine — so far as I know. But I've an uneasy feeling gnawing at my bones. Under all the humors of this Fair, I can feel an anger brooding...an anger that is more than the discontent of your people. I think it would be best if we found your son now, while we still have the time, rather than leave it for later when we might all be fleeing for our lives."

Colum's heart leapt at the thought. To see his son....

"But we agreed it was better to wait," he said reluctantly. "And you argued the loudest."

Myrddin nodded. "And now I counsel otherwise. I worried about Wodan's priests — the Norse druids that Guttorm will bring with him — but thought we could contain their mischief. Only now...now I can feel the land stirring restlessly under my feet, Wolf. This isle of yours is bound to its own laws — laws with which I'm not familiar. Tell me, what would happen if there was a peace-breaking at the Fair?"

"Why, the men would rise," Colum said. "The peace-breaker would be slain, his land salted. But...it's been longer than three of my own lifetimes since the Fair-truce has been broken. Who would dare?"

"Fergus?" Myrddin asked. "Or...when were there ever Norse at a Fair in Aerin?"

Colum nodded. Guttorm's men arrived today. There were other Norse in the houses beyond the rath of Emain Macha, though so far they had kept to themselves during the Fair. He had yet to see one of them. But today, when Guttorm arrived....How could Fergus keep his prospective son-in-law from joining the festivities of the Feis? And what would the Erse gathered here have to say to that?

Fergus trod a thinner line than perhaps even he realized, Colum thought. Sure disaster lay on either side.

"Beineon's an old man now," Colum said finally. "Since he's not here to judge the harping, I'd guess he would be in the Star of the Bards. Do you know the building?"

Myrddin nodded. "I saw it when we rode in. I think it's time I find out what I can concerning your son's fostering." As Colum rose to join him, Myrddin waved him back. "I'll go alone," he added. "Depending on what I learn, I might need to travel."

"I can—"

"You have to stay," Myrddin said. "Tomorrow you meet Donnan."

"But my son...."

"If you'd live to know him, you'll stay. Let me go, Wolf. Alone."

Colum glared at the druid. The child was his. Surely he was the one who should collect the boy from his fostering?

"You know this is how it must be," Myrddin said, as though reading his mind.

Colum nodded glumly. Reason won out, for all that his heart called him a fool. He knew that the fault lay with Fergus, not Myrddin. Fergus. The anger that smoldered in his chest awoke to flames, bringing a red mist to his eyes. If he could have that fat neck between his hands—

"Colum."

When Myrddin spoke his true name he seemed to hear it with his mind more than his ears. The word stole softly into his thoughts, delicate as a doe's footstep. But it was enough to cut through the red mist. He blinked to find Myrddin watching him, the blue eyes hooded.

"Keep a rein on that anger," Myrddin warned. "Your battle madness won't serve you well in this situation."

Do you think I can call it up or send it away at will? Colum wanted to ask the druid, but Myrddin had already turned away and disappeared into the crowd.

Frustrated, Colum returned his attention to the harping contest, but it no longer held any interest for him. He no longer cared for it or any of the Fair's festivities, underlain as they were with a hollow gaiety. Instead, he made his way back to Coinneach's hall, the dull anger still sparking inside him for all that he worked to keep it under control.

It will come, he promised the fires inside him. Our time must come.

CR⊗∽

That afternoon Guttorm arrived with three hundred men. They were housed with the other Norse in their halls on the hillsides north and east of the Mi-Cuarta. And that night in the great hall, seven years fell away from Colum for once again he looked on his lost love Meave as she was brought from the Stronghold of the Hostages to meet her husband-to-be.

She was as beautiful as he remembered — perhaps more so. Her auburn hair gleamed in the torchlight, her amber eyes glittered. She held her head high and proud as befit an Erse princess. But Colum could see the despair locked behind her cool gaze. And when Guttorm approached her, he saw her shrink back from the man — the movement so imperceptible that he was sure only he had seen it, and only because he'd looked for it.

Colum had dreamed countless times of this day when he would finally look upon her again, but he could never have imagined the moment to be so bereft of joy. His hand dropped to the hilt of his dagger as he stared at her chains. His shoulders trembled. The red mist came to his eyes so that everything in the hall was turned to the color of blood in his sight.

He tried to fight the rage. He ground his teeth together, but the blood was drumming in his temples making it impossible to think clearly. All he saw was Meave. Her chains and her torment. Then and there he would have attacked the Ard-righ, armed with only his dagger, if Coinneach had not laid a strong hand on his arm and pried his fingers from around the hilt of his knife.

"Peace," Lagan's King murmured. "Now is not the time."

Coinneach's warning by itself would not have been enough. But under his voice, Colum heard Myrddin speaking to him. His anger dulled to a coldness that settled like a stone in his stomach. The red battle-mist faded.

Carefully, Colum laid his hands on the table before him and looked around the room. No one had noticed him. All gazes were on the Norse King.

Guttorm had lifted Meave by the waist, his two huge hands easily spanning her narrow girth. Holding her up, he stood in place but made a slow circle, showing her off for all to see. The silence of the gathered Erse brought a grin to the Norse King's lips. His own warriors pounded their drinking mugs against the wooden table and shouted encouragements to their King. Setting Meave down,

Guttorm hoisted a huge flagon of ale. Crying a toast to his bride-to-be, he downed the ale in one gulp, then threw back his head and laughed for the pure joy of the moment.

Not an Erse in the Mi-Cuarta could miss the man's mockery of them. They looked to their Ard-righ, but there was a cold look in Fergus' eyes that would brook no defiance of his will.

Colum couldn't turn his gaze to the High King himself—that was asking too much of the hard-won restraint that he could barely maintain. Instead, he watched Guttorm, marking the man for weaknesses and finding none.

He was a huge man, a half foot shy of seven feet. His hair was yellow and hung down his back in a long twist of a braid; his beard was tangled and dirty. Under his sheepskin vest, corded muscles rippled with every movement. Incongruous to his ragged clothing were his armbands of solid gold and the chains hung heavy with precious stones that dangled from around his neck.

He removed one of the latter and slipped it over Meave's neck. "So!" he bellowed. "So do I name you Guttorm's bride."

His Erse was accented with the coarseness of his own tongue—making a mockery of the language as he made a mockery of its people. Despair sped through Colum again as he watched Meave's gaze rake the hall, searching for one man to stand up to her father and redeem the honor of their people.

Her gaze traveled from face to face, finding only shame, but no aid. Men muttered and looked away—some unwilling, some unable to face her reproach.

And then her gaze found Colum's face and he knew that she recognized him for all his dyed hair and moustache and the years that lay between them. Her eyes went wide with surprise, then she narrowed her gaze and looked away.

Did hope rise in her heart to see him here? Colum wondered, his own heart aching for her. Or was it the final insult to her shame that he too should be present at this luckless moment?

As she composed herself again as best she could, Colum surreptitiously looked about the hall, but no one appeared to have noticed her momentary surprise. He began to relax, only to find that the Ard-righ was studying him once more, eyes narrowed in thought.

Was he remembering another face? Colum wondered nervously. Did Fergus recognize the blood of a Faolta warrior in Colum's features?

Fergus leaned forward in his seat.

"My daughter was ever the errant child," he said conversationally.

An expectant quiet settled over the hall. Meave gave her father a worried look that Colum knew mirrored the one that his own features wore.

"She was forever running off," Fergus went on. He smiled and shrugged his shoulders as if to say, what can you do? "I remember the day my counselor Ludgaidh brought her back from her latest and last escapade—I believe it was about the time of my Gailana's victory over the Wolf clan. He told me that she'd been in the company of an outlaw when he finally tracked her down, but she would never give up the man's name."

He knows, Colum thought. He glanced at Coinneach and saw understanding dawn on Lagan's King as well. They were discovered and there was nothing they could do about it—not surrounded by Fergus's Gailana as they were—but Colum edged his hand towards the knife sheathed at his belt all the same.

He would not go down without a fight.

"There was one body not accounted for when the Faolta were slain," Fergus was saying. "Donal's son, the young Colum. Now I find myself wondering: what if he and this outlaw were one and the same?"

A questioning murmur rose up in the hall as the men considered their Ard-righ's words. Colum regarded Coinneach with bleak eyes, his fingers firmly gripped around the hilt of his dagger now. If he rose now and cast it at the High King....

Coinneach slowly shook his head. Do nothing, his eyes commanded Colum. Myrddin's voice whispered in Colum's mind in counterpoint to Coinneach's order.

Keep a rein on that anger....

It took the greatest effort of will for Colum to force back the red mists and obey.

"It doesn't matter to me who she was with or when," Guttorm said, misreading Fergus's reason for bringing the matter up. "She won't have known a man until she lies with a Valking."

The murmuring in the hall took an ugly tone at the insult.

Fergus shook his head. "That's between you and your bride," he said. "The question I have now is: what if this same outlaw were here…in this rath…seated among us like a kinsman when the King's Curse is on his head?"

Men looked at those with whom they shared their tables, then sent their gazes further through the hall to study their neighbors.

A Faolta? they asked. Here? Which of us…?

Fergus rose to his feet and pointed at Colum.

"My Gailana," he cried. "The King's Curse is on that man—Colum mac Donal. I want him dead!"

A chaos of noise exploded in the Mi-Cuarta.

"Seadna is—"

"Faolta."

"Donal's son."

"Wolf clan."

"Lagan's champion."

The only swords in the Mi-Cuarta were those of the High King's guards. At his command, they moved forward, steel bared in their hands, but Coinneach rose to block their approach, his own follow-ers and kinsmen holding Colum back as the brawny Erse struggled to meet the Gailana's attack.

"Would you break Fair-truce, Fergus mac Coemgen?" Lagan's King roared above the din.

"There is no peace in Aerin for the Faolta, Coinneach mac Conan," Fergus shouted back. He glared at his Gailana. "Why do you hesi-tate? I am your King. Kill the man!"

But there were others in the hall protesting now. It didn't matter to them that Colum had the King's Curse on his head. There was Fair-truce. There was honor. Donnan, the champion that Colum was to have faced tomorrow, drew his own short dagger and ranged himself beside Coinneach. Joining them a moment later was his own king, Fachtna, and the Kings of Kerry and Uloth. And then, tall and thin as an old battered pine, the grey-bearded Ghabhann, chief of the druids, arose from his seat to face the Ard-righ.

"No man of Aerin shall break Fair-truce," he said, his voice cut-ting across the noise in the hall. "Be he Ard-righ or a warrior of the lowest rank."

The chief druid's voice seemed to echo on in the silence that followed his dictate. His too-bright eyes stared down the Gailana, one by one.

Guttorm turned to Fergus, a grin on his lips.

"There's no Erse blood in my veins," he said.

Fergus shook his head. He could see all too well that to kill Colum now would lead to a Druid's Curse falling on his own head and for all his arguments with Coinneach, that was a thing which he couldn't afford at this time. He still needed Aerin. When the Grey Isles fell and he had the head of Artor Foes-slayer on a spear before his tent...when his ships were turning towards the mainland...then....

"Chain him," he said. "Bind him in chains and take him to the Stronghold of the Hostages. And then, when the Feis is ended, we will see to it that King's justice is done. Will that suit you, Ghabhann?"

The chief druid nodded, plainly unhappy.

Fair-truce gave freedom to all, outlawed or not, but to argue the point now would only lose them what they had gained. But the thoughts that ran through Ghabhann's mind lay all too plainly on the chief druid's face.

The Ard-righ grew too confident in his power. His gaze turned from the old gods and the old ways and only Lugh alone knew what the future held for Aerin with one such as Fergus mac Coemgen as its High King. But now was not the time, nor the place, for such considerations.

He stood aside, as did Donnan and then Coinneach and the other Kings. The Gailana pulled Colum's dagger from his hands and tossed it to the rush-strewn floor. They tore the colors of Lagan's King from his shoulders, then bound him hand and foot. Trussed like a raider's captive, he was carried from the Mi-Cuarta to the Stronghold of the Hostages.

Behind in the hall, the talk roared anew as men discussed who he was and why he'd come. The gazes of many men turned to Coinneach, speculation plain in their eyes. On the High King's dais, Fergus sat sourly nursing his ale. He looked out at his people and saw all too well how sentiment was running. Only the Norse were unconcerned, calling for more ale from the servitors as though there had been no interruption in the festivities.

On the dais with her husband-to-be and father, Meave sat silent, staring at the door through which Colum had been taken. She said not a word, gave no sign of the anguish that stormed inside her.

VII

Near midnight, as Fergus's Gailana were carrying Colum into the Stronghold of the Hostages in Emain Macha, Myrddin arrived at the dun of the Muireagain sidhe some leagues distant from the High King's Seat. He came in the robes of an Erse druid, with a holly staff in hand, but to the hidden gazes that watched him, it was the ancient strength and wisdom of an oak, hung with mistletoe, that gleamed in his eyes.

In front of the green knowe that housed the tulman of the sidhe, Myrddin tapped the staff on the packed earth at his feet. He called out a summoning word, then waited. The moon was full and rearing high in the sky, shedding its brightness of its borrowed light across the hills.

And the sidhe were near.

He could feel the weight of their many gazes on him, watching him from all sides. He could smell the apple-scent that followed them where they walked. He heard the sly rustlings and soft paddings of their light-stepping feet. They moved liquid as water. When they finally stepped out into the moonlight, it was as though shadows flowed from the deeper darkness where they had been hidden.

Myrddin stood, as silent as the moonlight, and regarded the gathered host. A good twenty of them surrounded him; there were more still hidden in the shadows.

They were the younger cousins of the Tuatha de Dannan and the Aelden of Artor's Isle. They reminded Myrddin of the Picta in northern Alban, for like the Picta, the sidhe were hill dwellers, too — slender and brown-skinned, with cloaks of fur and flint knives stuck in their belts, armbands and torcs of gold glittering bright. Bone arrows, feathered and flint-tipped, were notched in the gut strings of their yew bows.

"So," said one after silence had stretched between them long enough for the moon to have moved from the tip of one branch to the tip of another. "You've come."

"You know me?" Myrddin asked.

The sidhe stepped closer. His eyes were a dark unreadable glimmer that burned and flickered like wind-caught leaves, wheeling and spinning. They were eyes a mortal could lose himself in. Myrddin matched him gaze for gaze, letting the little man drink deeply from the druid blue of his own gaze.

"Myrddin," the sidhe said. "The Fox-without-a-home. We know you."

"And do you know why I've come?"

The small head bobbed. "For the bairn. You've come for our fosterling, haven't you, Old One?"

"His father sends me," Myrddin replied.

Bowstrings slackened in the moonlight. The sidhe spokesman nodded wisely.

"So. Has the time come so soon? Has the long wait ended? Will Morrigan's ravens feed at last upon the not-King's body?"

Myrddin nodded. "Men will die. Many. But more not born of Aerin, then her own sons."

"And the not-King? Will he die?"

"He especially."

"And you?" the sidhe asked. "You of the Grey Isle, the Pendragon's druid. What is it that brings the fox a-running to our door? The bairn alone?"

"Peace," Myrddin replied in a soft voice. "I seek peace."

The sidhe eyed him strangely. He seemed about to speak, then paused.

"It will be my final gift to the Bear," Myrddin explained. "He's fought for a long time, always striving in the name of peace. Now that he has found a certain measure of it, I would not see a new war laid upon him—and war there will be unless Fergus the non-King is stopped."

"Your Bear will still die in battle," the sidhe said.

"I know. But not soon. Not at the hand of Fergus's Gailana, nor at the hands of his Norse allies."

"No," the sidhe agreed. "He will die at the hand of his own—"

215

Myrddin held up a hand and the sidhe fell silent, his prevision unspoken.

"The more we give voice to such prophecies," Myrddin began.

The sidhe nodded. "The more likelihood there is that they will come about. But some futures lie embedded in the very bones of the world, druid. We can no more change them than we can the course of the stars."

"I would wish him at least a fighting chance in avoiding his fate," Myrddin said.

The sidhe shrugged. A tiny woman approached them, leading a boy of six summers by the hand. Myrddin took in the red-brown hair and the features that were those of a man he named friend, except that they were softened by youth in the boy's face. The woman placed the boy's hand in Myrddin's, then stepped back.

"Lugh's luck go with you," the sidhe spokesman said. "For it's that you'll need and more."

And then they were gone, the whole small host of them, vanishing as though the hill itself had swallowed them.

And so it had, Myrddin thought. They were all gone underhill. Safe in their tulman—the hollowed hill that was their dun. Safe underground while the war-birds flew overhead and Morrigan's ravens feasted.

The druid sighed. And then he remembered the look on the sidhe's face—that moment when he would have spoken, but forbore.

"What did they name you?" he asked the boy. "What was your sidhe-name?"

"Siochain."

Siochain. Peace.

"Were they so sure, then, that I was the one who would come?" Myrddin murmured, thinking aloud. "Did they know what I sought and for that reason named you as they did?"

"What do you mean?" the boy asked.

Myrddin shook his head. "Nothing, Connal-Siochain. Everything."

He looked eastward, then back at the boy.

"Do you want to meet your father and mother?" he asked.

"Oh, yes."

"Then we should be going now. The way's long for legs as short as your own."

CR&O

Myrddin set an easy pace—not so quick that his young ward could not keep up, but steady enough so that the hills wound away underfoot and they continued to put a good distance between themselves and the dun of the sidhe.

Aerin's old rounded hills made the travel easy, if one kept to the ridges. The boreens were choked with undergrowth where the land was wild; where it was cultivated, there were the farmers' duns to be avoided. Tonight Myrddin had no desire to meet with any man—Aerin-born or not—for it was Colum's son he had in his care and he considered the boy's safety a great trust.

Reared among the sidhe, Connal was hardier than a mortal boy his own age would be. He kept up the steady pace without complaint, but eventually his young legs grew tired and he began to lag. Myrddin carried him then, bearing the boy lightly for all the thinness of his own limbs, as though Connal had no weight to him at all.

They traveled in silence. Myrddin could not begin to guess his ward's thoughts, but he found his own turning more and more to the night itself, to Aerin and the feyness that seemed to ride her very air tonight. He sensed the approach of great deeds, the movement of gods, the presence of lesser deities. Once he thought he heard the baying of wolves and the winding of the Antlered Lord's horn—distant, but close-sounding as well.

It was like faring abroad on Samhain night, he realized, when all the denizens of the Middle Kingdom were awake and walking the starlit hours between dusk and dawn. The air was charged with otherworldliness, familiar…and that which was less comfortably so.

For the druid sensed something else at that moment.

A tenseness crept across his shoulder blades. It warned him to be as cunning as his namesake, the fox. He smelled the sea in the air—a sudden sharp scent that stung his nose with its salty bite. He paused, lifting his head, his nostrils flaring as he read the wind. He searched the dark hills with a druid's gaze—before, behind and around.

They were near their goal now. He could see the woods that bounded Emain Macha in the near distance. But closer...there was the sea...and something....

When the attack came, he was prepared for it.

But not enough.

He'd expected men and readied his magical arts to meet them. He'd set Connal down and called up the grey-gold flames of his magefire so that it blossomed from his palms. But he never had a chance to speak the sending words, nor cast the magefire at his enemies.

Invisible bonds trapped his mouth and arms — bonds as magical as any he himself could raise. They were the making of more than one mind and too strong for him to cast off. He delved deep inside himself, reaching for the strengths that were bound to the wild places of his soul, but he was too late. The enchantment that bound him writhed and snaked through his mind, robbing his strength and making clear thought impossible. He was trapped, like a fox by the hounds, and he could do nothing when the yellow-haired Norsemen came out of the shadows towards him.

Nothing but rage.

Beside him, he could sense Connal's confusion and fear.

Flee, he willed at the youth, but the boy seemed to be caught by the same magical bonds that entrapped himself.

The Norsemen stepped steadily nearer, their yellow braids bouncing on the boiled-leather of their armor, starlight glinting on their bared weapons — axe and sword. And then, behind the warriors, Myrddin saw the cause of his own helplessness: three Norse druids, priests of Wodan.

At the sight of then, he finally recognized the one-eyed god's touch in the magical fetters that held him. A cold icy breath of northern wind touched his cheek at their approach; a wind that Aerin's green hills never knew, not even in the dead of winter.

And then, their appearance striking him like the torch that lit the grave fire, he saw men of the Ard-righ's household walking among the Norse. By their presence, he knew they were truly undone. Fergus's Gailana would not be here unless they had already seen through Colum's disguise. So they were all the Ard-righ's captives now — Wolf and druid, the boy...and Meave, the boy's mother.

They'd been fools, Myrddin realized, and he the greatest one of all — walking the hills as though there were nothing in the world but fair men and justice.

How could he have been so blind?

He could see the strain on the faces of the Norse druids as they worked to hold him captive. That was enough to make him redouble his own attempts to wrest free of their influence, but strive though he did, he couldn't break the enchantment by which they held him. They were too strong and there was no more strength for him to call on.

This green isle wasn't his land. His magics drew their potency from the Grey Isles of the Bear, from the roots of its hills and its longstones, from Ullr and the Horned Huntsman, the Green Man of the Woods. They were kin to Aerin's gods, and so he could borrow strength from the land underfoot, but he couldn't borrow enough to defeat these three priests.

There was seawater in the flasks at their belts and stones from their cold home shores hung from leather thongs at their necks. Their foresight had given them their superior strength — a foresight that had eluded Myrddin when he sailed here with Colum a few short days ago.

Again he cursed his folly. If he had only thought to bring a handful of his own native earth with him. A few grains were all he would need to focus the attention of his own gods upon him.

The last thing he saw was the flash of a spear butt as it darted towards his head. It struck his temple with a sharp crack and then the darkness came to swallow him.

Oh, Colum, he thought as his consciousness ebbed away. Forgive me for failing you.

VIII

As Colum brooded in the darkness of his cell in the Stronghold of the Hostages, the years fell away in his memory. Seven years ago he'd been jailed as well, waiting on the King's justice. But he'd been young then, with a youth's ability to hope. Youth rarely perceives its own mortality; this time he knew all too well what lay in store for him at the end of the Feis. He was trapped like a badger in its sett, bolt holes blocked and the smoke wreathing down the tunnels towards him.

His chance to redeem his clan's honor had been stolen from him.

His father's shade would never know peace.

Meave was bound for a Valking's bed.

Their son was condemned to bear his clan's shame.

For there was no escape.

He was chained and guards stood watch beyond the stout wooden door that barred him from freedom — yellow-liveried Gailana and yellow-haired Norseman. And beyond them, in his hall, was the High King Fergus, celebrating Colum's capture, no doubt, and his alliance to the piss-haired Norse that was partly won on the bartering of his own daughter's body.

Colum ground his teeth in helpless rage. When the red mist rose to cloud his sight, he let it come. There was no Coinneach to soft-speak him to calmness. No druid to bind his limbs with enchantment. He let his anger dwell on the Ard-righ. On how, when they finally dragged him forth from his cell at Fair's end, he would, chains or no chains, bound or not, find some way to take Fergus with him to meet the Antlered God in his realm of death and reborning.

The red mist deepened across his gaze. His blood thrummed with useless rage.

At a sound that came from behind the door to his cell, he dragged himself to his feet. He struggled against the binding chains and gathered up as much of their slack as he could to strike out at his enemies. But when the door swung open, there were no Gailana standing in its threshold. No Norse.

Colum blinked through the red mist. He saw Coinneach and Muman's King, Fachtna. Beside Fachtna was red-haired Donnan, Muman's champion. Behind them were others of Coinneach's clan and men he couldn't recognize because they were in shadow.

It's a glamor, Colum realized. Sent to confuse me.

He gathered the chains more tightly in his fists, bunching his shoulder muscles as the man who wore Coinneach's face took a step closer.

"Colum," the illusion said in a hoarse whisper. "Have you gone mad? We're friends, man — come to free you."

Colum shook his head as the words fought their way through his mist-clouded mind.

Friends, were they? Then why did they have weapons bared in their fists? Why....

But then his gaze dropped to the ground behind the illusions where he saw the head and shoulders of a Norse guard. Neither was connected to the other.

Colum looked up to study the King of Lagan's features, blurry as they were in the red cloud of his vision.

"Coinneach...?"

At the King's nod, the red mist faded in Colum's vision. He staggered and Coinneach caught him before he could fall. Other hands steadied him while Coinneach unlocked his chains and then the night skies of Aerin were above him, Brigit's stars glittering and gleaming in their dark sea.

"Softly now," Donnan said.

He was supporting Colum on his right side.

Colum nodded and stepped free from the man's grip. The red mist was gone. His anger remained, but it was no longer a berserker's unthinking rage. It was cold now—fierce and bitter as only a winter wolf's can be.

As he was led from the Stronghold of the Hostages, through Fergus' rath and to freedom, the circulation returned to his arms and legs. By the time they were slipping through the camps surrounding Emain Macha, he felt fit enough again to do what he knew must be done. He stopped when only Uloth's green hills surrounded them, boreens cutting between them, the woods dark in the starlight.

"No further," he said. "You've my heartfelt thanks for freeing me, but now you lead me away from where I must go."

"But, Colum," Coinneach began.

"No. I won't be ruled in this. What comes next lies between Fergus and myself. Blood cries out to be spilled—for the wrongs done to my father and kin, for the wrongs done to Meave and my son, for the wrongs done to me. I won't listen to any more talk of waiting, Coinneach mac Conan. You, yourself, it was who asked me what I have done to right those wrongs in the seven years of my exile and I answered you, nothing. But I will right them now—in the Ard-righ's blood—and damn the consequences."

Coinneach faced him, not giving back an inch to Colum's anger.

"And you will listen to me, Colum mac Donal," he said. "It wasn't to spill blood that we rescued you. The Fair-truce still holds and—"

"Fair-truce? Then whose blood drips from your blade?"

"Norse blood, and Fair-truce doesn't hold for them."

Colum shook his head. "That's a question only the druids can answer. For my part I—"

He broke off, realizing that he was shouting. He took a deep, steadying breath to calm himself.

"Speak, then," he said. "Why did you rescue me? I owe you the courtesy of listening at least."

"You owe me the doing as well," Coinneach replied. "Unless the Faolta's word had become no more than the blustering of summer wind."

"I'm listening," Colum said, an edge returning to his voice.

"We're bound for Dairsean—the druids' wood," Coinneach said. "There you will meet with Muman's champion to settle once and for all, who will lead and who will follow."

Colum stared at him in shock. "Are you mad? You want me to fight Donnan while our enemies lie sleeping in Emain Macha, building their strength?" He turned to Fachtna, Muman's King. "Tell me it's not so."

Fachtna faced him, his hard gaze meeting Colum's incredulous stare.

"You fear to lose?" he asked.

"Fear to lose? You *are* all mad. You...."

Colum turned to look at the others in their small company and further words died stillborn in his throat. The men here....He was in the company of the Kings and champions of Aerin. Donnan and Fachtna of Muman; Coinneach and Oran, the King of Connacht. Seanan, Connacht's champion, Aed, Kerry's King, and his champion, Broen.

"You pledged me your word, Colum," Coinneach said.

"I...." Colum slowly shook his head. "My word, yes. But my fight's not with Donnan. This dye—" he tugged at his hair " —and this guise...the need for them is gone. I can no more meet Donnan at the Fair now than I can walk into Fergus's Mi-Cuarta and ask him for his daughter's hand."

"You'll meet Donnan there," Coinneach said, pointing ahead into the shadowed forest. "In Dairsean. Tonight."

"But—"

"Fight him and best him, and then together—with the united clans of Aerin beside us—we'll topple Fergus from the High King's Seat."

"It's madness," Colum replied.

But his decision was made. His features settled into grim lines and his gaze smoldered.

"Madness," he said again. "But you've my word in trust, so let us be done with it."

Coinneach nodded curtly and led the way once more.

IX

Hooded men met them on the borders of Dairsean Wood. Without needing to be told, Colum knew they were druids. Who else would they be in this place? For Dairsean was a druid wood and— more importantly to their present undertaking—the one place in all of Uloth that would never know the footstep of Fergus or his Norse allies.

Only one of the hooded figures let his features be shown. Colum recognized him from the Mi-Cuarta in Emain Macha earlier that night: Ghabhann, the chief druid. He gave formal greetings to the Kings, then turned his attention to Colum and Donnan.

"You may take nothing into the wood," he said. "Not metal forged, nor bough of tree, nor cloth woven, nor leather of beast, nor stone. Sky-clad the Goddess sent you forth; sky-clad you must meet this challenge.

Colum shrugged. Wordlessly he stripped.

"There is a glade," Ghabhann went on when both men stood naked. "North in the wood. You must circle it three times—nor let tree bough touch you, whether high or low, nor turn you aside for the same. The Goddess watches through our eyes; the Antlered God speaks through us.

"This is the first challenge. I will meet you in that glade to speak of the second.

"Now go!"

The druid's voice cut like a whip crack across the still night air. Colum paused for a moment, caught off guard, then he was running. But Donnan was already ahead of him, moving hard and fast. The big man ran like a hart and Colum marveled at the ease with which he dodged the tree boughs—here leaping one, there snaking under another that barely seemed to have enough room for a fox to squeeze under. He never touched one bough and, steadily, surely, he lengthened his lead.

Colum cursed. He could feel the eyes of the druids on him, standing hidden in the dark wood on all sides, marking each bough that slapped him, each one he failed to see. His bare legs smarted and stung. More than once he'd had to roll under a low bough through patches of nettles. He bled from a hundred tiny thorn punctures. His breath came in ragged gasps.

He wasn't used to this—not freshly arrived from the Grey Isles as he was, where he was a captain of horse troops, not infantry. He was making a poor showing, and this was only the first challenge.

He reached the glade finally and began his circle. Donnan was no longer in sight. Except for his own breathing and the slap of his feet on the ground, Colum didn't hear a sound.

He went more slowly now, marking the obstacles, thinking it better to go slowly, than make a worse showing of it by striding every second branch that presented itself to his bruised limbs. On his second turn of the glade, he caught a flash of naked skin between the trees on its far side, and knew Donnan was winning. He put on more speed. Dodging the boughs, low and high, was becoming easier now, but it was still no use.

Pain stitched his side by the time he completed his third circle and ran into the glade. Sweat beaded his brow, falling into his eyes. It stung the host of tiny cuts on his thighs and legs, arms and chest.

Ghabhann and Donnan were waiting for him.

The big man stood loose-limbed and relaxed, his breathing easy. But seeing the scratches on him, Colum took some small satisfaction in knowing that his opponent hadn't escaped entirely unscathed himself.

Columns gaze returned to Ghabhann.

How had the druid arrived here before them? He'd seen Donnan running ahead of him, but not Ghabhann.

"As the Goddess has seen," the druid said, "the first challenge is Donnan's."

Hooded figures stepped from between the trees, moving as silent as sidhe. They carried spears which they dropped at Colum and Donnan's feet.

"The way is uphill now," Ghabhann said. "You each have three spears and there are three targets between this glade and the next which is the heart of the wood.

"Go!"

This time Colum was prepared for the druid's abrupt signal. And throwing spears he understood.

He snatched up the spears and sprinted forward, weighing the weapons as he ran. The throwing spears were short — in the old Erse style — and perfectly balanced.

He was ahead of Donnan by a half dozen paces when he saw the first target — a flicker of white cloth in the starlight. He threw his first spear, pinning the cloth to the oak tree behind it with a dull thunk. Donnan's cast followed his like an echo.

Muman's champion drew abreast of Colum as they ran on. They raced uphill, dodging low boughs and the great oaks which appeared to lunge out of the darkness at them. On all sides they could sense the silent presence of the druids — watching, measuring — and then the second target was at hand.

Colum and Donnan threw as one man. Their spears winged towards the second target, but a bough deflected Colum's cast so that his spear struck Donnan's. Both weapons fell short.

Now only one target remained.

Colum ran as he never had before. The pain in his side was like a fire — piercing and deep. Underfoot, the forest's mulch gave his naked feet poor grip. Still he gained a pace on Donnan. Then another. He could see the last target now — just a tiny speck of white, far ahead of him. He put on a new burst of speed and drew ahead a little more. And then, when barely within range, he cocked his arm and let fly.

His spear struck true and he raced on. He heard the thunk of Donnan's weapon. A moment later, the big man was beside him and drawing ahead once more.

The glade was very close now. Colum could *feel* the opening it made in the great wood. And old though the forest was, in this second glade he could sense something older still.

He pushed at his protesting muscles. His legs churned, his toes digging into the mulch for purchase. Then he was abreast of Donnan once more.

They ran side by side. Just before they tore into the glade, Colum threw himself forward. He slipped on the dew-damp grass, skidded a half-dozen feet and tumbled into a roll. But he was on his feet almost before his back had touched the ground. Silently, he stood beside Donnan, trying to still the rapid hammering of his heartbeat, the quick heaves of air that he needed to draw in.

As he looked around himself, he saw the source of that feeling of age he had sensed earlier. A dolmen rose grey and tall into the night sky—an old longstone, a finger of the earth pointing Lughhigh. And standing beside it...was Ghabhann.

Now how...? Colum thought.

"The second contest is Colum's," the chief druid said. "The goddess has seen."

The wolf grin returned to Colum's lips. He glanced at Donnan, but the big man only shrugged and grinned back.

"Now let you two grapple, here beneath the sky that the Antlered God himself may see your struggle. Let one cry enough, or be struck senseless, and the third challenge is done.

"Let it begin!"

There was no more chance for Colum to catch his breath or to ease his cramped leg muscles. Donnan's hands were on him as soon as the druid cried, "Begin!"

Donnan was a powerful man—a bear, like Artor. And the wolf, who depended on his speed and guile, couldn't hope to prevail caught in his grip. He needed to be free, to strike, draw back and strike again. But Donnan's fingers were like vises; the power behind his shoulders as potent as that of the oaks which ringed the glade. He stood over Colum, forcing him down. In a moment, they would fall. And when they did, Colum would be on the bottom, helplessly pinned and with the last of his breath knocked from him.

There was no sense fighting the man, strength for strength, Colum realized. So he got a grip on Donnan's powerful forearms and let himself fall. He curled up his legs and curved his back. When they landed, Colum heaved up with his legs, arcing Donnan over him. The champion of Muman lost his grip as he flew over Colum's head.

Colum scrambled to his feet. As Donnan rose, Colum balled a fist and struck. Once in the temple. Again in the side of his jaw. Then he danced back — away from the man's flailing arms. He wouldn't be caught twice in that bear-like grip.

Donnan shook his head to clear it. A growl rumbled low in his chest. This time when Colum came at him, he moved like a cat.

He caught Colum's fist as it flashed towards him, his big hand enclosing it, and hauled Colum closer. A moment later, and he had engulfed Colum in another bear-hug.

Colum struggled to free himself, but the strength he needed simply wasn't there. The foot race through the woods had left him spent — too many years in the saddle had left him unprepared for this contest. Not so Donnan. He had trained all year for this day. And the man was strong.

In desperation, Colum brought his forearms up behind Donnan's back and clapped his open hands against Donnan's ears. The big man cried out. Shaking his head, he smashed his brow against Colum's forehead.

Colum's head rang. Lights flashed against his eyelids. Donnan increased the pressure of his grip until Colum could feel his ribs giving away. A moment longer, and they would crack. He needed air. He was dizzy from the blow he'd taken to his head and his ears still rang, dots dancing in his eyes.

Donnan increased the pressure again. Colum groaned, and then the red mist came spilling up to cloud his sight. Snarling, he struck Donnan's ears again, bringing to play all the force he could muster. The grip on his chest gave a touch. Colum struck him again, twisting his head to dodge the brow that came smashing towards him once more. This time it caught him only a glancing blow. The third time he struck the big man's ears, Donnan let him fall.

The battle-mist overcame Colum now. His knee lifted to drive into Donnan's crotch. As the man bent over in pain, Colum, struck him a savage blow across the back of his neck with a closed fist. Donnan dropped like a felled ox and lay still.

But Colum wasn't done with him yet. Still cursing, he leapt on the fallen man. He grabbed a fistful of red hair and raised Donnan's head, meaning to pound it into the ground.

It was Fergus he saw lying under him. This was no contest of champions. It was a blood-feud between the Ard-righ and himself —

a feud that could only end in one or the other's death. It could only end with the spilling of blood.

"Stop."

The word lashed Colum, piercing the red-mists that bound his mind. He lifted his head and saw, not Ghabhann standing there, but another. A tall man-shape from whose brow twelve-tined antlers sprung. The eyes that fixed their gaze on Colum were ageless, deep and knowing. Silently they spoke to him.

Would you break Fair-truce, Colum, Donal's son, and so be outlawed in truth?

The mist cleared from Colum's gaze—quickly and sudden, like the long grass of Kerry's plains parting before a storm wind. He realized whose head it was that he meant to batter against the ground. Gently, he laid it down. When he looked to the dolmen again, the antlered man was gone. He saw the chief druid regarding him with a curious expression in his eyes.

"Yours is the third challenge," Ghabhann said. "So the contest is yours."

Colum nodded in slow agreement. But still he regarded the druid. Still he knelt above Donnan, remembering.

"What is it, Donal's son?" the druid asked.

Colum shook his head. "I saw...another standing in your place. The Antlered One himself, I thought....But that couldn't be."

"And why not?" Ghabhann asked. "On this contest rested the fate of Aerin's High Seat. Such is a weighty matter, worthy of interest to the Lord of Death and Rebirth, wouldn't you think? Do we not speak here of the death of one Ard-righ and the rise of another to his Seat?"

"It *was* him, then, that I saw?"

The druid shrugged. "Perhaps."

"And is it such a common thing for you that you can shrug it off so easily?"

"Common? No. But his presence is always in this place—his and that of the Goddess who rules even him. Did you not feel it when you entered the wood—and especially when you entered this glade? The age of this place, and yet the agelessness of it? He is wild, our Antlered Huntsman, and this is an untamed place that is sacred to himself and the Goddess."

Colum shook his head again. "I don't know about such things."

Wearily, he rose to his feet.

"Donnan," he asked. "Will he...?"

"Live?" The druid nodded. "We will tend to him. Go to your companions now. There are deeds that still need doing on this night and the dawn draws near."

Colum straightened his back.

"I will do what needs to be done," he said.

Turning, he began to retrace his way back through the wood, his thoughts on Meave again, and on his son. On Fergus and the struggle against him that still lay ahead. But as he walked, his mind filled with visions of stags and stag-browed men, of wolves and ravens, and of a woman from whose eyes the light of the moon shone.

CRSO

The waiting Kings and champions of Aerin watched him step out from the wood and then pause. He said nothing for a long moment; he merely stood there under the trees — silent, dark-browed, eyes smoldering and fey. Not until Coinneach approached and threw a cloak around his bruised shoulders did he stir.

"I've fulfilled my side of the bargain," Colum said, "and in doing so, we have lost a strong warrior. So what now, Coinneach? Will you give me leave to do what I must do, or have you more madness in store for me?"

Coinneach gripped Colum's hand. His face was grim, too, but in that grip was the thanks for which he had no words. Then he turned to the others.

"Well, brothers?" he asked the Kings.

"We will follow you," Fachtna replied.

"Then this is what we do tonight," Coinneach said as he turned back to Colum. "Tonight we go to spill a not-King from the High Seat of Aerin and cleanse these shores once and for all of Wodan's curs."

Colum nodded. He ached in places he hadn't even known he had muscles, but he allowed no sign of it to show in his features. He had waited too long for this moment to allow his body's weakness to rob him of his part in the King-breaking.

"Let me dress," he said. "And give me a sword."

X

"Fergus knows," was the news that waited for them when they returned to Emain Macha.

With still an hour or so until the dawn, the darkness in the eastern skies was already lightening with a wash of grey. An owl dipped moth-like above them, wings silent in the dark air. More than one man marked it as a harbinger of doom.

"He knows?" Coinneach said to the man who gave then his news. "How can he know? Who's betrayed us?"

The gathered Kings and champions of Aerin moved closer to hear the reply. They fingered the hilts of their axes and swords, dark Erse gazes turned speculatively towards the twin towers that oversaw the Ard-righ's rath.

Flann mac Cu Uladh, the captain of Coinneach's who had come to them with the news, was more than a little ill at ease in the presence of such select company.

"It was no man of ours," he assured Coinneach. "But Fergus has Norse druids. It seems their *sight's* as keen as that of our own."

Coinneach nodded grimly.

"We've lost the element of surprise, brothers" he said, turning to his companions. "So the stakes are no longer the same. Are you still with me?"

"We gave you our word," Fachtna replied.

"And the Fair-truce?" Colum asked.

Coinneach spat on the ground at his feet. "Fergus will break it — and then we will break him."

"There's more," Flann said, his discomfort growing at the tide of bad news he was forced to bring his lord. "Not an hour past there were two new prisoners brought into the Stronghold of the Captives. One was your own druid Somhairle — "

"Somhairle?" Colum cried. "But that's — "

Coinneach put his hand on the Wolf's shoulder. His eyes went flat and hard.

"And the other?" he asked his captain.

"A boy," Flann replied. "I've heard it said that it's the Ard-righ's own grandson — the one that was fostered to the sidhe."

There were times when Colum cursed the red mist that came over him in battle—the berserker rage that fed false strength to his limbs and sent him charging at his enemy, bare-fisted if need be and without a care for his own safety. But at this news, with the weariness of his ordeal in Dairsean Wood still on him, he welcomed it as he might a dear friend.

There among the Kings and champions, he drew his sword. He viewed the world as though through bloody gauze. Shaking off Coinneach's restraining grip, he set off to finish the business he'd left undone seven years ago.

Fergus had stolen all that was dear to him—Meave, their son, his friend. But that was only one side of the coin. The other was, could he keep them?

"Colum!" Coinneach roared. "Will you throw it all away?"

Colum turned. His sword lifted until its point was at Coinneach's throat.

"Will you stop me?" he asked.

Coinneach retreated a step. There was something new in Colum's wolf-mask of a face tonight. The red mist clouded his eyes—that was plain enough—but this time he seemed to have a tight rein upon it, a control that made it appear all the more fey and deadly.

"Won't you ever listen to reason without first arguing?" Coinneach demanded.

"I'm done listening to Kings. I ask you again: Will you stop me?"

"Lord...?" Seanan, Connacht's champion began, stepping forward.

Coinneach waved him back.

"Let him go," he said. Then to Colum he added, "Listen to me, Donal's son. There will be no room in Aerin for a man who can't heed his King's word."

Colum met Coinneach's gaze, but saw in the King's features only Meave and Myrddin, and the features of a son whose face he had never known.

"Then there will be no home in Aerin for me," he said.

Turning, he strode away into the darkness.

Coinneach watched him go. His companions gathered silently around him, waiting on his word. When it came, his voice cracked the air like a whip.

"Gather the clans!" he cried.

CR&O

Colum stopped long enough to don his mail and gather up three throwing spears before he marched to the High King's Mi-Cuarta. When he finally stood in its courtyard, his mind was empty of all concerns except for his cold rage. His anger deepened still further — spinning against the borders of madness — at what he found waiting for him.

Guttering torches cast weird shadows across the courtyard, throwing their light upon a terrible sight. As was the custom with the Norse, when offering an enemy to their thunder god Wodan, they had nailed a man to an X-shaped cross.

This wasn't the first time that Colum had looked upon such a sight. But every other time it had been a stranger he'd found mistreated as was this man. This time....

They had bound Myrddin's mouth open with a part of his staff thrust between his jaws so that he could speak no spell. His fingers were broken so that they could not conjure. His head hung against his chest. Blood dripped from around the nails hammered into his hands and feet.

He lifted his head as Colum stepped into the courtyard. His eyes opened and in the flicker light of the torches and the growing dawn glimmer that spread from the east, his pained gaze found Colum's.

"Dogs!" Colum roared.

The door of the Mi-Cuarta crashed open and the Norse poured out. They formed a line two-deep in front of the great wooden building and locked shields. From the left and right sides of the High King's rath, more of the yellow-haired warriors appeared. Then Fergus stepped into the doorway. He leaned on a spear and regarded Colum with as much alarm as a man might a gnat. Guttorm came out to stand at his side, dwarfing the Ard-righ with his bulk, a mocking grin on his lips.

But Colum didn't see them. He had eyes only for the crucified man, nailed to the wooden beams behind the double-ranked Norse. Myrddin's gaze held his like a vise.

A spear, Colum thought he heard Myrddin say, the druid's voice echoing strangely in his head. *Cast it straight and true into my heart, Wolf.*

232

Colum shook his head.

He couldn't do it. Not while there still remained the smallest measure of hope that he could rescue Myrddin and cut him down. Until he was dead himself, he refused to give up that hope.

Cast your spear!

The druid's voice hammered in between Colum's temples. Colum shook his head again and then Fergus was speaking.

"This is a King-breaking?" the Ard-righ asked.

His voice was thin in the near-dawn air, filled with humor. He hooked thumbs in his belt and smiled down at Colum.

"One man?" he went on. "This is a sorry army that Coinneach fields."

"Not one man!" Coinneach cried from the shadows behind Colum.

They stepped forward then and arrayed themselves behind the last man of the Faolta clan — the Kings, champions and warriors of Lagan and Muman, Connacht and Kerry. There were even men from the clans of Uloth joined with then — the same clans from which Fergus took his Gailana. Though they were raising swords against friends and kindred, they could no longer stand aside.

"You disappoint me, Coinneach," Fergus said. "I thought you wiser than this. Do you not see how we outnumber you?"

It was true. There were at least two Norse for each man Coinneach had with him, and Fergus also had the Norse druids and his Gailana. Taking in the odds, Colum could only despair.

The Erse still disdained mail and shields, though their enemies had no such qualms. There was no room here for chariot work, It was man to man, and the Norse had the advantage. What use were spears and blades when the wall of locked shields would deflect them? The Erse would break on the Norse's ordered ranks like unarmed children falling under the blades of seasoned fighters.

He watched through the red mist that clouded his sight as more and more Norse arrayed themselves in front of the Mi-Cuarta. At directive from their captains, they began to circle around to enclose the Erse clans. Then Myrddin's gaze called him and whether he wanted to or not, he had to turn to look at the druid again.

Your spear, Wolf, Myrddin's eyes demanded of him. *Have you forsworn your trust in me as well? Cast your spear!*

233

Colum shivered and again broke eye-contact. He looked to Fergus. His hand tightened on his spear's haft, but when the first spear was thrown, it left the High King's hand, not Colum's.

Colum dodged the cast. Behind him, a man fell, the High King's spear sprouting from his chest like an extra limb. Erse blood soaked Aerin's soil.

The Fair-truce was broken.

Something keened on the wind as the speared man died. It was like a wolf's howl, or the cry of the Antlered Lord's Hunt. A banshee's wail. The earth shook with a tremor as she accepted the lifeblood of one of her children. Colum imagined the sidhe shivering in their burrowed duns. Brigit loosing her daughter's ravens into the sky. Lugh turning his gaze away as clouds rose up to cloak the dawn.

A kind of understanding dawned on Colum then—born of the fey powers that rode the air, rather than reason. He cocked his arm and threw his spear.

Fergus leapt behind Guttorm before he realized that he wasn't the target. The iron point of the weapon pierced Myrddin's chest, searched for and found his druid's heart.

A low rumbling moan grumbled like approaching thunder.

The Norse druids cast spells that proved useless as the clouds above the rath took on the shape of an enormous antlered man's head. The spear sprang from Myrddin's chest. The wound closed by itself. Antlers sprouted from his brow. The bindings that tied the broken haft of his spear into his mouth fell away. He spat out the wood.

"Cousin!" he cried to the face-shaped clouds above. "Will you let the not-King continue to torment your people?"

His voice was no longer his own. It was deeper, unearthly in its fey timbre. Thunder rocked the sky in response—sharp explosive cracks that set bones rattling. The voice of a god, Colum thought, though what walked the sky tonight was a god of Aerin, not the Norse's thunder god.

"I am the Green Man!" Myrddin replied.

Colum cocked his arm again, only this time it wasn't his own will that set his limbs to action. Another used him—the thunder in the sky, or that familiar stranger who hung crucified on the Norse's cross-beamed god offering. All he could do was watch the weapon fly, arrow-straight. It pierced the breast of the not-King Fergus mac

Coemgen — Meave's father who had caused Colum's father to die — and pinned him to the wall of his own Mi-Cuarta.

As though that spear cast had been a lightning bolt, a new peal of thunder roared across the sky. The cross to which Myrddin was nailed grew leafed boughs. The nails popped loose and spat across the courtyard, but the druid didn't fall. The cross had become a giant oak and one great branch lowered him to the ground.

Colum shuddered to see what Myrddin had become. The antlers on his brow lifted like the branches of a thorn tree, high above his head. He wore a cloak of green leaves. His feet were hooves, his limbs gnarled like the roots of some ancient tree. He turned to the Norse druids. Lifting a hand, magefire blossomed in his palms and leapt out at them. The druids ignited like bundles of dry twigs and were consumed.

"Guttorm," the Green Man said in a voice that was more Myrddin's now than a stranger's. "Is there still a place for you in these isles?"

Struck dumb, the Norseman could only shake his head.

"Then be gone from these shores."

Guttorm's men looked to him for guidance. Their hands were no longer on their weapons. Their shield wall was broken, shields hanging at their sides in slack grips. Preternatural fears clouded the burly Norseman's eyes. He gazed from the ashen remains of his druids, to his fearful men, to the weird being that faced him — antler-browed, more tree than man, with the magefire still crackling in his palms.

For a moment it seamed as though he would cast aside his weapons. His own fingers were slack around the handle of his axe. But then, with a hoarse curse, he swung up his weapon and charged.

Magefire leapt from the Green Man's hands to strike him, consuming him as it had his druids. And then, as Guttorm died, the semblance of the Green Man fell away from Myrddin and the druid pitched forward in his own shape to lie as still as death on the packed dirt of the courtyard.

For the passing of a few breaths, an utter and profound silence descended on the men in the courtyard of the Mi-Cuarta. Then chaos erupted as the two armies clashed.

XI

"They fought without heart," a Kerryman said.

"It's just as well," his comrade replied, "or there'd be still more of our own people lying here among the slain. As it is...."

The Kerryman nodded wearily. "Fergus is dead, but it's still a sorry day."

Colum was only half-listening to them as he searched through the corpses near the entrance to the Mi-Cuarta, looking for Myrddin's body, but he heard that last comment clearly.

It was truly a sorry day, he agreed. They'd broken the High King, but the price had been dear. Too many lay dead.

Then he found the druid and all further thought fled his mind, for Myrddin was still alive.

Colum handled Myrddin as though he was a baby, working him free from the press of the dead and carrying him to the doorway where there was a clear space. There, under the dead gaze of Fergus who still hung impaled from the wall of his rath, Colum bathed Myrddin's face and carefully looked him over. There were scars on his hands and feet, another over his heart where his chest showed through his torn robe, but no other sign of his terrible wounds. Even his fingers had been healed.

Myrddin's eyelids fluttered as Colum sat back on his heels.

"Wolf?" the druid murmured.

"I'm here."

"I was...mistaken."

"Rest now. There'll be time enough for talk later."

Myrddin ignored him. He sat up slowly, then leaned against the wall, spent by that small effort.

"When two men fight," he said, "and they're both Kings....What can there be but war?"

"It's over now."

The druid nodded wearily. "Over," he repeated softly. "You know, Wolf, the bards used to call me the Green Man and I...I always thought it a blasphemy of sorts. But now....What lies within each one of us, do you suppose?"

"Our hearts," Colum said. "And our wills. The need to be free."

"Wild as the Antlered man who walks the woods...in his eyes, the deadly beauty of a serpent....I *was* him, Wolf, for that moment, that flicker in time's shroud. I wonder...is he in me still?"

Colum was troubled to hear Myrddin speak like this. Myrddin, the druid. Who always gave advice. Who knew in the fall of scattered bones the days to come. Who could read the stars for portents. Who could ride the winds with his mind.

Had the god's touch on him stolen that sharp wit from him?

"Siochain," the druid said. His voice was suddenly stronger, not so fey. "I promised to bring you peace. Have you seen your son yet, Wolf?"

"I...."

Colum's mail was caked with the blood of his foemen and the many small wounds he'd taken in the battle. He was so tired that he could barely stand. His every muscle ached. Yet if one, or all, of these dead Norse were to rise, he knew he could find the strength to fight them all over again. But this simple thing of which Myrddin spoke...to go to Meave and his son....

That seemed beyond his present strength or courage.

Seven years was a long time. A woman might wait that long in a harper's ballad—but in this world? Wouldn't her eyes say as he approached: Why did you come now? Why did you not come sooner?

What had been done tonight—wouldn't it have been easier done seven years ago and so saved her the trials that she had suffered in between? What would he say to her when her eyes asked him these questions?

Myrddin's lips shaped a weak smile.

"Has the Wolf grown so timid?" he asked.

Colum shook his head. He drew a breath and started to rise, but then—

She was there.

There was no Erse sea, nor Nial's Arm, between them. No army of Norse, nor her father's Gailana. Only the space of three strides.

The morning sun caught her auburn hair and made it sing. She held the hand of a six-year-old boy whose features bore so striking a resemblance to his own that he knew it could only be his son. There was no reproach in her eyes—only a glittering light.

"I knew you would come," she said, as though they were, indeed, characters in some harper's ballad.

Slowly, wonderingly, Colum stood. He was as tongue-tied as a boy going to court his first maid at a Feis. But the words that were caught in his throat spoke through his shining eyes, until finally he found his voice.

"I would have come sooner —"

"Whisht," she said.

Then she was in his arms, ignoring the mail he wore and the blood of their foes that was upon it, seeing only the youth she'd loved, grown to be a man.

Young Connal regarded his parents for a long moment, then grew bored as their embrace lingered on, so he knelt down beside the druid. His small hand reached out to touch Myrddin's brow.

"They told me you had antlers," he said seriously. "Like Cernunnos himself."

"You can only see them in a certain light," Myrddin explained. "They are hidden things, it would appear. So well hidden that I never saw them myself."

"Is that my father?" Connal asked, pointing at Colum.

Before Myrddin could reply, Colum had turned. He lifted the boy and held him out at arm's length to look at him.

"I am, indeed," he said.

"They said you were gone."

Colum nodded. "But now I've come back, to make amends for the lost years, and I won't be leaving you again."

He held the boy close, snuggled into the crook of one arm while the other hugged Meave close to his side, and that was how they were found by Coinneach mac Conan, Ard-righ of Aerin.

"Colum," the Ard-righ said. "We had words, you and I, and now I wish they could be taken back. They were spoken in anger...."

"Though no less true for that. I can't stay, Coinneach. I'm done with the work of Kings."

"But where will you go?"

Colum looked at Meave. In her eyes he saw that she too was remembering a time seven years past when a young maid and her outlawed lover had spoken of the lands that lay across Atlanta where it was said the meaning of the word "King" was forgotten and no man or woman stood above the other.

"To Aerin Nua," Colum said.

"Is there no argument I could raise that would change your mind?"

"None."

Coinneach sighed. "I can't stop you. But if you should ever wish to return, there will be a welcome waiting here for you."

Colum nodded.

"We love this land," Meave added, "but it holds too many bitter memories for us. Perhaps someday — if the power those memories hold over us fades — we'll come back."

Her gaze traveled to where her father's body was impaled upon the wall of his Mi-Cuarta. She looked away, pressing closer against Colum's side.

"But I don't think it's very likely," she said.

"Go then," Coinneach said. "With a King's thanks, and a friend's blessing."

XII

They stood together on the shore, the Wolf and the Fox, the captain waiting at the ship's rail behind them for the word to raise anchor and be gone.

"You won't come?" Colum asked for what he knew would be the last time.

Myrddin shook his head. "But we'll meet again. Look for me when I'm least expected. There's work for me still in these isles — though not war-work, for which I give you thanks. When it's done...who knows where I'll wander?"

"You'll give my greetings to the Bear?"

"I'll drown his anger in a barrel of ale."

Myrddin paused, looking as though he had more to say, but then he simply sighed.

"Fare you well, Colum mac Donal," he said.

Colum clasped the druid to his chest.

"Farewell, Fox. Have a care with those spells of yours."

"It's apprentices that I've been warned against," Myrddin said.

Colum began to ask him what he meant, then thought better of it. Often Myrddin's explanations were more confusing than the ini-

tial question. At least the druid was back to his own self once more —
speaking in riddles.

He gripped Myrddin's shoulder, then turned and made for the
ship where Meave and their son were waiting for him, standing at
the rail with their ship's captain.

CR&O

Long after the anchor was raised and the ship rowed out to
deeper waters where her sails were unfurled, Myrddin stood there
by the sea, watching until the ship was just a speck, and then there
was only the sea with no sail at all upon its horizon.

"At last you have your peace, Colum," he said.

He thought he heard the fey murmur of sidhe voices. He cocked
his head to listen more closely, then shrugged. He wondered what
shape the people of the Middle Kingdom would take in that new
world to which Colum sailed. There would be secrets still, he was
sure. Little mysteries.

Finally, as the afternoon leaked away and the night drew close,
he turned and left. All that remained then was the sound of the sea,
lapping against the shore, and the unseen presence of the sidhe, looking westward.

In time, they too were gone, and only the sea moved in the glimmering twilight.

Damon

Damon: A Prologue

On Beltane Eve, in the Year of the Long Winter, Elfane Hall-bright of the House of Halmanor went walking through Wenwight Wood, under the baneful glare of a full moon. It was there that she was taken by a nameless daemon, her body and spirit ravaged by his insatiable lusts. On All Hallow's Eve, two months before her time, she gave birth to a son and he was named Daelin Wood-wise.

Though born of an unholy coupling between High Aelf and daemon, to all appearances he was one of the Elder Races: tall and bright, golden-haired and full of the joy of life. Yet there was one difference: his eyes. Where the High Aelves are golden-eyed, his were a dark — almost black — grey, flecked with gold and crimson red.

For many years he dwelt in peace with his kin and there was not one who told the son of Elfane Hall-bright the dark tale of his conceiving. But in the leaf-fall of the Year of the Dark Stirring, the House of Halmanor fell under the shadow of Noth Seganth — that foul sorcerer whose descendants will ever bear the name of Halmanbane.

All of his kin were slain that day save Daelin, for he had been far afield on an errand of Welkin Wander-star's — the eldest of his people. Upon his return, he was met with the charred ruins of the Great Hall and the bodies of his kin: hacked and disfigured beyond recognition by the loathsome minions of Noth Seganth. A madness came over him then and he made a pact with the Nether Gods: They would give him the strength and power to wreck his vengeance upon his foes if he would but renounce his aelfin heritage and thereafter do Their bidding.

So was Damon born for, in his madness, he agreed and true to Their word, he was given the power of a daemon – the power that slept within him and could be traced to his father's unholy blood. Gone then was the lithe aelfin body and in its place stood a mighty-thewed barbaric form. Great horns sprang from his brow and curled along the sides of his head in a full turn before they ended in wicked points. In his dark eyes, hell-fires smoldered and simmered and his strength was now many times that of aelf or man.

With Their gift of power, his revenge was completed so that utter destruction fell upon Noth Seganth and all of his cruel followers – yet his vengeance was of no avail. Nothing could return his people to him and – with his pact – he had damned himself and soiled the wonder and beauty of the House of Halmanor with the bloody fury of his revenge.

He rebelled against the Nether Gods – refused to do Their bidding – and for this They took from him all memory of the House of Halmanor and his kin. All he retained was the teasing remembrance of that House's name and his own: Damon.

They could not revoke his powers – there are things that not even the Gods may do – so They sealed his body and spirit within one of the menhir on the Moors of Boscawen. Within that standing stone he was trapped for two hundred years, as they are reckoned by the calendars of man.

CRSO

To those moors came two Wyslings or hedge-wizards: Robin Marrow and Coromorr Henchen. Sensing a living presence trapped within that menhir, they used their arcane arts to release whatever it might be from its bondage, for they were curious and prying – as wizards are and often to their own dooming.

So was Damon reborn into the Lands of Woldenar. Through hooded eyes, he looked upon the two Wyslings who had freed him. For a long strained moment his brow wrinkled as he strove to recall something of great importance. But then he shrugged his massive shoulders and, brushing the pair aside without a word, he stalked off across the moors…

Wings over Antar

I

He opened his eyes into the blinding glare of a noon-day sun. As he strove to rise, lances of pain shot through his hands and feet causing him to fall back with a curse on his parched lips. He shook his horned head in frustration.

By the Gods, they had nailed him to a rock!

He laid his back against its unyielding surface and, his massive muscles straining with the exertion, tried to release his limbs. His only reward was a fresh flow of dark crimson blood and the agony of the newly-opened tissues tearing against the cold iron.

A dark fury came over him. He braced himself for another effort, but then glancing up, he saw distant shapes circling — black against the brightness of the sun. One detached itself from the others and came diving toward him. As it plunged, he caught a glimpse of huge leathery wings and a long cruel beak. The thing looked like a nightmare cross between a bat and a vulture. Ignoring the pain, he strained anew to loose his impaled hands. But even with certain death approaching on the talons of this winged creature, suddenly the events that had led him to his present situation flashed across his mind...

II

It had been an hour after dusk when he had come to the West Gate of Antar. The two soldiers lounging on guard-duty stopped

245

him. As they questioned him, his long journey from the Peredur Mountains began to weigh heavily upon him and he broke in with:

"What do you call this hole?"

"Hole?" one of the guards spat the word out. "This is no hole! This is the City of Antar and the finest city it is, east of Calthoren. Watch your tongue, outlander, if you'd care to keep your head on your shoulders, Now. Your name and business?"

Through hooded eyes, hand on the hilt of the long blade at his left hip, he looked down at them from the tall back of his mount.

"I am Damon," he said. "Of the House of Halmanor. My business is my own."

As he spoke, one of the guards glanced nervously about but saw no sign of reinforcements to call on should they have any trouble with this self-assured barbarian. Then he took in the sight before him.

Mounted on an enormous leather-armored steed, Damon cut an impressive figure: heavy-chested with massive shoulders and well-muscled arms, and that one hand yet on the hilt of his blade named Banes-lord, ready for instant action. A great horned helmet framed a weathered face. Dark eyes glittered menacingly and there was a grim set to his jaw as he returned the guard's stare. His tunic was a dark green, with a brown cloak draped overtop that billowed in the rising wind.

The guard peered closer at the helmet and tried to imagine what beast those horns had been taken from. Why even his mount had a great horn set into the leather on its brow. He tore his gaze away and murmured something inaudible to his comrade.

"Pass through, stranger," he said, turning back to Damon, "but mind your manners while you're here. This is a civilized city — not some wild barbarian camp on the foothills of the Peredur Mountains."

Damon gave the man a long cold look, recalling how he had but recently been courteously received in those very camps. Then wordlessly, he nudged his mount through the gate and into the city.

He made his way along Antar's main roadway, his steed's cloven hooves ringing strangely on the cobblestone street and echoing against the silent lines of two-storied buildings that choked the road on which he traveled. At the first sign of a tavern he drew up and dismounted, wrapping his mount's reins about a post outside its door.

"I like this city no better than you, Storm-strider," he murmured quietly to him in the tongue of the High Aelves. "Give me but a half hour to wet my throat and we'll be away from its stink and back into the clean air of the mountains. Aye, and twice as fast as ever we came. Damned if I know why we're here in the first place."

So saying, he strode to the door of the tavern and stepped within.

He paused for a moment within the doorway, his dark gaze adjusting to the sudden light and roving about as he silently appraised the tavern's clientele. The tables were full with boisterous townsfolk and a harmless rogue or two at most of them. By the door, though, six soldiers sat at one table littered with empty flagons. Their scarlet cloaks stood out sharply against the more subdued clothing of the general crowd and they looked him over carefully as he stood framed in the doorway.

Pointedly, he ignored them. Then he saw an open spot, just across from their table, where two heavily-cloaked figures sat — heads bent together in deep conversation.

He strode over and sat down, stretching his cramped legs with a sigh of relief. Calling for a serving-wench, he was soon sipping a large flagon of a vaguely bitter ale. Then he looked up at the pair across the table from him.

One was a woman — and beautiful too, were it not for her hunched back. He wondered for a moment just what the rest of her body was like under that voluminous cloak. Her companion's face was in shadow, but it was obviously a man's.

His curiosity was short-lived and after that one glance, he soon lost interest in them and fell to staring into his flagon, brooding of days gone by. Deep in reverie, he never noticed the soldiers rising from their table and approaching his until one called out to the couple before him.

"Enough of this sham, vermin. We know you for the spies you are. Now, come along quietly or we'll run the pair of you through."

Damon looked up as the soldiers grasped the two and dragged them from their chairs. One of them cuffed the hunchbacked girl so that she fell to the floor, unconscious. The others were suddenly faced with the drawn sword of her companion. The soldier's blades were out in a moment and then they were upon the man. Damon turned away and, taking a long pull from his ale, fell to brooding once more. Disputes in an Antarian bar were of scant concern to him.

The battle was short, yet bloody. The girl's companion ran through one of the soldiers, but as he was drawing his blade free, another of them swept his sword up and opened the man from groin to chin. He fell back, stumbled against Damon's table and sprawled across it, knocking the Halmanorian's flagon to the floor.

There he lay before Damon: his entrails spilling onto his lap; dying eyes beseeching those of the grim warrior — burning into him to reach a part of him that he had thought long-dead. With a curse on his lips, Damon rose and drew his long shining blade and a short dagger. His cold eyes bore into the remaining soldiers and remembered his treatment by the guards at the city's gate.

"So," he said. "You'd call me a savage and a barbarian, would you, you murdering scum?"

"Ease up!" one of the soldiers told him. "This is not your fight!"

Damon laughed, a red glint growing in his dark eyes. "Aye, but I'll make it mine!"

So saying, he leapt forward. His gleaming sword cut down one of the Antarians, even as his dagger sank to its hilt in the breast of another. The three that remained drew back but, drawing a second dagger from his belt, he charged into them.

"Get behind him!" one of them cried.

A companion attempted to obey but a backhand thrust of Damon's blade slashed his chest to the bone. For a moment Damon seemed wide open to attack. In a concerted effort, one soldier struck at Damon's heart, the other at his midsection. The watchers in the tavern shuddered; no one could survive such an assault. They did not know Damon.

With lightning speed, the Halmanorian's dagger flicked across one soldier's neck. The Antarian fell back, blood seeping through fingers clutching spasmodically at his throat. The point of the other soldier's blade came within a hairsbreadth of Damon's breast before Banes-lord struck it aside. With a turn of his wrist, Damon plunged its point deep into the heart of his foe. Eyes flaming in bloodlust, he twisted his blade in the screaming soldier's chest.

"Drink deeply, Banes-lord!" he cried.

Then he turned to face the townsfolk but not one made a move toward him. They were terrified. Taking in the carnage, was it really such a surprise? Well, what was done was done. The Gods alone knew what he'd drawn onto himself into this time. He'd best be away ere the watch arrived. It was his head they'd want now, indeed.

He scooped up the surprisingly light body of the unconscious girl and made for the door. As he threw her across the neck of his steed, her cloak fell from her and his eyes widened at what was revealed. From her shoulders grew a pair of large feathered wings that had been hidden earlier in the folds of her mantle.

She was one of the winged-folk...the Halwaren. A legend come to life. But that only made him smile. Was he not a legend himself to most folk?

Putting aside his thoughts, he mounted behind her and set Storm-strider at a gallop toward the West Gate. Behind him one of the soldiers — clutching his stomach with a bloody hand — cried out for the town-watch. By the time they arrived, Damon was already at the gate.

The two guards there took one look at the fearsome apparition that thundered toward them and scrambled out of his way. Then Damon was through the gate and away into the night. From behind him, he could already hear the rising sound of pursuit.

III

Long and hard he drove Storm-strider. Still, they had come a far way that day and the day before as well, and even Storm-strider's seemingly tireless muscles were flagging under the strain. All too soon the pursuit was gaining on them.

Damon had a poor opinion of the Antarian soldiery. They were nothing but fancy-dressed puppet-warriors, what with their scarlet cloaks and city finery. Yet for all his belittling of them he knew that they must have some training, for they had lost no time in their pursuit of him. True, they had fallen like chaff before his blade, but they were many...too many.

Suddenly his daemon-born battle-lust boiled into a rage and roared across his thoughts, dispelling all reason. He drew back sharply on Storm-strider's reins and alighted to face his oncoming foes before his great steed had even stopped his headlong flight.

In the haste of his dismounting, the winged woman fell from Storm-strider's back. The jar of her fall brought her back to her senses. She looked about wildly — bewildered at her surroundings — then saw Damon facing the riders of the city as they thundered down the road toward them.

Full understanding dawned on her — he had rescued her from the Antarians and was now defending her against her foes, regardless of his own peril. It was sound reasoning save for the fact that it was not a man that championed her cause but rather a daemon enrapt in its own blood-lust. Yet how was she to know?

Dazedly she tried to rise and give him aid, but her legs wouldn't hold her. With trembling fingers, she undid the thongs that had strapped her wings to her slim body, almost passing out again from the exertion. Storm-strider the unicorn, pranced lightly on cloven hooves — uncertain as to whether he should aid his master or stand guard over the girl. Then Damon commanded their attention, both girl and beast.

Their pursuers were almost upon him as he stood there in the roadway, his long shining blade glistening bright and silver in the dark of the night and he charged the oncoming horsemen. They tried to draw back or aside — but it was too late. He was upon them like a fiend out of some inhuman hell.

With a wide sweep of his sword, he cut the legs of the foremost rider's steed from under him. Leaping up, he grasped another by the throat and hurled him to the ground. One swift stroke of his blade and that man lay gutted and moaning in his agony. Then with a backward swipe of a swiftly drawn dagger — that had been sheathed in the hilt of his sword — he caught the first rider across the chest and sent him sprawling into the darkness.

All that could be seen in that strange star-lit scene was Damon's silver blade, arcing and dealing death as his foes were cut down like ripe grain. It was like fighting a ghost, for Damon was never still long enough for an Antarian blade to find him. Yet the ghost had teeth and Antarian corpses littered the road.

For a moment there was a lull in the action as the soldiers tried to regroup in the darkness. Then they fell back in fear. Where Damon's eyes had been a dark-grey, flecked with golds and reds, they were now a pupil-less blazing crimson and his full daemon-strength was upon him.

He ran toward the Antarians, his tunic torn and splattered with the blood of both his foes and himself. Crying strange curses in an unknown tongue he struck with an uncontrollable rage. His blades were a vortex of unearthly lights as they wove their deadly dance — slaying and delivering their hell-born destruction. But there were too many foes and where first their fear had made them draw back, now it drove them at him in wild desperation. Not even his daemon-strength could prevail against two-score professional soldiers.

As the light began to dim in his eyes, his sword paled as well, and then he was overwhelmed by the sheer weight of their superior numbers.

At that moment the winged girl gave a wailing cry and rose into the air, half-drawing the short sword that rested in a sheath upon her back, nestled between her shoulder blades. Storm-strider stamped his hooves and screamed in his fury. But it was too late. He should have left the girl and aided his master. Almost, it seemed as if he would charge into the hopeless odds, but then he wheeled and disappeared into the darkness.

The woman sheathed her sword as she, too, realized the hopelessness of the situation. Her wings cut the night air with a slow and graceful rhythm and she rose higher and higher until she was but a shadow against the dim glow of the stars.

Damon had fallen.

IV

Damon snapped back to the present and, with one last burst of strength, tore his right hand free, iron nail and all. But not in time to stop the winged devil that dove at him. Yet, with his last effort, his upper torso had jerked forward and he lowered, then lifted his head, impaling the bird-beast upon his horns. It ripped at his leather helmet as his horns sank deeper into its soft underbelly. With a mighty twist of his head, he sent it tumbling from the rock, screaming its death throes. His helmet was locked in its claws as it plummeted to its doom.

Swiftly he fell to loosening his left hand. The pain was so excruciating that it burned into his very soul. Never had he felt such agony.

But finally that hand was free, too, even as more of the creatures attacked him.

Grasping two of them by their necks, he smashed their skulls together and tossed them away like limp dolls. Still more of the winged monsters swooped down, their beaks snapping and their eyes gleaming with hunger.

The exertion of this strife was rapidly taking its toll upon him. His strength was many times that of an ordinary man, but it had its limits. His feet were devoid of feeling, his hands a mass of blood and mangled flesh. It was not until he had slain three more of the creatures that they reluctantly drew back and circled in the sky again. Here was no helpless prey. As swiftly is they had appeared, they were gone, never realizing how close they had come to finishing him off.

Damon concentrated on the nails at his feet, tearing at the cold iron with numb fingers until at last he was free. He staggered to his feet and stood for a moment: his body covered with the yellow blood of the winged creatures; his eyes blazing with an unholy hatred for those who had dared to nail him there. Cursing, he vented his fury into the sky until he toppled over and fell back unto the rock—his pain too much for his conscious mind to bear.

CR&O

When he came to, the sun was westering and the sky was spinning. Before him swam the outlines of a human face. Then, slowly, the spinning stopped and he saw that it was the face of the winged girl, her lips pursed, her brow wrinkled with concern.

She had tended to him well. He was off the rock and resting against its base, hidden from prying eyes amidst a tumble of boulders. His hands were bandaged with strips of cloth torn from her flimsy shift. She had bound his feet as well, afterwards cutting open his boots—Where had she found them?—that they might fit over the bulky bandages. They were bound about his calves with thongs of leather.

Through the haze that yet clouded his vision, he took in the finer details of her figure and features. Golden-brown hair framed her worried face complimenting the deep, sudden green of her eyes.

When she spoke, though it was softly, her voice was clear and ringing like so many musical notes.

"Rest easy, stranger," she said. "I am Rhiannon gan Halwaren — of the winged folk — and your friend. Come. Drink of this. It will make you stronger."

She bent over him and lifted a small flask to his cracked lips. The fiery liquid he swallowed coursed through his body like a wild northern wind and he felt a surge of strength come over him. But his fearsome wounds were yet wearing away at his body and he laid his head back against the stone.

She sat back and regarded him thoughtfully, her gaze traveling from his pointed ears and great curling horns down the length of his heavily-muscled body. Aware of her scrutiny, he looked back at her though hooded eyes, but their lids grew heavy and he sank again into a deep slumber.

"What are you, I wonder?" she asked his sleeping form. "Aelf? Daemon?"

To herself she added: Or some unholy coupling of the two?

CREO

He awoke some hours later, clear-headed and feeling much less pain than he should have. Through the deepening twilight, he saw Rhiannon resting against a boulder across from him and realized that she must have fallen asleep while watching over him.

Slowly and painfully, he rose to his feet. Instinctively, his hand went for the hilt of his sword — but it was gone. Of course. The Antarians would have taken it: Banes-lord, a weapon so fair, yet so fearsome. One more deed amongst many that they must account for.

Antar, beware, he vowed. Long will you rue the day that you set yourself against Damon, last of the Aelf House of Halmanor — Damon of legend: Damon the Damned.

He crossed to where Rhiannon lay. For a long moment he looked down upon her, drinking in her beauty. Then he bent down and removed the small dagger strapped to her right thigh. She stirred in her sleep, but did not waken.

No warrior maiden, she, he thought. And yet…

Taking another swallow from the flask that lay by her side, he shivered as its fire raced through his veins, setting each fiber of his being alert and easing the ever-present pain in his wounded hands and feet.

She has yet her sword, he thought as he slipped her dagger into his belt, and that will see her safe until he could return this small blade.

Aching with each step, he hobbled down the side of the mountain, calling out softly in the language of the High Aelves. When he reached its base, Storm-strider was waiting. With an effort, he mounted the unicorn and rode again for the city of Antar.

V

It was long after midnight and Damon was slipping wraith-like through the back-streets of Antar. He had leapt from Storm-strider's back and slowly scaled the wall of the city — throttling the soldier who had had the misfortune of guarding that section of the city's fortifications. Now, armed with the guard's spear and sword, he crept like darkness itself until he came to the walls of the inner keep.

There was death in his eyes as he stood and surveyed that weather-worn structure. Death that blazed crimson as his emotions seethed within him. Then like a shadow with glowing eyes, he was over the walls and into the main keep proper.

Within, he wandered aimlessly about, trying to make some sense out of the endless winding corridors. Every so often a guard would come striding down one of them and Damon would melt into one of the many small patches of shade that pervaded the halls.

The pain of his many wounds — though ever-present — was greatly lessened now, both from that strange healing brew of Rhiannon's and his own daemon-bred resilience. Still, he could feel a sluggishness in his movements and a dulling of his senses. These signs he heeded not: vengeance was on his mind.

Without warning, he came upon a well-lit passageway, deep within the castle. From his vantage point in a small nook, he could see a door at its far end, guarded by a pair of soldiers.

It might not be Banes-lord that they were guarding, he reasoned, but something of value lay behind that door.

Noiselessly, he stepped into the corridor. He was halfway down its length when the guards first noticed him. Their eyes went wide with superstitious fear as the image of his horned figure was burnt into their minds. In that moment of panic, with death upon them, they realized that those great horns on his brow were not merely some decorative ornament on a helmet.

Before they could make an outcry, the Halmanorian's left hand loosed the wall-guard's spear at one. In the same movement, he flung the sword at the other. The weapons struck their victims almost simultaneously — entering their throats and impaling them against the wood-paneled walls in a shower of their own blood. There they hung like carcasses in a meat-merchant's stall.

There was a grim smile playing on Damon's lips as he ran down the rest of the corridor — wincing at each step of his loose-fitting boots. He threw his shoulder against the door and it burst inwards.

A fat man in an enormous bed sat up in fright. "W-w-who a-a-are you?"

Damon leapt from the doorway, drawing Rhiannon's dagger. He held its razor sharp edge against the man's trembling throat.

"I am Death, you fat little fool," he told the frightened man. "Come to take your bloated soul. Where do they keep it? Where is my blade?"

"I-I-I d-d-don't k-k-know wh-what —"

Damon leaned on the blade and a little trickle of blood dripped from where the dagger pressed into the fat man's throat. Gripping him by the shoulder, Damon dragged him from the bed and threw him toward the door.

"Lead me to where it's kept or by all you hold holy, I'll gut you where you stand. Now move."

Shaking with fear, the man arose and lead the way out of the room. When he saw his guards hanging in their own gore from the walls, he stopped short and was violently sick. Damon gave him a kick to keep him moving and glanced back into the room. There he saw a golden crown lying on a table by the bed.

So he had their king, did he? All the better!

The trembling king took him down many corridors. Damon grew restless as the minutes hurried by and he was no closer to his goal. He was about to cuff the overweight little man — as a small reminder to forestall any thoughts of treachery — when they turned into another well-lit corridor with, again, two soldiers guarding a door at its far end. Damon took a better hold of the king and set the small dagger against the monarch's throat.

"Drop your arms," he called out to the pair. "Unless you'd care to see your king's blood washing the floor! Now, open that door and enter before us...but carefully now."

The two guards took one look at the hell-fire smoldering in his eyes. The torchlight flickered across his horns so that they glinted wickedly and, shuddering, they hastened to obey. One unlocked the door and they scrambled within, leaving their weapons lying in a pile on the stone floor. Damon and the king followed them closely.

Glancing warily about, Damon saw Banes-lord lying upon an obsidian altar, strangely-carved with eldritch runes — runes that spoke of Nether Gods and dawn ages best forgotten. They woke a fleeting half-remembrance in him that pulled at his memory with eager claw-like appendages, but he shrugged his shoulders, shaking them from him, and crossed the room.

Grasping the hilt of his blade, he felt a sense of power flow up his arm and into his body, revitalizing him. There was one window in the room. Still holding the now gibbering king, he made for it and looked out onto a terrace, high above the main part of the city. Then there was a rustle behind him.

He whirled about to face a tall dark-robed figure framed in the doorway staring at him with luminous eyes. They caught his own and, as he fell prey to their hypnotic spell, he sensed behind the wizard — for wizard he surely must be — a half-score of the king's guard. His sword arm grew heavy and began to sink as the wizard's eyes bored into his soul.

With a curse, Damon shook his horned head and tossed the king at the dark-robed figure. The wizard fell back startled as the terrified monarch bounced at his feet. Then the Halmanorian wheeled about and sprang out the window to the terrace below.

Running toward its far edge, he heard doors crashing open. When he turned to look, he saw scores of soldiers coming at him. Ignoring the sharp jolts of pain in his feet, he sped on toward the far wall and peered over. The drop was too high. Then he turned to face the oncoming guards.

He slipped Rhiannon's dagger into his belt and drew forth his own from the hilt of his sword. In a low crouch, his dark eyes began to glow and then the pupils and whites were gone and they flashed crimson — with strange inner hell-fires smoldering in their depths.

He met the first line of soldiers with his full daemon-strength upon him. It was not battle; it was a slaughter. None could come near him. His two blades flashed and glowed in the growing dawn and wove a net that none could pierce.

The guards fell like flies: throats slashed, gutted, their chests crushed by the blows of Banes-lord and Damon in his full fury. But the ranks of the soldiers were endless. Ever more Antarians poured through the doorways and threw themselves at him, their blood-splattered bodies forming a mound before him.

Then out of the corner of his eye, the Halmanorian saw two winged forms dropping toward him from high in the morning sky. He knew the battle was over for him now. He couldn't fight the winged carrion-creatures as well as this endless stream of guards. But he was beyond reason now. There was but one thought in his mind and that was to slay as many foes as he could ere they slew him.

It would not be soon that they'd forget this day and the fury of Damon of Halmanor.

He ignored the winged menace and fall back to the struggle at hand with renewed fury.

"Drink, Banes-lord!" he cried above the clangor of battle.

Suddenly there was a rush of air and a roar of great wings beating. He felt himself lifted into the sky by two strong pairs of arms. He drew back his blades to cut their grip when he realized that these were not winged beasts, but Halwaren!

As soon as the knowledge flashed across his battle-fogged mind, he ceased his struggling and went limp, letting the winged men bear him high above the city. He looked down and saw the soldiers scrambling about like ants and he laughed as he thought of their frustration and dismay.

Fear not, little men, he vowed. You'll have another chance at me, for my blade is yet thirsty for your blood. There will be a final reckoning.

VI

Damon lounged in a large stone chair in the council chamber of the Halwaren. The room had high ceilings and its windows looked down from the southern heights of the Peredur Mountains. Cyfaill Caer it was called — this home of the winged-folk — and it was carved from the living stone of those mountains. In it, Damon felt strangely at ease; the long years of constant strife seemed to slip from his shoulders — years of reaving and slaying — and in their place was a hint of other times, times of peace.

He was clean and well-rested, for he had finally bathed the filth of the past two days' trials from him and slept for almost nine hours. While he was sleeping, the winged-folk had sewn a new tunic for him, emblazoned with the strange crest that he wore over his right breast. Rhiannon fingered it, when he woke.

"What do you call this?" she asked.

He looked at the circular motif with its three swirling lines and then shrugged his massive shoulders, saying:

"Why nothing. I've always worn it, never really questioning what it was."

"We call it a Triskell," she said, "and for us it symbolizes our world and our freedom of flight. Here. Take this, if you would."

She drew a similar symbol from a small pouch at her side and placed it in his hand. It was worked in gold and hung from a fine chain of the same metal. He nodded his thanks.

૭૪৪৩

Now, in the council chamber, Rhiannon sat to his right, her dagger once more in its sheath on her thigh, and smiled as she poured him another flagon of wine. Gwythlen, Lord of the Halwaren, was speaking.

"It began some three years ago, when King Glosar gained his new advisor. He called himself Caragh in those days, but soon revealed his true name: Noth Karsegrath, a dark wizard from foul and ancient Kasque. Cursed be the day he set foot in Antar.

"For you see, before his coming we could mingle freely with the Antarians and trade and take our ease within that city's walls. But after his arrival, strange laws began to be passed. Taxes rose — they seemed to double every month—and there were restrictions upon everything, even curfews. And so the people of Antar rebelled and that is when the king's guard gained its sudden influx of mercenary soldiers. They are hard and cruel men, though they fare better in groups than singly.

"Still, in a very short while, the rebellion was put down—before it ever really started—and Karsegrath's iron hand has ruled Antar since those days."

So he'd named them aright, Damon thought as the Halwaren Lord spoke. Puppet warriors, indeed! And yet—what with their numbers and a wizard's might behind them—they were a formidable force to contend with.

Then he turned from his thoughts for Gwythlen was still speaking. "About the same time, those evil winged creatures appeared on Mount Crithner—the Gods alone know how you escaped them. Fortune was with you in that Rhiannon was there to give you aid and, later, it was she who convinced us to send Tallowith and Mynth to rescue you in Antar, where she knew you had gone.

"But to continue: it was Karsegrath who convinced the townsfolk that the coming of those beasts was our doing. By Tarlwyth's Oaken Staff, as if we would have aught to do with those creatures, pawns of wizards as they are. No, they aid him in his spells and in return he offers them sacrifices. They'll not be so eager to aid him now that you've escaped, I'll wager.

"Still, for the most part, the Antarians believe his lies and now we are hunted as if we, ourselves, were the beasts. Their greatest sport—and these are mostly the mercenaries, mind you—is to take our folk alive so that they may cage us, only to torment and slay us later, at their leisure. There are some twenty of our kin in the dungeons neath Glosar's keep at this moment.

"And that was what Rhiannon was doing in Antar, when first you met her. We have yet some friends within those walls and there was one who had information for us...information as to how we might free our own from their dank cells. Alas, he is slain, as you know well enough.

"But this has gone on too long. We are determined to put an end to both this fat little king and his dark ruler, once and for all. And now—with your coming, Damon—I think we have a plan that will win this coming battle for us."

Damon looked up at Gwythlen, a question in his dark eyes. He thought back over the past two days, of that altar-like rock on Mount Crithner where he had been nailed. He glanced at his hands and a dark fury directed at the Antarians welled up within him again.

"And how is that?" he asked.

"Why," Gwythlen replied, "we would use you as our bait."

Damon rose from his seat and made a move toward the Halwaren Lord, his brow furrowed with sudden anger. But Gwythlen held out his hands.

"Hold, friend Damon," he said. "Hold your wrath and hear me out."

And then he told of the plan that he had conceived. As he spoke, Damon settled back into his chair and smiled as he learnt of his part in it.

He agreed readily enough.

CƏEO

The talk went on for sometime thereafter and at last Rhiannon drew Damon aside.

"The hour grows late, Damon," she said, "and some more rest would do you no harm. We'd not want you falling asleep on the battlefield. Come, I'll show you where you may lie down for awhile."

She arose and took him by the arm.

They walked until they came to the door of her bed-chamber and there she stopped and looked him in the eye. For a moment, she drew back from the dark side of his soul. But then she gazed deeper and was drawn into a warmth that was hidden behind the black shadows that frightened most from looking deeper.

She saw deep woods and rolling moors. She saw sunlight playing across the intertwined branches of summer bowers and twilights that were filled with the quiet peaceful ways of the High Aelves. With wonder, she saw all this and more and then she smiled and drew him into her chamber. Softly but firmly, she closed the door behind them.

VII

Three hours before dawn, two hundred pairs of wings lifted from Cyfaill Caer, which lay within the craggy claw of Mount Gwess, high in the Peredur Mountains. The sound of their rising was like a sudden thunder in the quiet night air. Gwythlen and Rhiannon were in the lead, closely followed by Tallowith and Mynth who were again bearing Damon in their strong arms. Once in flight, their passage was soundless save for the odd rattle of a sword's sheath against a long light spear.

There was still an hour left before the sun would rise when they came in sight of Antar. Noiselessly, they glided down toward her walls and like phantoms, sped over them and into the city. They passed unnoticed and, once within, they made for the main market square, which lay just before the walls of the inner keep. After dropping Damon down in an off-shooting alleyway, they hid themselves on the rooftops of the houses overlooking the square.

Dawn came.

With the growing light, Damon stepped from the alleyway and into the center of the square. He stood there — bathed in the rays of the morning sun — and shouted insults at the soldiers on the walls of the inner keep. They looked down at him in disbelief. He continued to taunt them and then drew Banes-lord, his long shining sword. Wielding it two-handedly, he shook it in their direction and dared them to come to their deaths.

From the walls, the guards hurled their spears at the demonic figure before them. With unbelievably quick flicks of his sword, Damon sent their spears spinning from him to lie broken and useless in the market square. Then the guards shouted for assistance.

Already from behind him, Damon could hear the approach of booted feet rattling on the cobblestoned streets as the soldiers from the outer walls came running. Before him, the great oaken doors of the keep's main gate opened with a protesting creak and from within spewed yet more of the king's soldiery. They were still fearful of him, but when they saw that this time he had no hope of escape, they laughed, clashing their swords against their spears as they ran. They were mercenaries and were paid to fight, not hide. Damon leapt to meet the first line of the oncoming soldiers.

Even as he charged and the soldiers filled the market-place, there was a sudden roar in the morning air that drowned out the clash of arms and the battle-cries of the soldiers. The sky above the square was filled with the Halwaren and they cast their spears in a shower of death. In less than a moment, a third of the soldiers lay upon the cobblestones, dead and dying. Their cries filled the air as they were impaled upon long spears that sprouted like extra appendages from their backs and chests. Then the Halwaren swooped down.

It was carnage. The soldiers were completely demoralized by the unexpected onslaught of the winged-folk. And then there was Damon: eyes blazing with a crimson fury as he wreaked havoc among them. The Antarians turned and fled for the keep.

They made it through the gates, but not in time to close them. It would have made little difference to the Halwaren, anyway. Still, Damon and the winged-folk were already there, swords flashing and sinking into the guards, leaving them screaming and wallowing in their own blood and entrails. Some of the Halwaren flew over the walls — striking down the guards upon them — and then plunging into the melee within the inner keep.

By this time, the people of Antar realized what was happening. They poured from their homes armed with kitchen knives, table legs with jagged ends, in fact, anything they could lay their hands on. They fell upon the soldiers as well. Whatever suspicions of the winged-folk that had been planted in their minds, they despised the mercenaries more. Insults, beatings, robbery and rape were on the citizens' minds as they dragged struggling soldiers down and tore them to pieces.

Into this chaos there came a sudden silence. Upon the steps leading into the main hall of the inner keep, a dark cloaked figure appeared. Noth Karsegrath! His strange luminous eyes glowed brightly — even in the glare of the morning sun — and they locked upon Damon's. Damon felt his strength fail him. His body went numb, sword arm dropping, and his spirit was grasped in a vise-grip that was slowly squeezing his very life's essence from him. Not a person stirred as all watched this eerie tableau that was enacted before them.

Damon sank to his knees beneath Karsegrath's soul-sapping gaze. Try as he might, there was nothing he could do. His body was no longer his to command. His chest felt as though it were on fire as he strove to free himself from this sorcerous enslavement of his will. Across his shoulders, his massive muscles rippled in involuntary spasms with his effort. The half-healed wounds on his hands and feet opened again and he felt his mind being torn asunder with the pain and futility of this unequal struggle. He was half-daemon, but Karsegrath had mastered greater daemons than he.

Then a small winged figure rose into the air behind the wizard. It was Rhiannon. In one hand she held her dagger, drawn from its sheath upon her thigh. For a brief moment she hovered, her wings beating a noiseless rhythm in the tension-charged air. Then she dove toward the back of the unsuspecting wizard. Her small dagger plunged between his shoulder blades and he staggered, but did not fall. He turned around slowly and lifted the ebony sword that he had held loosely in his right hand, throughout his confrontation with Damon.

The great black blade was high above his head and Rhiannon stared at it with a hypnotic fascination as she waited for it to sink into her soft flesh. She should have realized that ordinary steel could never slay a sorcerer. As this thought ran through her mind, the dark figure before her stiffened.

The point of Damon's enchanted sword, Banes-lord, came ripping through the wizard's chest, stopping with a jolt as its hilt rammed into his back. She was showered with a sickly yellow-green blood, too thick to be human's. With a horrible cry, Karsegrath understood that in breaking his concentration upon Damon, he had given his foe the opportunity he had needed to free himself from his spell of entrapment. Then the wizard was dead and he fell across Rhiannon, Banes-lord's point narrowly missing her slim waist.

Damon sprinted up the stairs to where the two lay, his body crying out in agony at the abuse he was forcing upon the newly-opened wounds on his feet. He ignored the pain completely. Reaching the pair, he gripped Banes-lord by its hilt and, pulling the blade free, he grasped the dead wizard by the nape of his neck and threw him to one side.

He lifted a shaken Rhiannon to her feet and spared her a warm thankful glance. Then whirling about, he faced the soldiers once more — shining sword in hand and thirsty for yet more blood.

During this time, winged-folk, soldiers and townspeople had all stood frozen as they watched the strange mind-battle between

the wizard and Damon. Now the mercenaries suddenly realized that their master — the one that had clothed, fed and paid them their ill-earned gold — was dead and they were at the mercy of his foes. As one, they dropped their weapons and held forth their hands in submission.

Damon looked down on them and laughed sardonically. Then he called out to Gwythlen:

"Ho! Wing-lord! The city is yours!"

VIII

It was much later in that eventful day. The hired soldiers had all been locked in the dungeons beneath the keep and the Halwaren that had been there were now released. The elders of the townsfolk had been meeting with Gwythlen and others of the Halwaren in the main hall of the inner keep to decide what must be done with the mercenaries and the town itself.

There was no need to decide the fate of Glosar — the fat little king — for he had thrown himself from the heights of the keep when he had seen how the battle had gone.

Suddenly, Gwythlen looked about.

"Where is Damon?" he asked.

Rhiannon sat up with a start and then all within the hall realized that he had not been seen for some time. One of the townsfolk spoke up and said:

"Gunther — one of our lads on the West Gate — mentioned him to me. He came there a few hours past. Seems he ignored them all and walked right out of the gate, calling out in some strange language. A great dark-brown steed answered his call — came out of the forest, it did, and had a long ornamental horn set into the leather that covered its brow.

"Gunther said he mounted the beast wearily and bent over to murmur something in its ear. Then they were away into the woods and he hasn't seen them since."

Rhiannon rose and made for the doorway but was halted by Gwythlen's words.

"Stay your flight, daughter. Damon was never meant to bide long with us."

Rhiannon turned about and glared at her father, rebellion flaring in her eyes.

But he continued speaking, saying, "O daughter, daughter, do you not yet know who it was that we had with us? Can you not recall the legends of our homeland—far to the north—the legends of Damon the Damned: half-aelf, half-daemon? The cursed last son of the House of Halmanor? Who did you think we had walking amongst us? Thought you that those horns were mere decoration?

"No, it is better for us all that he has gone this quickly, for wherever Damon is, ruin and death are soon to follow. I only wish that I could have thanked him properly for the part he played today. But it is too late, now. He is gone."

Rhiannon's shoulders sagged as he spoke and she made her way back to the council table, realizing the truth in his words. But deep within her heart she remembered a glimpse of light within a dark tormented soul and one golden night that would be forever etched in her memory. Then she knew that, someday, they would meet again and she wondered that she felt a tremor of fear at that thought.

Dark God Laughing

Death comes unannounced, abruptly he may
thwart you; no one knows his features, nor the
sound of his tread approaching.

—Glasfryn, Welsh, 19th century

Harad and Wryn rode into Safehid with the noon sun high above them. The town was lodged in the foothills of the Peredur Mountains and its name was apt enough, considering that it was the haunt of every outlaw from the foothills themselves to as far west as the wide sweeps of the Kormenick Woods. Here a man could rest in safety, far from the reaches of guardsman or bounty hunter.

A rich trade route ran between the wood and hills, tying Jarawen to the north with the rich coastal cities of Antar, Calthoren and Twenarp along the Southern Sea. From Jarawen came mule trains laden with furs, jewels, and gold; finely crafted dwarf-wrought wonders, worked in nameless metals, and treasures from the tombs of the Dead Kings; and slaves. The slaves were mostly women: sleek dark-haired wood-folk, full-bodied northern wenches with their flaming rust locks, and sometimes — though not often — slender aelfin maidens, shy as does, though tougher than tempered steel. There was a ready market for them in the south.

Harad was of the mountain-folk: strong as a bull, with a shock of black hair as dark as the underwing of a raven. He wore traveling clothes: plain brown trousers and shirt, unpolished mail, helm of

269

leather, boots the same. He had wide brows, heavy cheeks that bore the blue tattoos of the mountain-folk, and his eyes had a slight slant to their cast. A broad sword hung on his back. In his belt was a dagger, while in his hand he carried a heavy spear which he rested on the neck of his mount. The horse was mountain-bred as well: thick stocky legs, heavy body. It was built for endurance, not speed.

Wryn was of the Cities, standing a half-head under Harad's six feet. His slender limbs belied quick reflexes and surprising strength. His hair, too, was black, though thin and streaked with sudden greys. His clothing was similar to Harad's, save for his boots which were city-made. Black leather they were, with bright buckles that glistened in the sun. A narrow rapier hung at his belt; a short bow and quiver was slung over his pommel.

He shifted uncomfortably in the saddle, thankful that they were to rest. These mountain horses were sturdy, to be sure, but their gait was ungainly and awkward for one used to the slender mounts of the south and their smooth pace.

"Here then?" he asked Harad as they approached a sign heralding an inn.

The Roc's Nest, he read to himself.

Harad nodded. They dismounted before its white-washed walls, wrapping their reins about the hitching rail with practiced speed. Harad stretched, scratched his crotch, and grinned.

"In Safehid," he said, "any place'll do. In all the mountains, this one town is safe from king's men or bount'ers. We can hire our men here, too. There's always a cutthroat or two lying 'bout looking for a job."

"I'll be happy just to clear the damned dust from my throat," Wryn said, spitting on the road. An ale would taste like the gods' own nectar at this moment.

The sudden dark of the inn blinded them as they stepped over the threshold. Outside, the summer sun hung high and bright; within, it crept in through high windows set into the thick stone walls, creating pools of shadow, while offering little light. Once their eyes adjusted, they saw that the room was half full. Lounging at tables or playing knar were a dozen or so men: cutthroats, brigands, highwaymen—in short, men much like them. There was little that lay outside of the law that they hadn't tried. They had been thieves, slavers, paid assassins. Now they were to be treasure hunters, if the map and tale that had led them this far told no lies. Only the man who gave them the map knew for sure, and there was no use in asking him. He lay in an alleyway in Twenarp, his throat slit from ear to ear.

They made their way through the tables so that they could sit by the wall where the sunlight streamed over an empty one. Harad loosened a buckle on his shoulder harness and his broad sword slipped from his back, into his hands. Leaning it up against the table, he relaxed in his chair with a sigh.

"Good ale this," he said as the landlord returned to the bar, leaving them with four tankards on their table. "Stolen no doubt." He took another long pull. "Ha! And the better tasting for that."

He was well into his second while Wryn still nursed his first.

"Six men," Harad said at last, wiping his mouth on his tunic. "More than that and they'd slit our throats and take the booty for themselves. Less, and we'll have too much to carry."

"And a guide?" Wryn asked, his voice was slick with a cutting edge to it.

"Bedamned to a guide! So I lost us in the Quags. Can't you lay off about that? Haven't I lived my whole youth in this mountains? Don't I know every trail, every gully, every rise?"

"Then why've you waited till now to fetch the treasure?"

"I didn't know of it, till now." Harad's voice rose in anger. "I didn't have a map then, did I?"

Why was Wryn always baiting him? Eight years Harad had known him, and he'd not changed since that first night. Usually, he could put up with Wryn's taunting—after all, it was his way and Harad had become used to it. But these were his mountains. Riding through the lands of his youth had awoken a belligerence in him. He took the map from his belt and stretched it out on the table.

"See here?" he said, his voice still loud. "This is the trade route, and here—" he jabbed with his finger " —is where we leave it. Along here, then, till Cathan's Well, then along this cleft until…"

"Ye come to a dead end," finished a half-interested voice from behind them.

Their hands were on their sword hilts as they spun about.

"Who…?" began Harad. He shut his mouth and stared.

He knew Safehid well. It was an outlaw roost, a home for any brigand who had the gold to pay his way. Many's the strange being that Harad had seen in its streets and inns. There'd been winged folk from north of Antar, worm-riders from the far east, dwarf lords, and once even two exiled aelves; nothing like this, though.

He lounged in his chair as though it were a throne, with a comely wench leaning against him, one hand lightly caressing his leg, the other resting on his broad shoulders. Everything about him was large: chest, arms, legs. He was dressed in plain traveling leathers and boots with brass buckles. Leaning against a chest, close at hand, was a long sword, its hilt-guard carved into the semblance of many screaming skulls. But it was his head that brought an oath to Harad's lips.

Long curved horns twisted from his brow in a full circle, pointed ears sprang from his thatch of gold-brown hair, and his eyes shone with crimson lights deep within their almost black depths. Relaxed though he seemed, those eyes belied his intensity. A broad handsome face was his, yet it was overshadowed with these features which bespoke of a...

"Daemon!" Harad hissed.

"Aye," said the stranger, balancing a tankard on his knee, "ye've the name aright." Absently, he traced a design in the moisture that clung to the side of his tankard. When he joined the last line to the first, it began to smoke. "Now what could ye possibly be searching for in that hell-hole of the mountains?"

"Yadudd's Tem..." Harad began, forgetting himself.

He looked at the symbol on the tankard and shuddered. He tried to remember where he'd seen it before, even while he cursed his loose tongue.

"Yadudd's Temple," the stranger completed. "A strange place that...filled with treasure, it's said, and cursed to boot." He laughed. "Are they not all though? But Yadudd's...I'd not thought it still stood..."

Harad stood suddenly, spilling his half-full tankard as he scrambled for his map. Making it into a tight roll, he thrust it back into his belt.

"What matter's it to you?" he asked. "'Tis but a fable, as anyone knows."

His hands were shaking. To hide the fact, he grasped his belt with one, his still-sheathed sword with another.

CHARETTE 78

"Just so," said the stranger. "Naught but a fable." He peered closely at Harad, an evil smile awake on his lips. "Is there fear in ye, man?"

Man. To some it was a catchword, a way to address someone whose name was unknown. From this creature, though, it only served to emphasize his otherworldiness. All of Harad's childhood fears reared up in his mind. He remembered the tales told round campfires and in safe holdings of the daemons and devils that haunted the mountains: quick to anger, unforgiving, relentless in their pursuit of a chosen victim.

Aye, the ends of men daemon-marked were assured, prolonged and bloody. Once Harad saw a man brought back by hunters. They'd found him in a small gully, while tracking a pair of bighorns. Daemon-slain, they avowed, making ward-signs. Harad was no more than eleven at the time. Big-eyed, he crept forward and looked at the victim's corpse. Retching, he turned away. The man was yet alive. His chest was torn open, the heart ripped from it, and yet he lived. For three days and four nights, something kept the man alive. He writhed in pain and screamed during most of those long hours. When he died at last, there was no need to bury him. A black smoke issued from the gaping hole in his chest, spreading over his body. In moments, there was naught but ashes where he lay.

Harad's hand unconsciously shaped a ward-sign, as the memories washed over him. He could taste the bile in his throat again, could see that man's anguished face. Savagely, he shook his head and glared at the stranger before him.

"I do not fear you, if that's your meaning," he said.

But he turned on his heel and made for the door, before his fear broke loose.

Wryn followed him, angry at how much Harad had given away. He was puzzled at the exchange between Harad and the horned man as well; even more puzzled at his comrade's obvious fear. He looked back over his shoulder as they left. The stranger disengaged himself from a kiss with his wench and grinned at him, white teeth flashing, the red glint in his eyes stronger. Frowning thoughtfully, Wryn turned away.

"I'll not bide here tonight," Harad said when they were outside. "Let's gather the men we need and ride."

"But it takes time to get good men," Wryn said. He nodded back toward the inn. "He was fearsome enough, but he was only toying with you. What's to fear? There are men like him everywhere: picking fights, bored...I've seen them in every town I've ever ridden through."

Hared nodded. "Aye, but they were men. Listen to me, my city-born friend. You're not mountain-bred, so speak softly. When a daemon marks you — and he might have marked us — it is a time to fear. Naught can stop them...naught can sway them from you, if you're their chosen prey."

"He was no daemon," Wryn said. "What would he be doing here, amongst men, sitting in a bar like any common brigand, a wench on his knee?"

"Choosing, Wryn, choosing..."

CR&O

Harad and Wryn rode from Safehid a good three hours before the nightfall. The sun was westering over Kormenick Wood, lighting the slopes of the mountains on their right with a rich, crimson hue.

The mountains are bleeding, Wryn thought.

He shook the thought from his mind. He was beginning to sound too much like Harad.

Behind the pair rode a half-dozen men. They were all mountain-bred, save for the ebony-skinned Ismro, who hailed from the Plains of Tanbu, far to the west where the jungles of Kasque lie deep and impenetrable.

The better part of the afternoon had been spent in gathering men — making sure they were equipped and armed — buying horses, and supplies. Harad was like a madman: never bartering for the goods, accepting the first price with his eye ever over his shoulder. Wryn remembered a hundred trials they'd faced together — a werewolf in the north where they'd been slaving, an undead mummy in the tomb of the Dead Kings — and couldn't recall Harad ever being so nervous before. When, at last, they left Safehid, he'd sighed with relief. Harad's fears had communicated themselves to him. He shook them from himself and a sarcastic comment formed in his mind. He left it lying there. Harad seemed still nervous and there was little gain in baiting him now.

That night they camped along the trade route. Harad put the site under heavy guard. All that befell from his precautions was that they set the men a-grumbling. Harad had a feeling, though. He remembered the look in the stranger's eye and knew that they'd not seen the last of him—not by any means.

The next day saw his fears bearing fruit. Looking back along their trail, Harad saw a mounted figure silhouetted upon a hilltop. A gut-wrenching terror shook Harad, before he could take a firm grip of his fear. He stepped his mount ahead and spoke in a low voice to the dark-skinned Ismro. When Harad was done explaining, Ismro grinned. As they turned another corner in the trail, the black man put heels to his horse and made for the low hills. Harad smiled. A mountainer would have quailed at the task to be sure; Ismro had no qualms about ambushing their pursuer, be he man or daemon, aye, and he had no fear as well. Feeling that the situation was now well under control, Harad whistled a bawdy tune and relaxed somewhat.

Later in the day they met a heavily-guarded caravan taking slaves southward. Pointedly, Harad had the men ride as far to the side as they could, arms upraised to show that they offered no threat. In the ox-pulled wagons, dusky-eyed maids stared beseechingly at them; flame-haired northern wenches offered their ample bodies as an obvious reward for their rescue. Harad kept his men where they were, smiling and nodding to the guards. As the caravan passed them, they put spurs to their mounts and rode at a gallop until the wagons were far behind.

When they slowed down, Harad heard one of the men make a mocking comment about the wide yellow streak that ran down the back of Harad's vest. He rode up to the man, hand on sword hilt.

"Listen, Gart," he said, "and listen well. Those guardsmen would as soon cut us down for an imagined attempt against their wagons as a real one. The booty that awaits us in the Temple is worth the price of those sluts a thousand times over, and I'll not take a chance on losing it. Do you hear? But if you'd care to try my sword against yours..."

"Harad!" Wryn called, forestalling Gart's reply.

Harad glanced ahead to see Wryn dismounting. He picked up a leather sack that lay in the dirt and was unfastening its ties. Harad rode to his side and dismounted.

"What is it?" he asked.

"We'll see soon enough," Wryn said with a shrug. "'Twas lying here on the trail…"

His voice faded as he opened the sack. With an oath, he threw it from him. The sack fell with a dull thud to the dirt and from it rolled the grisly remains of a man's head. Ismro's head, Harad realized and he felt sick. Burnt into the brow was a twisting design—no, a rune. Harad recognized it. He had seen it on the stranger's tankard in Safehid, and before as well. He remembered a scroll that Wryn and he had stolen for a wizard from a small crypt west of Calthoren. That same symbol had sealed the tomb. Now he knew why he'd been troubled when the stranger had shaped it on his tankard. That was the signet of the Daketh, the Dark Gods.

Harad looked along their back trail. Wryn followed his gaze and they saw it together: a figure on a hill behind them. Harad could feel the cold smile in those hellish eyes and shuddered. Wryn glanced at him and raised his eyebrows questioningly.

"We go on," Harad said. "May the sun damn him, we'll go on."

CRSO

They made camp for the night, a mile or two up the trail. No one complained about their guard duty that night—not even Gart. They had all seen Ismro's head. The job had taken a darker turn.

"Do you think you were hired just for your brawny backs?" Harad cried, when one of them brought up a mention of more pay in lieu of the unforeseen dangers. "You'll have to earn your cut of the booty with honed blades and nerves better than you're showing now."

The talk of more pay ended there.

They left the trade route the next morning, cutting into the hills. The night had been quiet, and this morn they saw no trace of their pursuer. Ahead lay the trail to Cathan's Well, through a jumble of huge rocks, gullies, and blind alleys. Harad knew the way well, though, and he saw them through the maze without worry. The horses picked up their pace when they smelled the water ahead.

Within moments, they came to the Well—a large, natural basin set into the cliff face, spring fed and ever fresh.

"We'll camp here," Harad said, though it was midafternoon.

The horses could use a rest and so could he. He was a jangle of nerves. The stranger knew they were making for this Well. Harad looked up along the encroaching cliffs and rises. There was no sign.

He dismounted and led his horse to the water. Gart was on his knees at the Well's edge, his head under water. He lifted his head and grinned at Harad through the water that streamed from his hair.

"Kills the dust," he said.

He leaned forward to dunk his head again. Harad was kneeling himself, when he heard the whistle of a shaft. He scrambled for shelter as the arrow struck Gart in the back of the neck. The force of its flight toppled him into the water.

"Ambush!" Harad cried.

He fumbled with the buckles of his sword's sheath until the scabbard came to his side and the great blade was in his hand. Throwing the scabbard aside, he peered over the rocks to see a lone figure striding towards them. It was the stranger.

"Kill him!" Harad roared and his men hastened to obey.

As they charged the approaching figure, Harad retrieved his spear from where it lay by his horse's reins. He glanced at Wryn, saw that he was stringing his bow, and ran to the attack. With surprise, he saw that the stranger was not even armed yet. His blade hung on his back—who had fired the shaft then? His men were almost upon the stranger, when a voice spoke from the rocks to his right.

"Drop your weapons and I might let you live. Tyrr knows why he wants you alive, though."

He spun to see a woman stand from the rocks. She had an arrow notched and a full quiver lay on the rocks, close at hand. Harad's eyes widened as he recognized her to be the stranger's companion from the inn. She was no more than a bar-wench, though. The woman smiled, as if reading his thoughts.

"He said nothing about a shaft through the leg, though." Her aim wavered between Wryn and himself.

Harad took a step forward. The shaft struck him in the thigh and, before Wryn could bring his own bow into play, she had another arrow notched and covering him. Harad dropped his sword and spear to clutch at his leg.

"I'll call off the men," he said through gritted teeth.

"No need," she replied, nodding towards them.

Harad turned. Three of his men were already dead. The fourth was circling about the demonic figure of the stranger, his spear thrust out before him. He lunged and the stranger weaved back, grinning. The sunlight gleamed on his horns; his eyes were in shadow with a faint red gleam to them. The man lunged with his spear again. The stranger swept down his sword, cut the spear in two, and stepped forward. The blade lashed out, cutting through flesh and muscle tissue. Harad's last man fell forward, clutching his gut. The stranger's sword flashed downward and the man was still.

He cleaned his blade and returned it to its sheath before he walked towards them. He moved with grace, for all his bulk. Transferring his blade to his left hand, he took a wineskin from his shoulder and offered it to the pair. The thumb of his left hand held the sheath to his blade. One flick of his wrist and the sheath would fly loose, leaving the blade free. When he was near, he tossed the wineskin. Instinctively, Harad caught it.

"Drink ye deep," said the stranger. "I've saved the half for ye."

The woman put down her bow and disappeared behind the rocks. In that moment, Wryn set shaft to bow and let fly. The stranger's left hand flicked, the sheath flew from his blade and broke the arrow in its flight. Harad stared in disbelief.

"Drink up," said the stranger motioning to the wineskin. "And ye, my bonnie friend—" he spoke to Wryn, his voice low "—do ye mind ye save such tricks for another or I'll yet run ye through."

Numbly, with the stranger's blade threatening him, Harad drank. The wine was good—not sweet, nor yet too dry. He wiped his mouth.

"What's your game?" he asked, trying to hide his fear.

"My game?" The stranger laughed, baring his teeth. "Why I'd be riding to Yadudd's Temple with ye. I've business there, though I don't ken the way."

"You want a share of the treasure?" Harad asked.

Perhaps something might yet be saved from this seemingly doomed endeavor. If the creature wanted to come with them...well, a knife in the back when the moment was ripe, would slay even a daemon. As for the maid...

"Ye might say I wanted a share, aye," was the answer. "All in its own time. Are we biding here this eve?"

"Aye," Harad said.

There was a choice?

"Tessa," the stranger called.

His voice was low still, yet it carried far.

The woman appeared at his call, leading two horses. One was a mountain pony, while the other…the other was a fitting mount for its master. It stood taller than any horse Harad had seen before. It was a dark, almost black, brown and from its brow wound a long horn of purest ivory. A daemon mount for a daemon. Where had the horses been hid? Harad cursed himself for a novice. He'd been expecting an attack, and not noticed a thing.

The woman tossed a roll of white cloth to him.

"Bind it," she said.

He remembered his wound as she spoke. A sudden stab of pain ran up his leg as he moved it. Wryn hastened to his side to aid him. Over his shoulder, Harad appraised the woman. No, she was no bar-wench. Her movements were calculated and sure as she walked on the rough terrain. Where before she'd worn a thin shift, she was now clothed in leather trail-gear. She wore her auburn hair tied back from her face and her features, though not beautiful, were striking. The mouth a little too big, perhaps, the eyes too wide-set. For all that, he remembered her assured manner when she'd held them at bay. No, he decided, for all her obvious charms, she was too dangerous. She would have to die as well.

"What're we to call you?" Wryn asked as he finished binding Harad's wound.

"Ye may call me Damon," the stranger answered, grinning again.

Wryn met Harad's eyes. Though there was pain therein—and fear—it was tempered with anger and a determination to better their captors. For now, Harad could only shrug his shoulders helplessly.

CR80

They left at daybreak the next morn, along the cleft marked on Harad's map. He led the way, followed by Wryn, while Damon and the woman Tessa brought up the rear. It was hard for Harad to ride so. Continually, he wanted to look back at the creature, the daemon.

Again, he lived that moment when the hunters brought the dae-mon-slain man into their village. Aye, they were daemon-marked now — there was no doubt of it. Wryn could never understand. He was not mountain-bred. This was like far-seeing for Harad, a foul promise from his boyhood that reached into his future. It could not be explained in civilized terms.

Wryn was troubled, though not superstitiously so. City-bred he was, with a healthy respect for the strange doings and beings one might meet in the wilds, but he couldn't understand Harad's over-whelming fear. Anger, yes, that he felt. When the time was right, this Damon would feel a length of his steel bite into his back. They would see then how fearsome he truly was.

As for Tessa, she regarded her strange consort and wondered at his thoughts. They would be far from the present situation. That their captives would try and slay him he would have no fear of. He'd a strong arm, a quick ear, and reflexes that could blind a mor-tal; she'd seen them in action often enough.

No, his thoughts would be faring further back into time to where a slim aelfin youth returned to his homesteading to find all his kin slain. That youth forsook his aelfin blood, taking upon himself a mantle of daemonhood — bestowed upon him by the Daketh, the grim Dark Gods. Years had passed since then, since Damon had been that youth, since he rose against his masters. How many year-turn-ings he would never say. She could guess, though, from tales she'd heard.

Looking at the pair that rode ahead of them, she knew he cursed them. They had a choice in life, and what had they chosen? A life of blood and death, a life of scrabbling for wealth and power — swiftly earned, more swiftly fled. And what of he? Where was his choice? Made years ago as a child and irrevocable. Those others, they could end it whenever they pleased: one last haul of good booty, then off for parts unknown to lay down their blades and take their peace. How could Damon settle into a normal life with those horns, that flesh, his lust for blood?

She caught Damon's eye and smiled. Here was his chance, though; a chance to regain what he'd lost. In Yadudd's Temple lay hope. Damon returned her smile. She was a bonnie lass, he decided again, and had treated him well since that day two months past when they'd first —

A man leapt onto his back, cutting through his reveries. Cursing, he twisted and threw his attacker from him. He had time to thank his own foresight in leaving his captives with weapons, before he was grappling with another.

The shock of this man's assault threw him from his mount. They gripped each other for a long moment before Damon broke his grip and tossed him aside. He jumped on him—his boots and weight crushing the man with a terrible force.

How many more were there?

He saw Tessa fighting one, Harad and Wryn dealing with another three. There were more above on the rocks.

He drew his blade. The skull carvings on the hilt-guard seemed to glow, and when the length of steel cleared its sheath, its edge was blood-red and smoking. Banes-lord it was named—a weapon of the Daketh, forged for one of their own. Blood-red and smoking was the blade; blood-red were Damon's eyes...

"Drink, Banes-lord!" he cried and charged their attackers.

His lips were pulled back into a mirthless grin as he raced forward. He saw Harad cut a man open from neck to groin with one stroke of his broadsword, saw Wryn fencing with another, while Tessa rose from the corpse of her own foe. There was a long cut on her leg that was bleeding heavily and one arm hung useless. Then he was upon his own foes.

Banes-lord swung in a wide arc, slicing through one's forearm, shearing through the flesh and bone. Damon's eyes were blazing now. The two others that faced him dropped back to flee for the rocks from which they'd sprung. Damon stopped long enough to finish the first. Another wide sweep of his blade opened the man's chest in a welter of gore.

The other two were in the rocks now. The first he caught as the man clambered above him, Banes-lord ripping into his spine. He grasped the body and threw it below. That hand came away covered with blood: red like his eyes, red like his blade. The last man awaited him at the top of the rise. He threw his blade in desperation, meaning to skewer Damon and flee. The blade sang by Damon's head. Banes-lord swept out to cut the man's legs from him.

Damon topped the rise to stand over him and watch him die. As he stood, the light in his eyes began to dim. He cursed when he saw what he had wrought and sunk his blade into the man's throat to end his misery. Passing a hand over his brow, he looked below. His blood was still humming and singing through his veins, exulting in daemon battle-lust.

Harad stood by Wryn and looked up to where Damon was. He stood above them: behorned, red eyes still glimmering, the long blade in his hand smoking. He watched him descend and go to Tessa's side. She sat hunched over the corpse of the man she'd slain.

"The bastard," he heard her say. "He'd a hidden knife and cut me twice before I could finish him."

"Why?" Harad asked when Damon was done binding the maid's wound. "Why'd they attack us?"

Damon rose and lifted one of the corpses.

"Recognize him?"

Harad shook his head.

"He was in Safehid when ye were," Damon said. "I'm not surprised they waylaid us, not the way ye were throwing around the gold. They thought to find a good-sized booty on our bodies."

Harad caught Wryn looking at him, but he turned away and said no more.

CR80

"It's still a dead end," Damon remarked a day later.

They were at the end of the cleft with cliff faces rising on all sides save the way they'd come. Harad pulled the map out in response and passed it to him, saying:

"There's a way through. See the mark there? 'Tis a hidden door, built into the stone."

Harad and Wryn dismounted and went forward to investigate. Damon murmured a word to Tessa and she smiled.

"I'll live," she said simply.

Damon turned his attention to the pair then, stroking the neck of his horned mount's neck as he did. Storm-strider was its name. He came from the far northern wastes, where the trackless forests ran for leagues without sign of man; where there were grasslands and moors it would take a man three weeks to cross. Damon realized that his thoughts were drifting and shook them swiftly from him. Beyond this cliff was what he sought—no more delay. He moved Storm-strider ahead and dismounted before the rock face. Shoul-

dering the other two aside, he ran his hands along the rock, tracing every rift, every rill, every small cranny. At last, he stepped back.

"Ye be sure?" he said to Harad. "This is the place?"

Silently, Harad pointed to the map and Damon looked at it once more.

"Aye, so it is. Stand ye back then, if you value your lives."

An odd turn of a phrase, Tessa thought as he spoke, considering what he had in store for them.

The pair hastened out of the way.

Taking a deep breath, Damon placed his hands against the cliff and began to chant. To those listening, the words had no meaning. There was a familiar ring to them, though, as if they should have known them. Of an old tongue they were—aelfin, daemon; harking back to the days of the Tuathan. Damon's back was hunched. Beneath his shirt, his muscles rippled with his effort.

"What...?" Wryn said, his voice gone soft.

He gasped as tiny seams cracked in the rock. They emanated from where Damon had placed his hands against the stone.

On Damon chanted, his voice gaining in volume. Energy crackled in the air, building up upon itself, until there came a rumble from deep within the cliff. Harad and Wryn stumbled further back as the whole rock face trembled and shook. The seams by Damon's hands opened into cracks. Shards of solid rock fell about him. One final groan escaped the cliff before it fell in on itself, jagged rocks cascading about the daemonic form that had wrought its doom. The air filled with dust. Harad and Wryn stared aghast, trying to see through the cloud, while Tessa merely smiled.

As it slowly cleared, they saw Damon standing there: rocks piled to each side of him, his body coated with dust. Before him was an opening in the stone, black and ominous. Damon shrugged his shoulders to loosen his stiff neck muscles. Turning, he grinned, red glimmerings flickering deep within his eyes.

"Ye'll abide?" he asked Tessa.

She nodded her agreement. She was too weak to venture onward now. Damon beckoned to the others.

"Will ye come then?"

Still shaken, the pair picked their way gingerly over the broken ground to follow him inside.

"A torch...?" Wryn began.

It was utterly dark within, save for a small spot of light in the far distance.

"Can ye not see?" Damon asked. He turned and they saw his eyes glowing like those of some great cat's in the dark. "No matter. Follow me closely."

Now would be the time to strike him, mused Harad, only Damon soon left them behind. He strode sure-footed through the dark as though it were lit by a noon sun. They followed at a slower pace, testing each foot before them ere they set it down. When they reached the distant light, Damon was facing them once more. They were at the end of the tunnel.

Before them was a hidden valley with steep cliffs on all sides; the tunnel was its only entrance. In its midst was an enormous structure that could only be Yadudd's Temple. It was wide and squatted toad-like amidst a clutter of dead trees and grasses. Though the sun was bright, the building seemed to stand in shadow except for where the light gleamed dully on the metal seams in its dark stone. An aura of evil arose from it that spoke of the long night when the Old Gods trod Woldenar in its endless shadow, before the birth of stars or moon or sun.

"Yududd, Myken...Yurlogh...I smell your taint..." Harad heard Damon say to himself.

By now the brigand was having third and fourth thoughts about the wisdom of this venture. In Twenarp, it had seemed almost like a jaunt: ride up through the mountains of his youth, hire a few men for protection and cartage, then off for a life of ease and plenty in Calthoren, or perhaps even far Kasque. Now, though...there was this creature that led them...this daemon...

Suddenly, he realized that Damon was regarding him steadily with those hellish eyes of his.

Death...death...death...they seemed to chant.

He clasped the dagger at his belt. Now he must strike; strike now or never. The eyes bore into him, daring him to try. Harad recalled the speed of that sword that hung on Damon's back, recalled his battle-lust, his joy for slaying.

"The treasure..." he said. The words stuck in his throat.

"Aye," said Damon.

He turned abruptly and strode to the massive portal of the temple. Calling a word into the air, he watched it hover in the shadows lapping about the building and set his will to it. The word moved forward to dissolve into the huge doorway. Of what were they made, those doors...stone? Metal? Whatever they were, they swung open with an ominous silence and Damon stepped within. The pair followed.

It was dark inside, compared to the sunlight that burnished the cliffs without. Harad's eyes soon adjusted to the dim red glow that lit the interior. There seemed to be no source for the light that lit that vast hall. Walls—cliff-high and impossible, considering the squat features of the building as seen from the outside—reared up from a floor inlaid with precious stones. The jewels spelled out a rune: the signet of the Daketh. Harad was past his fear for the moment. It lay hidden and buried within him, buried under the weight of his lust.

The wealth herein was unbelievable. At the far end of the chamber was a huge bloated altar, cast of solid gold with shimmering gold drapes behind it. Before the altar was a pool of some thick dark liquid. Misshapen statues—also cast of gold—bordered it. Wealth hung in a blasphemous splendor throughout...only how could they retrieve it?

Break down a statue perhaps? Harad thought.

One alone was worth the whole of Calthoren itself. Only how to transport it?

"Unbelievable," Wryn murmured. "But how do we get it out?"

"My thoughts exactly," Harad said. "Still, with a little labour, we could break up a few of those statues and live in such wealth as could scarcely be imagined for untold years."

"If," Damon said, "you live that long."

They turned at his words, bewildered. Having forgotten his presence, he appeared more horrible than ever, especially in these surroundings.

"I had another destiny in mind for ye twain," Damon continued. His eyes were flaring into a bright crimson as he spoke. "Aye, ye twain can buy me something that all the wealth herein never could." His voice rose, echoing and rumbling throughout the hall. "I seek a form that I might wear and so walk among those of my own once again. To walk among men and not be spat upon, nor cursed as a daemon."

Harad's eyes widened and he began to understand. The creature wanted a mortal form, and they were to be his means of attaining it. His hand crept for the thong that would loose his broadsword from his back. He might die, but he would die fighting.

"With this form," Damon said, tapping his broad chest, "I can never know peace, can never lay aside my blade when I tire of the blood-letting."

"What is this to us?" Harad asked.

The strap was loose and slowly he lowered the blade at his back. Softly, softly...oh, let the daemon not see.

"Be ye still!" Damon cried. Echoes roiled in the air. "I curse ye, manlings, bloodsuckers, bedamned leeches! Ye'd sell thy own mothers, had ye the chance, and even so, shall I sell thee."

Harad's sword whipped from its sheath to leap for Damon's throat only he was no longer there. A twist aside and Banes-lord was in his hand. It licked out, spinning the blade from Harad's hand. Arcing above his head, it returned in time to strike Wryn's hastily drawn rapier, sundering it with a sudden crash that numbed Wryn's arm to his elbow.

Returning his attention to Harad, he aborted the mountain man's attempt to draw his dagger. Tossing Banes-lord into the air, he caught it by the blade and struck Harad across his brow with its hilt. Harad fell to the floor with blood dripping into his eyes, still scrabbling for his dagger. Damon's foot came down and his boot crushed Harad's hand against the cold stone, splintering the bones. Still holding Banes-lord by its blade, Damon swung it about, smashing against Wryn's skull so that he dropped with a dull thud. He smiled upon the fallen pair.

"The sacrifices await," he said, "though in none too good a shape."

ᏟᎡᎦᎧ

Harad awoke tied to the golden altar. His crushed hand throbbed with pain, and the arrow wound on his leg was open again. He could feel the blood wet upon his thigh. Beside him lay his comrade Wryn, eyes wide open and staring.

Shock has him, Harad thought until he saw the thin cut that severed Wryn's throat. It was the last thing he saw through his own eyes, for Damon's blade cut through his throat and ended his life.

Damon caught the blood in his hands and walked to the pool. He let the dark blood seep through his fingers and mingle with the waters of the pool. Retrieving Banes-lord, he stood by the edge and stared into its depths.

"Awake, Yadudd!" he cried in the old tongue, the tongue of gods, dark and light. "Awake, ye slimy godling! The price has been paid: two souls and fresh blood. Do ye think I ken not the old ways of calling ye? Awake, ye damned toad! Did ye think I would never come? Aye, I thought ye long gone and thy temple a ruin. I ken better now. Awake, Yadudd! Ye be summoned. Ye are in my debt now and must pay my reckoning. Awake!"

Beneath the surface of the pool, the waters stirred. Damon stepped back, smiling grimly.

Yadudd was awaking.

The water churned and bubbled; black gasses, that reeked of long dead corpses, filled Damon's nostrils. The waters grew still as a substantial shadow formed in the midst of the pool: shapeless, bloated, unnatural.

Yadudd was come.

"Ah, Daelin, Daelin Wood-wise," hissed a reptilian voice from that darkness. "Or does that name awake memories best forgotten? It surely no longer suits thee, sweet Daelin."

Damon shuddered at the sound of that name. Once he bore it, aye, once he wore the slim frame of an aelf and lived a life free from strife. 'Til Noth Seganth came to the holding of his kin; 'til he destroyed all that Damon held true and forced the youth into his cursed choice...

"What would ye of me, sweet Daelin?"

"An ending," Damon said quietly. "An ending to this curse. Ye be fed; ye owe me a debt now. This is my price: freedom from this form. Give to me what once was mine. Make me Daelin Wood-wise once more in truth."

"Unwise," Yadudd told him. "A poor choice. But ye speak the truth: I must give it to thee, though we lose the greatest reaper of souls that ere trod Woldenar. Must we go hungry for your whim, sweet Daelin? No more harvests of tasty souls?"

"I have spoken my wish."

"Then so be it, Daelin once named Damon. But for how long?"

The question hung in the air. Damon could not answer it. His body was wracked with an unbearable pain that seemed to rip the very flesh from his bones. Darkness swept over him like a living thing: encasing him, tearing at him, shattering his soul. He retched blood and bile, writhing in torment all the while.

Until it ended.

Slowly, he got to his feet. Standing shakily, he looked down at himself. He was lithe and slim; the terrible weight of the horns was gone from his brow. The clothes that had fitted snugly on his huge frame, hung like rags now. Sudden joy rose up in his heart and he shook his arms defiantly in the air.

"Praise be!" he cried. "I am freed at last."

As the echoes of his cry faded in the great hall, a whisper of sound arose from behind him. He turned with a sinking heart to see a great mass of hellish beings dancing throughout the hall: daemons and ghouls, weres and the long-dead. The daemons all had great curling horns stringing from their brows. They capered and mimed obscenities about a huge bloated man-like figure in their midst; its features more toad-like than human. In the thing's swollen hand was Tessa.

"Yes," the toad-thing said in Yadudd's voice, "we found this pretty maid without, awaiting thee." A daemon leapt up, clawing for her. "I think she needs thy protection, sweet Daelin...but can ye save even thy own life?"

The massed creatures scrambled for him. Cursing, what once was Damon reached for Banes-lord where it lay at his feet. His movements were too slow, too sluggish, and the blade...he could not lift it. The pack was upon him, howling and slavering. He fought as best he could, cursing the weakness that now was his. Talons ripped into his chest and tore the flesh from him.

In the back of his mind a voice whispered, *Die; and the curse will still be broken. There can still be an ending to it...*

He could not give in; the will to live was stronger than any death-wish or longing to end his curse. He strove, though every inch of his flesh was being flayed from him, though his guts lay strewn on the floor before him, though he could do naught.

"Such a reaper of souls we lost," Yadudd's murmured voice through the chaos. "Such a gallant champion of death."

The daemons had torn him to ribbons. Yet still he lived; still he could see, feel, know pain that no being should know. Before him he saw Yadudd's long claws teasing Tessa's flesh. She screamed.

"No!" Damon cried, through a mouth that hung in tatters. His voice was muffled and blood spat from his lips as he spoke. "Curse these feeble limbs! I renounce this flesh. I revoke thy debt!"

Again a darkness ripped at him — more painful than the tearing of the daemon's claws, the ripping of their sharp teeth. Through it, he heard a terrible cry:

"DONE!"

CRSO

Tessa awoke from a nightmare. She cast fear-filled eyes about the huge chamber in which she lay. It was lit with blood-red lights from some unknown source. She strove to remember. There had been daemons, hellish creatures...

Before her she saw Damon. He was tearing at the stone floor with his hands; his huge broad back was bowed with defeat and his horns flickered in the light. Hesitantly, she stood on shaky legs and stepped towards him.

"Damon?" she said softly.

He made no reply. Through his mind echoed the harsh laughter of one of the Daketh, the Dark Gods, laughing and laughing. The mockery in that sound, the futility it encompassed, built a fire of rage within him. He tore at the rocks in his fury, ripping the stone to shards.

"Damon?" she repeated, laying a hand on his shoulder.

He started at the touch and rose threateningly before he stepped back from her. His eyes gleamed with crimson fires. Tessa shuddered with fear, remembering the nightmare again. Those creatures, she realized, had not been very different from the being that stood before her.

The lights in his eyes dulled. He moved to her and enfolded her in his arms, careful of his strength. She held him, uncertainly. Then she gave in to his need.

In Damon's skull, the laughter slowly faded into a dying echo.

Liavek

The Rat's Alley Shuffle

Saffer was sitting on a flat stone on the strip of land between the salt marsh and the Levar's Highway about a half mile or so west of Liavek. She had her back to the road, her feet in the couchgrass and her cittern on her lap. The song she was working on was a new one and it was going well, except for the bridge between the verses. She'd tried a dozen different bits and pieces, but nothing fit. It was much more interesting watching the birds in the marsh.

Closer to the sea, black and white oyster-catchers with their long orange bills were feeding among the stones, catching mostly marshcrabs. Four or five terns were hovering over a stretch of open water, slender wings and long tails outstretched as they dropped down to skirl the surface. A cormorant flew from right to left across Saffer's field of vision in a straight purposeful line and she wondered where it was going in such a hurry. Near where she was sitting, a group of ducks were watching her, hoping for more of the bread bits that she'd shared with them earlier.

The song, she decided, should have been about birds. Especially if she was going to work on it here. But this was one of her private quiet places — even so close to the road as it was — and she had to get the song finished. Liavek was noisy at the best of times, unless one could afford private lodgings in the Canal District or a house on the here-now/gone-again Wizard's Row. She lived in Rat's Alley and the only privacy she had there was a box of a room that was stifling at the moment. If only she'd learned magic instead of music, she thought sometimes, invested her luck in a nice little bauble that she could hang around her neck perhaps, things might have been different.

But as it was, it was the month of Heat, she was always next to broke, the city was too noisy for her to think, and she had commission from Tapper Tan Burnie that would be delivered late if it wasn't finished today. She was supposed to write a catchy little piece for him, something that prominently mentioned his tavern the Quick's End, with a tune simple enough for any streetsinger to sing and perhaps a touch of something hidden in the music to make listeners thirsty.

She played the newest version of the bridge through a couple of times, lightly plucking the cittern's double strings, and frowned when it still didn't sound quite right.

"Duck farts," she told her attentive mallard audience. "That's what it sounds like."

"But coming from you," a voice said from the road behind her, "even farts sound melodious."

Recognizing that voice, Saffer didn't bother to turn around. "What are *you* doing here?" she asked.

"I've come to make you rich."

The ducks swam off as the newcomer came down from the road and gingerly chose a stone of his own to sit on. He gave Saffer a grin and stretched out his long legs. Narrow spidery fingers adjusted the knot of the scarf tied at his throat. He seemed to be all angles and bony limbs, but anyone thinking him awkward was in for a rude surprise if they sat down to play cards with him.

"Hello, Saffer," he said. "Lovely day, don't you think?"

"Hello, Dumps. How did you find me?"

"I asked Meggy Thistle. 'Meggy,' I said, 'Where's Saffer who I plan to make rich?' and she sent me down here. She told me you were hunting tunes — or was it loons?"

"Well, I've found my loon," Saffer said as she laid her instrument down on its quilted bag by her feet.

"Is that the way you always talk to those who mean to make you rich?"

"The last time you meant to make me rich, you almost had us both sent to Crab Isle. We're just lucky it was my brother in the Guard that picked us up and that everyone got their levars back."

Dumps waved off her worry. "Sink 'em if they can't take a joke. Anyway, this time I've got a commission for us that's perfectly legal."

Saffer leaned towards him. "If you want to make your fortune, Dumps," she said, "why don't you just go ask Elmutt for it?"

Dumps shook his head. "I've laughed at that old ragpicker too often before he became a fortune maker to chance his goodwill. Did you hear what he did to Cankera? Melted her on the spot, I heard." He fluttered his long fingers at her. "Not for me, thank you very much. Now come on. Say you'll help me."

Saffer shrugged and picked up her cittern. "I've already got a commission," she said.

"It'll be perfectly safe—lose my luck if I'm lying."

Saffer shook her head and began her tune again.

"Ten levars for you," Dumps said. "And *no* risk."

The tune faltered. "Ten levars?"

"Guaranteed."

"No risk?"

"None at all."

"I don't have to get dressed up again?"

"Not so much as a glove."

Saffer gave it a few moments of serious consideration. Her chestnut hair was cut very short at the front, top and sides, but fell in a long braid down her back. This had come about from one of Dumps' plans at disguising her as a young man for some trick or other that never quite got off the ground. She'd ended up liking the raffish look it gave her—but that came only weeks after walking about in a big floppy hat. She ran her hand through the short hair at the top of her head, still undecided.

"Just as you are, and your cittern as it is," Dumps said, following the motion of her hand. He knew what she was thinking.

"All right," Saffer said. "I'll listen."

"You won't regret this, Saffer. Odd's End, but it's sweet."

"I said I'd listen, Dumps. I didn't say I'd do it. Whatever 'it' is."

"Then listen," he said. "Listen and weep for the beauty of it."

CR&O

At least one good thing had come from listening to Dumps, Saffer thought later as she was walking down the Street of the Dreamers. She had the bridge for Tapper Tan's commission worked out—she'd just drone for a couple of bars between verses. Tapper Tan had liked both words and music and paid her on the spot. The first thing she did with her new wealth was buy a fresh set of cittern strings at Whistler's Corner which, while it wasn't as fine a place as the Tiger's Eye a few doors down, was still dear to her heart for one very good reason: Its goods were cheap. With her purse a touch lighter and the pocket where she'd stuffed the strings a tad heavier, she made her way over to Levar's Park where she bought a cup of kaf and a few sticky buns, then sat down in one of her favorite nooks to watch the crowds go by.

When she was finished eating and had carefully licked her fingers clean, she considered putting out her hat for an hour or so. She could always use the practice on her cittern. On the other hand, with her purse still weighty from Tapper Tan's commission, and with Dumps' commission in the offing, she didn't really have the proper air of desperation to do any streetsinging today. She just wasn't feeling poor enough to put on a proper show. At that moment her friend Kaloo—on the way to Market from the Mug and Anchor where she worked—plonked herself down beside her and settled the whole question.

"My you're looking prosperous today," Kaloo said.

Saffer nodded. "I finished up that commission for Tapper Tan *and* I've got a new one."

"Don't tell me—let me guess. The Levar's asked you to play for her on her luck day!"

"Nothing so grand. I'm providing the music for a night of private bidding—Dumps's arranged the whole thing."

"What'll you be dressed up as this time?" Kaloo asked. "An Ombayan parrot?"

Saffer laughed. "At least I wasn't named after the Kookaloo."

The Kookaloo was a wild songbird that left its eggs in other birds' nests. From someone else, Kaloo might have taken this as an insult, but coming from Saffer, she just laughed along with her friend.

"Be that as it may," she said, "I saw Dumps at the other end of the park having a most earnest conversation with Coniam—the *wizard* Coniam," she added.

"I know those who're wizards and those who aren't," Saffer said.

Coniam lived at 13 Wizard Row, just a few doors down from The Magician, and while he wasn't the most powerful magic-worker in Liavek, he wasn't exactly a slouch either. But what business could Dumps have with him?

"What were they talking about?" she asked.

Kaloo shrugged. "Who knows. I could ask L'Fertti, but he's not all that mad about cardsharps—especially not dandies like your Dumps. When's this bidding party anyway?"

"Twenty-eighth of the month."

"Can you use a whistle player?"

"Who? Meggy?"

Kaloo nodded. "She's looking for work."

"How is she on Ka Zhirian tunes?"

Kaloo pulled a face. "Awful. I don't like listening to all that modal stuff either. Is that what Dumps wants you to play?"

"Nothing but. He says it's to add a little tension to the game, to keep the bidders on a sharp edge. They'll play better—*and* pay better."

"How much better?"

"Ten levars for the evening," Saffer said smugly.

"Ten…?" Kaloo shook her head. "Oh, that doesn't sound right, Saffer. If it was anyone but Dumps…."

"He's not so bad," Saffer said, but she was beginning to have her own doubts again.

Ten levars was enough to clothe and feed two families of six each for a month. And she didn't like to hear about Dumps being seen in the company of a wizard.

Just then Count Dashif went by and the two of them fell silent. They watched him saunter through the park, his dark curly hair catching the sunlight with flickering highlights. The path he took seemed to magically clear before him as people moved out of his way, then paused to follow his progress once they were cut of his line of sight.

"I have to go," Kaloo said suddenly.

"Me, too," Saffer said.

She slung her cittern bag to her shoulder.

"Don't go off in a huff," Kaloo began and Saffer joined her to finish with: "Just go!"

Laughing, Saffer gave her friend a jaunty wave and set off in search of Dumps. Kaloo smiled until Saffer had turned away. Then the humor drained from her face to be replaced with a look of determination as she walked off in the direction that the Count had taken.

CRSO

Saffer found Dumps in a tavern that night — the Kondy's Brew off the Rat's Alley — and he immediately proceeded to alleviate her worries with two brimming mugs of ale and protestations of innocence that, knowing him as well as she did, were as preposterous as they were anatomically impossible.

"It's just a luck's day party," he finished up with. "That's all. And Coniam's footing the bill. These're his friends, Saffer — remember friends? They're the sort of people that one trusts and depends on."

"What do you mean by a 'luck's day party'?"

"Well, it just so happens that each of our five fine — and might I add wealthy — guests were born on that same day, at approximately the same time. Coniam's thinking of organizing a club for them."

Saffer studied her ale for a long moment. Was this still her first, or a second? It was so smoky in here and ale always went right to her head that it was difficult for her to work it out. What she did know was that the more she heard about this bidding party, the worse it was beginning to sound.

"They're friends?" she tried again.

"The very best."

"All born around the same time?"

"So Coniam says. Actually, I think they're more his friends than each others'. This party's for them to all meet and form this — "

"Club. Yes. You mentioned that."

"Would you like another ale?"

"I don't think I should. And so they're going to have a friendly game of Two-Copper Bid, while I play Ka Zhirian tunes to make them tense….This sounds mad, you know that, don't you, Dumps?"

"I prefer the word 'eccentric.' Poor people are mad; rich people are eccentric. I read that in *The Cat's Street Crier*."

"Yes, well, I don't think I want the commission anymore," Saffer said.

"Oh, but you can't back out now — Coniam wouldn't like it. Not now that I've told you all about it."

"What's he going to do?" Saffer asked. "Turn me into a frog?"

But then again he *was* a wizard and the trouble with wizards was that they were liable to do anything.

"Oh, I don't like this at all, Dumps," she said. "Not one bit. You *promised* me there'd be no trouble."

"And there won't be. Just come and play some music, collect your ten levars, then tra-la-la, off you go."

Saffer took a long swig of her ale. She was still thinking about frogs and what it would be like to be one.

"I don't like it either," Dumps admitted, "but what's to do? He *is* a wizard."

"What's in it for him?" Saffer asked. "I mean all this talk about a club — that's just nonsense. So what's he got planned?"

"Think about it."

Saffer didn't want to because she was feeling somewhat woozy, but she gave it a try.

"There'll be five of them," she said. "All playing cards, all concentrating their luck on those cards...on their luck day...right in the hours of their luck, the only time it's really potent for anyone who isn't a wizard....Oh, Dumps! He means to bind their luck into a pack of cards!"

Dumps nodded glumly. "And they're so keen on the chance to play when their luck's at their best, they can't even see it. When the night's done, Coniam will be able to use those cards and no one will be able to beat him. They'll never guess that he's cheating. In fact, it doesn't even have to be him using the cards. *Anyone* who uses them will be unbeatable."

That was the worst thing that you could do to someone, Saffer thought. Steal their luck. And these players, they'd lose their luck for as long as the cards existed. And if their luck was bound into them and if the cards were somehow destroyed...they'd all die. With that control held over them they wouldn't even be able to do anything to Coniam once they found out for fear he'd destroy the cards.

"But why us?" Saffer asked. "Why would he pick us?"

"Well, he wasn't too happy about my bringing you in — your brother Demar being in the guard and all — but I know he approached me because...well, who could I tell? Who'd listen to old Dumps if he tried to pass around a story like that? I'm like the lad who cried troll once too often."

"What are we going to do?"

Dumps shrugged. "Nothing. I'll run the bidding and you'll play your music and, after it's over, we'll both go home a little richer."

"But those players—what about their luck? What if they come after us when they realize what's been done?"

"There's no way for them to know, Saffer. They're not wizards. The only ones who'll know will be you and me."

"And Coniam."

"And Coniam," Dumps agreed.

"And he's a wizard," Saffer said, "who could conceivably turn us into newts or toads so that we couldn't spread the tale around."

"Or he could just kill us."

"Dumps! You promised this would be safe!"

"Or he could just pay us and let us go, because who'd believe us anyway?"

"I suppose," Saffer said, a little mollified. "I wonder what he needs those cards for. You'd think he'd turn his wizardry to a more honest way of making a living."

"Depends on what his luck is. I don't think it's anything useful or he wouldn't be trying this, now would he? I've also heard—just this evening, mind, so don't start on me again about my leading you into danger—I've just heard that Coniam owes a certain Brugsti a great number of levars."

"Brugsti? This just keeps getting worse, Dumps! He's a thug."

"Agreed. A very rich, powerful, unpleasant-if-you-cross-him thug. He also happens to be completely resistant to magic—"

"I didn't know that."

" —which makes things difficult if you're a wizard and have decided to renege on your debts to him. Brugsti's paid a lot of levars to a lot of powerful wizards for that immunity, so it's either pay up with him, or get thumped."

"Or worse."

"Or worse," Dumps agreed.

Saffer commandeered an ale from the tray of a waiter going by, gave Dumps a nod that he should pay, and took a long gulp. Was this her third, or her second? It didn't really matter, not when life as a toad was potentially in the offing.

"What are you doing?" Dumps asked her as he paid the waiter.

"I," she announced a little unsteadily, "am going to get levarly drunk. It's the twenty-sixth today, so I'm going to stay drunk until sometime on the twenty-ninth, whereupon I shall sober up—if I'm still all in one piece."

"But what about the commission? Can you still play when you're soused?"

Saffer finished the ale in a second long swallow and regarded him blearily. "I play mussh better," she assured him and promptly fell head forward against the table. Dumps caught her before her forehead was introduced to the oak slats and propped her back up in her chair. Her head lolled to one side.

"I don't suppose it would help if I said I was sorry?" he asked, but he wasn't really expecting an answer.

C&SO

When Saffer woke the next day it was late afternoon. She immediately discovered three things. The first was that her head felt as though someone had mistaken it for an anvil and had spent the better part of the night hammering away on it. The second was that if she moved very slowly and squinted rather than opened her eyes, the pain could be almost bearable. The third was that she had woken in Dumps' bed with Dumps snoring beside her. She gave him a poke.

"Huh—whuzzat?"

Saffer squinted daggers at him.

"What," she began, grimaced, then quickly lowered her voice, "am I doing *here?*"

"You *were* sleeping," Dumps mumbled and began to turn over.

Saffer poked him again. "Did we...?"

She'd been a little lax with her Worrynot of late.

Dumps rolled his eyes. "Odd's End, Saffer! I've told you before, you're too skinny for my tastes. Now either go back to sleep, or go away."

Saffer thought about thumping him, but decided that in her present state it would probably hurt her more than him. Instead she got up, found she was still fully clothed, grabbed her cittern bag from where it was hanging on the end of the bed, and made for the door. Dumps sat up in sudden alarm.

"Where are you going?" he demanded.

"Out."

"You're not planning a repeat of last night's performance, are you?"

"First," she informed him, "I'm going to look up Marithana and see what sort of a cure she can sell me for this head of mine, and then I'm going to the marsh to look at the ducks."

"But you *will* honor the commission?"

"We'll see," she said maliciously and closed the door. His shouting after her, while it made her head throb more, was still music to her ears. Let him stew a bit, she thought. Serves him right, the rotter, for getting me into this in the first place.

CRBO

"Fold."

"I'll see your bid and call."

"Fold."

"Fold."

"His Lordship has a filled tower," Dumps said as Lord Shin, the Count of Grandeth spread out his cards, "Mages high."

He looked expectantly at Mistress Olna, the Vavasor of Chem's Way who had seen the Count's bid, but she shook her head and threw in her hand. Dumps pushed the pot over to Shin and collected the cards.

"Ante up," he said as he began to shuffle the deck.

His Lordship was doing very well tonight, Saffer thought, though all five of them would be the losers before the night was out, if Coniam had his way.

She was sitting in a corner, playing a Ka Zhirian version of an old ballad known in Liavek as "My Love's Left Me and My Luck's All Gone" on her cittern. The irony of its title would be lost on all of them, except perhaps the wizard.

They were using one of the backrooms at Cheeky's for the party. Besides the Count and the Vavasor, there were three wealthy merchants in on the game, Dumps was the dealer, of course, and she was the entertainment. Judging from the irritated glances that were cast in her direction every so often, she was fulfilling her commission properly, if not pleasing the guests.

Two dancers from Cheeky's had been hired to keep a steady supply of drinks and pastries at each player's elbow. Saffer didn't know either of them and they hadn't bothered to introduce themselves, which suited her just fine. Not present, though certainly watching from a peekhole, was the host of the party. Coniam had made no mention of his "luck's day club" which meant that it had either simply been a ruse to get Dumps to agree to play his part, or it had been another part of the cardsharp's inventions. After briefly introducing the players to each other, Coniam had bowed out because of other "pressing business."

Saffer sighed as she started up a new tune. It would be at least another hour before the party wound down. Her fingers were getting stiff, though not so stiff that she wouldn't be able to play her own card when the bidders' game was done. Given two days to think about it, she knew that Coniam wouldn't be physically present. And this afternoon, while supposedly checking the room's acoustics, she'd found the chalk markings that encircled the underside of the table, confirming her guess. These five citizens had been chosen because their luck times all coincided with his. At this very moment he was somewhere very near, investing the cards with his own luck as well.

Oh, Coniam was a clever sod, Saffer thought, yes, indeed. It was just too bad for him that he hadn't taken into account the fact that there might be an honest rogue or two in Rat's Alley.

Another hand had ended, one of the merchants being its winner, and Dumps was dealing the cards anew, seven to each player. Two-Copper Bid, Saffer thought. Levar's blood! There was more wealth on that table than she'd ever seen before in one place. They should have called this game Ten-Silver Bid. Each of the players discarded two cards and then the bidding began again. Saffer started up another tune.

∞

"Every cramp in my fingers has its own cramp," Saffer said as she was putting away her cittern.

She slung the bag from her shoulder and wandered over to the table where Dumps was sitting wearily. She flexed her fingers in front of him for a moment.

305

"See?" she said, then added, "Time to pay up."

As Dumps bent down to get at the money box by his feet, Saffer picked up the cards and gave them a quick shuffle.

"Don't touch those!" Dumps cried and snatched them from her.

"Oh, grumpy, aren't we?"

"Don't start, Saffer. Here's your ten levars."

Saffer counted them out very carefully, grinning at the annoyance on Dumps' face, then stowed the coins in her purse. Making sure that it was still firmly attached to her belt, she buttoned it shut and gave it a pat.

"One last favor," she said as she headed for the door.

"What's that?"

"Don't do me any more favors."

Dumps looked as though he was seriously considering throwing something at her.

"Sink you, if you can't take a joke," she said and stepped quickly out of the room.

CRSO

The pounding came at her door at approximately an hour before sunrise—a full half-hour later than she'd been expecting it to.

"It's open!" she called out cheerfully.

Dumps stormed in. "You ungrateful wretch!" he cried. "Give me the card!"

"What card?"

"Don't play innocent with me. The Rikiki card that you filched from the deck tonight."

"Oh, *that* card."

"Did you really think you could get away with switching it for one that wasn't a part of the binding? Saffer, he's going to kill me if I don't get it back."

"How? With some terrible spell?"

"He's a wizard, sinkbrain! Get that through that tiny mind of yours."

Saffer smiled. When she was in the room that afternoon she'd made sure that the smudged and worn Rikiki card she was going to have hidden up her sleeve that night matched the pack they were using. After that, with the sleight-of-hand tricks she'd picked up from hanging around with Dumps, it had been child's play to exchange the two when she gave the pack a quick shuffle at the end of the night.

"A wizard without his luck is all he is," she said. "He doesn't frighten me."

"And Brugsti?"

"Well, he's a different matter, but he's Coniam's worry — not ours. Brugsti may be a thug, but he's not stupid enough to come after us because Coniam can't made good his debts. The Alley'd get together and sink him in the harbor."

"Saffer, *please.* Maybe Brugsti won't come after us, but Coniam can certainly hire a few thugs that will."

"But then he'd never find out where I hid his card, would he?"

"Saffer, don't do this to me."

"All right," she relented. "Tell Coniam that I'll meet him on the docks tonight — ten sharp. We'll work out a deal."

"A deal? Are you mad?"

"No. But I plan to be eccentric some day."

"Saffer — "

"Ten tonight. On the docks. Near Yonner's Netting. He can come alone, or bring his merry luck's day club with him — I don't care."

"Saffer — "

"Goodnight, Dumps."

He stared at her for a long moment, then slowly backed out the door and slammed it behind him. The look on his face, Saffer decided, made this all very worthwhile. It was about time he was on the receiving end of things going wrong.

CR8D

Coniam was prompt — Saffer had to give him that — and very sure of himself. The only person accompanying him to the meeting place was a very miserable looking Dumps. Even without his luck, the wizard was a formidable figure. He was a head taller than Dumps, which made him two heads taller than Saffer. She looked up into his lean features and swallowed thickly at the blaze of anger that brooded in his eyes. He wasn't the sort one would want to meet in a dark alley — with or without his spells. He was also quite rude, Saffer thought, as he came directly to the point without even a few words of preamble.

"Do you have the card?"

Saffer nodded and drew it from her sleeve, being very careful to maintain a distance of more than three paces between them. Unless Coniam was an utter fool, he'd have the rest of the pack in one of his pockets. "Rikiki's here," she said. "What've you got to offer in trade?"

"How does your life sound, child?"

"Melodious as a lark."

"Saffer!" Dumps cried. "Don't egg him on!"

The wizard lifted a hand in Dumps' general direction and the cardsharp immediately fell quiet.

"What do you want for it?" Coniam asked.

"Let's see....The use of the cards for one night? But of course that wouldn't do, would it? Since you've invested your own luck in the pack, it'll only serve you, won't it?"

"How much in straight coinage will you take for it?"

"Well, it depends. You *did* infuse it with more than your own luck, so that should make it worth—but then there's my keeping quiet about it as well. I don't think Lord Grandeth or any of the others would be all that happy to find out that you've, shall we say, 'borrowed' their luck."

"You are trying my patience, child. You won't say a word about it to Lord Grandeth or anyone else, or I'll simply have to tell them that it was the pair of you up to your usual tricks. Who do you think the judges would believe if it came to court? A respected wizard, or a pair of guttersnipes from Rat's Alley?"

"Well, that depends," Saffer said, "on whether or not one of those guttersnipes has a brother in the guard."

"You wouldn't dare—"

"But I already have." Grinning, Saffer tore the playing card in two.

"My luck!" Coniam roared and he charged her, but two grey-clad shapes stepped quickly from the shadows to intercept him. After a very brief scuffle, the two Guards had the wizard under control.

"That's one I owe you," Saffer's brother said to her.

He was the taller of the pair, not as broad-shouldered as his partner, and his hair was the same chestnut brown as his sister's.

Saffer shook her head. "This is payment for pulling me out of Dumps' last scrape."

Demar shrugged. "Fair enough. This might mean a promotion for us."

"Wouldn't that be grand."

"Try to stay out of trouble now, won't you? Promise me?"

"Singer's honor," Saffer said, crossing her heart.

Her brother and his partner exchanged weary glances.

"Go on," Demar said to her, "the both of you. And be quick about it—before we change our minds and run you in as well."

"But, but...." Dumps was spluttering.

"What's wrong?" Saffer asked him.

"The five players. When you tore the card in two...."

"They're fine," Demar said. "Saffer just tore up a fake. The real card's in a very safe place."

Coniam glared at Saffer, but she just grinned back. Her brother took the wizard by the arm and led him off.

"One day...." the wizard called back to Saffer.

"Oh, I don't think so," Demar said. He tightened his grip on Coniam's arm. "I'm afraid it's Crab Isle for you, Master Wizard, and I doubt you'll be coming back."

∞

The morning was warm, the sky blue, and the ducks had returned. Saffer was back on her stone between the Levar's Highway and the salt marsh, playing a new song to them. She didn't break off when she heard a footstep on the road, just waited for Dumps to sit down.

"I thought I'd find you here," he said. "What're you doing?"

"I'm writing a new song—free of charge—that will make us both famous."

"The one you were just playing? That's the tune you're using?"

Saffer nodded.

"Sounded like duck farts to me."

"Actually, I was thinking of calling it 'The Duck's Fart Shuffle.'"

"Odd's End, Saffer! Sometimes you really make me wonder."

Saffer gave her purse a whack and it replied with a jingle that sounded most tuneful to her ears.

"I'm just eccentric," she said. "That's all. Sink you, if you—"

"—can't take a joke."

Saffer laughed. Giving Dumps a poke with her toe, she began to play a jig on her cittern.

The Skin & Knife Game

(with Lee Barwood)

Thunder drummed in Saffer's room, as if a madman had been let loose at a set of kettle drums. Saffer groaned and burrowed her head deeper into the twist of blankets on her bed. She wished desperately for the storm to move on. As though in answer to her prayer, for one brief moment there was a lull. Then the thunder started up again.

Poking her head up from out of her nest of bedclothes, she squinted at the bright light coming in through the window. How could she be hearing thunder when the sky was so blue it hurt to look at it? Her squint tightened, then focused on the door to her room which was vibrating with the thunder.

"Open for the Guard!" a deep voice cried in the next lull.

Saffer continued to stare stupidly at the door. The Guard? Sink them. What did they want with her at this hour of the—

The thunder started up again.

"All right!" Saffer shrieked, then immediately clutched her temples to keep her head all in one piece. In a much softer voice she added, "I'm coming."

Sitting up very carefully, she stretched a hesitant foot towards the floor.

Stumbling to the door, she swung it wide to blink at the pair of large Guards in their grey tunics.

"Demar wants to see you," one of them said.

Saffer winced. Demar. That figured. Trust her brother to have her roused at—

"What time is it?" she asked.

"Almost noon."

"Already?"

"I wouldn't keep him waiting," the Guard told her. "He's in a mood."

Lovely. Her head was ready to split and Demar was in a mood.

"What am I supposed to have done this time?" she asked.

The Guard shrugged.

Saffer sighed and stumbled back into her room. Fumbling about in the small remedies bag that hung from the end of her bed, she finally closed her fingers about a little pouch of herbs that contained one of Marithana's hangover cures.

"Can I get dressed, or is it a come-as-you-are sort of a party?" she asked as she sprinkled some of the mixture on her palm.

Pulling a face, she swallowed it dry.

"Five minutes," the Guard said, then closed the door.

Saffer replaced the little pouch in her remedies bag. She rubbed her hands over her face, then ran her fingers through the short hair on the top of her head. The seven braids hanging behind her felt heavier than the Levar's purse this morning and she draped them carefully over each shoulder to take their weight off her aching head.

Going over to the window, she stared out for a few moments, trying to remember what she could possibly have done that would entail her brother sending a couple of his men round to pick her up. Odd's end. She hadn't been in a decent scrape since Dumps had left the city to work the railroaders' camps with his card tricks.

A sound at the door—still loud, but identifiable as a knock now—roused her enough to get dressed, hurriedly splash some water on her face and join her unwanted traveling companions. About the only good thing for this morning, she thought as she trailed along between them, was that Marithana's hangover cure was beginning to take effect.

❦

Demar took one look at Saffer and frowned. She was decked out in the current fashion—baggy Zhir-styled trousers and a tight undershirt, topped with a loose jacket, all in pastel shades of mauve and pink. Her face was puffy from the previous night's drinking and her hair was a snake's nest of braids spilling to her shoulders.

"You look like a clown," he said.

"Oh, don't be such a dried old toad. This is all the rage."

Demar sighed. When she tried her best winning smile, he didn't allow himself to react.

Demar had Saffer's chestnut brown hair, but he was taller than her by a head. He was lean and rangy, thick-wristed, with a lightness to his step that came from years with the Guard. Looking at his sister with her lopsided smile made him think that half those years had been filled with pulling her out of one scrape or another.

"What is it you think I've done this time?" Saffer asked finally.

"You'd better come with me," Demar said.

Saffer gave him an odd look. "Oh, don't go all sinking officious on me," she began.

Demar cut her off with a wave of his hand and led her down the hall. He wouldn't speak until they entered another room in the guardhouse. Lying on a cot in the center of the room was the bruised and battered body of a young man. The guardsman who had been tending him left the room when Demar gave him a nod. On another cot by the wall lay a girl a few years younger than the young man, one leg twisted and thin.

Saffer blanched, but she stepped forward to take a closer look all the same.

"Are...are they dead?" she asked.

"The girl is. The man's taken a bad beating, but he'll live."

Demar studied his sister, watching her reactions.

"Do you know them?" he asked.

"No. Should I...." Her voice trailed off as she got a closer look at the man's face. "Kerlaf," she murmured. She turned to look at her brother. "I met them last night. I had a commission at the Luck's Shadow and he was there with—" she glanced at the body of the girl " —with his sister, Ayla. Demar, how did you know I knew them? Odd's end, I only met them last night."

"The man had your name on his lips when he was brought in."

"Truly, Demar. I went straight home after the party and collapsed on my bed until your thugs dragged me out of it." Her gaze drifted back to the pair on the table. "Poor Kerlaf. He really cared about Ayla. You could just tell by the way he took care of her."

"So the last you saw of them was at the Luck's Shadow?" Demar asked.

Saffer nodded.

"That's a wizard's inn, isn't it? Is he a wizard?"

"Ayla was—sort of. I never really got to talk with them about it. But they were there with me. I met them on my way to the party and they looked so bedraggled that I brought them along and snuck them in. They looked like they could use a bit of fun."

That was Saffer, Demar thought. Always willing to pick up any stray dog.

"What happened to them, Demar?" she asked.

"Nobody knows. A couple of guards found them in Fortune Way and brought them in just an hour ago. When the man—you said his name was Kerlaf?"

Saffer nodded.

"When he mentioned you by name, I had you brought around straight away. They're not from the city, are they?"

"They used to live here a long time ago. I got the impression that they'd been away and only just returned, but I didn't get much of a chance to talk to them. I was working, you know."

Her gaze drifted back to Ayla.

"And you're sure there's not more to this than you're telling me?"

Saffer looked away from the dead girl's face. Swallowing hard, she shook her head.

Demar sighed. "Will you take responsibility for them, Saff? Neither of them had even a copper to their name."

"I can put Kerlaf up at my place, I suppose, but Ayla...."

"If she stays here, she goes into a pauper's grave."

"Send her to an undertaker in my name," Saffer said. "I'll go by later to make the arrangements."

Though who knew where she'd get the money.

"I'll see to it," Demar said. "You'll want some help getting him back to your place...?"

Saffer nodded.

"I'll get those two 'thugs' to help you."

Demar could tell his sister wasn't in the mood to smile, but she touched his arm to let him know that she wasn't just being sulky.

"But if you hear anything...?"

"I'll tell you right away."

"That's all I wanted to hear."

Taking her by the arm, he led her back to his office.

CR§D

After seeing that Kerlaf was comfortable in her room, Saffer spent the rest of the afternoon making the funeral arrangements for Ayla. It took the last of her money, plus some that she had to borrow from Meggy Thistle whom she ran into in Levar's Park. She'd also been at the party at the Luck's Shadow the previous night and was an old friend of Saffer's.

"Mind you," Meggy said as she handed Saffer the coins, "I'll need it back before the end of the week. I thought I'd wander up towards Trader's Town for a week or so and see how well the railway men are paying these days. I was going to ask you if you wanted to come. We could've had a bit of fun and collected a copper or two while we were at it. I've heard they're starving for good entertainment."

"Don't I know it," Saffer replied. "Dumps is up there right now, cardsharping his way through their wages. Say hello to him for me if you see him."

Meggy shook her head. "Not likely, Saffer. I want to stay on the good side of the railway men."

Saffer knew just what Meggy meant. Dumps was better at getting Saffer in trouble than she was herself. His latest escapade involved a series of pamphlets that promised to reveal everything from Zhiran love secrets to the best way to summon Rikiki. Using uncommon good sense for a change, Saffer had managed not to involve herself in any of them, although Dumps had pleaded with her for the better part of a week to write a cittern tutor.

"I'll get this back as quick as I can," she said, holding up the money Meggy'd lent Saffer. "Thanks again."

Meggy nodded, but just as Saffer turned to go, she caught her arm.

"Now I remember," she said.

"Remember what?"

"I had something to tell you and it just drained out of my mind the moment I saw you. Remember the big woman at the party last night, the one who looked more like a baker than a wizard? She had the little yapping dog that thought it knew every tune better than we did."

"I remember her. Her name was Teshi, wasn't it?"

Meggy nodded. "She was by looking for you."

"For me? What for?"

"She didn't say. Maybe she has another commission for us."

"Then why didn't she talk to you about it?"

Meggy shrugged. "I don't know. Anyway, I sent her round by your place."

Wonderful, Saffer thought. Her brother thought she was up to no good, she had a patient in her bed, she'd just spent all her money on a funeral for someone she hardly knew at all, and now a wizard was looking for her. She just hoped that she hadn't done something stupid at the party last night while in a beer-silly mood.

"She's probably been and gone by now," Meggy said.

Saffer nodded glumly, not believing it for a moment. After thanking Meggy again for the loan and promising again to pay it back as soon as she could, she hurried off for home.

CR&O

According to her landlord, the wizard had been and gone by the time Saffer returned to her room. Upstairs, Kerlaf was still imitating a man-sized lump on her bed. After fussing about with his pillow and blankets, she went and sat in her windowseat. There she indulged in a soliloquy while plucking the odd note from her cittern and staring off through what little view there was from her window.

"It's not so much that Demar doesn't trust me," she said, "as that sometimes I wonder if he isn't right. Maybe I do just bring trouble on myself."

She plucked a few notes from the cittern's double strings, then a chord.

Ting, ting, kring.

"I didn't have to bring them along to the party, but they did look so forlorn, and I just knew there'd be all that food there that was only going to get thrown out in the morning."

Kring.

"And no one really seemed to mind, what with Ayla being a...was it a herbalist or an astrologer?"

"She was an astronomer, actually."

Saffer blinked with surprise at the reply to her question. She looked at the bed, but Kerlaf hadn't moved, little say spoken. Then her gaze went to the door.

The wizard Teshi stood there. She was a short, friendly-looking woman, plump with short curly grey hair, dressed in voluminous robes that glimmered with a rainbow effect. Huge gaudy rings, all gold and silver and with far too many large gems, glittered on her hands. Her eyes twinkled, but there was something in their blue depths that made Saffer feel a little intimidated. She found it hard to look away. It wasn't until Teshi broke eye contact to look at Kerlaf that Saffer blinked and set aside her cittern. Then she spotted the little mop of grey fur with the big dark eyes that had accompanied the wizard.

"I don't want to seem rude," Saffer began, "but —"

"What am I doing here?" Teshi replied.

"Something like that."

"It's because of Kerlaf's sister," Teshi said.

She turned from the bed and sat down on its edge so that she was facing Saffer. The little dog began to explore the room.

"She does star charts," Teshi explained. "*Did* star charts. I was planning to commission some from her, but then I heard the horrible news. This sort of a thing.... You'd think we were in Ka Zhir or something."

She gave Saffer's clothes a sharp look, but Saffer managed to ignore it. Saffer thought about her patient and his sister. News certainly traveled fast. Half of Liavek had probably known about it before she had.

"I took rather a liking to them," Teshi finished, "and thought I would see if I could do anything to help. Whoever did this shouldn't be allowed to get away with it."

"Well, the Guard's looking into it," Saffer said.

"Yes, but they have so many things to look into. If we can lend them a hand, I doubt they'd mind."

"You don't know my brother."

"I'm sure I don't."

Saffer shook her head. "That's not what I meant. Demar's in the Guard and he told me I was absolutely not to meddle in this. Odd's end, he'd kill me if—"

"We caught the attackers and delivered them without his having to lift a finger?"

"He wouldn't be happy."

"Nonsense."

Before Saffer could argue any more, Teshi had turned back to Kerlaf. She laid her palms on either side of his head. The air seemed to glimmer around her for a moment, then Kerlaf's eyelids flickered and his eyes opened. Saffer left the windowseat and stepped close. He had, she decided, the nicest pair of clear blue eyes that she'd seen in awhile.

"A-Ayla...?" he murmured.

"Ah...she's not...ah...."

"She's dead," Teshi said softly.

Kerlaf's gaze went back and forth between them, then his eyes clouded with pain.

"I...I remember," he said and he began to weep.

Saffer had never had a grown man cry on her before. She gave Teshi a beseeching look. The wizard nodded and gathered Kerlaf up in her arms.

"Maybe you should get him something—tea, or soup," she told Saffer.

Saffer backed away to the door.

"I'll see what the landlord's got on," she said.

But they weren't listening to her. Kerlaf's body shook with great shuddering sobs. Teshi held him against her, murmuring comforting noises. Biting at her lower lip, Saffer hurried downstairs to the kitchen, grateful for something to do. The wizard's little dog followed at her heels.

By the time Saffer returned with a steaming bowl of beef broth, Teshi and Kerlaf were sitting on either end of the bed. Kerlaf's eyes were bleak with his loss, but he was no longer weeping. Saffer remembered her first look into them last night and then again a few moments ago, when Teshi had brought him around. The guileless clarity that had attracted her was gone, replaced with a sorrow that went beyond despair.

"Can you remember what they looked like?" Teshi was asking him. "The men who attacked you."

Kerlaf blinked. It took a moment for him to find his voice.

"It wasn't men," he said finally. "It was the woman—the one who ran the boarding house."

"What woman?" Saffer asked.

"Her name was Bica. We rented the room when we arrived yesterday afternoon—it was cheap and clean and when you don't have much, that's enough."

"I don't know her," Teshi said. "But this isn't my part of town. Saffer?"

"I know of her," Saffer replied. "Everyone in the Alley does. She's this crazy old woman who runs a rooming house a few blocks down from here. I don't know anybody who's stayed there."

Teshi's eyes narrowed.

"No," Saffer said. "It's not because she's dangerous or anything. She's just—too weird. My friend Meggy was going to rent a room from her, but she got the creeps and never moved in. The thing is...."

Saffer hesitated, looking at Kerlaf. Odd's end, you'd think he could take care of himself against some old spinster.

"She's not tough or anything, you know?" she said. "She's just a crazy old woman."

"What did she do?" Teshi asked Kerlaf. "Did she have others with her?"

"No one else," Kerlaf said. "She...she gave us hot spiced milk when we returned to our room last night—a welcome cup, she called it, and then.... The next thing I remember was her standing over me. I was on the floor and Ayla was beside me, so still. She must have drugged us only I didn't finish all of my drink. I tried to rise, but she hit me with something. I started to pass out, but she just kept hitting me, and Ayla...I knew Ayla was already...I knew she was...."

He didn't weep again, he just closed up. His eyes went bleak and he slumped against the headboard.

"If I wasn't so...so sinking weak...."

Teshi and Saffer exchanged glances.

"We'd better tell my brother," Saffer said. "Demar can—"

Teshi shook her head, her eyes cold and hard as diamonds.

"Let me deal with this Bica," she said.

"I don't think that's such a good —"

Something flickered like fire in Teshi's cold eyes and Saffer suddenly remembered that this was a wizard she was arguing with, not one of her friends.

"All right," she said. "Sink the Guard. Let Demar dump me on Crab Isle when he finds out. What do I care."

Teshi's dog jumped onto the wizard's lap and she patted it absently.

"Twig and I, we look after our friends," she said. "Even when we've only just met them."

"Fine," Saffer said. "Perfect."

And do you know any spells to get one off of Crab Isle? she wondered.

Teshi rose. Twig leapt to the floor and danced eagerly by the door while the wizard laid a comforting hand on Kerlaf's shoulder.

"I'll be back," she told Saffer, and then she and the little dog were gone and Saffer was alone with Kerlaf.

"Ah…you really should try some of this broth," she told Kerlaf.

Her patient made no reply. Lovely, Saffer thought. Not that she blamed him. But looming larger in her mind than Kerlaf's grief were her own worries about Demar. He was going to kill her.

∞

The dead woman sat upright in the chair. The day was wearing to its end outside, but it was always dark in the cellar where the corpse sat. In the flicker of the lantern light, its features almost seemed alive. But the corpse was mummified and tied to its chair. Its withered cheeks were hollow and gaunt. Its skin clung like dry leather to its limbs. Dark hollows lay where its eyes had been.

Across from the corpse sat a living woman. She too had a wrinkled face, but her eyes glittered darkly like a crow's as she stared at her dead companion. Her hair was a faded salty-yellow and hung limply past her sloped shoulders.

"He went and stayed alive," she told the corpse, "and Bica doesn't like that. He'll bring Guards, he will, and maybe wizards. You'd like that, wouldn't you? Maybe the wizards will put your soul back in your body, or set it free — I'm sure you don't care, just so long as you can get away from Bica. But Bica has a plan, you know. Bica will just find him and cut his throat and then no one will know that Bica had anything to do with it."

She grinned at the corpse, exposing long yellow teeth in poor condition.

"Maybe Bica should bring him back here to be with you and then you wouldn't be so lonely. Would you like that?" She cocked her ear. "Oh, you'll have to speak up, or Bica will keep him for herself." She listened a second time, then rose to her feet. "Well, Bica gave you a chance to speak, but it's too late now. Bica's made up her mind. It's the knife for him and the dark cellar for you."

Catching up the lantern, she held it up to the dead woman's withered features.

"It's almost night now," Bica told the corpse. "Soon Bica will go out and find him and play a game of skin and knife with him. Do you remember that game? It's the one Sadabel played on Bica before Bica tore out his heart. See this? See it now?"

She lifted her blouse to show the dead woman the scar tissue on her abdomen.

"You peel the skin back, bit by bit. And then you cut a muscle here, and another there. And then you twist the blade, just a touch, until the blood's running freely. And then you peel some more skin back. It's a fine game, isn't it?

"Remember when Bica played it with you? You didn't like it. You kept crying for Bica to stop, but Bica remembered that you had a little power. Bica knew that you'd helped Sadabel hurt her, so Bica had to cut away, cut, cut, cut, until there was just the skin left to cure and the bone left to wire, and then the puzzle to put all back together again.

"But you're still here, aren't you, and don't you look fine? Oh, yes. Bica didn't want to send you away. Bica wanted to keep her eye on you. Like Bica should have done with Sadabel so that she didn't have to keep killing him, over and over and over again..."

CRSO

Teshi stopped by her rooms in the Luck's Shadow after leaving Saffer and Kerlaf. She stayed only long enough to change, then left by the rear, transformed into a shabbily-dressed woman by the simple magic of a disguise. Her beautiful robes and jewelry were replaced

321

with well-worn clothing that was too large for her, while her fingers glittered with rings of polished tin and brass set with great chunks of brightly-colored glass. She carried a bag over one shoulder, and a small disheveled bundle of fur dogged her footsteps as she headed towards Rat's Alley.

She paused across the street and eyed the battered three-story dwelling. Twilight lay thick on the streets, but the building was dark, giving it a gloomy look. The door was an odd-colored green — the paint chipped and flaking, she discovered as she crossed the street to approach it. She was about to knock when the door opened.

Teshi took a step back and Twig growled while hiding behind her ankles. The woman who opened the door leaned on a knobby stick of a cane and glared at them until she spied the bag on Teshi shoulders.

"Looking for lodgings, are you?" she asked.

Teshi took another step back. An unpleasant odor hung about the woman that grew more pronounced when she opened her mouth.

"Don't be shy, don't be shy. Bica's got room enough for everyone, isn't that the truth?"

"I haven't much money," Teshi began, but Bica waved that notion off.

"Paugh! Bica likes to help people and, in turn, people like to help her. Bica always has room for those that need it, don't you know. You can pay a little and help out a little...." Her eyes narrowed slightly. "Do you know any magics?"

Teshi shook her head.

"Too bad, too bad. Bica likes to trade lodgings for magics, especially guardspells." She leaned close and Teshi held her breath. "There's some that don't like old Bica, you know. They live up there." She pointed straight above them.

"What — on the upper floors?" Teshi asked.

"No, no. In the sky. In the moon. Bica's far too clever for them, though."

When Saffer had described Bica as a crazy old woman, Teshi realized, the young cittern player hadn't been exaggerating. She felt Twig still rubbing nervously against her ankles so she hoisted him up into the crook of her arm.

Bica eyed the dog with sudden suspicion. "Where are you from?" she demanded.

"Not from the moon," Teshi said.

"So," Bica said after a long moment of silence. "You want a room?"

Teshi blinked, then nodded. "Yes, but—"

"Oh, don't you worry about your little dog. Bica loves animals, doesn't she just."

She put out a hand to Twig—who suffered a rough pat with only a little trembling—then turned and led the way inside. The room she offered Teshi was the first on the right from the front door. Leaving the wizard to inspect it, Bica bustled off, "To get you a little welcoming gift, and wouldn't that be nice?"

Teshi studied the rented room. In different circumstances, it would have been amusing. The room was clean, but it was such a crazy-quilt of colors that it made her head spin. Bica must have furnished her house from the pickings of Fortune Way—but only after a more thorough cleaning than anyone else would want to get close enough to give the various articles. She sighed and turned to Twig. The little dog sat in the middle of the room, fastidiously wrinkling his nose.

"Yes," Teshi said. "There certainly is an air of—" Bica chose that moment to return with a tray and two steaming mugs of spicy milk. "—a charm about the building," Teshi finished.

Bica nodded. She smiled, but the revelation of her yellowed teeth only made her look worse.

"There is something about these old buildings," she said, "isn't that the truth?"

She put the tray down on a table by the door and handed Teshi a mug. Then before she picked up her own, she muttered something about that shade not hanging quite right. As soon as Bica crossed the room, Teshi surreptitiously exchanged the mug she'd been given for the one still on the tray. Twig barked a warning.

Teshi caught a glimpse of Bica with her knobby cane in her hand, then the cane hit her head as though powered by the force of one of the new railway engines and she collapsed to the floor, her milk mug spilling from her hand. Twig growled as Bica approached his fallen mistress, but the old woman swung the cane at him and he had to back off. She chased him all the way to the front door, coming closer and closer to hitting him with each blow, until he finally turned and fled out onto the street.

"Bica likes to eat dogs!" the old woman screamed after Twig before slamming the door. Her momentary ill-humor at the dog dissolved as she stood over her newest victim.

"Thought Bica wouldn't know you had a new body, did you now? Thought you could fool her, but Bica's too smart. Always was, always will be. And this time Bica knows what to do with you. It's the skin and knife game for you, and won't that be fun?" She paused long enough for Teshi to answer, but the wizard lay limp on the rug. "Oh, yes," Bica nodded. "It'll be such fun, wait and see."

CRSO

Saffer was sitting in her windowseat, working on the particularly intricate bit in the middle of a reel called "Wrap Up and Roll." Winny Lind, the bones player, had showed it to her on Meggy's whistle once and, while it wasn't quite a cittern sort of a tune, Saffer had always wanted to learn it. With Kerlaf asleep once more, and Teshi still gone, it seemed the perfect thing to keep her mind off her troubles.

She had just about got the three rolls of triplets that were giving her the most trouble when she happened to glance out the window. Surprised, she started to lean over the ledge, then quickly ducked her head back in. Demar was out on the street, heading for her lodgings.

Perfect, she thought as she laid down her cittern. She gave the bed a glance, but Kerlaf was still asleep. Maybe she should curl up on a pillow and pretend to be asleep as well. Demar would peek in, see them sleeping, and then—

Demar's characteristically loud knocking interrupted any further planning. Was that the first thing they learned when they joined the Guard? How to knock down doors with their knuckles?

"I know you're in there!" Demar called through the wood.

Saffer swung the door open and lifted a finger to her lips.

"Will you keep it down? I've got a sick man sleeping in here."

Demar gave the bed a quick glance. "Sorry."

He caught the door before Saffer could close it on him. Taking her by the arm, he pulled her out into the hall where he was standing and then shut the door.

"We have to talk," he said.

"About what?"

"Let's start with the wizard you had in your room this afternoon."

"Demar, have you been spying on me?"

"Only as much as you've been holding back."

Saffer tried a fierce frown on him, but it did no good.

"It wasn't my idea," she began, then told what had happened since Teshi had arrived.

As Demar listened, a storm gathered in his face.

"Saffer," he said grimly. "I warned you what would happen if you held back on—"

"Odd's end, Demar! She's a wizard. What was I supposed to do? Stand in her way and get turned into a frog or a newt?"

"Wizards don't do that kind of a thing."

"It happened to Dumps—he told me so himself."

"Do you believe everything he tells you?"

Saffer shook her head. "No, but—"

Demar held up a hand to cut her off. "Please, Saffer. No more."

"What are you going to do?" she asked as Demar turned to go.

"Talk to this Bica and your wizard. We have laws in this city, Saffer, and a Guard to see that they're obeyed. Both you and Teshi are in a lot of trouble."

"But—"

"I want you to stay in your room and don't budge until I send someone around to collect you."

"But—"

Demar took a step towards her. Saffer skittered back into her room and closed the door on him. But when she heard him going down the stairs, she crept out into the hallway again. As Demar went out the front door, she bolted out the back, meaning to make her own way to Bica's rooming house. But in the alley that the back door opened onto, she almost stepped on a little bundle of fur.

"Twig!" she cried when she recognized it. Then her heart lurched inside her. If the little dog was here, alone, what had happened to his mistress?

Twig gave a bark.

"Aren't you a clever little thing," Saffer murmured. She scooped him up and, holding him against her chest, took off at a run for Bica's once more.

CR80

The dead woman in Bica's cellar had company now. Teshi was tied to a chair, just as the corpse was. All her clothes had been stripped from her, every belonging from the small bandage on one ankle where her sandal had been chafing to the tiniest of her rings. It all lay in a pile at the far end of the cellar, well beyond Teshi's reach.

Humming to herself, Bica sat in a third chair. Lamplight spilled from the copper-based lamp on the table beside her, lighting both the corpse, which stared straight into eternity with its sightless gaze, and Teshi, whose head was limp against her chest. The melody that Bica hummed was one that Saffer might have recognized. It was a Zhir knife-sharpening song and Bica honed away at her knife with a whetting stone as she hummed.

From time to time, Bica tested the blade against her thumb. Then she went back to her sharpening, her own eyes glittering like a carrion bird's as it dropped from the sky to feed.

When Teshi finally regained consciousness, the first thing she saw was the dry weathered skin of the corpse's face. Its dark eyeless sockets gazed emptily back at her. That, combined with Teshi's own nakedness, the coolness of the cellar, and Bica's humming, sent a shudder through her body like a wave.

"Awake now, are you?" Bica murmured.

Teshi lifted her head and turned it slightly so that she could see her captor.

"Didn't think Bica would recognize you in that body, did you? But Bica's no fool. Bica always sees right through the skin — don't you know that by now?"

Teshi's gaze went from the woman's mad eyes down to the long wicked blade that she was sharpening.

"We're going to play a game," Bica said. "The skin and knife game. Bica's let you go free too many times, so this time you'll stay with Bica forever, just like your lover has. Bica's going to wrap your soul around your bones, then sew it all up in your skin and then won't you look fine?"

Teshi remembered Saffer's argument about leaving this to the Guard and wondered why she hadn't done just that. She strained against her bonds, but the ropes were tied too tightly. Her gaze lit on the pile of her belongings. Her luck was invested in a small gold band that she normally wore under her larger gaudier rings. She could sense it lying there, just across the cellar. But it might as well have been on the moon for all the use it was to her now.

"Looking for your power, are you?" Bica asked with a grin. "Bica's got the power now, wizard. You should have plunged your knife straight through Bica's heart instead of teaching her the skin and knife game, isn't that the truth?"

Teshi saw something change in the madwoman's eyes — just for a moment. There was flash of anguish, a weight of pain for which there could be no measurement, but it was quickly suppressed. The fire returned to Bica's eyes, glittering and mad.

"I've never met you before," Teshi said quietly, but firmly.

"Isn't that a laugh?" Bica said to the corpse. "Our good friend Sadabel doesn't remember us." She looked back at Teshi and held up the knife. "Bica thinks you'll remember quick enough, and won't it be fun, won't it just?"

She returned to working on her knife's edge and began to hum once again. Teshi stared at her, then at the corpse. Bica had called her Sadabel. Teshi tasted the name, trying to recall why it sounded so familiar. When the memory finally came to her, she shuddered again.

Bica looked up with a grin. Testing the knife against her thumb, she set the whetstone aside and stood up.

"Bica thinks Master Knife is ready to play," she said.

CR&O

Though Twig protested, Saffer refused to go round by the front of the rooming house. She made her way by the back alleys, holding the little dog so that it couldn't run away. By the time she reached Bica's back door, she was out of breath and had to lean against the dirty wall.

Some rescuer she was going to be. She'd come in looking like a guttersnipe and — oh, what was she even doing here? If Teshi who was a wizard was in trouble, what could she possibly do?

She heard hammering from around the front then and realized that Demar must have arrived. That was why she was here, she told herself. If Bica could deal so easily with Teshi and Kerlaf, what mightn't the old witch do to her brother?

Stealing her nerve, she pulled a length of wire from where it was hidden in the sole of her left shoe and began to work the lock on the door as Dumps had taught her. It was hard to keep a grip on Twig, who was squirming to be let down, and work the lock at the same time, but finally she was rewarded with a satisfying click. Replacing the wire it its hiding place, she cracked the door open and peered inside.

CRSO

Demar arrived at the green door of Bica's house and brought his fist down against its wooden panels. Once, twice, again. He waited a moment, then repeated the hammering. When no one came after a quick count to twenty, he reached for the doorknob. But before he could touch it, the door swung open and a shabby old woman who could only be Bica stood there leaning on a cane and studying him with small glittering black eyes.

"Oh," Bica said. "What's this? A Guardsman looking for lodging with old Bica? Isn't that fine."

Demar rubbed a finger lengthwise against his lips.

"Er, not exactly," he said.

While the old woman was probably a few bricks short of a load, she didn't exactly appear to be the villainous madwoman that Saffer had painted her.

Bica fluttered her eyelashes grotesquely. "What? Have you come courting old Bica then?"

Demar took a half step back.

"I'm looking for the wizard Teshi," he said in his most formal tones.

"Ah, the wizard." Bica revealed her yellowed teeth in a grin. "Of course. The important wizard." She stepped aside. "Come in, come in. Don't be shy. Bica doesn't bite."

Demar nodded uncomfortably and moved past her. "I just have to ask her a few —"

Before he could finish, Bica hit him from behind with her cane and he went stumbling to his knees. He stopped his fall with his hands, but she hit him again, across the shoulders, then once more on the back of his head. The floor turned black and swallowed him.

Bica pushed at him with her cane. When he didn't move, she cackled to herself. "Bica's blows are worse than her bite," she told him. Laying aside the cane, she grabbed his shoulders with surprising strength and began to haul him down to the cellar.

CREO

There was no one in the kitchen when Saffer crept inside. She closed the door behind her, then scurried across the room, one hand around Twig's muzzle to stop him from making an outcry. When she poked her head around the doorjamb, she was just in time to see Bica dragging her brother down the hall. Twig squirmed in her arms, but she clamped him to her chest with panicked strength and ducked out of the old woman's sight. Not until she heard Demar's boots hitting each stair that led down to the cellar did she dare peek around the corner again.

The hall was empty. The door leading to the cellar stood ajar. Swallowing dryly, Saffer crept to the landing and peered down.

Oh, Demar, she thought. If she's hurt you, I'll...I'll....

She didn't know what she'd do. She didn't know what *to* do. Run to the Guard and call them in? What if they arrived too late? What if they thought it was just some joke and didn't come at all?

Oh, why did this sort of thing always have to happen to her?

Bica's laughter came drifting up the stairs and Saffer knew she couldn't wait any longer. Gathering the tattered bits of her courage, she eased her way down the stairs, stepping close to where they joined the wall and praying they wouldn't creak. By the time she reached the bottom, she was a walking tangle of nerves, tautly wired and ready to flee at the slightest provocation. But then she looked into the room from which Bica's laughter was coming.

She saw Teshi first. The wizard was tied naked to a chair. Her position might have seemed humorous if it hadn't been for the withered corpse tied to another chair and Bica standing over Demar, tugging off his trousers with one hand, a big gleaming knife in the other.

Saffer froze. She wanted to rush to her brother's rescue, but every muscle in her body knotted and she couldn't move. Then Bica turned and saw her. With a shriek she dropped Demar's trouser leg

329

and brandished the knife at Saffer. But while Saffer still couldn't move, Twig surged out of her arms and attacked the mad woman, yapping madly.

Bica swung the knife at the little dog, missed, tried to kick it. Twig dodged each of her blows, ducked in and took a nip out of pale leg, then dodged away from the next slash of the knife. The flurry of action was enough to unlock Saffer's paralysis. With a shriek as piercing as Bica's, she picked up the first thing that came to hand — a chipped statuette of Andrazzi the Lucky that was standing amidst a pile of junk on a table by the door — and charged the madwoman.

Bica lifted the knife to meet Saffer's attack. Twig launched himself at Bica's calves and bit through to the bone. Bica wailed. The statuette in Saffer's hand came down with enough force to shatter against the madwoman's head. Bica stumbled, her weight on her unhurt leg, her arms flailing to keep her balance. She tripped over Twig who was attacking her good leg and then fell over Demar's body. The knife twisted under her and she fell onto it, then rolled over.

Her cries were pitiful as the blood pumped from the hole in her stomach. Saffer took one look at the wound, then turned to retch in a corner. She continued to retch, dry-heaving long after Bica had finally expired. It was Teshi's voice that finally brought her around to free the wizard from her bonds.

Teshi held Saffer tightly, then steered her towards the stairs.

"Go on up," she said. "I'll see to your brother."

Saffer stared at her, wide-eyed with shock. "I never meant...I didn't...she just...."

"Go," Teshi ordered softly.

She waited until Saffer had reached the top of the stairs, then slowly turned back to the room.

CR£O

Two days later, Demar was still off-duty. He sat in the common room of the Luck's Shadow, nursing an ale, his head wrapped in a swath of bandage. Saffer sat beside him, much subdued. Teshi was across the table from them, Twig on her lap, daintily eating the little fishsticks that the wizard fed to him, one by one. Kerlaf, his bruises a hundred glorious shades of purple, yellow and blue, sat beside her.

"Sadabel and Kitani—it was a great mystery when they vanished," Teshi said.

"But where did Bica fit in?" Kerlaf asked.

Saffer shuddered at the sound of the old woman's name. Her head filled with visions of gaping wounds and the high-pitched sounds of her shrieking.

"We can't be sure," Teshi said, "but my guess is that she was Sadabel's apprentice. From the old scars on her torso and what little of her rantings I had the chance to hear, it seems Sadabel and Kitani had been torturing Bica. Somehow she managed to kill them both. Kitani you saw in the cellar—Bica cured her skin, then sewed it back up again with the dead woman's bones inside. As for Sadabel...I doubt we'll ever know exactly what happened to him."

"But...but why was she killing people?" Saffer asked.

"She thought they were Sadabel, come back to have his revenge upon her," Teshi explained.

"No doubt she killed him in a place where the body was easily disposed of," Demar said, "then came back to deal with Kitani."

Teshi nodded. "Only to live in fear of Sadabel's return."

"That poor woman," Saffer said softly.

Kerlaf shook his head. "I've no pity to spare for her."

Saffer looked at him, at the bleakness that still lay in his eyes, and didn't bother to argue with him. All she knew was that Bica had been a poor mad creature and the weight of her death lay on Saffer's soul.

Demar put his arm around Saffer's shoulders. He said nothing when she turned to look at him, just gave her a squeeze, but it was enough. He hadn't said a word about her following him, nor anything to anyone about how she and Teshi had interfered with Guard business.

"Did you know," she said, "that you look like a camel-driver with those bandages on?"

"Watch it, camel," he told her sternly. "You could still end up in the Guardhouse for a day or two."

Saffer smiled for the first time since the events in Bica's cellar and laid her head against his shoulder.

"That's better," she said. "You were being so nice to me that for awhile there I thought you didn't like me anymore."

Demar looked at Teshi, but the wizard only rolled her eyes and went on feeding Twig his fishsticks.